Eclipse the Flame

When Ingrid Seymour is not writing books, she spends her time working as a software engineer, cooking exotic recipes, hanging out with her family and working out. She lives in Birmingham, AL with her husband, two kids and a cat named Mimi. She can be found on Twitter @Ingrid_Seymour

www.IngridSeymour.com
www.facebook.com/IngridSeymourAuthor

LONDON BOROUGH OF BARNET
D1424351

Also by Ingrid Seymour

Ignite the Shadows

Eclipse the Flame

INGRID SEYMOUR

HARPER
Voyager

HarperVoyager
an imprint of HarperCollins*Publishers* Ltd
1 London Bridge Street
London SE1 9GF

www.harpervoyagerbooks.co.uk

This Paperback Original 2016

First published in Great Britain in ebook format by HarperVoyager 2016

Copyright © Ingrid Seymour 2016

Ingrid Seymour asserts the moral right to
be identified as the author of this work

A catalogue record for this book
is available from the British Library

ISBN: 978-00-0818149-9

This novel is entirely a work of fiction.
The names, characters and incidents portrayed in it are
the work of the author's imagination. Any resemblance to
actual persons, living or dead, events or localities is
entirely coincidental.

Typeset in Sabon by Palimpsest Book Production Limited,
Falkirk, Stirlingshire

Automatically produced by Atomik ePublisher from Easypress

Printed and bound in Great Britain

All rights reserved. No part of this publication may be
reproduced, stored in a retrieval system, or transmitted,
in any form or by any means, electronic, mechanical,
photocopying, recording or otherwise, without the prior
permission of the publishers.

MIX
Paper from
responsible sources
FSC˚ C007454

FSC™ is a non-profit international organisation established to promote
the responsible management of the world's forests. Products carrying the
FSC label are independently certified to assure consumers that they come
from forests that are managed to meet the social, economic and
ecological needs of present and future generations,
and other controlled sources.

Find out more about HarperCollins and the environment at
www.harpercollins.co.uk/green

Para mi padre
Por poner el viento en mis velas

Chapter 1

The heavy bag swings gently from side to side under the dim lights of the empty dojo. Sweat drips down my forehead and into my eyebrows. My chest pumps in and out with the exertion.

Again.

I tighten my black belt, then hit the bag with a combination of jabs and kicks, my bare feet swishing against the rubber tatami floor. My white uniform jacket and ankle-length canvas pants snap. The slap of my bare hands and feet striking the leather reverberates through the rectangular room. I end the attack with an elbow strike and a loud kiai.

My side hurts. My throat bobs up and down. The floor-to-ceiling mirrors on the back wall reflect my hunched over shape. Several karate masters watch me with still eyes from wall-affixed posters. I look toward the unopened water bottle on the floor. I'm so thirsty I could guzzle the whole thing in one big gulp, but I'm not even close to the required level of pain.

Again.

I hit and hit the bag. Twenty minutes pass. My uniform is soaked, my extremities red and burning from smacking the leather bag. I bend over, holding my side and panting. After a moment, I straighten and stare at the now-still bag with near hatred.

No doubt I'm hurting, now. Time to try this crazy scheme.

The punching bag hangs from a wooden beam in the ceiling. I stare at it and reach with my mind, willing it to swing. I narrow my eyes, narrow my attention to the chain that holds it in place. The tendons in my neck pop, ready to snap.

Move. Move!

Nothing happens.

"Damn it!"

The bag mocks me by just hanging there all shiny-black and sturdy. I concentrate, gather all my pain and project it forward, trying to nudge the bag just a bit. The veins at my temples throb with the effort. Just two weeks ago, I pushed a multi-ton van full of half-crocodiles into an abyss and saved the entire IgNiTe crew after blowing up Elliot Whitehouse's fertility clinic, all while laying half-dead on the frozen ground. Now, I'm as alive as a freakin' newborn and anything heavier than a box of bonbons gives me problems.

"Screw this!"

Maybe I'm wrong. Maybe pain isn't the key to spur my telekinesis into action. It's time I try something else. Imminent peril, perhaps?

Hmm, I guess one hundred pounds of sand can be categorized as imminent peril when combined with velocity. I stare at the heavy bag.

"All right, then." I press my open palms against the bag's cool leather and push it as hard as I can. The bag swings like a pendulum. I push again and again. Momentum builds. The bag goes higher with every oscillation. The supporting chain groans. Damage to my kisser should qualify as imminent peril, right? When the bag reaches its apex, I take a deep breath and lower my face into the path of the advancing wrecking ball.

My eyes grow wide.

Oh shit! A heavy-ass heavy bag is headed straight for my nose.

Stop, I command, my mind stretching, taking the shape of a pacifying hand, but the black, limbless monster ignores me and keeps coming my way. It's not even slowing. Not one bit.

Stop! Stop . . .

Next thing I know, I'm groaning on the floor, its rubbery smell twisting my stomach further. My eyes blur, then blur some more. I blink and hold my head. The right side of my face throbs. I turned away in the last instant, so my cheekbone got the smack-down.

Well, that was stupid and useless. The back of my head pounds. I sit and look up at my leather-clad attacker.

"Who's the punching bag now, bitch?"

I can almost hear Sensei 'Moto shaming me from his favorite spot in front of the Japanese flag I helped him pin to the wall.

Pain and imminent peril both fail with a giant "F".

What do I have to do to jump-start my skills?

God, I give up.

I stand and sway on my feet as the room spins. I sigh, finally convinced that only meditation will help me improve. The problem is I'd rather get hit by a hundred punching bags than face meditation without another Symbiot's help. Every time I've tried it, I've practically needed CPR to survive it, since the shadows take the opportunity to attack me and send me into convulsing fits whenever I try it. It's been just over two weeks since James kicked me out of The Tank, so training has been reduced to these lonely, pathetic attempts.

Damn, I wish I could be back there, wish James would let me explain that my brother isn't a spy. I've sent him several emails explaining what I've found out so far, but he's ignored them. I've snooped enough on Luke's *extracurricular* activities to know there are only three things on his mind: football, parties, and girls. If he's a spy, then I'm Jean Grey from X-Men—which clearly I'm not since I doubt floating bonbons are her telekinetic specialty.

Shuffling toward the dressing room, I pick up my bottled water and chug it down. My throat relaxes. In the shower, I turn the water to searing hot. Now it's my muscles' turn to relax. I practically moan in ecstasy. Why do I do this to myself?

Fifteen minutes later, I'm ready to go, clad in my leathers and carrying a new custom-painted Scorpion helmet under my arm. It's a beauty with a reflective visor and a sweet design of neon blue zeros and ones raining down the sides. I was sick of wearing the one I dented when Xave and I wrecked the bike and skidded into the woods. I head for the door, key in hand. I'm grateful to Sensei 'Moto for trusting me and letting me use his dojo after hours. Lately, I've been spending *a lot* of evenings in here—more than I'd like to admit.

A few steps from the front door, a familiar buzzing begins in the back of my head. I freeze, heart in sudden havoc. I drop my gym bag and whirl, expecting some manner of monstrous creature to be right behind me. Disoriented, I face the front door again and realize the threat is outside.

Two strolling silhouettes appear behind the frosted glass, out on the sidewalk. I try to calm down. The buzzing in my head— the telltale sign that infected humans, Eklyptors or Symbiots, are around—is nothing new these days, not after the coordinated attacks from IgNiTe cells destroyed enemy fertility clinics all around the world. Clearly, they're getting bolder.

Whoever is out there is not moving on. I put my money on Eklyptors: dangerous humans with a full-fledged parasitic brain infection. It has to be. Symbiots from the IgNiTe gang wouldn't stalk me. The infectious agent in their brains would also make my head buzz, even though it hasn't taken them over. But I know IgNiTe wouldn't be this overt. No, if they wanted to see me—not that they do—Aydan would just hack into my computer to deliver some cryptic message. But James kicked me out and hasn't looked back. I haven't heard from him in fifteen days. I hate that I'm counting.

I swallow and take a step back. The buzzing in my head lessens and, like many other times, I wonder about its purpose, wonder why Eklyptors announce their presence to each other in this irritating manner. If I could only turn it off.

The two shadows outside lean their heads into each other as if conferring. After a moment, they approach the window front, cup their hands against it and try to peer inside. The back of my head hums a little harder. I walk backward until I hit the far wall and the buzzing stops completely.

They can't see me.

Breathe. One, two . . . a million.

They can't see me.

But they try. They move along the length of the entire front, trying to catch a glimpse through the letters that spell "YAKAMOTO MARTIAL ARTS – KARATE – SHOTOKAN." They even rattle the door, which I always lock when I'm in here by myself. After a few minutes, they walk away. I slide down the wall, sit on the floor and hug my shaky knees. Bastards. It seems every day there are more and more of them out there.

Before I knew what the buzzing meant, I used to sense them occasionally. Now it's a daily affair: at school, at the arcade, on the streets. For me, Seattle's entire vibe has changed. I can feel it in the air—much like a briny, stagnant breeze blowing off Puget Sound. It's nothing regular humans would necessarily notice. I doubt I would have if it wasn't for the constant brain signals. It appears they're preparing for something. I fear what is coming, what they must be planning. I cringe to think how many people they've infected and how quickly they'd be able to get to us all.

5

And then what? What when everyone has a parasite in their heads? Kristen, IgNiTe's resident scientist, says their hosts are perfectly capable of giving birth, but the babies aren't infected. They're human, and to turn them into Eklyptors the beasts implant parasites in their spines. The thought is so terrifying and vivid in my mind that I have nightmares about it all the time. If they infect us all and this becomes their only option to acquire new hosts, we would never be free of them. We would forever be slaves, vassals.

And it's not just Seattle. They're getting bolder in other cities where local IgNiTe cells also orchestrated attacks against Eklyptors. I guess now that we're aware of their existence and organized against them, all bets are off. Xave says James and the entire crew are on edge.

Well, whoever was outside seems to have moved on. Their shadows disappeared from the window several minutes ago. But what if they're still out there?

You can't hide here forever, Marci. I get to my feet.

I approach the door and, with every slow step I take, I expect the buzzing to pick back up. It doesn't. Silently, I key the lock, poke my head out and look up and down the street. The lamp-posts are on and the sky above bruised in dark blues and purples. There's no one around. My heart thinks otherwise, though, and it beats at a fight-or-flight rate. I pull back inside, press my head to the door and take several deep breaths, still alert to any mental disruptions.

For years, I've stayed late training at the dojo and it never scared me before. A black belt tends to make one confident like that. But when living nightmares roam the streets, the same black belt seems about as useful as a bib.

A coward. I've turned into a coward.

I check my watch. Mom's preparing dinner tonight, and I'll

be just in time if I leave now. Fighting the urge to hide, I step out of the dojo, lock the door and, as I head toward my bike, pretend my legs aren't shaking. There are two cars parked by the quaint coffee shop with the red awning, but all the other vehicles that were here two hours ago are now gone, which has left only my Kawasaki on this side of the narrow, asphalt street. Most of the other businesses—a small hardware store, a florist, a seafood restaurant—are closed.

My helmet swings back and forth in my hand as I rush down the sidewalk, staying as close to the edge as possible, away from the dark servicing alley that runs alongside the dojo. The passage is a safe cut-through during the day, host to little more than Dumpsters and wrought iron fire escapes a bit gone into the rusty side.

A broad-shouldered figure comes out of one of the cars by the coffee shop and begins to walk at a clipped pace down the opposite sidewalk, headed in my direction. I stop and judge the distance between us. If he was an Eklyptor, my head would be droning by now. He's no more than fifteen feet away. I shake my head, reminded that I need to toughen up and stop being such a wuss.

I hurry ahead, skipping off the sidewalk and slipping on my helmet, ready to get out of here. Mom will kill me if I'm late and spoil the evening. She's cooking lasagna which she found out is Luke's favorite.

Reaching in my front pocket for the key, I'm about to straddle the bike when the guy calls out.

"Hey!"

He's crossing the street, heavy boots stamping the pavement, and a twisted smirk plastered on his face.

I hesitate, instincts in full alert, even if my head isn't humming with his proximity. Because how can I forget that James can sense

Luke loud and clear, even when I can't? It would have been nice for that telltale buzzing to be fool-proof, but nothing is ever that easy, is it? This guy could still be an Eklyptor.

I consider jumping on the bike and driving away, but I don't have time to start the engine and tear off. That would just make me vulnerable: a prime candidate for being tipped like a cow before I have the chance to get too far. So instead, I open my visor and give Mr. Smirk the most acidic look I've got.

His hurried stride and stupid grin don't falter as he asks. "Hey, babe, what faction are you with?"

My heart slams against my chest all at once, then goes into a wild tempo. I wish I'd thought of putting the bike between us. "Excuse me?" I say, facing him, flexing tingling fingers at my sides.

He stops a few feet away. "Don't be a dumbass. I know what you are." He rubs his knuckles. There's a huge ring on one finger and small tattoos—in all ten of them. His flat-top haircut looks as if it was made with a precision laser.

I know what you are.

I know what you are.

I know what you are.

Such a familiar message.

"I know you ain't with Hailstone, so who you with?"

Hailstone? There's a faction called Hailstone?

After the question, his smile switches, changing from friendly to knowing to something sinister. His eyes flick surreptitiously. He glances behind me, over my shoulder, into the depths of the alley at my back. In the next instant, my head begins to drone, first faintly then all at once, like hail after light rain. My eyes spring wide-open as adrenaline of the purest kind infuses my veins.

Noticing my reaction, Mr. Smirk tries to grab me by the shoulders, but I roll to the side and land on all fours, facing the alley.

I glance into its shadowy confines and see nothing, except I know *something* is approaching. And fast.

To my right, Mr. Smirk puts his hands up. His large ring reflects the light from the nearest lamppost. "Hey, chill, bitch. We just wanna have a little chat. That's all."

The buzzing in my head is reaching its climax. I straighten, weighing my options. I could turn tail and run, but judging by the speed at which the buzzing is increasing, I have a feeling I wouldn't get very far. I narrow my eyes at the darkness of the alley and, this time, I see a shape moving close to the ground, rushing toward me in a bizarre sideways gallop of hands and feet. Haunted by that horrible night at the fertility clinic, visions of misshapen half-crocodiles fill my mind.

Whatever is headed my way right now is different, though. This creature moves fast, bounding, covering yards and yards at a time.

Worse yet, it's just leaped out of the alley and into the air.

Chapter 2

I scream, expecting a monster to swoop down on me with huge, leathery talons. Instead, I realize it's a man, leaping like a giant ape, pushing with elongated arms and too-short hind legs. His teeth are bare, his hands aiming for my throat. His flat, wide nose flares.

"You ain't going nowhere. We gotcha!" Mr. Smirk yells in an excited tone, as if I'm some sort of piñata and candy will spill out of me when I burst open.

Years of training kick in, and I throw a front kick. My foot connects with Ape Man's jaw. His momentum dies and he stumbles backward. In succession, I release a roundhouse kick that slams into his temple and sends him sprawling onto the pavement. Wasting no time, I twirl and drive an elbow right in the middle of Mr. Smirk's stomach, knocking the wind out of him with an audible *whoosh*.

I go for the bike's keys in my front pocket and run to the other side of the bike to place a barrier between me and them. But, too quickly, Ape Man recovers and jumps back to his feet as if I didn't just kick his face with a thousand pounds of pressure.

He bounds from the blacktop and flies in a diagonal line. Mouth agape in a hideous cry, he soars straight over the bike and wraps his arms around me. I fall backward, the back of my helmet slamming the ground, my neck bending painfully.

My eyes blur for a moment, enough for my attackers to get the upper hand. Quickly, Ape Man pulls me by the wrists to a sitting position, while Mr. Smirk slips an arm around my neck and puts me in a chokehold. I try to kick back, but Ape Man pins my legs under his huge weight.

"Help!"

Mr. Smirk snaps my visor shut.

"In the alley." Ape Man grabs me by the ankles.

As they lift me, I writhe and buck. My struggle slows them down, but it doesn't stop them from dragging me into the shadows. Once under the cover of dark, they slam me to the ground next to a foul-smelling Dumpster.

Ape Man straddles me while Mr. Smirk pins my arms over my head. My helmet scratches the ground as I thrash and wriggle. The smell of dead whale is so strong it finds its way into my helmet. I blame the seafood restaurant for the lovely perfume.

"Settle down, little girl." Ape Man's flat nose flares. "We're only trying to keep our territory under control. You don't belong here. Answer our question and we may let you go. Who are you with?"

Their territory? What is going on here? He sounds as if they've carved Seattle up like a pie at an all-you-can-eat buffet. This city is not theirs to divide. This city doesn't belong to Eklyptors.

"Who are you with?" He gets his face right up to mine. His meat-ridden breath makes me gag.

I turn aside, cringing. "I'm by myself."

"You sure are. Let me rephrase. Who would care if I decorate this alley with your intestines? They can make very pretty garlands, you know?"

A piece of corroded pipe that lies next to the Dumpster catches my eye.

"Answer my question while you still can." Ape Man grabs my helmet, yanks it off and throws it aside. It rolls toward the sidewalk, making a hollow sound. He wraps gnarled fingers around my neck and squeezes.

"E-Elliot Whitehouse." I make a strangled whisper and fight for my next breath, which gets past my throat with a weak whizzing sound. I focus on the pipe. It doesn't move.

"Whitehouse, huh?" Ape Man spits the name out. "What do you do for him?"

"Nothing."

He squeezes harder. My eyes feel as if they'll pop out of their sockets right into the fetid clam chowder juice that leaks out of one corner of the Dumpster.

Move, I command the pipe, but it mocks me.

Shadows enter the edge of my vision, like curtains flapping at the edge of a window.

Cinnamon kisses.

Dual core processors.

Murdering pipes.

My thoughts jump at the speed of light, chasing each other down a rabbit trail of random, loosely connected ideas, doing their best to stay away from the ravenous specters.

"So I guess he won't notice when you go missing." Ape Man laughs, his lips pursing then opening wide in an *ooh-ooh, aah-ahh.* My skin prickles with fear. It's a jungle out here, with beasts marking territories, leaving their rank odor at the bases of trees and walls. Hardly a place to fight for, especially when there's no one to fight with.

"Die." he constricts my neck until blood pounds in my jugular, fighting for a way into my brain. My tongue lolls out, a dead thing. My eyes cross as, in one last effort, I stare down the pipe.

The pressure around my neck abruptly ceases. I gasp. Chilled air rushes into my lungs, burning, prickling, filling me with glorious oxygen. I cough and gasp, cough and gasp.

Ape Man cocks his head to one side, his brown eyes giddy. "Or . . . you could tell me something *useful*."

My face tingles as blood rushes in. I eat two mouthfuls of air, feeling the way a newborn must feel when pulled into the nightmare of life. My head clears. My vision sharpens, bringing the rusted pipe into startlingly clear focus. A ball of power surges from my core and floods into my mind. What a second ago seemed impossible, becomes a pulsing certainty, an undeniable truth. And here it is. This is what I needed to be able to do, what I've failed to accomplish for two weeks. No hours of sweating and self-inflicted pain—just *very* real, *very* deadly imminent peril.

I can do this.

The pipe vibrates for a split second, emitting a faint rattle. Then, as if infused with a life of its own, it shoots up into the air with a *zing*. Ape Man looks up in shock. The excited flush of his cheeks turns paper-pale and, as the pipe plummets back down, his eyes go round and fill with innocent wonder—the kind of awe of a child at Santa Claus or the Easter Bunny. "Look, there's an honest-to-god flying pipe headed my way," his eyes seem to say. "And wouldn't you know, it's about to impale me."

With a wet *crunch*, the rusty tube pierces through his clavicle and embeds itself deep into his chest. He hovers for a moment, then falls limp to one side, wearing the same childlike expression.

Even though a part of me twists with primal guilt and horror for what I've done, I do my best to ignore it. I know better than to dwell. Guilt and uncertainty about how moral it is to kill an Eklyptor have no room in my world. Kill or be killed. That's the edict by which I now live. Them or us. The choice is easy because there isn't one.

So I rock from the hips, swinging my legs up and back over

my head. Like a pair of wild scissors, I wrap them around Mr. Smirk's head and pull back down as hard as I can. He rolls over me and lands with a thud, back slamming onto the ground. I jump to my feet, take him by the lapels of his jacket and heave him upright.

Rage boils in my blood, like acid ready to spill all over his face. I want to disfigure him, leave a lifetime reminder of what it costs to put me in a chokehold. I push backward and slam him against the wall.

"You filthy traitor." I grab him by the neck with my right hand and squeeze. I want him to feel what I felt, to beg for a gulp of air.

His eyes roll, then look toward the ground in amazement. Something in the incredulous quality of his gaze makes me look down. His feet are dangling several inches off the ground. Panicked, I let him go. He crumples to the ground, holding his neck, regarding me as if I'm much worse that his ape-like companion.

I am not. I am nothing like that.

He gets to his knees. The accusing look in his eyes causes my panic to morph once more. Rage electrifies me. I slam my fist against his jaw, putting all my weight into the punch. He screams—a cry so shrill it makes my ears hurt—then falls to the ground and twists in pain.

"Tell your leader this territory won't go unchallenged." My voice is a near growl. "Elliot Whitehouse's faction will control *all* of Seattle soon, so don't get too comfortable."

I have no idea what I'm saying, but pitching Eklyptor factions against one another can't be bad. If they're too busy fighting each other, it can only help IgNiTe's cause, humanity's cause.

"You broke my jaw," he whines, a hand pressed to his chin as tears spill down his cheeks.

I squat next to his crumpled shape. He recoils, pushing closely to the wall and pressing his forearms against his face.

"You're lucky I don't kill you." As if killing is on my daily checklist next to doing my homework and brushing my teeth.

Other words try to push their way past my lips, but I cage them behind clenched teeth. I want to know how he can betray his own kind, how he can act as decoy to approach unsuspecting members of other factions, why he's a freakin' human pet to the Eklyptors. I already messed-up and called him a traitor which to him would make no sense since in his mind I'm fully infected. I wonder what he thinks I meant. Symbiots are a secret to anyone outside of IgNiTe. I can't risk saying too much.

"Run to your masters and deliver my message, *little pet*."

I stand to give him room. He sits, holding his jaw, and looks up at me, full of doubt. He can't believe I'm letting him go.

"GO!"

He clambers to his feet and hobbles away, slipping on Ape Man's blood before getting traction and scurrying like a chastised dog.

I stare at a swirl of light as it dances in the depths of the crimson puddle and do my best not to let my eyes wander to the impaled corpse. I picture his rabid expression as he tried to strangle me. He was *not* a victim. He was an attacker, a nightmarish predator.

"Survival of the fittest," Kristen would say.

Easy for her to justify killing when all she does is look through her electron microscope, trying to find a cure that will never be enough to avert the chaos that already haunts the city. I turn my back on the inert body. Shutting my eyes, I imagine a different world around me. A happy place where the darkest thing is a night with twinkling stars and a bright moon. A warm home with a family who understand me. A boyfriend I don't have to lie to and I could talk to about my infection without fear that he would leave me forever. Or, at the least, a group of people who are like me and don't shut me out, people who let me fight against the horrors that get in the way of the life I want to live.

Forcing my chin upward, I walk to my helmet and pick it up. The custom paint job is ruined. With a foul word on my lips, I slip the helmet on and lower my visor. I'm so late for dinner there'll be no understanding at home tonight.

Chapter 3

On my way home, I zoom through empty streets that used to have a decent amount of foot traffic just a week ago. The well-to-do Seattle citizens sure consider it advantageous that the presence of hookers and drug peddlers is on the decline. The authorities must be doing something right, for once, right? Well, think again. The *cure* is certainly worse than the disease. I don't have to think too hard to know where these people ended up.

I park my bike, rush up the porch steps, open the door and skid to a stop in the foyer. With a deep breath, I turn to the entrance mirror and run twitchy fingers through the flat mess in a vain attempt to get rid of my helmet hair. Not that it makes much of a difference. I'm wearing my leathers, anyway.

"The hell with it," I mumble as I start to turn for the kitchen, which is when I notice the finger marks around my neck. I swallow, feeling the ache deep in my throat. The sight makes me want to kill Ape Man all over again. I cringe at my cavalier thoughts. Death should never be the butt of a joke, even one nobody gets to hear.

I zip up my jacket all the way to the collar to hide the marks. My hands shake. I don't need this family stress right now. I could have been killed tonight. My nerves are shot. But what choice do

I have? Besides, I've promised myself to try. For Dad. It's what he would expect of me, if he was still with us. I brace myself for Mom's murderous blue eyes and Luke's "I don't mean to be such a good son" expression.

I picture them waiting for me in unprecedented mother/son bliss:

"Oh, Mom, you're such a good cook." Yum, yum.

"Well, thank you, son. I'd cook an orca whale for you, if you'd ask me." Blink, blink, charming blue eyes.

What I get when I step into the kitchen is nothing like that. And I mean: *nothing* like that. Instead, I find mom sitting at the table by herself, staring at the flame of a half-spent candle, her eyes rimmed in red and smudged mascara. Untouched food platters are expertly positioned behind empty porcelain dishes and wine glasses I didn't know we owned.

I freeze and look over my shoulder, wondering if she has noticed me, if there's the slightest possibility I may sneak to my room without finding out what happened here. I take a step back.

Mom's chair scrapes across the tile floor. I wince and look back. She's staring straight at me, her expression a petrified mask of disappointment.

"So finally someone shows up." She barely looks at me as the wavering flame of the candle holds her attention.

"Uh, sorry. I ran into a bit of trouble," I say, my tone as apologetic as I can manage—which isn't much in this strained relationship.

"It's always the same with you, Marcela. Nothing is ever as important as what you want."

"I guess that's why you have your model son now," I say, matching her bitterness.

Her eyes twitch visibly, then her gaze falls on a bowl of mash potatoes in an oddly repressed expression.

"Wait . . ." I look around. "He's not here, is he?" I want to laugh, but even I'm not that heartless. "He's not here and you're giving *me* a hard time about being late."

She lifts her nose defiantly, but says nothing.

"At least I showed up," I say. "At least I remembered and would have been here earlier if I hadn't been delayed. Did he even call to say he wasn't coming?"

"I'm sure he has a perfectly good reason." Her tone is a weak parody of the one she was using just a moment ago.

I doubt Luke has been attacked by Eklyptors. He's only in danger of being assaulted by blonds and brunettes with well-proportioned limbs, and not ape-like creatures with a proclivity for strangling.

Mom lets out a heavy sigh. "I want so badly for us to be a family, a real family. I'm trying. Is that so bad? I know I'm not perfect. I have my faults, but no one seems to remember I have feelings, too."

I blink, taken aback by this unexpected, candid moment.

Have I disregarded her feelings? My insides twist into knots, because I know the answer is *yes*. I've been too busy being jealous of Luke to remember that all I've wanted from the beginning was for us to be a family. Guilt straddles me like an expert jockey.

"I'm sorry, Mom." My voice breaks, but my sincerity is clear enough. Mom gives me a sad smile and something passes between us through a connection I thought had died forever. I smile back and take a step forward, a step in the right direction.

"It would be a shame to let all this good food go to waste," I put in.

We don't say much after that, but the fact that we get through an entire meal without a mean word gives me hope for that family I've been craving.

After helping Mom with the dishes, I enter my room and close the door behind me. Luke is still missing and, after the last hour with Mom, I'm even angrier at him. It's only been a month since Luke moved in, but I think—for his part—the rose is *way* off the bloom. Not that I can blame him. Mom has been extremely overbearing, expecting him to abandon his previous social life for his newfound family, more specifically his new mom. Now, more than ever, a serious chat between us is in order. He has to make an effort. He *will* make an effort. He'll get a taste of black belt if he doesn't.

I wonder where he is, though.

More out of habit than anything else, I log into my computer and check Luke's email. I hacked into his account two weeks ago and have been monitoring his every move, hoping *not* to catch him in any illicit activities that may mark him as a spy, as James suspects. So far—to my relief—I've observed nothing but normal jock/popular guy behavior. I've told James that much in countless emails, but no matter how much I assure him he's wrong, his decision to keep me out of IgNiTe hasn't changed, that's assuming he's even had time to think about me.

I browse Luke's inbox, sifting through what is mostly junk mail from sporting goods stores. A read email from almost an hour ago catches my eye. The "Subject" reads: "We need to meet NOW!" Clearly, the culprit for his absence.

Clicking it open, I read the message while holding my breath. Dread fills me every time I do this. I don't want one of these emails to prove James right. I don't want to find out that Luke isn't the brother I've longed for, or that he's a monster with a plan that somehow involves my family. Because, in spite of everything, I still feel a connection with him, something unique that I can't explain.

Luke,

Meet me at the same place as last time. I'll be there in thirty minutes. Don't make me wait. I promise you won't regret it.

Xoxo,

Zara H.

Really? What is this? A booty call? This girl is desperate.

She has been trying really hard to get Luke to succumb to her charms. I think this is her fifth email. I don't know. I'm losing count. I followed him to what may have been their first date. She was all over him, flipping her blond hair right and left like she was trying to shoo away flies or something. Luke, for his part, couldn't have looked more disinterested, which was kind of a shocker given his philandering history. Still, her emails keep on coming and I've no idea if he's rising to the challenge—pun intended—or blowing her off. Either way, she's definitely a non-suspect. She's just another horny admirer, ready to offer all her physical goods to the handsome jock who seems determined to taste every pretty girl in school.

Just to be on the safe side, though, I pick up my phone and go to my "Find Luke" custom app. Just yesterday, I swiped his phone while he was showering and installed a small Objective-C program that gives me access to his GPS. It took me days of surreptitiously looking over his shoulder to get his passcode, but I managed. Now, I'll be able to know exactly where he is at all times.

When my app opens up, a red balloon marks the spot on the map. I zoom out and see that he's in Belltown in some nightclub called *Shadowstorm*. Figures! Why didn't he tell mom he wouldn't be here and would be shaking his booty along with some ditsy blond instead? He can't be this callous.

I rub my brow and take a deep breath, trying to keep the budding anger in my chest from climbing into my head. Something needs to give! James can't keep me away forever with this bogus reason. I'm tired of stalking Luke all over the city just to find that he has another date or has been invited to yet another party. It's a waste of time. I could be helping IgNiTe, hacking systems for intelligence against Eklyptors, going on missions to destroy their fertility clinics. I was helpful last time, wasn't I? I could also be training, meditating, getting my infectious agent, the damn parasite living in my brain, to cooperate with this telekinesis absurdity, which is as useful as a gun with disappearing bullets.

A quick buzz from my cell phone pulls me away from my mental rant. It's a text message.

Xave: Miss ya! Hows family dinner?
Me: Better than I expected
Xave: Good to hear
Me: Where r u?
Xave: M.A. Starving!
Me: Miss ya, too. Be right there?
Xave: Sweet! Can't wait 2 c u!

He's at Millennium Arcade, probably playing pool. A smile creeps to my lips, which turns back into a frown when I see Luke's email staring back at me from the computer screen.

"Screw you, Luke," I say, locking the desktop and jumping to my feet. He seems to be the source of all my headaches lately. It's time I stop wasting my time with him. There have to be other ways I can help IgNiTe and prove to James and the crew that they need me back, that I can be useful.

For now, though, all I need is a hot cup of java . . . and an equally hot boyfriend.

Chapter 4

As soon as I enter Millennium Arcade, my head buzzes, a reminder that this Seattle isn't the same as the one of the pre-IgNiTe attacks two weeks ago. My eyes drift toward the pool table, where Xave puts the laws of physics to the test with his insane skills. I immediately identify the usual crowd: diehards who might as well keep sleeping bags under the green-velvety tables. They never seem to leave. Behind Xave's friends, watching the game over the rim of her glass, I spot the tall brunette who's responsible for the buzzing in my head. She gives me a raised eyebrow. I do my best to ignore her. She's here scouting future victims, I'm sure. It takes all I've got not to cause a scene and act as if I don't know our city has gone to crap.

Fortunately, Xave is not among the pool players. Instead, I spot him by one of the red, faux-leather booths.

I nod and change direction, boots padding on the space-themed carpet. He must have really been hungry. Normally, I find him, cue in hand, wringing a few dollar bills out of foolish amateurs who don't realize they'll never be able to beat him. The computerized sounds of gun fire from one of the video games mark my steps.

He stands and wraps me in a tight hug. I relish his solidity and the fact that he lingers for several, long seconds. As he pulls away, I look up, surprised.

"Hey," I say, my cheeks going warm. Being Xave's girlfriend still makes me feel self-conscious and nervous and wonderful. I'm not sure I'll ever get used to it. He's a bear of a boy, tall and muscular, with a penchant for slightly tight t-shirts and ripped jeans.

"I didn't think I'd get to see you today," he says. "Don't take this the wrong way, but I'm glad family dinner didn't last very long." Before I can reply, he places a hand on my cheek, gently lets it slide to the back of my neck and pulls me in for a kiss.

His lips are warm and supple as they move against mine, sending such a wild current down the length of my legs that I feel like I'll take off and shoot through the ceiling. I wrap my arms around his waist and pull him closer, forgetting where we are. He responds by sliding a hand down my back and deepening his kiss. I'm at the verge of moaning in pleasure when I remember myself and manage to break the kiss.

Xave growls in frustration, his forehead pressed to mine. My eyes surreptitiously check the room, noticing a few people watching—one of them a girl that looks as if she'd trade places with me even if it meant growing a third eye.

I clear my throat. "People are watching," I say.

"It never mattered to me before," Xave says, brushing my lower lip with his thumb, "but you make me care."

With his previous girlfriends, he had no qualms about making out in public. With me, he always stops before it gets out of hand. My heart smiles like an idiot.

His beautiful hazel eyes are warm and happy. He gestures toward the booth. "I know you already ate, but I ordered you the special, anyway. Rolo had one of his Southern creations today."

"Oh, yum!" I sit and my mouth waters at the sight of a plateful of Cajun jambalaya. I much prefer Rolo's specials than the regular fare and Xave knows that. Is he a wonderful boyfriend or what?

God, I love him.

I stab a piece of sausage and stuff it in my mouth just to stop me from baring my heart in those three words. It's too soon. We've only been dating for two weeks. I don't want to freak him out. And what if he doesn't say it back? I think he would, but what if he doesn't? I frown. Ugh, what is wrong with me? Have I become one of those spineless girls who bases her every action on how her boyfriend will react? No. I can't allow that. I should tell him. Right now. I look up.

He's watching me closely. "Everything all right?"

"Um, yeah. I—I . . ."

Xave looks concerned. I realized that I *have* become one of those spineless girls. Stuffing another forkful of spicy sausage into my mouth, I chew and make sounds to indicate how delicious it is—although all I can really taste is the worst kind of girly cowardice. I'm not any better than all my boy-crazy classmates.

"Did family dinner get you rattled? Wanna talk about it?" he asks.

I shake my head and finish my mouthful. "I was late."

Maybe I should tell him about Ape Man and his squeezy fingers, but that'll just worry him, and I don't want that. I want him to have a clear head at all times and only worry about himself. Not me. He's still working with IgNiTe, going on who knows what kind of dangerous missions. I wish he could tell me about them, but James instructed him not to share any details with anyone.

Xave thinks James is being unreasonable by keeping me away from the crew, thinks the man's just trying to make an example out of me for being reckless, for taking unnecessary risks that almost get me killed *and* for hanging out in coffee shops when

I've been told specifically not to do that. He says once James is done making his point, he'll come around and let me back in. God, I hope Xave's right.

I sigh and continue, "And Luke didn't show. At all. I think he had some hot date or something."

Xave winces.

"Yeah," I spear a piece of shrimp this time. "So, at first, Mom decided to take it out on me 'cause, of course, her precious son can do no wrong."

"That's bullshit!" He tosses a ketchup-soaked fry in his mouth. He went for a Philly steak sandwich tonight. He's not much for exotic cuisine. "If you had to get a twin brother, why couldn't you get someone cool like Luke Skywalker or Quicksilver?"

"Yeah, I wouldn't mind being Darth Vader or Magneto's daughter. That would be ultra-cool."

"Oh, my dad would be *so* jealous."

I laugh. Xave's dad never grew out of his comic book obsession, so much that he named all his kids after fictional characters: Xavier, Clark and Selina.

Xave checks his watch, then rubs his chin. "Though, if you were Magneto's daughter that would make us enemies."

"To the death, Professor Xavier," I say.

"Hmm, I guess we'll have to put up with Luke. Couldn't imagine you being my mortal enemy." He reaches for my hand.

I smile and shy away from his touch, suddenly struck by the irony of the situation. If he only knew how close we are to being mortal enemies, how a small miscalculation could turn me into a full-fledged monster, one of the very beings he's sworn to destroy. How much must I keep from him? I'm worried about my inability to tell him I love him, when what I should be worried about is this monumental lie that would split us apart if I ever put it out in the open. My mouth goes sour with the untold secret.

"Damn, I hate that they had to spoil your Friday night like this," he says, blaming my slump on Mom and Luke. "Don't think about it. Eat your jambalaya."

"The truth is that it wasn't all bad. Mom and I sort of had a moment. I think she's decided to try on *reasonable* to see if it suits her. I kind of think it works very well."

"Well, that's something. I'm glad to hear it."

Xave works on his sandwich. I pick at my jambalaya. In the expanse of thirty minutes, he checks his watch too many times for me not to notice. When we're done with our food, he empties our trays and walks back, wearing a worried look that makes me suspect he's hiding something, something that can make a girl jealous, like a date with a clandestine bunch of misfits en-route to kick some Eklyptor ass. God, being away sucks. I even miss Blare and Aydan. Well, maybe not Aydan with his ridiculous lab coat, genius-status aspirations, and huge ego. At least Blare only suffers from a bad temper and a stick up her *colonitis*.

Xave checks his watch yet again. Something is definitely up. He's never this twitchy, not on a Friday night and surrounded by the electronic sounds of pinball machines and billiard balls clanking against each other.

When he reaches the booth, his anxious expression changes to one of determination. Without saying a word, he takes my hand and pulls me outside.

"Where are we going?" I ask as we exit the arcade onto a neon-light splattered sidewalk. Millennium's sign flashes in the night, bathing Xave's face in a red glow.

He doesn't say anything, but pulls me to the side of the building and pushes me against the wall. I'm about to ask him what is going on when his mouth falls on top of mine, robbing me entirely of breath. He presses me against the rough brick with a passionate intensity that should make me slap him across the face considering its caveman-like quality. Instead, the traitorous female inside of me arches her back and gives into the kiss with equal force.

My fingers get tangled in his shaggy brown hair, pulling him closer and relishing the silky feel. His hard body pushes into mine with desperate determination, caging me in a way that makes me want to be his prisoner forever. My hands fall to his chest, exploring the contours that I've just begun to discover, but have all intentions of becoming very familiar with. Hormones rage through my blood and I forget where I am and how I've always loathed girls who make out in dark, but obvious places. The thing is, I never understood, never knew how the body takes over the mind, how you become this primal thing, this single-minded creature who wants and wants and wants.

Xave's lips leave mine and make a trail to my clavicle. "I'm sorry. I just can't help myself. I kept watching you talk and dab your lips with that napkin. You were trying to drive me crazy."

"Me?! I didn't—"

"I know. I know. You weren't doing it on purpose, but God, you might as well have been."

Two guys exit the arcade and peer our way. One of them wolf whistles. Xave leans his shoulder on the wall, turning his back on the rubberneckers and hiding me from view.

"Come home with me," he says once they have walked away. "Some privacy would be nice."

"Privacy?" My mind reels. What is he asking, exactly?

"Just for a bit, so we can talk and maybe . . . kiss a little more." He touches his wet lips to the spot beneath my ear.

I shudder, wanting very much to go with him. We don't get many chances to be alone. *Kissing* would be nice, and maybe I'm even ready for something else.

"Kissing a little more, huh?" I tease him, too, catching his bottom lip between my teeth.

He makes a sound in the back of his throat that sends goose bumps marching like pert little soldiers all down my back. Grabbing me by the waist, Xave ushers me toward my parked motorcycle.

"Hop on," he says. "I'll get my helmet and ride with you." He rushes toward his ever-improving Yamaha, retrieves his helmet, and jogs back. Clark let him have the bike after we crashed it against a tree and, every day, I'm amazed by how meticulously Xave is bringing it back to tip-top shape.

"Why are you still standing there? Hop on, I said." He puts on his helmet.

"Why don't you just ride your bike?"

He snatches my helmet from the handlebar and plunks it on my head. I'm grateful he doesn't notice the scratches. Clearly, his mind is somewhere else.

"'Cause I don't want to be separated from you for more than a few seconds," he says. "I can get my bike back tomorrow. Go, go!"

I straddle my Kawasaki, laughing. Xave gets on behind me, presses his chest against my back, and places his hands around my hips, pulling me into him. I drive toward home, the heat of his touch seeping through my leathers, my every nerve hyper-aware of all the areas where our bodies are in contact.

I can't wait to get there, so I speed and let the chilled wind take some of the heat away.

Chapter 5

When we get to our neighborhood, I park the bike by home, then we walk across the street to Xave's small, one-level rambler house. We pass the large trees in the front yard, walk to the back and climb through his bedroom window as we always do, except this time it feels very different. Secret and exciting, right and wrong, all at the same time. We've both been so busy in the past few weeks that we've barely had time to see each other, much less be alone.

At school, he's a year ahead of me, so we don't share any classes. And afterward, he spends most of his free time with the IgNiTe crew, mainly helping Rheema on all sorts of mechanical duties, like keeping the surveillance van running smoothly, customizing engines for higher torque and improving James's already souped-up, expensive cars. Something Xave enjoys more than he's willing to admit to me, since I don't get to be part of anything—not even the most mundane hacking chores that Aydan would consider beneath him.

I go in first. Xave follows. I stand in the middle of the room, looking around, drinking in every detail of my boyfriend's bedroom. It still feels good and new to say *my boyfriend*. The one good thing about being kicked out of IgNiTe is that I don't have to invent an excuse for hiding our relationship from the crew. The truth is, at The Tank, we couldn't have acted like a couple, and any reasons for secrecy I could have offered Xave would have been nothing but more lies.

If only I could create a world where neon signs flashed our names within big hearts and no one would disapprove. If only I could tell Xave the truth and not lose his love. Too often Kristen's words echo inside my head. She told me our relationship was a bad idea, asked me what Xave would think if he found out what I truly am, said that being with him would endanger IgNiTe and the trust among Symbiot and non-Symbiot members, assured me that a relationship based on lies was nothing but doomed.

Her words swirl so much inside my head that I'm always thinking of comebacks, things I should have said to challenge her negativity. Most of all, I wish I could have recognized the hypocrisy in her words, wish I had asked her to be honest about whatever she has going on with James.

Xave's bed is unmade; his bedside lamp is on, casting its glow on the olive green walls. There are a few library books on his desk—*Holley Carburetor Manual, The Classic Indian Motorcycle, Muscle Car Source Book*—and a huge tilting stack of *Motorcycle Mechanics* magazines by his scuffed night table. He stands behind me, pulls my jacket off and throws it on his cluttered desk chair on top of a red metal toolbox. He sheds his hoodie and tosses it on top of my jacket.

Gently, he gathers my hair to one side and kisses my neck, nibbling up and down until my head is thrown back against his chest.

Wrapping his arms around my waist, he draws me close. "This is great. Just us."

"Yeah, it is."

He makes me turn and face him. His eyes search mine as if I

hold a treasure he deeply desires. He fiddles with my hair, brushing it away from my forehead and tucking it behind my ear.

"You're beautiful," he says.

I smile, feeling anything but beautiful. The only person to ever call me that was Dad, so it's been a while since I heard it. I guess I stopped believing it. "I'm glad you think so."

"I *know* so."

His mouth inches toward mine. When he's millimeters away, he pulls back and lays a small peck on the corner of my mouth. My stomach drops in disappointment. He's toying with me. Well, he's about to find out he's not the only one capable of torture.

I slip my hands under his t-shirt and run my fingers over his solid abdomen. Xave sucks in a breath and looks at me in surprise. He lowers his mouth to mine, but I dodge him and leave a trail of moist kisses along his jaw, sliding my hands toward his back, then letting them travel the length of his spine.

"*You*," he says in a breathy, accusatory voice.

Suddenly, Xave pushes me onto the bed and lands on top of me. Something pokes my ass. I reach back and find the sturdy motorcycle gauntlets I gave him for his birthday. I toss them aside. Before I can evade him again, he captures my mouth in his and kisses me like never before. His lips move with abandonment and confidence. There's no one here to snoop or judge and that seems to make all the difference. I never knew he was holding *so* much back, keeping *so* much passion locked inside of him. But it's free now. Free and tumbling all over me, stirring my own desire and making me feel alive.

His hands find their way under my shirt. I squirm with the intensity of the sensations that keep growing within me, as if I've always lived folded into a little square and I'm finally getting to be as expansive as I'm meant to be.

I pull the t-shirt over his head and fling it across the bed. He props himself up with his left hand and looks at me in surprise. It's like he can't believe I have this in me, but he has no idea what he has awakened. A sexy, lopsided smile slowly materializes on his face. His eyes search mine, then flick to his watch in the most shameless way.

I open my mouth to ask why the hell he keeps checking the time, but he gives me no chance. He lowers himself and kisses me again, catching my hands between his chest and mine. All thoughts go out the window as the solidity of him assaults me. He's all muscle and ridges and warmth. And I had no idea I could be such a fool for a nice set of pecs and washboard abs. I want to memorize his exact shape, every dip and rise of his beautiful torso.

His hands tentatively push my shirt up, exposing my abdomen. He stops to check if it's all right, if he can go on. My eyes scream "yes," so he removes it, tosses it aside and allows himself a leisurely look down my chest, a look that might as well be a match on my very, very flammable skin.

We go back to kissing, but my attention is now someplace else, specifically, on the way our agitated breaths make our heated chests move against each other, pushing gently together then moving away just to return faster than before, fiercer than ever.

Xave lets his fingers memorize me, the same way I'm memorizing him. He explores my shoulders, my stomach, my back, but especially the skin around the outline of my bra. When he boldly begins to trace kisses down the length of one of the straps, my heart stops, frozen with expectation. As he ventures lower and lower, I gasp, overwhelmed by his daring, his skill, his gentleness.

He stops. "I—I'm sorry." His breaths are fast, out of control. "Please don't get mad at me."

"Mad?" I say dumbly. Who told him I was mad? Is he insane? I've never been happier. Well, maybe happy isn't the word, but I've never been *this*, whatever it is. And I like it. A lot.

"I shouldn't. I promised myself to take it slow, but I . . . *I want you*. Can't seem to think of anything else but . . ."

He wants me. He thinks I'm beautiful. And just like that he boosts my ego and makes me feel feminine. I've always been such a tomboy that, more than once, I've wondered if a boy could be seriously attracted to me. Now Xave has left me no doubt.

A moment later, the rest of his words register. He promised himself to take it slow. Why? I don't want him to take it slow. Slow is all it's ever been for me in the relationship department. I want to go on the fast lane; the Autobahn is nothing compared to the speed I'm thinking of. Call me whatever you want, but I'm ready. Ready because my body is telling me so, because life doesn't have the same leisurely shape it used to, because everything feels askew and finite, the way it must feel to a terminal patient.

"I want you, too," I say, because I need him to know I'm ready—not that he wouldn't be able to tell. I imagine I've made myself pretty clear.

He growls and rolls to the side, taking me with him so I end up on top of him. "You're killing me."

I trace a pattern on his chest with my fingernail. He shivers. "You don't . . . have to take it slow." Unable to keep eye contact, I let my gaze wander about the room. I focus on the red Ford Mustang Boss poster taped over his bed.

Xave sits up and rests his head on my chest. Now it's *my* turn to shiver. "I do."

"No, you don't. Maybe a few months ago I would've agreed, but not now. Not with all that's going on."

"I hate thinking that way." His voice goes low.

"Me, too. But I can't help it. Sometimes I feel I have an expiration date and it's not that far off. I think the Quick Mart would have me at a discount already."

"Don't say that."

34

"I mean it." The mood has shifted. My shoulders feel heavy again—the way they do most of the time nowadays.

"Well, you seem mighty fresh to me." He squeezes my sides and takes in my scent. "God! Your scent both drives me crazy and grounds me. It feels new and exciting and, at the same time, comfortable and familiar. I love it."

His breath is warm on my skin as he exhales. I hold him tight. His words resonate inside of me, because I know exactly what he means. I feel the same way. We stay still for a long moment.

When we pull apart, his gaze drifts to the alarm clock. "Oh shit!"

"What?"

"I—I . . . there's this thing. Um, I have to—"

I push away and stand. "No need to lie, Xave. I know perfectly well what's going on. You've been checking your watch all night." I pick up my shirt, suddenly feeling quite cold and bare. I slip it on, trying not to appear rejected. I understand the state of things too well to blame him for bringing me here even when there isn't enough time to dawdle in each other's arms for hours. He's just trying to make the best of what little time we're allowed to have to ourselves.

Xave rubs his forehead with a sigh. "Clark is picking me up in a few minutes. We're going to check out this place." He also snatches his t-shirt and puts it on. My mouth goes dry with disappointment.

"This sucks." I slump on the bed. "When is James going to stop punishing me? I'm sick of this. I want to help. I want to go with you."

"He'll change his mind. Though I kinda like it this way," Xave says in a furtive tone.

I give him a dirty look.

"Well, I like knowing you're safe."

"Oh, that's bullshit. Don't give me that crap. I can take care of myself better than you can. And what? You think I don't worry about *you*? Think I don't wanna be there to save your sorry ass in case you need it?" If he knew the half of it, he wouldn't patronize me this way.

"I can take care of myself just fine, thank you very much. I'm not the one who screams at the sight of half-baked Eklyptors."

What the hell? That happened only once, and it was the very first time I saw one. Besides he has no idea what it feels like to discover you're a monster. I punch him in the arm, a nice jab with a lot of bite.

"Ow! Why are you getting violent?" He rubs the spot and tries not to laugh.

"This is funny to you?" I want to stay mad, but I can't.

This isn't his fault. If James kicked him out, I would be relieved, too. I don't want him to go out there and risk his life, but it's not like we have a choice. Someone has to stop this horror, this latent doom that could be the end of us all. And lately, with my head buzzing wherever I go; with factions clamming Seattle, carving it in sections like an orange; with violent crimes and missing person reports on the rise, I know *everyone* should be fighting. I don't think it's something IgNiTe can keep under control by itself, no matter how many cells they have around the world. They've tried to contain it, to eradicate it before it becomes public, before chaos ensues, but it hasn't been enough. Because not even James knows how widespread the infection is and how many levels of society they have infiltrated, including the top ones, *especially* the top ones.

They've sabotaged us and, now, fighting for survival is left up to people like Xave—a boy whose only dream was to fix broken things, to love a girl who loved him back, and have a normal family with no superhero names.

So he *has* to go. He has to be wherever Clark is taking him, dangerous or not.

My anger drains. He sees it and walks to me, arms outstretched, ready to receive me. I take a step forward, into him, and let all that he is, strong and tender, gather me against him.

"It's not your fault. I shouldn't take it out on you," I say. "I should kick James's ass. *That's* what I should do."

He smooths the hair down my back. "I think I'd like to see that. Sometimes he can be such a pain in the butt. It'll be fine. After this, maybe we can take a break, do something nice. How about a date? You could wear a pretty dress and we could go out to dinner to a nice place."

"Sounds good, except for the dress part."

He chuckles. I rest my head on Xave's chest and concentrate on his heartbeat. It's strong and even and, I'd like to think, partly mine. Because I can command it. I've made it go fast, real fast. And I've soothed it, too, made it beat in sync with mine.

"Be careful," I say.

"I will be. The crew has each other's backs. Clark is pretty annoying, acting like my babysitter half the time."

I know it must kill him to say this—proud male that he is— but he's doing it for my sake, to make me feel better about him going off into the night to fight misshapen humans. He's doing it to remind me that he's not alone and has the rest of the crew.

And he's not. I'm here for him, and he's here for me, too. More than ever. Because with the way things are at home—Mom love- sick with her son and Luke cooling off on his initial *hey-look-I-have-a-mom* notion—and with James kicking me out of IgNiTe, Xave is the only solid thing left in my life.

The realization hits me with its veracity.

I knew this. I did. I've thought about it plenty of times. I just didn't want to believe it. I want to think there's hope for my family, but Mom's newfound awareness could come to an end at any minute. Maybe it's too late for a second chance with Mom and the twin brother who should have grown up alongside me. I also wanted to fight next to IgNiTe, wanted to make a difference, but that's gone, now.

So all I really have is Xave and he's mine in a way no one's ever been—in the same way I'm his. And nobody, *nobody*, should have a say in that. Nobody should be allowed to keep me away from him, especially those who don't give a damn whether I die in an alley unable to defend myself or whether I live trapped in my own head while a parasite morphs my body into "The Fly" or something equally disgusting.

I hold him tight, so tight that he gives a little exhale. He squeezes me back and I know he feels it, this need to be one, to be with each other at all times, ensuring nothing bad happens.

"Xave," I say. "I—"

"Shh, it's okay. I'll be fine. I promise. You know we *have* to do this. There's no choice." His warm breath tangles with my hair. His chest rumbles with the intensity of his words, with the zeal spilling from his lips.

"We can get through this. Promise," he adds. "We're strong. *You're* strong. More than anyone I know. And I'm so glad for that 'cause—even though I worry about you—I know you can take care of yourself, no matter what." He kisses my cheek and pulls away. His fingers trace a line down my jaw. "I'm so proud of you, for that and for so much more." Something glints in his eyes. "Marci, I . . ."

He trails off and his expression changes and I'm reminded of Xave, the child, before his features sharpened and his voice deepened, before the tough exterior closed him off and made him into the man he's supposed to be. He's open, so open, that I know exactly what he's about to say. And I want to hear it. And I don't.

My heart beats in a wild pattern. Air knots itself in my throat. My cheeks flash with a strange heat. I can't even remember the last time someone said those three words to me, and—for some stupid reason—I'm scared and full of shame. Why is it so hard to give yourself fully?

Without making a conscious decision, I push on my tiptoes and press a silencing kiss to his lips. For a second, he doesn't kiss me back. And, then, the moment is gone and his lips move against mine, telling me without words what they meant to spell out.

Relief and regret mix in my chest. I want so badly to hear him say it. I want so badly to say it back. But I think each day I'll grow a little more and, soon, there'll be nothing to stop me.

Chapter 6

Tonight is a night to rebel.

A night to do, rather than wait.

To decide and never again be *told*.

My headlight is off and my reinforced leather motorcycle pants tight around my bike. In the distance, I see Clark's taillight. I've been trailing them for ten minutes, headed south, parallel to the I-5 Express. A chilled breeze blows from Lake Union, cooling my nerves. I've wanted to do this for a while, but have always refrained for Xave's sake. I don't want James to kick him out, too. As much as I'd like to know my boyfriend is safe, I also respect his decision to fight. Today, though, I'm done holding my breath, waiting for James to call me or for Xave to return from one of his missions.

The guiding red dot of Clark's taillight turns right toward Belltown. I turn, too, keeping my distance. They drive onto Aurora Avenue, all the way to the waterfront, smack against Elliott Bay. To my right, lights sparkle on the waterfront and tall white masts signal the presence of unseen boats. In the distance, the Ferris wheel shines blue and pink against the dark sky, each gondola giving its passengers a sight of the bay and the Bainbridge Island ferries. We pass several restaurants and bars that would be inviting, if they weren't so busy. In spite of the cool March weather, many

40

occupy outside sitting areas and enjoy glasses of wine or something stronger to keep themselves warm. Couples walk arm in arm along the tree-lined sidewalks, the women dressed in fur coats and tall boots, the men in warm coats, all appropriate for the ongoing party that Belltown seems to be.

What can IgNiTe possibly want in this area of town?

Clark continues onto the main strip and parks his Harley. I stop forty yards away and watch Xave cross the one-way street, while Clark stays behind. A long line of people stretches the length of a black-painted building with strips of golden lights along its outline. They're waiting to enter . . . what? A new restaurant? A club?

To my surprise, Xave joins the back of the line. He's clubbing? No. Xave wouldn't lie to me like that—not that I could call it a lie when all he did was let me assume that this outing had something to do with IgNiTe.

Shaking my head, I push my doubts aside. I *know* he didn't lie.

After a moment, Clark rides down the street and disappears around the corner, leaving his little brother behind. What the heck is going on?

I get off my bike and, from across the street, move in Xave's direction, ducking under the bright signs and streetlamps. When I reach the front of a small coffee shop, I stop, finally able to make out the name of the place. My hands go cold. I push my back into a recessed wall, hiding under its shadow.

Shadowstorm Nightclub.

The same place Luke chose over our family dinner.

I rub my fingers together for warmth, thinking this has got to be a coincidence. Or is it? Is James after Luke? Has he discovered something I haven't?

The faint sound of dance music reaches my ears. Anxiety

ripples through me, making me restless. My hands twist and twist against each other. My feet march in place. My eyes scan the waiting crowd—women in tights and miniskirts, their sequin clutches twinkling as they gesticulate in conversation, along with men dressed mostly in black, like it's a uniform. I go up and down the line, from the bouncer at the door to Xave, until I spot a familiar face. A red-headed bombshell wearing a tight, black minidress and four-inch heels. In spite of the wig, I recognize her. It's Blare. And next to her, Aydan, also dressed in a black uniform, his matching pale, pale skin making him look like Blare's brother, not her date.

I nervously scan the crowd again, trying to spot the rest of the crew. I search for James, Oso, Rheema, but they're not there—a least not in line, though they could be inside already.

Xave fidgets, looking over his shoulder as if waiting for someone. He looks my way. I push deeper into the shadows. The *clip-clop* of high heels comes from my right accompanied by a sharp buzz inside my head. An Eklyptor!

Fumbling in my pocket, I snatch my cell phone and press it to my ear. There's no hiding, but I manage to obscure my features a little more. A woman wearing a blue glittery skirt and silky black blouse walks past without minding me. She crosses the street and heads straight for Xave. They acknowledge each other with a showy kiss on the cheek. He wraps an arm around her waist. She leans into him, looks my way and shakes her head at me.

Rheema!

She knows I'm here. Great. I stare bullets into her brown eyes. Jealousy tastes like bile—something I never knew. But I guess there's a first time for everything, even if it's unfounded. They're here on a mission, doing what needs to be done. I know a lot of pretending goes into these situations, like Blare and James acting all cozy at Elliot Whitehouse's party. I have no reason to feel this way, even if *my* boyfriend has been spending *a lot* of time with the cute blond, playing mechanics.

The feeling simmers to a slow boil as I struggle to lower my heated reaction, chanting "this is just a mission" inside my head over and over again. No matter that he changed into his best gray button-up shirt and the black jeans that hug his butt like no one's business.

Just a mission.

I wait as the line slowly moves forward, the bouncer at the door accepting or dismissing patrons as if they were cattle. Blare and Aydan are a few yards ahead of Xave and Rheema. They ignore each other entirely. I wonder if they'll let them in, if they have a plan. Or maybe they'll just bribe their way in. But heck, Aydan and Xave are minors. There's no way they'll get through, is there? Not that Eklyptors respect the law, especially lately.

Biting my thumbnail, I pay attention to who gets in and who's given the slip. My mind flies through the attributes of those who are allowed inside. There seems to be no rhyme or reason. Clothes, looks, race, age, height, nothing seems to make a pattern.

A pattern?

I know a pattern, and the Blare/Aydan and Xave/Rheema combos just happen to fit it perfectly. I move closer to confirm my hunch, making sure to stay hidden, even if my cover is blown—with Rheema, anyway. At least she doesn't seem to have mentioned my presence to Xave. She was always nice and friendly, was even rebuilding a Harley engine for me last time I was at The Tank. Another reason *not* to be jealous of her, right? Because this is all in *my* head.

As soon as I get within fifteen feet of the nightclub, my head begins to buzz, divulging the presence of way too many Eklyptors—monsters that I could believe human from a few paces

43

away, but that might hide some terrible deformation under their clothes or might one day grow claws. I take a deep breath and stretch my neck from side to side, my thoughts jumping like bunnies on steroids.

Dance music.

Clustermess.

Glitter.

A couple is let in. She's a victim; he, a predator.

Next comes a girl. She's by herself, looking hopeful, bouncing on the balls of her feet and sucking in her stomach. They turn her down. Too young? Too short? Too human? Too alone?

Lucky, lucky girl.

A tall guy in jeans and a black leather jacket walks right in. One less buzz thrills through my head as he disappears behind the large doors. Another girl walks up, alone like the last one. She's also human through and through, except the bouncer lets her pass.

No!

Unlucky, unlucky girl.

Why? Why? Why?

Then it hits me. They let the guy in the leather jacket in. He went alone, so she's meant to balance the ratio. One to one. Victim to predator. Human to monster.

It's Elliot Whitehouse's party all over again—another venue for Eklyptors to bring in a human they can infect, to contribute to the growth of their species—and Xave is about to go in, which is a terrible idea considering what happened last time. At least Rheema won't freak and scream her head off when she sees the creatures, so he might be all right. She knows everything about the monsters already. Heck, she's half of one, neurotoxin-ridden fangs and all.

Another couple steps up to the front of the line. Now that I've figured out the pattern, my attention focuses on other details. They've paused in front of the bouncer. He asks them something. The freak half of the couple answers. The bouncer—a massive hulk of an Eklyptor—nods and lets them in.

There's more than a pattern. There's a password, too.

I move closer. My head vibrates like a piano string out of tune. I stare at the lips of the next Eklyptor in line, trying to make out the words. I get nothing. Super hearing would be nice at the moment.

Blare and Aydan are next. The bouncer puts a hand up, asks for the password straight away, without carding Aydan. Cold sweat slides down my back. Aydan's lips move, speak the words and must deliver the right ones because he goes in, his arm intertwined with Blare's, his slender body stiff and elegant, made more so by the bombshell walking at his side. Whatever he said to the bouncer starts with an "A" or an "E," I think. Oh, who am I kidding? I couldn't read lips to save my life.

Squinting at their mouths, I watch people get processed by the bouncer. I'm trying very hard, but I'm getting zero. My hand flies into my hair in frustration, ready to uproot it. I need to get in there. My brother's inside and my boyfriend is about to make it to the bouncer. I can't stay out here waiting, waiting, waiting until I've eaten all my fingernails *and* the crud beneath them.

A night to rebel rather than wait. Isn't that how it went?

Frustration bubbles up my chest and I want to scream. I'm pacing in place, thinking about crossing the street to try and overhear the password, when my cell phone vibrates with a text message.

Unknown: You look desperate there :)

I jump, press my back to the coffee shop window with its huge display of mouth-watering treats. My gaze darts in all directions until I catch Rheema giving me an amused smirk. I look down at my phone and consider a reply.

"Bitch"?
"Go to hell"?
"That's my boyfriend, you skank"?

I rub a hand across my mouth, considering. The buzzing in my head gets worse, incited by stress. I take a deep breath that seems to get oxygen to my bone marrow. My cell phone vibrates again. I blink my eyes open.

Unknown: "Hailstone Reign" will get u in. Ur welcome.

Hailstone? The faction fighting for territory against Whitehouse's faction? Oh, shit.

My gut twists with a strange feeling, something I can't quite put a finger on. James says I have ESP abilities. We're yet to agree on that, but if this is what being psychic is like, the hell with it. Half-baked premonitions are about as good as half-baked baguettes.

My eyes cut to Rheema, but she's not looking at me anymore. She and Xave have made it to the bouncer. Like Aydan, Xave isn't asked to show an ID. Rheema's mouth moves very slowly, enunciating every syllable, leaving me no doubt as to what I need to say to get in, giving me more than what I need to look after my boyfriend. And my brother. That's if I'm not here to find out something that will cause me to lose him again. Because what the hell is he doing in a place that belongs to an Eklyptor faction strong enough to challenge Elliot's?

Chapter 7

I rush into the coffee shop's bathroom, trying to shove my premonition to the background. Not caring if anyone sees me, I strip off my leather jacket and ratty shirt, and I'm left in my black push-up bra. The mirror in front of me reflects a bleary-eyed girl with black hair matted to her head.

A twenty-something walks in and looks me up and down as if I'm infectious. If she only knew. She slips into a stall.

The sweet aroma of coffee and the hissing sound of an espresso machine pumping steam into milk gets through the door before it closes. The coffee shop was the most accessible place to do this, not to mention my need for a very strong dose of joe with *lots* of sugar. No way I'm going anywhere near that nightclub without some backup.

I throw the shirt in the garbage can—been meaning to do that, anyway—and put my jacket back on. I zip it but only to my breastbone, leaving what little cleavage there is exposed. Thank God for Victoria's Secret. The bruises on my neck will just have to pass for hickeys. Leaning forward until my long hair hangs over my face, I work my fingers into it and muss it around for some much needed body.

I look up and check my efforts in the mirror. My leathers are tight-fitting and can pass for some Catwoman wannabe outfit—pretentious enough for a night out at the club. Not bad. As a final touch, I pinch my cheeks and wet my lips.

A toilet flushes and the woman walks out of the stall. When she sees me, she does a double take and raises her eyebrows. I smirk and walk out. Can't wait until Xave sees me.

While I order a large iced coffee, I catch several looks. They're all from yuppies pretending to stare at their drinks and looking mortified by the way their eyes have wandered to a not-yet-legal girl.

Amused by their discomfort, I dump ten packets of sugar in my coffee and guzzle it in a matter of seconds. I shake my head to dispel a sharp brain freeze, then dump the empty cup in the nearest bin. I square my shoulders and look out the window toward the club. I search the crowd until I spot a young guy standing alone.

"All right," I say under my breath, then walk out and cross the street, my hips doing their best to keep up with the forced sashay that seems appropriate for the situation. I feel like a fool.

My breaths quicken as the buzzing inside my head deepens and the uneasy feeling doubles. I can only imagine how it'll feel inside the nightclub, *if* I manage to get in.

Just breathe, Marci.

Breathe.

The premonition is no premonition at all, just nerves. The buzzing can't hurt me. It's annoying in a you-might-soon-be-a-monster kind of way, but I can handle it. I've done it before.

I plaster a smile on my face, hop on the sidewalk and head for my target. He's looking straight ahead, fidgeting and getting on tiptoes to look at the front of the line. He seems nice and non-threatening in every imaginable way, especially since he is perfectly human. Most importantly, he's alone. Just what I need to make the *perfect* couple.

With certainty, I can say the word "outgoing" has never been used to describe me. Unfortunately, that's exactly what I need to be right now, which seems about as creepy as turning into a full-blown Eklyptor.

"Hi, there," I say as I sidle next to the guy. By my estimation, he's over twenty-one years old, probably a college student out to have a good time. He wears glasses that make him look bookish and approachable.

His head snaps my way and he looks me up and down with wide, blue eyes. "Um, hi."

"You, uh, have no chance of getting in, you know?" I smile.

Like *I* have a chance! They might find me too young and send me packing. I'm counting the buzzing will give me the edge I need. Also the fact that Aydan and Xave got through without problems is an encouraging sign.

"I don't? Why not?" he asks a bit defensively, eyes widening behind his horn-rimmed glasses.

"Oh, nothing against you." I flip my hair to the side. God, I feel so out of my element. "I don't stand a chance either and I *so* want to get in."

He gives me another once over.

"They're letting in mostly couples," I smile again, this time provocatively, I hope. I'll need a good shower after this. How do women stand to act this way? How do men fall for it?

His eyebrows do this little wiggle that seems quite involuntary. "Well, then . . ." He crosses his arms, leans his weight on one leg and relaxes the other one. His smile twitches, then he nervously strikes a different pose. Man, his attempt to be smooth is more pathetic than mine and that's saying a lot.

"Know what?" I say with a sigh. "Let's just agree to help each other get in, okay? And FYI, I'd be helping *you* more than you would be helping *me*."

"Oh, yeah? How do you figure?"

"Well, there's a password and I know it."

"Oh." His shoulders drop about two inches.

"What do you say?"

"Yeah, sure."

For some reason, he looks as if I just ruined his evening. I feel terrible, especially because he has no idea that, possibly, I've ruined more than just that.

Pretense gone, we take small steps as the line slowly moves forward. When it is our turn to face the bouncer, my heart begins to hammer in time with the bass thumping through the club's entrance. I've never liked the song that is playing, but the bass house mix the DJ is working is a definite improvement.

The meathead looks me straight in the eye, not even acknowledging Mr. Smooth by my side. The man is unnaturally wide with a small head, ears the size of cashew nuts, and gloved hands. He leans into me and asks for the password with a simple nod.

"Hailstone Reign," I say in a hushed tone that cracks at the end and might give me away. To make up for it, I add a smile. But my mouth trembles, so I press my lips together and eye my supposed pet human as if he's a chunk of succulent meat I'm ready to devour.

The bouncer gives me a knowing nod and waves us in without a second look. I walk in, my heart slowing for only a fraction of a second, then speeding up again when my head explodes into a mad cacophony of dance beats and Eklyptor brainwaves. I have entered the mouth of the beast once more, this time fully aware of what I'm doing. I'm scared and can definitely say this is one of the dumbest things I've done, but I can't let Xave go through this alone. This fight is also mine.

The world before me sways in blinding lights and smothers me in body heat. There are so many people inside I don't see how I'll be able to find anyone before I suffocate.

So much for rebelling.

Chapter 8

I blink against the light and smoke wafting through the air. My eyes and ears take a while to adjust to the relentless assault of strobe lights and synthesized, blaring music. I stand off to the side, waiting for the world to make sense again.

Everywhere I look, people seem to throb in and out of existence. One second they're there as if under a camera flash, the next they're nothing but a shadow. My stomach flips and it takes a tremendous effort to breathe deeply, to stay and not run back outside.

"That thing is huge," someone says.

I'm startled, a little surprised to see that Mr. Smooth is still here. I'd forgotten all about him already. His chin is pointing upward as he focuses on a rather large disco ball. It hangs and twirls fifty feet above the center of the building, sending glittery outbursts in all directions. The club seems to be designed around a large circular dance floor. Above it, on the second floor, there's a balcony. It is also circular and allows full view of the revelers below. Small tables are arranged around the cylindrical middle. Further back there's more, but it's hard to see past the snug crowd.

"Retro cool," Mr. Smooth says, lowering his eyes to mine.

"Um, thanks for your help, but I have to . . ." I hook my thumb in no particular direction.

He shrugs and gives me a regretful look.

"Be careful," I say, feeling awful for helping him get into this hellhole.

"Sure." He frowns as if that's the dumbest thing I can say.

I take a few steps back, wave, then march in the opposite direction, hoping he gets home safely tonight.

Squeezing between the oppressive bodies of Eklyptors and humans alike, I make my way around the club, trying to spot a familiar face. All I see are strangers; though, strangers I quickly catalog in a species chart: homo sapiens who don't make my head buzz on the left and worthless parasites on the right.

The DJ's voice bursts through the club's speakers, encouraging everyone to clap. He's up on a stage at the front of the crowd—surrounded by multiple mixers, controllers, amplifiers—and wearing nothing but a pair of white pants and matching fedora hat. He must be some famous DJ to be in such a prominent position, though I don't recognize him. His skin is dark and gleaming with sweat. From this distance and due to all the buzzing signals around me, I can't tell whether he's human or not. He seems to be having the time of his life, dancing and mixing music. The crowd is totally feeling him, shuffling, fist pumping, and even twerking to his beats.

I make my way up the stairs to the second level to get a better view. From here, the disco ball looks even bigger, like a toy for some giant princess with a taste for shiny things. It's hideous. I make my way to the railing and wiggle my body between two human women, earning a dirty look from each of them. I ignore them and stare at the round dance floor below.

There are doers and there are . . . well . . . non-doers. Right now, the ones below are clearly the former, while we—up here—

are content with just gawking. And it is a sight, a spectacle that sends icy tremors straight into my veins.

Below is a pit of sweltering bodies moving, sliding, grinding against each other. They're prey and predator in a literal dance, a morbid ritual of doom and extinction. There's wicked pleasure in the movements, in the sensual allure of a camouflaged hunter. Eklyptors tempt their victims with their stolen human camouflage and—unconscious of the danger—the helpless quarry takes the bait.

A shadow rises inside my mind, groping, ravenous for control of my senses. It swarms all at once but I start thought-jumping.

Glittering lights.

Blinking LEDs.

Server racks.

I shut my eyes. My hands grip the railing with white-knuckled strength. My chest pumps and I force myself to breathe purposefully and focus. My eyes want to roll to the back of my head. I shake myself, flex my neck, loosen my shoulders. To anyone on the outside it might look like a nervous tic, but it's my defense mechanism, a way to tell myself that I'm here, that this is *my* body. The almost-ritual reminds me of President Helms, and how, in a video of one of his State of the Union Addresses, I learned he has acquired the same affectations.

As I blink my eyes open, feeling back in control, I see a familiar shape cutting across the dance floor below, forcing his path between the throng of bodies, making his way toward the back of the building. I try to see exactly where he's headed but it's impossible from up here. A pang of sadness hits me in the gut, twisting my insides into a tight knot. James doesn't trust me enough to let me help, to let me fight against this evil. But it's not his call, is it? I can fight just the same, because everyone should if we're to survive.

I push past the crowd behind me, eliciting more dirty looks and some insults. The stairs leading downstairs are jam-packed in both directions. I try to get ahead but only manage to overtake a few drunken guys before a bouncer yells at me to slow down.

Grinding my teeth, I wait and descend the stairs at an infuriating rate. When I finally make it to the main floor, I follow James's path, eyes flickering from face to face, but fail to spot him again.

I push further back, right of the stage from where the DJ enthralls the dancers, and try to see past the thick crowd and find a slick bar lined with backlit panels that give a cool blue glow. People sit in front of it, atop expensive leather barstools, ordering drinks. A staggering array of bottles adorn the illuminated back wall, looking like some modern piece of art, instead of what it really is: a foul collection of overpriced intoxicants meant to rob you of what little control you have over your life.

My gaze sweeps down to the other side of the bar and I notice an additional room at the end of it, marked with three large, gold letters: VIP. I make my way in that direction and stop a distance away from the entrance. Two cashew-eared bouncers stand at either side, looking as inaccessible as the door. I curse, guessing the crew must be in there since I haven't been able to spot anyone out here and that was the direction James was headed.

I'm fidgeting restlessly, wondering what to do, when I spot my brother at the bar. My feet become lead blocks, and I just stand there, staring, as he talks to a middle-aged woman instead of the girl he was supposed to be meeting. His head leans into hers in an intimate way. His expression is almost feral, completely foreign to me, and I feel I'm looking at a different person to the guy who lives under my roof. The woman puts a hand on his shoulder and pats him. He nods, but looks frustrated as hell, as if whatever comfort she just offered him isn't nearly enough. Her copper-colored hair hoods her eyes and half of her face, making it impossible to get a good look. All I can say is that she makes my head feel like it's been invaded by yellow jackets.

Luke runs a hand through his blond hair and shifts in his seat, his whole body turning my way. I panic, whirl around and stare at the dance floor. There's a sudden hiss and a jet of dry ice releases from above. It descends on the crowd like a macabre fog, enveloping everyone and turning their faces into bleached skeletons.

My heart hammers. I chance a glance over my shoulder, barely turning my face back to the bar. Luke and the woman aren't there anymore. I look around, searching for a tall boy with beautiful blond hair. He's nowhere in sight.

I curse myself. I should have questioned him, should have confronted him about his knowledge of sentient parasites. I should have assumed his mind was already ravaged rather than choose to believe he can fight the infection like me. Have I been wrong about him all along? Is that why James hasn't responded to my messages and reassurances that Luke isn't a spy? That must be it. James knows something I don't know and it involves my brother.

Because he is a spy. God, he is.

But he can't be.

He's my twin brother. Max. Mom's new pride and joy. His presence here means nothing.

The world tilts. Music pounds in my ears. I look around, hoping to find a friendly face, a big smile and assurances that *everything* will be okay.

Xave. I have to find him.

I walk toward the VIP room. One of the bouncers puts a hand up to halt me.

"Password?" he says.

I say the only thing I know, "Hailstone reign."

"*That* won't work over here. Please enjoy the rest of the club." He smiles in a cold way that suggests he doesn't expect me to enjoy anything but his foot on my ass. I'm opening my mouth to say something that will probably get me thrown out when the doors to the VIP room explode open and a crazed crowd bursts out, pushing, trampling, screaming at the top of their lungs; though, not loud enough to drown the strident cracks of gunshots.

Chapter 9

Before I have time to fully register what is happening, I stagger backward, fighting to stay on my feet. More shots resound inside the VIP room, a million times faster than the bass of the song blasting through the speakers. The crowd's euphoria morphs into a different kind of insanity. Screams rise above the music. The heavy techno beats stop. The DJ freezes, hands poised over his electronic equipment.

A very human, very scared girl shrieks in my face and pushes me aside. I try to catch my balance, but I only manage a few short, awkward steps that aren't enough. I fall backward and hit the floor. A crushing battalion of feet passes to either side of my head. I wrap my hands behind my neck and roll out of the way. Someone steps on my back. I groan in pain as a high heel stabs me between the ribs.

After a couple of turns, I roll onto my hands and knees and crawl out of the way. Pressing my back against the wall, I stand, panic like a stake through my heart. Eklyptors and humans alike try to run on top of each other on their way to the exit. For a moment, I'm hypnotized by this odd sight: the fact that they're all equally afraid of dying.

Eklyptors are predators, hunters, stalkers. It's how I've always seen them. I would never think of a lion running alongside a zebra, both escaping from something more horrifying. Except these Eklyptors are new, freshly made, like a delicacy that might soon rot into a foul, deformed mess, if they choose to morph. They're as vulnerable as humans, with dull teeth, weak claws, supple skin. They can't defend themselves.

Not for the first time, I marvel at the fact that we climbed to the top of the food chain, way above stronger, mightier creatures, and we've stayed there, unchallenged, for so long. It gives me hope, even in my panic, because the Eklyptors are screaming as loudly as the humans, pushing as hard to get outside and save their fragile necks.

A feral, unearthly growl breaks me from my trance. My skin crawls in goose bumps made of primal fear. The growl is shrill and long. It's then followed by another and another. At the sound, the crowd pushes more desperately, tripping over each other, trampling those who fall. Fearful of the creatures capable of such sounds and reminded of the night I almost died, gruesome images of deformed humans with yellowed fangs and snapping mandibles rush out of my memory gates and flood my mind. I'm frozen, completely unable to move, stuck to the wall with fear. Smoke wafts through the air. Glittering lights dance in random patterns. Static plays on the speakers. I stare into nothingness, rooted in place, doubting my decision to come. I have no business being here. I should be home doing my homework.

My fists clench. This is what I wanted, wasn't it? To help Xave? To fight? Well fight, then. Don't be a coward.

Pushing aside the unwelcome memories, I come away from the wall and turn toward the VIP room. A bullet whizzes past my nose. I jerk back and drop to one knee, making myself a smaller target. When I look again, I see Rheema, Blare, and Aydan shuffling backward out of the room, shooting one round after another into the darkness from which they came.

"I'll cover you. Go!" Blare commands.

Rheema and Aydan turn to leave, but find themselves surrounded. Three bouncers wait at the edge of the dance floor, with two more pushing their way through the thinning crowd. They are all tall and broad, their gloved hands dark and twitching.

Finding themselves surrounded, they stop while Blare shoots one-handed at a staggering speed. I look around for something I can use as a weapon. There's absolutely nothing.

Blare lets out an uncharacteristic scream, staggers back and crashes into Aydan. They fall in a heap on the floor just as a hunched shape flies above them, narrowly missing them. In the commotion, Aydan's gun flies from his grip and slides away from him.

The leaping figure skids to a stop, digs long, clawed fingers into the floor and whirls around to face them. A hideous creature with an elongated snout and a bright red line along its nose opens its large mouth and growls. The word that immediately comes to mind at the sight of it is: *mandrill*. Coarse hair covers its torso, a pair of cropped jeans its bottom. Canine teeth the size of my forefingers flash, dripping drool. The beast pushes back on its curved haunches and bounds.

Everything happens in slow motion. Rheema slams shoulder first into one of the bouncers and falls back. Blare struggles to untangle herself from Aydan, while he blindly slaps the floor, looking for his gun. Adrenaline explodes in my chest and my not-so-useless powers rise to the challenge one more time. Before I know the thought has formed in my mind, Aydan's gun zooms from the floor toward my hand, all while the creature soars through the air, extremities forward, claws ready to rip their targets.

The gun's metal grip slams cold and hard between my fingers and, in the next instant, I'm aiming, squeezing the trigger, shooting.

The shots ring in my ears. My hand kicks *back, back, back.*

My bullets slice the space between us. One shot hits the monster in the abdomen, two in the chest. Its body jerks with each impact, blood exploding from the wounds like water from a leaky balloon. But it makes no difference, because the creature continues on its path as if the bullets are nothing but minuscule gnats. I aim and shoot again, but my shots go wild. The Eklyptor lands on Blare and Aydan, tearing with its claws and huge teeth. I run to them, gun outstretched, but the three bodies are a writhing mass on the floor.

Human limbs. Animal limbs. All a tangled mess.

Leg.

Blood.

Arm.

I move the gun up and down, from side to side, trying to get a clear shot. My hand shakes. Blare's wig sails across the room and lands inside a yellow martini on an adjacent table. Aydan's face twists in pain. Crimson blood flashes in my eyes. I have to do something. I start to squeeze the trigger, my finger too stiff to comply. A series of muffled shots sound between the fighting bodies. They go stiff. Aydan's face is frozen in an awful grimace.

Oh God.

NO.

Blare growls and pushes the beast off. It falls aside, riddled with holes and squirting blood.

"Take that you piece of shit." Blare spits and wipes her forearm across her face, smearing speckles of blood to one side, making them look like red shooting stars.

I fall to my knees. "Aydan!" There are claw marks running down his shoulder, a gash that seeps and soaks his shirt.

He blinks and looks at me in surprise. He's alive.

"What are *you* doing here?" He's still grimacing, and I can't tell whether he's annoyed to see me or just hurting. With him, it's easy to guess.

"You're welcome," I say. "Just saved your worthless life."

"No time for warm reunions," Blare says and runs to help Rheema whose neck is in the clutches of a bouncer, her feet dangling off the ground.

Shots keep ringing from the VIP room.

My eyes snap in that direction. "James? And . . . Xave?"

Aydan stumbles to his feet. "They're still inside."

The battle sounds from the VIP room are fierce, and James and Xave are alone.

"I gotta help them." But I only manage to take one step before Aydan stops me.

"No, don't go in there. James ordered us to get out."

I push him aside and open my mouth to curse him, then notice the bouncer coming at him from the back.

Reflexively, my hand flies upward. "Duck!"

Aydan's dark eyes open so wide that, for a moment, he looks like a crazed deer. As soon as my meaning dawns on him, though, he throws himself to the side, giving me an unobstructed path to the charging bull headed my way. I aim for the man's chest, the biggest target, and shoot. I hit the mark, but barely slow him down. His gloved hands reach out for me. I dodge and sweep his legs from under him with one quick swipe of my foot. He crashes face first to the floor like a stone statue.

He's stays down for only a beat, then tries to stand. With a filthy oath, I jump on top of him and bash the butt of the gun against the base of his skull, putting all my weight into it. He slumps forward and goes still, fingers splayed open on the polished surface of the dance floor. For some odd reason, his hands catch my attention and I realize he's not wearing gloves. His hands are black, covered in tough, leathery skin with blocky fingernails just as black as the skin. They're sturdy, monstrous hands, large enough to snap a human neck like a twig.

I jump to my feet just as Xave runs out of the VIP room, another mandrill-looking creature right on his heels. He has a gun like mine and is desperately trying to reload it, the magazine slipping between his fingers.

The creature leaps, teeth bared.

My blood runs cold, chilling me to the bone.

Chapter 10

"Xave, behind you!" I scream in warning, then raise my gun.

For an instant, surprise at the sound of my voice is the only thing that registers in his expression. Then, just as quickly, the surprise flits away and is replaced by awareness. In one fluid motion, he drops to the ground, letting his legs become two useless rags. The Eklyptor overshoots its jump and flies over Xave in an arch. I shoot, but the creature changes course in midair and my bullet goes amiss. I aim and pull the trigger again. An unsatisfying *click* informs me the magazine is empty.

The monster lands on the other side and begins to turn. My heart lurches toward Xave. He's on his knees still having problems with his gun. Eyes darting around, I look for help. Blare, Aydan, and Rheema are busy, completely overwhelmed by more bouncers who seem to have sprung from the walls. There's no one else who can help. I'm it.

With a war cry, I spring toward Xave without a second thought. As I'm about to reach him, he finally manages to get the magazine into the gun. Quick as humanly possible, he lifts the weapon and takes aim. Except, as it turns out, humanly possible isn't good enough anymore—not in this new world of altered minds and enhanced bodies. He's too late, and the Eklyptor is on him, clamping its jaws to his shoulder and shaking its head from side to side, intent on ripping him to pieces.

"No!" I scream, my voice devolving into an angry growl, a visceral sound that would be perfect for scaring naughty little children.

Xave cries out in pain, his legs and arms caught in the indecision of thrashing and pushing away his attacker. An instant later, I ram into the beast, expecting it to loosen its hold, but it's like running into a wall, and all I manage to do is infuriate it. The thing shakes its head harder. Xave screams, his vocal cords ripped open by pain.

Blind with desperation, I jump on the creature's back and hook an arm around its neck. Bristled fur pricks my hands as I clasp them in a headlock and squeeze with all my might. I throw my weight back, exerting enough force to choke a man as thick and strong as Oso. My neck and head pulse with blood. My teeth clench with vicious pressure. Every tendon, every atom in my body is engaged in one unprecedented force grip and yet, nothing. My efforts are worthless.

Not enough. Not enough.

Until, suddenly the creature gives, just a little, enough to let Xave find the strength to pull out his gun from between his chest and the beast's. Wincing in pain, he presses the barrel to the Eklyptor's neck and releases a deafening shot that makes my ears ring and ring.

I fall to the side, the weight of the world on my chest. I cough. Xave helps get the dead weight off me. He's pale as death, but wears a small smile and a grateful expression.

He weakly wraps one arm around my neck. "You saved me," he says.

I push him away, too worried to feel any relief or believe that this thin moment isn't ready to snap. I assess his wound. It's bleeding, soaking, draining life. He needs a doctor. Right now. His face is contorted. He gags as if ready to vomit.

I press a firm, cool hand to his forehead. "You're going to have to be strong. We have to get outta here and stop your bleeding," I say, my voice as firm as my hand. He needs to know how urgent this is. I need all doubts he might have about the seriousness of his wound gone from his mind.

"The others," he says.

"They can take care of themselves. Get up. NOW!" I order.

He flinches, then takes a deep breath and stands. I drape his uninjured arm around my shoulder and turn. The view isn't pretty. Several enemy bodies lie on the dance floor, but Blare, Aydan, and Rheema still have their hands full. Blare has lost her gun and is fighting two men by the bar to my left, keeping them at bay with what looks like a metal leg from one of the many upturned, broken tables. She's fast with it, enough to handle both of her attackers.

Rheema is exposed in the middle of the dance floor, but still has her double guns and she's shooting, shooting, shooting—back to back—but barely slowing the barrage of attackers trying to get her under control. Aydan is the closest to the exit and has found another gun. He's also shooting. Compared to Xave, they're doing great, so I urge him on, without regret. He's my priority. All I've got.

I lead him along the rim of the dance floor, away from the heat of the fight, even if cutting across would be a faster way to the closest exit. After a few yards, he falters, panting, his eyes rolling to the back of his head. I give him a few seconds to rest.

"C'mon, you're doing great. Just a little more," I whisper in his ear, no one has noticed us, and I want to get him out of here like this, in stealth, indifferent to what may be happening to anyone else.

He nods and we're about to continue forward when a strange breeze whirls around us. I stop, blink and look to my left.

My skin crawls with an eerie feeling. "James?" I whisper.

Then he's standing right beside me, bloodied, clothes torn, eyes bruised. He's been in the VIP room, fighting who knows what horrors, buying time for his team to escape.

"Guerrero," he says, not surprised at all to see me here. "You two get out, now!"

And, in the next breath, he's gone. Fast, though not fast enough to give his supernatural skills away. Now, he's by Blare, helping her, luring one of her attackers away, engaging him in hand to hand combat.

They'll be fine, now. James is with them.

I begin to move until I notice one of Rheema's weapons fly across the room. One of her attackers has gotten within arm's reach. With a high kick, he knocks the last gun out of her hand, grabs her by the throat and slams her down onto the floor as if she were nothing but one of her greasy mechanic's rags.

Ignoring my budding guilt, I tell myself she will be fine and readjust Xave's weight against my body. I only manage to move two more steps before I look back. Rheema's still fighting, still trying to free herself from the massive weight perched on top of her. My guilt grows a little more. I'm still wavering with indecision when a barrage of shots resounds through the night-club. An instant later, something groans, then snaps with a metallic, almost musical quality. I blink and look up as if in slow motion, already aware of what I'll see before I even catch a glimpse of the thousands of tiny, reflective mirrors raining from above.

The glitter ball is falling. Falling straight toward the middle of the dance floor.

Falling toward Rheema.

Chapter 11

"Rheema!" Her name slips past my lips, a worthless warning.

I don't know if she hears me, but, in that instant, she pulls her face away from the attacking bouncer, fangs dripping with deadly neurotoxin, lets the body roll to the side and notices, too late, the plummeting, car-sized disco ball that is well on its path to shatter her world into a million pieces of sparkling oblivion.

Once more, I act before I know the thought has formed in my head, overtaken by the need to act, the need to stop another tragedy, another waste of life at the hands of these beasts whose only aim is extermination and dominion.

Like a pre-programmed robot, I'm stepping away from Xave, leaving him to balance on his weak legs. My hand is outstretched, my fingers twitching and reaching and guiding. Whatever invisible force I possess flies from my hand. I can feel it like never before, a powerful tingling, full of purpose and will. It extends away from me like an unseen arm. My body quakes, writhing in a serpentine motion that seems to carry strength from every molecule in my body straight into my hand.

Suddenly, it's like I'm right there and the weight of the massive ball is on me, on my very shoulders, crushing me down. It slows, but barely enough. My knees bend. It's falling, gravity doing its job, like a reliable worker that never relents, never takes a vacation, never fails.

I scream with the effort, with the ache in my tendons and the electricity that seems to course through my veins. Rheema's below me, eyes shut, tight-faced, ready for death. My back bends and I feel I've been at this for hours, but know it's only been an instant, a life-saving or life-ending nanosecond.

And I can't, I can't, I can't.

I'm breaking under the weight. I'm crumbling.

Suddenly, there's a *whoosh* and blur of movement, and I break into an infinity of shards. Bits of me slide through the floor like snowflakes caught in a strong wind, tumbling end over end and leaving a beautiful trail of dancing light and whimsy glamour. I'm all over the floor, wasted, destroyed.

Then I'm not, and I jolt back, a thousand rubber bands snapping me into place. The tension is gone. I'm whole again, not broken, but still a failure.

"Rheema." Her name a word that, at first, spells regret, and then it doesn't. "Rheema!"

To my shock and relief, she's not under the shattered disco ball. She's standing away from it, safe in James's arms, shaking her head, disbelieving her luck and still-beating heart, then believing again. James lets her go and gives me an acknowledging nod.

I did it. I gave James enough time to pull her from under the wrecking ball. A fleeting smile touches my lips, but then it's gone, driven into a hard, cold line by a chill racking its finger down my back.

I turn, almost in slow motion, almost wishing this second would split into two again and again, so I could keep turning forever, until the end of the world.

Xave is standing there, staring at me with wide, hazel eyes that betray so, so much. Even in the poor light of the club, I see it all, see the surprise, the doubt, the hurt. I see James's and my secret facing the light, coming out into the open where no explanation will suffice, where the truth will mean the end of IgNiTe's subtle balance.

But then, just as the secret shatters, so it rebuilds and hides again, retreating back into the dark, drowned by the emptiness that replaces all emotion in Xave's eyes. I reel at the abruptness of his vacant, lost expression. He looks exactly the way I thought he would before I turned with that chill on my back.

I blink, follow his drooping gaze to his chest and lose my mind, my heart, my soul.

There's a stain blooming on his abdomen, a wet circle that seeps and leaks what little strength was left in him.

Xave falls to his knees, a hand pressed to his middle.

"No!" I catch him before he hits the floor and lay him gently on his back. "Xave, Xave, Xave," I call his name as if he wasn't here in my arms.

My fingers fumble with his shirt. I tear it open. Buttons fly and fall to the floor, making small *tip-tap* sounds. His torso is dark, dark red. His shoulder torn. His middle seeping and spurting blood like an oil spill.

He's been shot. I turned for a moment, left him for just a moment, and a bullet found him—a bullet did this.

I press a hand to the wound. Blood sneaks between my fingers. I press harder.

"Xave!"

I search his gaze, but his eyes are closed.

"XAVE!"

His eyes spring open, swivel from side to side, trying to find me.

"I'm here. I'm here. Please hold on, hold on."

He takes a labored breath. His eyelids begin to close.

"Open your eyes."

They close. All the way.

"Open your eyes. Please, baby."

They open. He looks at me and smiles.

His lips move. "I . . ."

"Don't talk. Save your energy." I look behind me, waiting for someone to come help, for James to scoop Xave up and save him, just the way he saved Rheema. James is fast and strong. He can take Xave out of here, take him to . . .

" . . . never told you," Xave says in a wet voice.

"No, no." I shake my head, swat tears away with a bloodied hand. This *isn't* happening.

No. No. Please.

Red rubber boots.

Cinnamon breath.

Untold love.

Xave coughs, then pushes the words he desperately wants to say out of his too-pale lips, "I love you." For a moment, his hazel eyes fill with tenderness and something I've never seen in his gaze before, not in the twelve years I've known him. And my heart swells at this new emotion and at the intensity that, even in his weakness, he's been able to conjure with three simple words.

A reply burns on my lips, and I bite it back. I squeeze my mouth tightly because the thought of saying "I love you" under these circumstances feels final, feels like the end to something that has barely even begun. I bite the words back because I can't accept this terminal notion that has entered my mind, because I refuse to believe that life will do this to me.

These can't be the terms under which we tell each other "I love you" for the first time. They can't be. I won't accept it.

"Don't be an idiot," I say, trying to smile. "You don't need to go all gooey because you hurt a little. You're going to be fine. You promised."

His eye narrow, and it's the best he can do to show me he's actually amused. Then he blinks and his gaze drowns in sadness; a sadness deep and total that tells me he knows, irrefutably, that he won't be able to keep his promise.

It is then that the pretense, the denial that is holding me back, vanishes and it's replaced by soul-crushing sorrow. My bones turn to powder. My heart flattens, squeezing all the blood out and denying it further entrance. The useless muscle in the center of my chest refuses to work and my lungs fight for oxygen, pumping and pumping.

"No no no." I grab Xave by his shirt collar. "Please don't leave me. Don't leave. Don't don't don't."

He fights to stay and make good on his promise. His eyelids blink open in slow motion, but a dark force shuts them back down.

"No, Xave. Stay with me. I need you. I need you forever and ever and ever. I'll do anything you want. I'll wear a dress and go out on a girly date with you." I press my forehead to the very center of his chest, then raise it right back. There's a flicker of light in his beautiful eyes, but it's faint, so very faint.

Then I *know*. I feel it with damnable certainty. I realize that this is his last moment, the last glance over his shoulder before one last step into the unavoidable beyond.

And whether or not he'll remember this moment once he walks across the line, I owe him better than this. So I take a deep breath and hold it until my lungs ache and burn and incinerate my rage.

I close my eyes and imagine his crooked smile and the happy-green hue of his eyes. Tears spill down my cheeks and, from the wasteland of my fury, my heart fills with tenderness for him, for my first and truest love. For Xave.

And with that, I open my eyes and look at him, hoping to give him something worth remembering wherever he's going.

"I love you, Xave," I say with conviction. "I love you," I repeat, then I kiss him goodbye.

Chapter 12

When someone pulls me away from Xave's still body, I'm done being strong.

All the reasons are gone and, in their place, I see only ghostly shapes of the things that used to matter; the things that made fighting worth it.

"Marci," someone says. Hands slide under my arms and separate me from Xave.

Aydan. Horrible, despicable Aydan who makes my head buzz like one of the monsters.

No. I don't want to move. I want to stay with my head on his chest, because at any second his voice will rumble, his heart will beat. I have to stay, stay, stay. Every part of me fights to remain, except my body, my defeated limbs. I try, but barely manage to lift a hand.

"No, Xave." James kneels next to him, index and middle fingers against his neck, desperately looking for a pulse. "Damn it." There's a growl deep in his chest.

Blare stands behind him, eyes dark and in a trancelike stare that anchors her to Xave's slackened features.

I was supposed to save him if he needed it, and I failed him. My head falls to the side, slumps against Aydan's chest.

Steps. Someone running.

"C'mon, c'mon, let's get outta here." Rheema runs past, too pumped on adrenaline to notice anything except the two guns she's using to fire backward, over her shoulder, and forward, opening a path toward the exit.

James curses, gets to his feet. "Go! I'll cover. GO!"

The command is fierce and snaps Aydan and Blare into action.

"Marci, we have to go," Aydan says.

My eyes lift to his with disinterest. There's something like shame on his face. He knows what he's asking for is cruel beyond measure. I can't leave. I have to stay with Xave. He can't stay here all alone, growing cold, no one to guard him from the trampling beasts in this godforsaken place.

"Help yourself!" Blare urges me, not unkindly.

"Please, Marci. Get up. Help me," Aydan says.

His arms struggle with mine and, limp as they are, I'm impossible to wrangle. My dead weight is more than he can handle. I don't even need to fight him.

Shots. I think it must be James, trying to buy time, prolonging the inevitable. He thinks we can defeat this evil, but we stand no chance. We are outnumbered and weak. Eklyptors have sneaked up on us, have corroded our world right under our noses and we're no match for them. Not even close. Humanity holds no aces up its sleeve. Just like others didn't stand a chance against us and met oblivion at our hands. The irony will be sweet and Mother Nature, the gods, and whoever else, will laugh and laugh, and we will deserve it.

"Damn it," a curse from Blare as she helps Aydan sling me over his shoulder.

The world is upside down as I dangle at Aydan's back, unsure of how I got there. And for a moment, it doesn't matter, until Aydan begins to walk and we move away from Xave.

"Put me down," I order.

Whether or not he hears me above the shots and animalistic growls that break behind us, Aydan tightens his grip on my legs and begins to run. My head bounces up and down. I make my hands into fists and beat on the back of his black jeans, wriggling and hating him more than I've ever hated anyone. I had thought him weak, but he doesn't relent, barely even wavers. Shimmering bits of glass twinkle from the floor. The smell of spilled alcohol drills a path into my sinuses.

"Don't! Let me go, you bastard. I have to stay with him. Don't you see?" My throat strains with the shouts, feeling as though it might tear open and bleed all over Aydan.

A cool breeze hits my wet face as we step outside.

"He's alone. He needs me." Tears run out the corners of my eyes, onto my forehead and into my hair; then I confess the truth, the knowledge that is tearing me apart molecule by molecule, atom by atom. "Please, I—I need him."

My voice dies, drowned in a fit of coughs brought on by my exploding words and the sheer force of my anguish. With my voice so leaves my will to fight him. I fall limp again and just dangle, useless and beaten, wrung empty by sorrow and something else that grows and grows at a prodigious rate.

Guilt.

Guilt because I turned away from Xave, because some unknown force in me chose to turn away and save Rheema. Guilt because if I wasn't the freak I am, I would have never abandoned him to perform mind tricks; I would have taken him to safety, to . . . to his brother who's suddenly here, helping Aydan push me into the back of a van.

"Shit. What the hell is she doing here?" Clark asks, hoisting me onto a seat. "Where are you hurt? Fuck, so much blood." His eyes, so much like his brother's, sweep the length of my body.

He wipes my face, and he doesn't know. Oh God, he doesn't know the blood isn't mine.

Blare and Aydan pile into the van, too.

"Where are James and Xave?" Oso asks from the driver's seat. His kind, brown eyes peer into the van's dark rear.

Blare exchanges a quick glance with Aydan. Clark doesn't miss it.

"They're coming, right?" He looks outside through the open sliding door, his body leaning forward as if he's about to take off running into the club. No one answers. He steps out of the van and onto the sidewalk. "They're coming, right?!" he asks again, this time in an angry shout.

The hum of electric streetlamps and traffic fill the silence. Clark's chest pumps and pumps. I absently stare at the back of his neck, foreseeing his pain and the huge crack that will tear him in two never to be put back together again.

Suddenly, he whirls. "Is somebody going to fucking answer?" he screams, then shudders with the force of a fear that twists his face into a terrible grimace. He looks from Blare to Aydan to me. "Marci?!"

I jump at the thundering sound of my name. His eyes search my face then lock with mine, looking for the answer my lips won't give him. But there's nothing in my gaze. Nothing. I know because I feel it. A great emptiness, a void, a depthless expanse like a black hole.

Clark shakes his head, understanding inching its way into the beginning fissures of the crack that will be his undoing. Except, he doesn't let it grow and tapes it over with denial. "No!"

A determined expression shapes his face and he begins to turn. He's going inside because that would be a lesser madness than standing here, splitting in two.

"Don't!" Aydan exclaims, understanding Clark's intention all-to-well.

But Clark never gets to turn all the way toward the nightclub, because the madness comes to him instead, breezing into the van in James's arms, then landing on the floorboards in the shape of his brother's lifeless body.

"Go, go, go!" James's voice, hoarse and desperate.

A volley of shots rings in the night. The engine revs as Oso steps on the gas. One of the mandrill-like creatures bursts out of the nightclub into the street and bounds toward the van like some sort of projectile. James snatches Clark by the collar, pulls him inside and slides the cargo door shut. There's a deafening thud followed by an inhuman shriek. The van rocks slightly with the impact. Outside, tires screech against the blacktop while, in here, Clark begs his little brother to please wake up, but Xave will not talk to us again. He's still and I try to pretend he's asleep, but it doesn't work. His handsome face holds a pained expression that makes it impossible. I long to see his expressive hazel eyes, but they are forever empty now. I want to clean the blood that stains his fingers, but what good will it do?

In my peripheral vision, the shapes that make up my world run downward like wax, like rain, like so much blood.

Shadows.

Then I realize that *outside* has become far worse than *inside* has ever been.

So I shut my eyes and let them take me.

Chapter 13

I wake up in a familiar room with white walls, white ceiling, white lights, white sheets . . . white everywhere, still I feel the darkness, right behind my eyes, beckoning, calling me back. I wonder why I'm still here. Why surrender isn't working.

I'm alone, curled on my side on a stiff, hospital-style bed. I've been here before when I first found out Symbiots have accelerated healing powers.

The Tank. I'm back. Go figure. Yippee.

There's a tube connected to a needle in my arm. I yank it out and let it fall to the floor. Dark blood beads in the crook of my elbow and I watch it, absently, until images from a living nightmare spring into my mind. I shut my eyes and curl up even tighter, ready to try again.

C'mon. Take me away. I dare you.

"Been waiting for that sedative to wear off," a voice says behind me.

My eyes spring open. I roll over slowly, almost without meaning to.

James is sitting by my bedside, the too-white, fluorescent lights reflecting on his shaved head, hurting my eyes. I squint. He wears clean clothes: jeans and a black t-shirt with the "IgNiTe and FiGhT" logo on the breast pocket.

"Sedative," I repeat without enough breath to even make it a question.

"Something Kristen formulated to help Symbiots in times of . . . duress. It keeps the mind clear, so the agent can't take advantage of the situation."

So that's why I'm still here.

"Bummer," I say.

James frowns and pushes to the edge of his chair. "You can't be thinking about . . ." He starts but can't finish. He takes a moment to consider. "Marci, there's still much to fight for." His tone is tired, but there's great conviction in his stormy, gray eyes. He truly believes this.

"Maybe for you. Though I doubt it. I think you're just lying to yourself. It's a hopeless battle. We've lost. Too little, too late. They're everywhere. My head won't stop buzzing, no matter where the hell I go. So let me be or give me some more of that *sedative*."

"We can't give up. There's always hope. Kristen is working day and night to find a vaccine and maybe a cure."

Maybe a cure, an idea that used to give me the hope he talks about, except that was . . .

Before.

My cynicism is such that it even gives me the will to laugh, even if in a dry, throaty way. "We've already failed."

"We'll only fail if we stop fighting," James counters.

"Bullshit! We fail even when we fight. The way I failed *him*, because this thing in my head took over when he needed me most."

I suddenly realize that I'm sitting up in bed, face hot, throat torn open, eyes melting into tears I didn't invite. James is telling me to calm down, to breathe, to get a grip before I end up *shad-*

owed, imprisoned in my own brain without the use of my body and any of my senses.

Ha. Bring it on. I deserve it. My life is pointless as it is.

"He needed me and something that is NOT me chose to play the superhero for the wrong person. He was all I had left and now he's gone he's gone he's gone."

"They will pay for it, Marci. I will make sure they do. He was just a boy. He was brave and wanted to fight, but he—"

"Shut up!" I can't take James's anger, his empty words. "Shut up!"

Something that James pulls out of his back pocket pricks my arm. In an instant, the ache in the middle of my chest goes numb. My hysteria dies with it. I blink several times, look up at James who takes me by the shoulders and gently lays me back down.

"Rest, Marci. It'll help you find the strength you need."

My arms and legs feel like remote appendages with uncertain functions. James brushes hair off my forehead and kisses me above my right eyebrow.

I grind my teeth and, as I slip into oblivious sleep, I curse the pity in his gaze.

* * *

"You woke me up for this?" I say in a groggy tone.

"Your mother will need you now more than ever," Kristen says again. She's standing by the foot of my bed, her previously pristine, high-end haircut looking anything but. I bet she'd kill for an appointment with a pair of sharp scissors. The circles around her eyes are so huge that, for a moment, I try to make myself believe James has been beating her. Fat chance.

"Don't pretend you know anything about my life, lady. You didn't want us to be together. You're probably happy he's . . . he's dead. Now you don't have to worry about our relationship endangering our little Symbiot secret. Now I'm not a risk to IgNiTe and they don't have to know there are *freaks* in their ranks, especially when their supreme leader, James 'Flash' McCray, is one of them. You're a hypocrite. Do you think I'm blind and didn't see there's something between you two?"

Dr. Kristen Albright is the master of cool. She doesn't even flinch and, to her credit, doesn't try to deny anything.

"Xave was a good boy." Her green eyes are steady and full of sadness. "He didn't deserve to die."

My throat falls in the grip of a giant hand, and I hate her, hate her because she has no right to make me feel anything but contempt for her presence here.

"I got to know him while he was here," she says. "He wouldn't want you to waste your life like—"

"Oh great! Now you're presuming to know what he would want. You know what? Just leave. Go to the hair salon or something."

"What a waste!" She walks to the side and drops a syringe on the end table. "Here you go. There's plenty more where that came from, in case you're planning to run from your problems forever," and with that she walks out.

I would curse at her, but, for that, I'd have to care. I don't. She means absolutely nothing to me, except as my drug peddler, I guess. I grab the syringe, uncap it and stick the needle in my arm. Numbness spreads through my mind and body like a gift from some chemist god.

As I wait for the world to blink out I wonder who they'll send next, because this is definitely a pattern.

* * *

I laugh, really laugh.

They've sent Aydan. Aydan of all people. He's even wearing that stupid, white lab coat which now has his name stitched across the front pocket: Aydan Varone. The arrogant dick. He's standing at the foot of the bed, in the exact place where Kristen stood just hours ago, or maybe it was days or weeks. Who knows? Who cares?

If I'd had to guess who would be next, I would have said Clark, but, for all I know, he's in the next room, lying on a bed like mine, struck by the same realization as me: none of this matters.

Fighting or not fighting, both amount to the same.

"Save it," I say. "Whatever you've come here to say, just shove it."

"Classy." One of his dark eyebrows arches against his pale skin.

"Give me the syringe and get the hell out of here."

"This?" He pulls it out of his lab coat pocket and holds it up for me to see.

My limbs ache at the sight of it. I crave the numbness, the oblivion its contents will bring.

He uncaps it and pushes the plunger in one swift motion. Clear liquid squirts into the air. I sit bolt upright and watch the sedative form a momentary arch, then spill down onto the floor. He gives the plunger one last push to make sure all the liquid is out, then throws the syringe over his shoulder with a wicked glint of satisfaction in his black eyes.

"There," he says, "you can lick it off the floor if you want it *that* badly."

My upper lip twitches. Hatred seethes in my chest, tries to push its way into my unwavering stare. I'm imagining his heart in my hand, between my fingers, beating his useless life away, one thump at a time. Suddenly, red flashes in front of my eyes, a confusing network of tissue and bones, the inner working of a body. A throbbing heart! Primal fear seizes me. I pull back, shut myself to my despicable impulse.

Aydan flinches and takes a step back, eyes open wide, betraying surprise for just a moment. His mouth opens to take a deep inhale. He makes a fist and pounds his chest with it, a quick, jump-starting type motion.

He clears his throat. "Well, I guess the saying 'if looks could kill' becomes a reality with you. *Nice*. If you were to use that skill against your enemies, that is."

I shake my head—denying my murderous instinct and wondering why my skill has come to me at this moment. I am not in imminent danger, even if I'm in the worst kind of pain imaginable and Aydan is pouring acid into the wide-open wounds. Maybe I just hate him *that* much.

He moves closer to the bed, his legs almost touching the foot of the mattress. He should be scared of me, running for the door, but he only looks disgusted.

"They sent me here to talk sense into you." There's a mocking quality behind his words, as if he thinks I wouldn't know *sense* if it bit me in the ass.

He looks longingly toward the door, the desire for escape written all over his face. "I'm surprised that, with all that's going on, they still give a damn." His depthless gaze returns to me. "Because I sure don't. There are too many people who need saving to worry about someone who's too weak to fight."

Aydan pauses as if to let that sink in, then continues, "James is under the delusional impression that you can help IgNiTe, that you can help save our city. But he couldn't be further from the truth. You're wasting everyone's valuable time here. He doesn't want to accept you're too self-absorbed in your own misery. How could you save others, if you won't even save yourself? I don't know what makes him think you're worth keeping around."

He pauses and waits for me to say something, but my lungs are in hyperdrive. If I could, I would shout, curse at him, but I can't. Oxygen is shocking me, too much, too fast.

"At a loss for words?" he asks, his expression arrogant, perfect to cast in stone for posterity, if he was as important as he thinks he is. "Well, that has to be a first."

His eyebrows go up, giving me another chance to say something. Only curse words come to mind, nothing logical. Nothing.

"You're mute because you know I'm right. If you don't get your act together, all you are is a waste of good space and even better time."

A vein throbs on his temple, blue-green behind his white skin.

"You're not the only one in pain," he continues. "You're not the only one who's lost somebody. In order to get out of this one, we need to be the strongest we can be. Weak people are of no use to IgNiTe, to Seattle, to the world. It is survival of the fittest, after all. Humanity and altruism only exist when there's a Starbucks around the corner. When the world becomes a jungle, the weak fall through the cracks."

My throat works. My lips move.

"What?" Aydan asks. "Did you say something? Speak up if you wanna be heard."

"I am not weak!" I shout.

Aydan opens his mouth to say something. He looks ready to tear into me, to tell me how worthless I am, how he would rather be picking his nose than be here talking to me. But he stops. For a moment, he seems to ponder what to say. His face relaxes. All the fight goes out of it and morphs into something that, if I didn't know better, I'd call kindness.

He walks around the bed and stands next to it. His inscrutable eyes reveal nothing. His face is back to the usual mask of conceit and self-importance. He lifts a hand as if to touch mine. I pull

85

away. His fingers twitch, then still as he presses them against the edge of the mattress.

Jaw clenched, he leans forward ever so slightly.

"Prove me wrong, then," he says and walks out of the room.

Chapter 14

After Aydan leaves, I cry and cry and cry.

I allow myself to be weak, to be the girl who lost her boyfriend and sees her future melting away into nothing, not even a miserable puddle in which to see the reflection of what used to be.

I let grief, fear, anger, guilt, all my emotions, seethe in my chest. I rock back and forth, hugging my knees. I become what I've never been before.

Weak. Frail. Pathetic.

My hands shake with need, with the desire to lose myself in the dreamless, empty sleep of Kristen's sedative. Pulling my fingers inwardly, I make fists and press them against my eyes. It takes all I've got not to jump off the bed and retrieve the syringe to see if there's anything left in it. A metallic taste fills my mouth. Blood pools under my tongue. I swallow it even as I gag, wanting to spit out.

My whole body trembles as I fight and, suddenly, I realize that the grief and tears don't mean I'm weak. On the contrary, they are what I've been hiding from, what I've feared, thinking I wouldn't be able to survive them. Except I'm still here. Even as my heart shrivels and shrivels. Even as the pain tears me down, and I put myself back together just to shatter again.

It's not easy, but it seems I *am* strong enough.

Just as Xave said I was.

You're strong.

You can take care of yourself.

Strong enough to withstand the crashing waves of pain, the loneliness, the tears. Strong enough to face this reality fully awake. Strong enough to speak and shape words to make an oath against Elliot, Zara, Luke, anyone who dares call himself an Eklyptor. To make them pay for what they've done. Strong enough not to let my enemies cancel me out without a fight.

Strong enough to shine through this darkness and not be snuffed out like a candle.

Because I'm meant to burn. I'm meant to ignite the shadows.

And so I will.

* * *

Hours later, as I walk into The Tank, where the large area is divided into clear-wall quadrants, I do my best to hold my head high and stifle the shame that keeps forcing my eyes toward the polished wood floor. I'm dressed in my leathers which I found folded on a chair together with my keys and cell phone. My lace-up boots were on the floor next to the chair and, now, reveal my presence with a *tap-tap* that echoes throughout the expansive area.

The first one to notice me through the clear partitions is Rheema. She looks up. Surprise fills her dark brown eyes. Leaving her work behind, she exits the auto-repair pod and walks in my direction. I stop and wait for her, focused on her blue, grease-stained coveralls. When she's only a few feet away, she pauses and smiles. Her eyes search my face, then, without words, she wraps me in a hug and holds me tight.

At first, I'm stiff, reminded of all the reasons why she's still here and Xave isn't. I squeeze my eyes shut. My throat aches as if a white-hot iron has been pressed against it. When the urge to dissolve into pieces goes away, I remind myself that being vulnerable requires more strength than shunning all my feelings and sticking my head in the sand. I relax and pry my heart open, letting the tidal wave of emotions move in and out. It takes everything I have not to fall to my knees and beg for drugs, for shadows, for death, anything that would be easier than this.

But it was my strength which Xave admired most. He told me that much. So I imagine armor plates clasping around my legs and knees, and I stay upright, return Rheema's hug and spill not a single tear. She pats me on the back and pulls away after a long minute. With a final smile, she turns and leaves—never having said a word. One down. How many more to go?

After a few steps, I spot Oso coming out of the kitchen area. A broad smile appears on his gentle face as soon as he sees me. I stop, trying to reinforce my armor, wondering if he'll be the one to undo me.

"Hey, little girl," he says. "It's a good thing to see you up."

"Thank you."

He seems unsure of what to say next, then he turns to what he's comfortable with. "Are you hungry? You name it, I'll cook it for you."

"No, not really, but I appreciate it."

He nods several times, then his thick hairy arm comes up and he lays a hand on my shoulder. "It may not seem that way right now, but it gets better. I lost someone, too. It's never the same, but the pain eases up enough that you can breathe again."

I look at his boots. He pats my shoulder and walks away. The angle of his shoulders and his entire posture spell sadness; so much so that I doubt the truth in his words.

I press forward. Kristen is in the lab pod, head down, nose practically touching the large notebook that rests on her work area. As I walk by, she barely acknowledges me. Her green eyes peer up for a second, then turn back to her work. She's not friendly by any means, but not hostile either, which is more than fine by me.

When I reach the computer pod where James and Aydan are so deep in conversation that they don't even notice me, I clear my throat. James looks up. When he realizes it's me, surprise flashes across his face, but he hides it quickly. He stands and gives Aydan a quick nod that looks like a "thank you" and an "I knew you could fix her" all rolled into one.

I think a smile curves Aydan's lips, but when I look closer, he turns away and rolls his chair to a gutted computer that rests on one of the many work tables.

"How . . . do you feel?" James asks.

"I'm fine."

"You were sedated for three days. It might take a few days to feel completely normal after . . ." He pauses, searches for the right words.

"You don't have to walk on eggshells," I say. "I won't fall apart again. I promise."

Strong. Be strong.

James nods slowly. Out of the corner of my eyes, I notice Aydan's hand become still and hover over the motherboard he's repairing. His ear is cocked in our direction.

"That's good to hear, Marci," James says, then sighs. "Especially since I need to talk to you."

I frown, feel my chest tighten.

"I wish you could have more time to rest and clear your mind, but, as you well know, time isn't a luxury we've had in a very long time."

"I know," I say, hands locked tightly behind my back, fingers stiffening and relaxing compulsively.

"Good, give me a moment to talk to Kristen, then we'll go into one of the conference rooms."

He pats my shoulder and leaves. I stay back, shifting my weight from one foot to the other, looking in every direction except Aydan's. I focus on all the pictures of geniuses he has taped to the server racks and CPUs that occupy the pod. A few of them have underlined quotes written in quick scroll. I get closer and read a few of them.

"Reality is only an illusion, albeit a very persistent one." – Albert Einstein.

"Intelligence is the ability to adapt to change." – Stephen Hawking.

As I pretend to deeply ponder each quote, Aydan slips on a pair of goggles, then picks up a soldering gun and begins to deposit a few drops of solder here and there. His hands don't look very steady. He must be tired. My eyes flick back and forth from Einstein's frizzy hair to Aydan's trembling hands.

His words ring in the back of my mind.

Prove me wrong, then.

I don't care for proving anybody wrong. I just want to prove Xave right.

"No!" Aydan exclaims, setting the soldering gun in its stand. "Crap."

He picks up the circuit board and looks at it closely. After a moment, he straightens his back, rolls his neck and takes a huge inhale. I know just how frustrating this type of work can be, especially when you're tired.

Aydan pushes his goggles up to his forehead and bends his head over the circuits once more. On autopilot, my feet shuffle closer to him, curiosity getting the best of me. When he notices me, his head moves almost imperceptibly in my direction. I stop, but he doesn't say anything. Instead, he acts as if he hasn't noticed me and continues to work.

Infuriating prick.

And even as I curse him, I peer over his shoulder, thinking it would feel good to lose myself into work, doing some productive hacking or hardware rigging, anything to take my mind to better places.

From the looks of it, he's trying to replace the motherboard's capacitor. There are a few key places where he needs to solder the leads. It's delicate work, but nothing to cause him this type of frustration.

"If I could just . . ." he says under his breath, pointing at one of the tight spots where he needs a connection. His index finger twitches. A strange crackle fills the air. The back of my arms erupt in goose bumps and Aydan's jet black hair stands on end. I frown.

Suddenly, a blue spark erupts from the tip of his finger, zaps and fries the small circuits in front of it. In one quick, freaked-out motion, he rolls back in his chair and jumps to his feet.

"What the crap?" He looks back from his hand to the now smoking motherboard. His gaze drifts to mine, dark eyes round and full of questions and incredulity.

"Something the matter?" James asks, returning from his discussion with Kristen.

"Uh, not really." Aydan frowns at the ground. I frown at him.

"I just burned my finger," he says.

I turn to face James and, as I do, Aydan catches my gaze and shakes his head ever so slightly. I turn my back on him without acknowledging his request. I don't owe Aydan anything. Why shouldn't James know there might be some power brewing inside of one of his crew members?

I leave with James, without a backward glance. As we walk, I'm on the verge of telling him what I saw but, in the end, I say nothing. Aydan may be an asshole, but his suffering is none of my business, just like mine isn't any of his.

Chapter 15

"Take a seat, Marci," James instructs as we enter one of the small conference rooms.

He slumps on a chair at the head of the mahogany rectangular table and runs a large hand over his bald head. I sit to his right.

"Things are getting out of control, moving too fast." He presses a thumb to his temple and smooths a bushy eyebrow with his forefinger. He looks extremely tired. "I'm sure you've noticed. I flew to Washington on business last week. My head never stopped buzzing. TSA guards. Cab drivers. Even a few people I used to know." He sighs, ending the *small* talk. "Anyway, there's no easy way to start this conversation, so I'll just go straight to the point."

I wait, teeth clenched.

"I know you're convinced Luke isn't a spy, but—"

"I saw him there, at the nightclub. I'm sorry," I say, admitting my mistake.

James nods. "He led us there. It looks like that place was one of Hailstone's main spots of operation. Hailstone is another Eklyptor faction."

"I know."

James frowns questioningly.

"I was attacked by two guys the other night," I explain. "They asked what faction I belonged to. They didn't like it when I said the 'Whitehouse faction'"

"I see. Well, they're Elliot's biggest rivals. They've been establishing territories around the city. The police members who are still human think they're dealing with gangs. Luke is clearly with Hailstone, Marci. He was meeting with Zara, Zara Hailstone. She's their leader."

"Crap! I'm so stupid. He's been getting emails from her. I hacked his account."

"I know. I received your reports. Sorry if I didn't respond. It's been crazy busy and I didn't want you involved since Luke is your brother."

So this is why he kept me out? If only he'd said, I might have understood.

"But he must have known," I wonder out loud, "must have been trying to get me off his trail. I followed him to one of the meetings they arranged. He met some blond chick at a restaurant and sat there looking bored while she made goat eyes at him. I thought she was one his many admirers, so I lost interest. It was all a freakin' show."

"We saw those emails and followed him, too. Every time. Everywhere," James says.

I curse under my breath. My hands are shaking. I wring them and think of Kristen's oblivion drug. My tongue feels swollen and heavy. I don't see a way to go on.

"Don't blame yourself. We simply had more resources to dedicate to the task."

Pressing a hand to my forehead, I wince at the pounding sensation in my temples. "I don't understand. Why can't I sense him? I don't feel a thing. No buzzing, not even one bit. Why is that?"

"I don't know. Maybe it's a fluke of some sort," James says in a puzzled tone.

"Why would he come to us? To join his long, lost family?" I let out a derisive chuckle. "To infect Mom? 'Cause he has to know I'm already a goner, right? None of it makes sense," I say.

"No, it doesn't. That's why I think we should find out all we can about him, which is precisely what I wanted to talk to you about." James places his elbows on the table and leans forward. "He has been staying at your house, right?"

"Yeah," I say, suddenly jolted by my total disconnect from the real world. I sit straighter. "How long have I been here? Is he still . . . ? Mom?!"

"Calm down. Luke hasn't been back there. It's only been three days. Clark went by your house and talked to your mom. She was fine. He explained about Xave. Told her you were with some friends, trying to . . . you know."

A lump builds in my throat. The back of my eyes burn. How will I go on? How?

"Anyway," James continues, "we thought you might be able to get some of Luke's DNA. Hair from a comb, toothbrush, anything like that. Kristen would like to take a look. Can you do that?"

I feel strangely numb. The room looks colorless in spite of James's art hanging on the walls. "Yeah, sure."

"Great. If you're also able to get something that belongs to your mother that would help."

"My mom? Why?"

"For cross reference, maybe. I really don't know. Kristen is the expert."

"Yeah, I guess that's fine."

"Good. Good. Well . . ." James stands and straightens his shirt.

"Is that it?" I ask.

"Yes." It sounds like a question, which makes me think there's more. "I didn't realize you'd seen Luke at the club, so I thought

it'd be harder for you to hear that he's involved with Hailstone."
He looks relieved I didn't melt into a puddle of tears.

I stand, following his lead. "The hardest thing that'll ever happen already happened."

James nods and looks at me with pity, making me feel as if I'm just an ignorant child who has seen but the tip of the iceberg. To hell with him. What does he know about the way I feel? What does he know about the measure of sorrow? And whether or not my grief for *one* person is bigger than what he's felt for the bunch he may have lost in his forty-something years of life.

He walks to the door, then stops and looks back. "Just send in the samples with Clark. You should take some time to rest. Go home. Spend some time with your mother. Grieve. This isn't the best place for you right now."

I open my mouth to protest, then clench it shut, fighting the anger that swells in my chest. His gray eyes are stern and unwavering, making it clear that he has no time to argue but, most of all, that *I* have no right to argue, that my presence here is entirely up to him and no one else. I thought Aydan said James wanted me to help them fight? I guess that was a lie. This is not the best place for me? He just doesn't want me here. He must think I'm more trouble than it's worth, and maybe I am.

James leaves, and I stay behind, hating myself for swallowing the lies they fed me just so they could get me out of The Tank and off their consciences.

The colorless room swells around me, exemplifying the emptiness I will endure from now on. Before, it hurt not being with IgNiTe and the Symbiot family I thought I'd become part of. But at least then I had a brother I could still trust, and I had Xave, the one person who gave me hope and happiness and could have kept me going, even if the rest of the world came to a screeching halt.

Now all I have is my mother and, ironically, I've never really had her, and now that there's no way in hell I'll play family with Luke, the chances of reconnecting grow slim again.

* * *

I exit the conference room a few minutes after James. When I step outside, Oso is waiting for me, a tan shoebox cradled in his large hands.

"I thought you would like to have this." He offers the box. I take it. "It's a few of the things Xave left here."

"Thank you." I'm so touched by his thoughtfulness that my response comes out in a mere whisper. Staring down at the lid, I think of opening it, but quickly realize it would undo me. I whimper in the back of my throat.

Oso takes a step closer. "It's okay to cry, kiddo. It don't mean you're not tough."

"I know that."

"Good. I'm glad you do. It took me a while to realize that. Tough guy like me, crying, not a pretty sight, but sometimes you can't help it." He chuckles.

I smile sadly and see his warm expression through wavering tears. His eyes are full of paternal kindness. His crow's-feet fan out from the corners of his eyes as he smiles back. His cheeks shine under the white, harsh lights overhead.

"Take care, kid. We'll be here when you feel ready to come back."

If only my return was up to Oso.

"We'll fight for Xave." Oso's eyes fill with fury. "His life wasn't given in vain. We'll make sure of that."

I thank him again, unsure of what else to say, and walk away. Box tucked under my arm, I make my way toward the metal stairs that lead out of The Tank. My feet drag. My chin rests on my chest. I don't even know the time and whether day or night await on the surface of this high-tech, underground hideout.

As I pass one of the corridors that lead to the sleeping quarters, a hand grabs my elbow and pulls me into the passage. I stagger, then stare blankly at the bodysnatcher. Aydan.

I look at his slender hand and, with detachment, notice the length of his fingers and the perfect shape of his fingernails. My gaze goes from his tight grip around my arm to his near-black eyes. Suddenly, he pulls away from me as if I've become too hot to touch.

"Sorry." The tips of his ears turn red.

Unblinking, I wait to hear whatever asinine thing he has to say. Must be something important if he's willing to lower his high standards to talk to me.

"About . . . the thing." He lifts his index finger as if that explains everything.

I narrow my eyes, trying to decide whether to play stupid or not, but I find I have only enough energy to stare and sneer the way *he* always does.

He runs a hand across his mouth. "Did you tell James?"

"No. He was too busy kicking me out."

Aydan's left eyebrow goes up, calling attention to itself. I examine it with indifference, the same way one might look at the curves and angles of a passing car, while the rest of one's mind is immersed in an endless daydream that has all the markings of a nightmare. I blink and try to focus on the words spilling out of his too-red lips and, instead, I end up wondering whether his lips always appear red because of his pale skin or because he wears some sort of balm. I blink again.

". . . not kicking you out," he's saying. "He says you need time to rest, to grieve, and I think . . . Well, it doesn't matter what I think. It's none of my business. I just wanted to ask if you had told him about what happened."

"Believe it or not, it didn't even cross my mind to mention it. It's also none of my business. So no, I didn't."

He nods and, for a moment, I think I see a glimmer of emotion in his eyes. At first, I try to define it, then decide it's hopeless, like trying to name the first tune played by a four-year-old violin student. So not like the real thing.

Aydan's gaze strays to the wall, to one of James's many classical paintings in his gilded art collection. "Um, I don't know what that was." He rubs his soldering finger absently. "It's never happened before. It's probably nothing and I don't want James worrying and wasting time on me when he has better things to do. So . . . thank you."

Gratitude? The emotion in his eyes was gratitude?

Well, I think the devil just took a cold shower.

A hundred smart-ass responses form in my mind, my favorite being: "It was just a discharge of excess self-importance. The human body can only take so much snobbery, you know?"

Instead, the words that come out of my mouth are civilized and reasonable, so undeserved by the likes of Aydan, but yet appropriate given that I owe my—what to call it?—*wakefulness* to his arrogance.

"I understand. Don't worry. I won't mention it. To anyone."

We stand there for a few seconds, looking at everything but each other.

"I'd better . . ." He points toward the computer pod.

"Right. Me, too."

Our feet shuffle. Our eyes shift from side to side, and then we part—Aydan back to work and I out into my life, which will be both old and new, but mostly terrible.

Chapter 16

I leave The Tank and walk to the closest bus station. After a twenty-minute wait, I decide to take a cab instead. The drivers, the passengers, cause my head to buzz and give me meaningful glances that make me want to kill them. If I ride with them, I'll never make it home in one piece.

The first two cabs are just as *infected*. I wave them off. I finally catch one with a quiet driver who wears a lime green Hawaiian shirt and gives me a pleasant smile. When we get within a mile of home, I get the urge to walk, so I pay my fare and get off. Walking slowly, I turn into my street around 2 P.M. The moment I see the familiar pothole in front of Mrs. Jenkins's house, my shoulders morph into two steel beams, stiff and heavy. I shut my eyes and open them every few seconds, just enough to make sure I'm still on a straight path. I count the cracks on the sidewalk and don't look to the left, across the street, where Xave's small house rests under the cover of many shady trees.

I know the lawn will be deserted, so I try to picture Xave—one shoulder pressed against a tree trunk, one foot folded lazily over the other—waiting for me. He's smiling, hazel eyes in their happiest shade of green. His brown shaggy hair curling by the ears and two-day stubble darkening his face.

"'Bout time you showed up, Marci," his voice echoes. "Been waiting for you."

"I knew you'd be waiting," I whisper after a deep breath.

The smell of cinnamon gum fills my senses. I think of those firefighter boots he was wearing when I first met him twelve years ago, the flames tattoo over his back that I helped him select, the way his strong arms felt around me when I allowed myself to be vulnerable. My thoughts jump from one thing to another, every tiny scar, freckle, and crooked smile. All of them Xave, keeping the shadows away as I step closer and closer to home, my breaths firing at a thousand per minute, my neck tense and ready to snap.

When I reach home, I turn my back, never having looked across the street, except in my imagination. I notice my bike parked by the side of the house in its usual spot. Clark brought it back, I'm sure—strong and protective and still functioning among the living, in spite of it all.

I unlock the front door and go in. Mom will still be at work at this time and on a Tuesday. She won't be home for another four or five hours, long enough to sweep the house for what James wants: my mom and brother's genetic secrets.

I set the shoebox with Xave's things on top of a narrow table by the entrance. I still don't have the heart to look inside. Walking through the white-painted foyer with its modern black picture frames, I move toward my room, but a slight creaking noise makes me stop. Slowing down, I peer into the living room. No one's there. Next, I check the kitchen and that's where I find him, sitting at the table, reading a book and sipping a Coke.

Luke.

My thoughts reel. I stand still, trying to understand. I didn't expect to find him here. James said he hadn't been back. Not after what happened at the club, after we found out he's part of Hailstone . . . after Xave. Blind rage builds up inside me. Here is one of the many monsters that bear the blame. Luke is with Zara—whatever he might be to her—and together they're the masks this evil wears, two of the three that will pay for ruining my life.

Taking several big breaths, I do my best to stow away my fury. Luke never saw me at Shadowstorm. He has no idea I was there and saw *him*. I suppose that's why he's still here, that's why he thinks it's still safe. Well, maybe I'll prove him wrong.

I back up a little, then walk forward again, taking firmer steps. As I pass by the kitchen, I stop and do my best to look surprised. Luke lifts his eyes from his book and matches my startled expression.

"Marci!" He stands, walks to me and wraps me in a tight hug. He's wearing a pair of loose, gray sweatpants, a white t-shirt, and sneakers. He's the picture of comfort, of I-don't-give-a-shit-who-died.

My skeleton turns to concrete.

"Oh, Marci." His tone is charged with regret I would buy if I didn't know better. "I'm so sorry. That was just . . . you must be devastated."

I swallow my disgust, doing my best to ignore the burning sensation in my throat along with the bitter taste of bile.

He holds me at arm's length. "Are you all right? Where have you been? Mom and I have been worried about you."

Lowering my head to conceal the hatred in my eyes, I walk away from him and enter the kitchen. "I'm fine," I say, my voice hoarse with a million emotions. I clear my throat and walk to the white porcelain sink. I pour a glass of water and drink it in one gulp.

"Clark said you were with some friends. Mom had me call everyone I could think of. I talked to a few of your classmates, but they didn't know where you were. I told Mom you weren't close enough with any of them. So, of course, they didn't know. Marci, *where have you been?*" He sounds like a father asking a naughty child how many cookies she stole when he knows exactly what is missing from the jar.

"It's none of your business," I say.

"Oh, don't be like that. I *love* you. I've been worried about you."

My skin crawls at the word "love". I rack my brain, trying to get hold of a loose thread in this game he's playing, but all I see is a big, tangled ball with no end and no beginning. This started the minute he was kidnapped from the neonatal unit sixteen years ago, I'm sure of it. If only I knew why they took him? Or, more importantly, why they sent him back?

"Come." He puts a hand out and points toward the cherry-stained table. "Sit. I can't imagine what you must be going through. Everyone at school is shocked. Is there anything I can do? Let's talk. Sit. Please." His blue eyes brim with compassion and under-standing. At the moment, he's all-loving, amazing Luke, a version of him that always makes an appearance when Mom's around. I feel like puking.

My heart hammers, rage-infused adrenaline fueling its wild rhythm. It's going so fast it's practically climbing, clawing its way up my throat, choking me. The fury builds and builds and builds, until red is too mild a color to mark how far it's gone.

"You're a two-faced bastard!" I scream.

Luke takes a step back. "Marci," he says, looking as innocent as a lamb.

His blue gaze fills with hurt and, for an instant, I consider the possibility that he doesn't have a clue about what's going on, that he's innocent, a pawn, a victim in someone else's game. Maybe it's Zara's doing or that man who kidnapped him, or some other monster. I don't know who, just someone else.

The doubt lasts *one, two, three* breaths, then it's gone. Gone, because I've always known something about Luke isn't right, because the way he treats me sometimes is creepy, so unlike a sibling. Because the way he looked while talking to that woman revealed yet another side of him; one that fits him perfectly, more than any of his other favorite costumes. The jock and perfect son, even the womanizing bastard disguise don't quite cut it. They strain, ready to rip at the seams, or are too loose, leaving him indefinite and shapeless.

He's not what he pretends to be, nothing like it.

Nothing.

Fake.

Three dollar bill.

Bogus.

I point straight at his face. "I know about you."

"W-what are you talking about?" he asks, but only halfheartedly. More than anything, he seems surprised I've finally decided to confront him.

"Tell me something, Luke. It's the only thing I want to know, then you can leave, can get the hell out of my life, or I swear I'll kill you." I pause, then point in the general direction of my head. "Why, why can't I sense you? Just answer me that."

His perfect blue eyes tighten at the corners, his blond eyebrows press together. "What do you mean?" The question, at face value, still makes him sound clueless. His expression, however, is a different story. He knows precisely what I mean. Yet, alongside this understanding there's also confusion; the discovery of some puzzling piece of data that doesn't fit his scheme.

I shut my mouth, determined not to unwittingly give away something that may provide an advantage. I wait for his answer. He offers none. Instead, he takes a deep breath and paces in front of the kitchen table, staring at his titanium sports watch.

After pondering for a moment, he says, "Karen will be here any minute."

"'Karen'? What happened to 'Mom'?" I ask, feeling as if the walls around me are cracking and will soon begin to crumble right over my head.

Luke shrugs. "I'm afraid the act isn't necessary anymore. Besides, I really have the hardest time thinking of her as my mother, in spite of it all."

"What the hell do you mean?"

"I guess it's your turn to be *confused*," he says with a perfect smile and a flick of his head that makes his blond hair sway to the side. "It's all so puzzling, even for me. I've known all along that something was wrong with you. You can really *sense* others?" He sounds as if I just told him I can fly. "We just assumed you couldn't, because *I can't*." He adds the last two words as if they should explain everything.

For a moment, my brain goes perfectly still, like the calm before a storm unleashes hell on Earth. Then a million questions sprout, mature, take shape. I gather everything I know, try to see patterns in hopes of puzzling the answers to some of my most demanding questions. But what I come up with looks more like an exam rather than the bullet point facts I want to find; an exam with a few true or false questions, a fair number of multiple choice entries, and a hell of a lot of essay-style doozies.

1. *Luke is an Eklyptor True False*
2. *Luke is my brother True False*
3. *I'm supposed to sense Eklyptors*
a) Always b) Never c) Sometimes d) The hell if I know
4. *Explain what the heck is going on?*

He takes a step closer. "We can make it all better, Marci. We can fix whatever is wrong."

"And by *we*, you mean Hailstone?"

He nods once, looking very gracious, as if he's referring to some altruistic society and not a group of freaks trying to exterminate humanity.

"Have you been with them since the beginning?" I ask, as a great hole opens inside of me, letting my newly formed concept of family fall through a depthless crack.

"If I had known you could sense it," he says ignoring my question, "I would have never allowed them to . . ." He shakes his head. "I'm afraid it will upset you."

"What? What will upset me?" I demand.

He sighs and is about to explain when we hear the front door open.

"Hello," a voice calls out in a sing-song.

Mom is here? Luke sighs again and runs a hand through his hair, a weary expression on his face. The *tap, tap* of her heels sounds against the foyer's floor. I'm trying to figure out how we'll play this out when a low hum begins in the back of my head. I step back, imagining a hideous creature walking on clawed feet, getting ready to burst into the kitchen and attack me. I look over my shoulder toward the glass panel door that goes from the kitchen to our small backyard. If it's locked, would I have time to unlock it and escape? I eye the Coke can on the table, my brain performing all kinds of calculations that could facilitate my escape. Except some part of me is stuck on Luke's words and they play again, as I struggle to understand them.

If I had known you could sense it. I would have never allowed them to . . .

"Mom?" my lips move in an involuntary murmur.

My gaze drifts toward the threshold.

I peer over Luke's shoulder. He moves out of the way to let me witness this next horror in its full glory: Mom, or the body that used to host her consciousness, walking into the kitchen, destroying what little was left of a life that's almost never been worth living.

The only person I had left in the world is now one of *them*.

Chapter 17

My cheeks are wet. I thought my tears were spent for the rest of my life, but I was wrong.

"Is something the matter, kids?" Mom . . . *it* . . . asks.

Luke shakes his head. "There's no need for pretense. She knows."

"Oh," she says.

My head hums, and I want to turn and find someone else to blame for it, but it's coming from Mom. She looks the same, her blond hair long and smooth, her nails red-tipped and manicured to perfection. She has on a blue tailored suit, like the many she owns and wears to work. But it's not her, no matter how identical. Mom has been pushed aside, imprisoned in her own mind, replaced by a parasite that, for some reason, signals its presence to its kind. Or has she? Is there any hope she could be a Symbiot?

"Mom?" I ask.

Luke cocks his head to the side. He's probably wondering why I called her *Mom* when I can sense she's been infected. He doesn't know about Symbiots and that's something I can't give away.

I search Mom's eyes, reaching, hoping to find that nothing has been stolen from her.

"Oh, Marcela," she says. "You must be *so* confused, honey."

I take a step back. "What have you done?" I ask Luke, breath drifting through my lips in a cloud of hatred.

This is not my mother.

Tears stand frozen at the corners of my eyes. This can't be happening. It can't. I have to go. I have to get out of here.

Back door.

Key in my pocket.

"Please don't be upset," *Mom* says, making a pacifying gesture with her hand. "Take a breath. Think. Don't act on impulse and without all the facts." She takes a step toward me.

"Yes, we can help, Marci." Luke nods and gives me an understanding, sympathetic look.

"We can be a family, just the way you've wanted all this time. The way we've never been since your father died," Mom adds.

How dare she mention Dad?! I should scratch her eyes out for thinking she can use Mom's old memories against me.

"We'll explain everything and it'll all make sense. I promise." Her words seem to drip with caramel. She never talked to me this way, not even when I was little. And this creature should know that, but it thinks I'm vulnerable.

But I'm not! I shake my head. "Stay away from me, you f-freaks."

I snatch the key from my pocket, whirl and run up to the back door. I try the knob, but it doesn't turn. My ears ring with panic. I fumble with the key, my breaths erratic and shallow. Darkness presses against my eyes, making the lock appear and disappear from view. The keychain slips from my fingers and hits the floor with a metallic *ding*. I spin on my heels and press my back to the door. My heart booms in my ears as it knocks against my ribcage. I look at them the way a laboratory mouse might look at an approaching hand.

I blink and blink, so blinded by panic that it takes a moment to realize they're simply standing there, looking at me as if I've gone insane.

"Please, Marcela," *Mom* begs.

"We don't want to hurt you," Luke says in a quiet voice. "On the contrary, we want to help, take away the pain. You've lost your way, somehow. Please, let us fix it." His tone is the type of tone that inspires trust and comfort. It's tempting, so tempting, to be rid of the hurt, to feel, for once, that everything is right with the world, with me. To at least have my family back, to save it somehow. And why not trust him? Why not, when I feel this strange connection with him, some shared invisible bond?

He approaches, tentatively, his feet barely making any noise on the tile floor. Taking my hand, he locks his blue gaze with mine. I look up into his eyes and am overwhelmed by the need to believe him.

"Marci, I promise you won't regret it. Give us a chance, give . . . *me* a chance"

The last few words are charged with a meaning that slithers around me and makes my skin crawl. He's my brother. He can't possibly mean I would give him *that* kind of chance. I stare at him with disgust and slowly push my confused panic away. Whatever he can offer, however tempting, I could never accept it. Even if he possessed the last lifeline to ever be cast my way, even if the most torturous of deaths was to become my fate, I would never go with him.

Xave died fighting this evil. To give into it would be to dishonor him, to make his life mean nothing—even for my family, even if there's the slightest hope to get it back.

I look at Mom one last time, saying a silent farewell inside my head. Even if she was but half the mother a child deserves, I loved her and it hurts to think she's gone forever. A part of me wants to mourn her, but I can't allow it. I push away my sadness and shove it behind one of the many doors I've built through the years, doors I've always used for secrets and compartmentalized emotions. And it's so surprisingly easy to do that it scares me, makes me think I'm irreparably broken, because no one should be able to stop grieving a dead parent so easily. Except I know this isn't true. I'm not broken. Not irreparably, at least. I still mourn Dad and doubt I'll ever be able to push my memories of him past any doors.

As all doors shut on my mother, my gaze returns to Luke's. He's watching me, expectant, waiting for the chance he has begged of me.

A satisfied smile stretches one corner of my mouth. He thinks it's that easy to convince me. His eyes search my face, then focus on my lips. I shudder, repulsed by the hungry quality of his gaze. The smile freezes on my face, a rictus that must show how dead I feel inside.

Luke lifts his free hand and presses it to my cheek. "I knew you would—"

Unable to stand his touch one more instant, I grab his wrist and, in one swift motion, twist his arm behind his back and push him face first against the door. One of the glass panels cracks. He groans and tries to break free, but I move fast and elbow his kidney with everything I've got. With a howl, he arches his back and falls to his knees.

I turn and face the thing that once was my mother. She digs in her purse.

"Don't even think about it," I growl, snatch the bag from her hands and shove her away.

Rabid, she launches at me, teeth bare, blood-red fingernails ready to claw my eyes out. But this thing hasn't anymore fighting ability than Mom did, so I just step out of the way and watch her stagger past. Unbalanced in those stylish, auburn stilettos, she falls on top of Luke.

I stare at them for a moment, watch them get untangled as they struggle to their feet. I swore an oath to make Luke pay. I just wish I knew what I could do to make him hurt to the fullest extent. I may not know what that is right now, but I'll figure it out.

Snapping out of it, I look around. I have to get out of here, have to run away from my own house. Staying isn't an option, not seeing how determined Luke is to "help" me.

Taking a few backward steps, I move away from them. As I pass by the dining table, I snatch Luke's Coke can and, as an afterthought, the hoodie that hangs on the back of the chair. That and Mom's purse should give James what he wants. I step backward into the hall and look both ways, trying to decide what to do. My bedroom lays to the right, the front door to the left.

"Marci, wait!" Luke calls in a pained voice. I look in his direction. He's on all fours, still trying to get to his feet.

I should head for the front door as fast as I can, but all I have are the clothes on my back. To survive, I, at least, need money and—

"Marci!" Luke is now standing, one hand against his lower back and the other one on the table for support.

I curse and run toward my bedroom. I push the door open, rush inside—throwing a regretful look at the shoebox by the foyer—then click the lock behind me. I look all around, trying to remember where I left my backpack. After a desperate moment, I spot it lying by the side of the bed and fall to my knees next to it. I unzip it, make sure my laptop's there, then stuff the Coke can, hoodie and small purse inside. Sliding toward my night table, I throw the top drawer open. A money envelope rests under Dad's copy of Neruda's book of poems. I snatch both and put them in the pack. After securing the zipper, I sling the bag over my shoulder and stand.

The doorknob rattles. I turn. A loud pounding makes me jump.

"Leave me the hell alone or I'll crack your skull open," I yell.

"Please, come peacefully, Marci. I promise everything will be all right." A pause. "Tauro, I need some help here," he says in a different tone. "Yes, Marci's house. She's not seeing reason."

He's on the phone with someone?

"Marci, c'mon!" He pounds on the door, clearly trying to bring it down.

Peacefully, huh?

Stepping on the bed, I jump to the other side, push the heavy, black curtains out of the way and slide the window open. Daylight pours into my ever-dark dungeon. I throw my leg over the sill just as the door flies open and Luke bursts into the room. He squints at the bright light, then rushes in my direction. Glad the house only has one level, I jump into the backyard and, without a backward glance run around the corner, thanking Clark for rescuing my Kawasaki and bringing it back.

I hop on the bike. The engine roars to life as I key the ignition. I ride away, this time allowing myself a passing glance toward Xave's house. It looks nothing like the way I imagined it a few minutes ago. The trees cast too many shadows and the shabby front door suggests that only emptiness and sadness can be found behind those wooden panels. Funny how the same paint-chipped surface used to look so inviting.

I ride without a compass, just away from here. The urge to give up resurfaces. I don't even have a home anymore, so why try? What point is there to living and fighting now that *every* aspect of my life is destroyed? I speed up and hold the image of Xave's smile. He tells me he admires my strength as he holds me.

You're strong.

You can take care of yourself.

I will the heaviness in my eyelids to go away.

The shadows don't hold any power over me, not today, not

114

ever again. I will hold Xave's memory like a torch and its brightness will keep away the specters that hunt me. Nothing will ever eclipse the fact that he was and is a great part of my life.

For him, I will fight. For him, I will be strong.

Chapter 18

Four hours later, I plug in my laptop and collapse on the lime green beanbag that sits in one corner. I'm miles from home, in a bright internet café. In spite of their fluorescent harshness, I welcome the overhead lights, as well as the cheery, modern decor of greens and yellows.

Eating a croissant turkey sandwich accompanied by a kiwi smoothie, I wait for the battery to charge just enough to power my computer on. I haven't used it in a while and it's completely drained. I watch the attendant as he makes an espresso for a college girl. Several tables are occupied by patrons who type away on their ultra-quiet keyboards and wear huge headphones.

My fingertips tingle, eager to get online and set my life on track. I need to find a place to stay. Somewhere I can rent temporarily, nothing fancy, just a place to crash and not freeze at night. For the *nth* time, I consider telling James what happened, but I don't want him to take me in as some charity case. If he doesn't think I can add value to IgNiTe, I will do this on my own, prove him wrong, and *make* him invite me back.

I finish my food and lick mayo off my fingers. I started eating without appetite, just because I knew I needed it, but I can already feel my energy levels increasing. I fire up the laptop and walk to the counter to order a cup of coffee while it boots to life.

After dumping several packets of sugar and cream into the steaming cup, I sit back on the beanbag and use a padded lap desk to rest the computer on my legs. I've never been to this internet café, but I have to admit they have a comfortable setup, good food and reasonable prices. *And* no Eklyptors, which is the main reason I chose it.

Determined to change my current situation, I crack my fingers and begin typing at the speed of light. First, I perform a few searches until I find a small motel that rents rooms on a weekly basis. It's in a sketchy part of town, along the northern side of Aurora Avenue where many such motels exist in abundance to support the numerous prostitutes and their *trade*. But it's the best I can do, considering my limited cash reserve. Three hundred and twenty dollars looks like a lot less when you find yourself on the street.

Feelings of panic and despair rear their heads every few minutes, but I push them down, shutting myself to all the recent memories that want to keep playing inside my head like cheap horror shows.

Instead, I immerse myself in a world of zeros and ones, the bits that somehow seem to float in front of my eyes every time I sit in front of a computer. The cyberworld presents itself like a series of switches and paths. The decisions are easy: *ON* or *OFF*. Everything makes sense. There are no emotions, just cold logic.

I check my protective programs to make sure they're in place. This laptop is as secure as my mammoth system at home. It may not have the same kind of power, but I have made sure the activities I perform from this device are just as untraceable as from home. To be sure, though, I won't use this café again, at least not for a long while.

After making sure everything is 100% secure, I log in to the H-loop. I wish I didn't have to, but I need to do something about my money situation, and I normally find my hacking gigs among some of the most diehard, veteran members of the loop. Whenever they have a gig they can't take due to time restrictions, they hand it over to others like me, who hack only occasionally, for extra cash, not to actually make a living out of it.

I browse the users who are logged in, looking for Hazard-US or SMASH, but they are not here. I stare at the cursor blinking, blinking next to my user handle.

$Warrior> |

The small flashing stick looks as lonely as I feel, beating away without purpose, without anything useful to do. I squeeze my temples and shut my eyes against the loneliness that seems to be winking at me, even from my computer monitor—from the cyberspace that has always been my haven—the one place where I can hide.

Angered by my self-pitying mood, I begin to type, my fingers deciding what to do way before my mind does. I go in a mad trance, the kind I've known only a handful of times since computers and hacking became my thing. I stay on the beanbag, chin pressed to my chest, fingers moving over the small keyboard, mind rolling from one line of code to another, until two hours later, when the large cup of coffee takes effect and I have to rush to the bathroom. It isn't until I get back and look over the code I've written that I fully realize what I've done.

I've created a hack to allow me to break into IgNiTe's network.

Doubtful of my motives, I scroll through the code disbelieving my eyes. For the most part, I know Aydan keeps IgNiTe's vital systems off-grid, completely inaccessible to anyone outside of

The Tank. However, he can't keep the network as an island—not if he plans to be aware of what is going on in the world. For that reason, he maintains one outside connection, a way out to the Internet, behind a firewall plus an amazing custom-made security system, one that I know well enough to find its weaknesses.

I frown, wondering why I've done this and what I can gain from it. If James finds out, he will probably kill me and then throw my remains into a pit full of hungry Eklyptors.

As I scroll through the program, absentmindedly chewing on my bottom lip, I spot a few problems and fix them. I think of Aydan, his arrogant ass and how he would react if he caught someone perusing around his sacred domain. Would he suspect *me?*

My own arrogance makes me think I'd be the first one he would suspect. I chuckle sadly, realizing that we have more in common than I'd like to admit. No wonder we rub each other the wrong way.

My index finger twitches over the enter key. I tap it just enough to make a hollow sound, but don't press it all the way down. I go back and forth between caring and not caring about what James will say or do.

I have the DNA samples. There should be saliva in the can and hairs on the jacket. Mom had a comb in her purse. I could call and say I'm coming over to personally hand him what he asked for, but something tells me he would take what he needs and then send me on my way to "rest". He has no time to deal with a messed-up, out-of-her-mind teenager who doesn't know the meaning of discretion and has nervous breakdowns when she should be grieving quietly and with dignity.

The hell with that.

I have waited long enough for him to change his mind. I can't wait anymore.

With a strong surge of resentment toward James and his decision to keep me away, my finger bears down on the enter key and unleashes my hack against IgNiTe's closed doors.

Ha. And they thought they could keep me out forever.

Chapter 19

The screen flashes with an "ACCESS DENIED" message.

I curse, feeling a giant bruise blooming on my ego. I'm not as good as Aydan, after all. I've almost decided this failure is for the better when I spot the problem, fix it and run the program again. After a long, breathless moment, the screen flashes and I'm in.

A week ago, I would have jumped up and cheered or, at least, thrown a fist up in the air. Today, I barely manage a smile. I look around at the patrons and the guy behind the counter, imagining they see the guilt in my expression. I've always restricted hacking activities to the comfort of my bedroom, and the targets have invariably been corporations whose CEOs go for coffee runs in private jets. Now, I'm out in the open and invading James's network. The shame feels like slime on my face. They don't see it, though. Everyone is too focused on their own devices, most of them just burning neurons in Mr. Zuckerberg's anti-social media site.

I look back down, wondering what I'll find. Hopefully some useful information that could give me an opportunity to help. I crack my fingers, ready to begin perusing around, but before I press the first key, random characters pop onto the screen, first slow, then faster and faster, until the entire surface fills with them and, finally, goes blank.

"Shit!" I exclaim.

Heads turn my way. The barista frowns at me, but doesn't say anything. I bite the end of my thumb and curse again, this time under my breath.

Damn Aydan! Did he just fry the only computer I have?

I press the space bar, expecting the worst: a dead laptop. To my surprise, the screen comes to life again, spelling a message with large letters made out of ASCII characters.

```
   /___|                    |  | |     |  |
  | |        _   _   __ _   | |  |  |_
  | |       / _` | | | |/ _` | '_ \| __|
  | |___   | (_| | |_| | (_| | | | | |_
   \_____|  \__,_|\__,_|\__, |_| |_|\__|
                         __/ |
                        |___/


                            _
                           | |
           _   _  __ _     | |
          | | | |/ _` |    | |
          | |_| | (_| |    |_|
           \__, |\__,_|    (_)
            __/ |
           |___/
```

It spells "Caught ya!"

$Specter> I knew you'd come
$Warrior> |

A handle with my H-loop username waits for me to type a message. I stare at it, seething with anger. How the hell did he find out my handle? I've never chatted with Aydan, on or off the H-Loop—at least not to my knowledge. I wonder if he was ever part of those forums. Admittedly, I've spent endless hours on the H-Loop. That's where I learned many of my tricks and soon started showing up every script kiddie who dared challenge me. Everyone there works anonymously, so it's a possibility. I doubt it, though.

One possibility . . . I was logged in to the H-Loop the time he hacked into my computer at James's request, when IgNiTe was trying to recruit me. That must have been when he saw my handle, and since "Warrior" is my last name in English, it would have been easy to remember.

After a moment without my response, Aydan types a new message.

$Specter> I left an open door for you. Build it and they will come ...

That arrogant bastard.

$Warrior> Sure you did
$Specter> No one else could have found it
$Warrior> Even your compliments sound like insults

He doesn't reply. I imagine him typing, then deleting some mean response. Even through messaging, silence feels awkward with him, so I type my cover-up story.

$Warrior> I got what James asked for. Mom and Luke's DNA

$Specter> He'll be glad. Are you okay?

Huh? It's not like he really wants to hear that my life has gotten worse since last I saw him or that I don't even have a home to go to anymore. I don't need his pity.

$Warrior> Since when do you care?

The cursor just blinks, no answer comes for a moment.

$Specter> I'm sorry

I stare at the words, shocked. He's sorry? About what? Asking? Never caring before? Aydan never apologizes. I start to wonder if this is even him I'm talking to. I have no response to this, so I backtrack to the one topic that really matters.

$Warrior> How do I get these DNA samples to James?
$Specter> I can meet you, get them from you

That's how low I've fallen. I'm not even welcome at The Tank anymore. Not only that, I have to meet Aydan, of all people. We make arrangements for the next day.

$Warrior> Anything else I can do to help?

I hate myself for asking, but that's why I hacked into their system, isn't it? To find out if there's anything I could do for *the cause*. Now that I've been found out, though, all I can do is ask because, surely, whatever door Aydan left open for me in their network will be gone after I log out.

$Specter> Nothing for the moment, but I'll let you know if something comes up. Something always does

My guess is I'll never hear from them again.

$Specter> If you need anything, ping me here

What? He'll leave this open for me? I frown, confused.

$Warrior> Will it be safe to leave this open?
$Specter> Yes. This is only

The typing stops. I wait for it to resume, but the cursor flashes on, spelling nothing. Did the connection drop? Someone's cell phone rings, then another and another. I look up, stare at a mussed-haired guy as he presses an iPhone to his ear. His brow furrows. His eyes dart from side to side as the caller speaks.

"What the hell is that thing?" a guy with blond hair and a dangling earring asks as he stares at his computer monitor.

I look at the other patrons who are also on the phone or laptops. Their eyes are wide and shifting, too. A sense of panic builds in the air like a cloud of steam. In the corner of my eye, I notice activity on my screen. I look down.

$Specter> It's happening!
$Warrior> What?

My heart beats and beats. I didn't really need to ask that question. I know what he's talking about. I've been waiting for it, seeing it like a flashing light in the distance, dreading it for weeks.

$Specter> It's all over the news. I have to go

I have no idea what to type, so I just sit there, staring, the steamy panic that hangs in the room seeping into my bones like the chill of winter. I shiver.

$Specter> Marci, please be careful!

Aydan's last message sits on the screen for a few seconds. I stare at it as if it were a rare museum piece that got filed away in the wrong exhibit. Words like "please" aren't in Aydan's normal vocabulary, not to mention the sentiment behind them. After a moment, the window in which we've been chatting goes away, giving me a clear view of my wallpaper: the image of a platinum-colored Vyrus 987 C3 4v road bike.

Numbly, I pull up my browser and click on the news link. If I thought my life had gotten as bad as it possibly could, I was deeply mistaken.

Chapter 20

I secure the door behind me and draw the curtains, making sure to cover the window perfectly. The room reeks of cigarette smoke, old carpet, and muffler exhaust—which is entirely my fault, but there's no way I'm leaving my only means of transportation outside. I've rolled my Kawasaki into the room and placed it next to the bed.

Feeling rather vulnerable, I check the small bathroom to make sure it's empty. The area is tiny, but thankfully clean. I leave the light over the sink on and close the door halfway, then turn off the lamp by the double bed. The less it looks like someone is in here, the better.

Kicking off my boots, I sit on the bed and press my back against the wall-attached headboard, feeling fortunate I got here before things got any worse. My hands shake over my lap. I squeeze them into fists and concentrate on breathing and conjuring random, off-the-wall things.

Souped-up road bikes.

Machiavellian.

Double espressos.

The ideas run out as images of what I saw on the news insert themselves in the middle. Fires. Tear gas. Pike Place enveloped in

127

flames. People running, trying to escape the chaos. Police officers wearing gas-masks, holding shields. Shaky camera shots of hunched figures slipping in and out of dark alleys, snatching men and women from the sidewalks and pulling them into the gloom where no one dared follow.

I think of the terrified faces of the café patrons as their lives suddenly went from run-of-the-mill existences to run-for-your-life, apocalyptic nightmares.

A police siren wails outside, faint at first, then loud, then gone. I stand, skirt around my bike and peek outside, pulling the dusty curtain back just a bit. The street is dark, only a "Vacancy" neon sign shining on the sidewalk. There isn't a soul roaming around, not even cars driving by on the adjacent road.

I sit on the edge of the bed and stare at my sock covered feet.

The world is not what it was yesterday, and it never will be again.

Monsters are real, and they're no longer afraid to come out and show themselves. On the contrary, they are eager, prepared and organized—more than I could have ever imagined.

Their coming out was nothing less than a concerted effort. They are on TV, radio, Internet. All the news channels are reporting their existence at once. Some are calm and quite inform-ative on what will happen next. Others are frantic and unable to express what their eyes are seeing. It is clear which news organ-izations are run by Eklyptors and which aren't.

Depending on their news source, citizens around the world are being encouraged to seek help and information from their local authorities or to stay home and lock their doors. Depending on their trusting natures, people are either going out looking for answers or barricading their windows and gathering anything that can be used as a weapon. Depending on their choice, some citizens aren't human anymore and some have quickly remembered how to pray.

I shiver thinking of our failure. We could have warned them. We could have done something, but we were utterly unprepared for something of this magnitude.

The extent of their invasion is staggering. They are everywhere. Police departments, fire stations, hospitals, news channels, government organizations. Every place imaginable. Their numbers are beyond my wildest calculations.

My stomach flips, a combination of fear and disgust. My life is destroyed in every possible way, and there's no solace in the fact that I tried to fight. Because it all amounted to nothing and, now, everyone is to share my fate or actually worse.

Whatever hope there was, it's now gone. They will persecute us until every last one of us is one of them. The CBS anchor said: "*There is no point in fighting. We are stronger in number and strategy. Our plan has been in motion for many years. If you are learning about it now, it is because we are well past the point of no return. The scales have finally tipped in our favor, and there is nothing, let me repeat, nothing that anyone can do to stop this. So . . . come peacefully and join our ranks, we promise you and your loved ones won't be harmed. Listings are available through the link below for locations where you can seek information and learn more about our new society. We promise you it will pale in comparison to anything seen before. Lastly, I entreat you to ignore any deranged reports about our movement. They are blatant lies, mere Hollywood stunts.*"

It is laughable and terrifying at the same time. In spite of the full-fledged Eklyptors— "creatures" as some news reports are calling them—that attacked law enforcement agents and appeared on some of the newsfeeds, they're claiming none of it is real and want people to believe that it's all ridiculous lies worthy of a sci-fi movie; for when has anyone seen half-human monsters pouncing on policemen and ripping their throats out?

"My God! My God!" an independent news reporter exclaimed as she and her camera crew filmed one of the beasts from a distance. *"It's a . . . it's a sort of animal. No, not animal . . . creature. I've never seen anything like it."* Her voice went raw with fear. *"I don't know if you can see, but it's massive. It's got huge claws, and they're . . . they're bloody. Oh, Jesus. Back up! Back up!"* The image shook as they moved further away. *"God, it can stand!"* she said as the Eklyptor reared on its hind legs and pounded its chest. It looked a lot like Ape Man, except bigger and further gone into *nightmare*.

Even with that, most members of our *oh-so* jaded society think the horrifying, quickly disappearing, YouTube videos are part of some elaborate hoax. Because who in their right mind would believe that honest-to-god monsters are walking our streets? Who would believe in men leaping over cars, tearing people in half with their bare teeth, blocking bullets with their exoskeletons, delivering poisonous bites?

No one.

Not when we've grown up in this CGI era and have become used to end-of-the-world special effects and plots.

If children don't believe in monsters under the bed the same way they don't believe in Santa and the Easter Bunny, of course adults don't believe in werebeasts. That it's all a big, fat joke or a twisted reality show created by Hollywood is really the only logical explanation. Forget locking the door and hiding. That's for losers and deranged conspiracy theorists. Most will trust the authorities and walk into a nightmare suspecting nothing, a nightmare they'll never, ever walk out of.

I lay back and stare at the ceiling, wondering what the members of IgNiTe are doing at the moment, how they are reacting to this turn of events. Did they know this was coming so soon? Are they prepared to fight? Will James call me now? Am I more valuable in this new world?

Jumping off my bed, I pull out my laptop and set up a hotspot with my cell phone. I sit cross-legged on the floor, run the program I wrote and access the pathway that Aydan left open for me.

I wonder if there is some mechanism that notifies him. Hoping that's the case, I wait for him to notice my presence, but he doesn't. I roam the system for a while, hoping to find something useful, but there's nothing. Not even "read.me" files. Aydan was thorough cleaning everything up, which suddenly strikes me as odd. Why do all of this just to leave a door open for me? Why not just block all access? Why create the means to communicate with me?

It makes no sense.

The whole world makes no sense any longer.

Chapter 21

I close the laptop, a feeling of disorientation falling over me. The world is truly bent out of shape and I don't know which way is up anymore.

Dragging my limbs, I head for the double bed and crawl under the covers. The comforter—if it could be called that—is rough, with the colors and patterns of a week-old bruise. Exhaustion clamps around me like a heavy suit of armor. My body gives into it, finally overtaken by the events of the day. I pull my knees into my chest as a tremor makes me shake all over.

My mind follows, collapsing under the weight of all the thoughts I've managed to keep behind a locked door.

Another shuddering wave rocks me. My chest contracts, causing me to inhale all the air in the room in one huge gulp, then letting it out in a barely repressed wail. I call out his name between sobs. In the last few hours, the world has become unbearable but, for me, without him, it's more than that.

It is agony.

I'm split in two—one part of me dead and the other one in total anguish, wishing to also die, but staying alive just to honor Xave's memory.

I yearn for sleep and, when it doesn't come, for Kristen's sedatives.

The street, the motel, the room are quiet, and I wish I could step outside, out of my own head—to a place where a stream of random thoughts isn't necessary to live under the light, where hunting specters don't try to imprison you during every waking moment.

I am one hundred percent awake. Time ticks by and by. My eyes are wide-open and dry.

A light knock at the door makes my blood go cold.

Before my heart finishes its next beat, I'm on my feet, eyes darting around the room.

The lamp!

I grab it and pull it hard enough to wrench the cord off the wall. I throw the small shade on the bed.

No one knows I'm here. No one but the guy at the counter— the tattooed, hippie-looking man who checked me in. He wasn't infected. He was riveted, watching the news on a small TV, biting his fingernails off, but he isn't one of them.

"Marci," a stage whisper from outside the door.

What? Is that—?

"It's Aydan. Open the door."

My heart climbs into my throat. If anyone could have tracked me here, it's Aydan. But why? I walk to the door, lamp in hand, tiptoeing on the worn carpet. My heads begins to buzz. I look through the peephole and catch a glimpse of his profile.

"Hey, I know you're in there," he says.

"What are you doing here?" I ask, suspicion building and building against my will.

My hands tingle as adrenaline bursts through my veins, because a new realization just hit me: how can I, after what has happened, trust anyone who makes my head buzz? How can I let Aydan, Rheema, Kristen, and James get close again? How? Yes, I've trusted them all along. I fought beside them and wanted to do it again, but that was before the world tipped on its head and left us grasping at straws. Eklyptors are out there now, acting with impunity, infecting humans and confronting their own about faction allegiances. What if someone got to Aydan?

How can I tell monster from friend anymore?

"Damn it, let me in before someone sees me!" he says.

"What do you want?" I ask.

"Really?! Open the door. You're gonna get me killed."

"We're not supposed to meet till tomorrow. How do I know you're not—?"

"You can't be serious."

I say nothing, which is answer enough to show him *I am* serious. The peephole obscures a little as he leans forward and presses his forehead to the door.

"I guess you're just going to have to trust me," he says. "Kristen has a test for it, but it's not the pee-on-a-stick kind of test. It takes blood and a microscope and who knows what else, so just open the freakin' door, all right?"

My hand grasps the doorknob and sits there for a moment, unmoving.

"If you don't open the door, I'll leave, okay? Then James can send whoever else is stupid enough to come get you."

"He sent you?" I ask.

Aydan doesn't answer. Does he really think I'm being unreasonable? He would probably do the same thing, if he was in my position. I look through the peephole again. Nothing, just the empty parking lot and the lonely night. He's gone. I fling the door open, stick my head out and look right and left.

"Hey!" I mock-whisper.

Aydan looks over his shoulder and gives me a tired look. He turns and walks back. "I suppose the entire place knows we're here, now," he sneers as he walks in the room, his eyes drifting toward my motorcycle.

I close the door and twist the bolt. "Why did you come? Did James really send you?"

He looks at the room, a neutral expression on his face. He's wearing his typical black jeans and black shirt, a perfect match for his jet black hair and eyes. His pale skin stands out against all that dark. I guess sitting all day in front of a computer doesn't help his complexion in the least.

"I tracked you to the café. You were sloppy covering your trail," he says.

"I didn't think I needed to worry about you but, clearly, I was wrong."

He keeps going as if I haven't said a thing. "But you were already gone. Then I went by your house, but you weren't there either. No one was there, as a matter of fact."

I walk to the bed and sit down, my familiar *Aydanphobia* growing by the second. "Yeah, both my mother and brother are Eklyptors now," I say.

"Your mom?" he asks.

"Yeah," I say, making it clear I don't want to talk about it.

He nods, then asks. "What are you doing here?"

"I asked you first."

"Fair enough. Anyway, I thought you might try to hop on our network again, and I was right. You did. So I tracked you a *second time* and, now, here I am."

"In all your glory," I mumble and roll my eyes.

"I came to get you. Like I said, James sent me."

I frown. "You could've just called, texted, emailed. Why come all the way out here."

"Um, James didn't want to take a risk and have you go out by yourself."

I scoff. "I can take care of myself. So he really sent you? He wants me back in the team?" I hate how hopeful and pathetic I sound.

135

"Yeah," he says, but it sounds more like "duh".

"He kicked me out, Aydan," I remind him. "Twice."

"He didn't. Before, he was just mad at you for being so careless and not telling him about your brother. Can you blame the guy? After . . . the nightclub and . . . you know . . . he was glad you were there to help. But, with what you were going through, he just thought you needed to rest. Get your mind off things for a bit before coming back."

"Did *he* say that?" I hate how much I care about James's opinion. I hate that I admire him and want to impress him, especially when he can be so inflexible and set in his ways. I wish I didn't give a damn. Besides, it's a stupid question. He told *me* that. I was too busy being dense.

Aydan walks to my bike and pats its leather seat. "He worries about you, Marci. Worries about all of us, but he's especially protective toward you. Yes, he *did* say that. He also wanted me to do some reconnaissance. See what the situation is like out in the streets. I hacked into the traffic system and navigated my way around using their cameras. I was able to avoid the worst areas."

Smart. Not sure I would have thought of that one and, even though it makes me hate him a little more, it also gives me a twinge of admiration for him.

He shakes his head. "It's messed-up. As soon as people heard of the chaos on the news, a bunch of them took to the streets like it was Black Friday or something. The idiots try to score a TV and end up with more than they bargain for." Aydan taps his temple. "I guess Eklyptors were counting on some trying to profit from the mess. All of downtown is out of control, Pacific Place, the shops by Rainier Square, Pikes Place . . . people went to raid those and it was like a big trap. Tons just got snatched and, well, I'm sure the bastard *Spawners* will have a busy night infecting people. At this rate, half of Seattle will be taken over in a week. From there, it can only get worse."

"What are we gonna do? Does IgNiTe have a plan? They must." In spite of my need for answers, I try to relax. I don't have to fight alone anymore. James wants me back.

"I don't know. He talked to us today and said that things are much worse than any of the IgNiTe leaders around the world had anticipated. I mean, we knew Eklyptors were getting ready for something like this, but no one suspected it would happen so soon and on such a global scale. We knew they were organized, but this . . . this is beyond what anyone expected. We have to regroup, have to figure out what we're going to do to fight them. Apparently, IgNiTe lost two of its cells tonight in Austin and Barcelona. The Eklyptor factions there knew about them and blew up their headquarters even before all hell broke loose."

I rake trembling fingers into my hair, hoping to calm the nervous tingling in my scalp. This sounds really bad. It's not just any nightmare. It's a hellish ride designed by the devil himself who, by the way, is laughing all the way to the bank. Because the madness is collective: a vicious psychosis of the highest stakes. So why wouldn't he?

Aydan walks to the other end of the bed and sits, elbows on knees, head between his hands. He heaves a sigh and turns to face me. "Are you all right?" His dark eyes search mine. His gaze is intense and heavy, almost like a touch. There's nothing superficial about his question. He truly wants to know and is demanding a real answer, not something off-hand.

What the hell? Aydan has always been a jackass to me, pedantic, arrogant, with a holier-than-thou attitude that makes me want to strangle him. So this new side . . . it's really throwing me for a loop. They say bad times bring the best out in people and maybe it's true. Maybe now I just have to decide if I'm capable of forgetting the times he acted like I was dirt on his shoe.

I'm tempted to reciprocate his past behavior, to snub him and tell him to bug off. But when I open my mouth to speak, I can't do it.

Instead, I offer him a noncommittal truth. "I've been better."

He presses his lips in a thin line, making them go as pale as the rest of his face. He appears unsatisfied by my answer and looks as if he'll press me further. After a moment, though, he nods and seems to decide that, given everything, this is actually a civilized answer, even more than he deserves. Okay, maybe *he* doesn't think that, but I certainly do. I'm all for getting along, but if he turns out to be one of those neurotic people who suffers from severe mood swings, I'm *not* going to put up with that.

"We should leave." He stands. "The Tank will be safer and I'm sure there'll be plenty for us to do."

I put on my leather jacket and sling my backpack over my shoulder. "How did you get here? Car? I can follow you on my bike."

"Would you be opposed to leaving it here? My car is rigged with a laptop. You can look at the traffic to help me navigate. It would be faster and safer that way. It's a good thing the cameras are still running. Although that surely means Eklyptors in high places."

I look toward my bike longingly. I'd like to take it with me, but I guess Aydan's right. "Okay. The room is paid for two weeks, so I can get it later."

"Good." He walks to the window and peeks outside. "Do you have the DNA samples?" he asks without looking back.

"They're in my backpack."

"The coast looks clear. Let's go."

And with that, we step out into the night where, more than ever, the shadows seem to possess a life of their own. We walk briskly to his car, a small VW Jetta. The air is crisp and charged with a strange silence that makes me feel desolate. In my mind, I imagine the terrified cries of an entire city riding the wind, desperately casting outward in hopes of reaching someone who can deliver them from evil.

It hurts to think that, at the moment, no one can.

Chapter 22

We've made it to downtown where, from what I gather, the bulk of the mayhem is concentrated. As we head south, the entire length of Westlake Avenue looks deserted: an odd sight. We pass The Westin hotel with its two cylindrical towers and cross under the inert-looking monorail. Signs for parking, rental car places, pharmacies, and other businesses shine in all their rainbow neon glory. In the quiet, I can almost hear their electric hum. Aydan's hands grip the wheel in a way that would make any Driver's Ed teacher proud. He's leaning forward, staring fixedly at the road, the way old people do.

"What next?" he asks.

I look away from him, stare back at the laptop. It's mounted on a swivel on the center console. He said it's detachable, that he rigged it a while back as a custom navigation system.

"There's no activity on this road as far as the traffic cameras are concerned," I say.

My hands are sweating. I wipe them on my pants. "I have a bad feeling."

"Shut up," he says—not meanly, though, but in a you-read-my-mind kind of way which makes me even more worried. Maybe James is right and these bad feelings are truly premonitions.

We pass a few intersections, ignoring their traffic lights. They continue to function, shining red-yellow-green against the night sky, as if nothing has happened and the hustle and bustle of the city is the same as it was yesterday. I imagine ghost cars waiting for pedestrians to cross, then speeding up when it's their turn to go. In my mind, I picture Seattle vibrant and active, and try to ignore the terrifying idea that the city I love is lost forever.

A west-bound breeze blows with enough force to make the stoplights sway and creak on their wires. Aydan drives, ignoring all rules as if they never existed, but the tension in his shoulders gives him away. They tighten every time he runs a red light. This sudden lawlessness unnerves him as much as it unnerves me.

"Crap!" he exclaims, startled.

My heart jumps. I look up and follow his gaze. A tall man in a long, black coat is walking up to the edge of the sidewalk a few yards ahead.

"He just came out of there." Aydan points at a three-story, brick building with a copper-plated awning over its large glass door.

The man is alone. No other sign of life around him. As we drive past him, my head buzzes. Aydan looks straight ahead, but I make eye contact. The man stares at me, unsmiling, then taps the side of his nose with a forefinger. He watches us as we move away. I crane my neck and stare backward until I lose sight of him.

I face the front with a sigh of relief. Aydan and I exchange a look.

"Assholes," he says.

"We should turn coming up. Let me double check." With a few clicks on the touchpad, I open the feed for the nearest cameras. Grainy black and white images show me our route. "Three streets ahead take a left. It still looks clear, as far as I can tell."

We're still a few miles from IgNiTe's headquarters, and every single one feels like a thousand.

Aydan taps his turning signal, then snorts. "A turning signal, ha! 'Bout as useful as a two-digit password."

He smiles a crooked grin I've never seen before. His lower lip trembles, revealing his nerves. What a geeky comment. Still, I smile, because he's right. Short passwords *are* absolutely useless.

Aydan turns the corner, craning his neck even more. My eyes do a quick sweep of the street. It's empty. I exhale with relief. Tapping on the keyboard, I see what other cameras are available.

"A few more minutes and we'll be there," I say. "I really—"

The car comes to a sudden stop with a screech of breaks.

I jerk forward and have to brace a hand against the dashboard. "What the hell?!"

I blink, wishing I didn't have to see what made Aydan stop, but what choice do I have? I look up. Three shapes stand in the middle of the road, about forty yards away. They all wear long coats and stand legs apart, like gunslingers in a ghost town.

Cursing, Aydan whips his head back and puts the car in reverse. Before he has time to press on the gas, though, a large, red truck rounds the corner and blocks our way.

"Shit!" Aydan shifts gears again. "There's a gun in the glove compartment, but maybe we won't need it. Maybe they'll let us pass if we tell them we're in the Whitehouse faction."

"Don't count on it," I say. "Run them over."

"Are you sure?"

"Trust me."

"I think—"

But before he finishes the sentence, there's a loud crack and the driver side window explodes into a million pieces. A pair of thick hands wrap around his neck and yank him out of the car as if he were made out of virtual bits.

"NO!" I try to grab one of his legs, but he's gone too fast. I stare for an instant, open-mouthed and unsure of what to do, then my reflexes kick into gear and I'm moving, hands opening the glove box and gripping the weapon.

I throw the door open and jump outside. Holding the gun above the car's roof, I aim it at Aydan's attacker, the Jetta between us.

"Let go of him, you asshole!" I order, my voice firm, like I mean it when, in truth, I'm shaking inside. "What the hell's the matter with you? We're on the same team," I bluff. They stare at me with mocking expressions, don't even bother to pull any weapons out.

Condescending bastards. I only hope I have the chance to teach them a little respect.

Aydan struggles, clawing at the massive arm around his neck.

"Are we?" the guy asks in a deep voice that seems to rumble like the engine in an old car.

Two more guys join him, then a third one—the same one we saw a few blocks away and seems to have been driving the truck that blocked our way. All four of them are in their early thirties and look perfectly normal—no claws, no fangs, no scaly skin— just normal as far as steroid-ridden, meatheads is concerned. They defer to the one choking Aydan; he's their leader, I suppose.

"If we're on the same team, why didn't you *lovely* kids get the memo then?" He tightens his grip around Aydan's neck and sniffs his hair, nostrils opening wide at the inhale.

I curse inwardly, wishing I knew what he was talking about, but the best I can do is keep on bluffing. "Who gives a crap about memos?" I sneer, focusing my aim, wondering if I could hit the guy without hurting Aydan.

"You should," he says. "Who are you with?"

"Wait, I think I know her," one of the other meatheads says.

My eyes flick in his direction. Have I ever seen him before? Mind racing, I try to process the possibility. His leathery face does look familiar, but I can't place him.

"Yeah!" he exclaims, then leans into the guy holding Aydan and whispers something in his ear.

The leader's eyes go wide. "Is that right?"

A knowing expression registers on Aydan's face. He's heard whatever the man said. "Marci run!" he screams and renews his struggle to get free. "Run," he growls when he realizes I'm not going anywhere.

What does he think? That I'm going to abandon him—not when there are four perfectly killable Eklyptors in front me—one of which I'm growing more and more certain I've seen somewhere, if I could only remember . . .

"We should bring them in, then." The leader licks his lips as if he just found a captain's booty. A satisfied smile twists his big mouth for an instant, then it's gone.

"Stanton, Jack. Get her!" he orders.

Stanton, the meathead who recognized me, and one of the others move forward on bent legs, ready to pounce. I take a step back, aim the gun from one to the other. I open my mouth to threaten them again, but what is the point?

So instead, I brace myself and pull the trigger. The shot echoes down the empty street. The recoil hits me like a mule and I lose my focus for a moment. Disoriented, I blink and look for my next target, except my first one's still upright, wincing a bit, but certainly not out of commission as he should be.

"That wasn't nice," Stanton says.

A hole in his trench coat marks the spot where my bullet hit him. Wrinkling his bulbous nose, he presses a huge hand to his shoulder and rubs. Something about the deep grooves on his face triggers my memory, and I remember where I've seen him before.

It was at Elliot Whitehouse's party, in that room while Xave knelt on the floor, facing scrutiny after I freaked and gave us away.

The burning hatred in my gut flares, igniting every fiber, every atom in my body. I prepare to shoot again, but, this time, Stanton and Jack charge, the former running in front of the Jetta, the latter behind it. They move fast. I aim right, shoot. Stanton ducks just in time. The bullet misses. The guy to my left rounds the back of the car. I move backward trying to get a better angle. I shoot again—this time in the other direction. The bullet strikes Jack's thigh. It barely slows him down, even as he limps. I shoot two more times, hit him once, but he's still coming, head down, charging, growling like a beast.

Under the pressure and panic something clicks inside of me, sending my instincts into warp speed. Suddenly, I'm part of Aydan's car. A door with metal parts and a latch. I fling myself open. Jack's face disfigures in surprise, eyebrows up, mouth a shocked "O". He's going too fast to stop and slams against the door. He hits the ground with a heavy *thud*. He's a felled tree, a massive waste of space.

I whirl to shoot at Stanton, gun tracing a semicircle around me, but it's too late. He's on me, grabs my wrist and twists it. In a blur, he sidesteps, gets behind me and pushes me stomach first onto the hood of the Jetta. I scream as he bends my wrist to the breaking point. My fingers go numb. The gun drops to the ground. The world undulates before my eyes.

"You little bitch," Stanton says, a hand on the back of my neck, bending me over, forcing my face down until it hits the still-warm hood.

"Let her go, you bastard," Aydan yells.

I strain to look in his direction. He kicks and squirms from side to side, teeth bare, hands trying to yank the arm that has him in a headlock. His face looks red, disfigured with the worst kind of anger and impotence I've ever seen. A vein pops up on his temple as his captor applies more pressure to the headlock, determined to strangle him.

I want to tell him to stop, to give up, or he'll end up dead, but going down without a fight isn't an option. Not really. So I writhe, kick harder and try to harness my pain to jump-start my skill, but my head's swimming. The pressure around my neck is cutting blood flow to my brain and I can hardly breathe.

"Stop or I'll truly bash your head in." Stanton leans his weight into me, increasing the pressure on my neck, compressing my cheekbone into the hood until it dents inwardly. Pain radiates through my skull, then it stops as he lifts me and whispers in my ear. "No use in fighting. You're coming with me. Whitehouse will be pleased." And with that, he slams my head against the car so hard that white sparks flash in front of my eyes, practically blinding me.

My body wilts, knees folding in on themselves. Eyes rolling toward the back of my head, I fight to stay awake. Stanton catches me, then my feet leave the floor and I'm tossed over his shoulder. The world rolls over. Up is down. My head swings. My arms dangle.

"MARCI, MARCI!" a hysterical voice screaming my name.

I blink at the blur the world has become. There are flashes, patches of darkness, wavering surfaces. I blink again, reaching for the slippery thread of my consciousness. I grab hold of it, take a deep breath to secure my grip. Aydan's still struggling, lost in a mad rage that will be his undoing.

"I'll bring her in," Stanton announces.

"NO." Aydan cries out, then reaches backward, slapping his hands over his attacker's ears. "NO," he yells again.

Suddenly, sparks fly out of his mouth, and I think I'm losing it, slipping out of awareness and into dreams. A blue-white flash flickers on his chest, then explodes outward, crackling down his legs and up his arms. An electric hum fills the air. Stanton swears, fear riding his voice. A pang of nausea rocks my stomach. My head pounds and I can't understand what is happening.

Then there's a blinding flash, and I think it's coming from Aydan's hands, but it can't be. His attacker's head lights up like an electric bulb. The man's hair stands on end. He jerks and jerks, the whites of his eyes flashing in a Christmas tree display.

Aydan's hands glow brighter and brighter. Veins of energy run from his chest up his arms and into his fingers, white rivers flowing against gravity, driving into the Eklyptor's head an unrelenting electroshock.

My head pounds. I vomit and my sick runs down Stanton's pants. The thread of my consciousness slips from my grasp. The world bounces up and down as I move away from Aydan. He's fighting the other Eklyptors, shooting electricity in all directions, screaming my name. I reach a hand out, but he's getting smaller. And he glows and glows and it's beautiful. Light everywhere, running over the blacktop, surging, oscillating, sizzling through the air.

The world rolls over again. Up is up as it should be. I'm thrown to the ground like a disposable thing. No, not the ground. It's too soft to be the ground. My eyes roll from side to side, fighting the heaviness, the sickness. Something slams shut. A door? I'm . . . I'm in a car.

"Aydan," I croak.

My head swims and my eyes blur like I'm in a pool, sinking, drowning, going under . . . under . . . under . . .

Chapter 23

He's wearing one of his scarfs—the ones he prefers, in the color of cat's puke—and a tailored, dark suit. His golden eyes drill mine, unblinking, unnatural.

Fake.

Barbie and Ken.

He made them into that shade. No one is born with eyes like that.

I'm in an office, presided by Elliot Whitehouse behind an executive desk. He sits on a black leather chair with a back taller than his head.

My throat bobs up and down. There's an incessant pounding between my temples brought on by the loud buzzing of his presence. I wish the droning to stop. It doesn't relent one bit. Nausea hits me in waves, undoing me from the inside. The word "concussion" has a real meaning for me now. I know my Symbiot healing powers are at work, but they don't work fast enough.

I eye a heavy-looking statue that rests off to the side on a pedestal and imagine it ramming against Elliot Whitehouse's temple. It doesn't move. I imagine squeezing his heart like an overripe peach. Nothing.

Instead, daggers of pain lance from the top of my forehead to the back of my neck, skewering my brain through and through. I hate him with all that I am, so why isn't that enough? If I could only handle meditation . . . if I wasn't so weak . . . if my brain didn't feel ready to split in two . . . if . . . if . . . if . . .

Freezing air blows from the air conditioning vents. I shiver, wish for a blanket, a bed, a pillow, but all I've got is a hard chair and a nasty old man who's staring at me with terrible eyes. He stands, comes to pace in front of the desk. His expensive patent shoes creak with every step. He looks warm in his suit and scarf or cravat—whatever the hell it's called. And I want to pull that silky mess off his neck and stuff it deep, deep inside his throat.

My hands twitch behind the chair. The zip tie cuts into my skin.

Not for the first time, I wonder what makes this man a leader to these monsters. He's no match to the beasts I've seen. They could spike his old ass in seconds. There must be a reason.

"*Ms. Milan,*" Elliot says with a smirk. "What a pleasure to see you again. How do you do?" He still remembers the fake last name I gave him at his twisted party.

"Just swell," I say, my upper lip twitching.

"So glad. And how about our mutual friend, our *dear* James? How does he fare during these *trying* times?"

I take a deep breath. My nostrils flare and feel too narrow to inhale the air my lungs demand. Shadows swim around the edges of my vision, fueled by my anger and impotence. They try to disseminate my thoughts, hoping to snuff me.

Puke cravat . . . inside his throat.

Bring fluorescent lights . . . Electricity.

Aydan . . . Bright, bright hands.

God, I hope he got away.

I swallow and answer, "I don't know. James isn't my friend."

Elliot pinches the edge of his sleeve and pulls on it, adjusting

149

it. A golden cufflink sparkles with small diamonds. "Is that so? Did you have a falling out?"

"Yeah, you could call it that." The jerk is high if he thinks I'll tell him anything about James or IgNiTe.

"Was that before or after you destroyed my cryo lab?" he asks in a calm, cold tone.

I frown, try to look surprised. "I don't know what you're talking about."

He leans against his desk and crosses his arms. His pupils are black horizontal slits surrounded by flecks of gold. "Let's agree not to insult each other's intelligence, *Ms. Milan*. Shall we? I know you were there. You and James and Veronica and others I don't know."

It takes me a moment to remember that Veronica is Blare's fake name, and another to puzzle over how he could have managed to see us. Aydan disabled the cameras. The only ones there were the guards and they all died.

"I can see you're baffled," he says. "Your team had an easy back door into the security system, what with James being the owner of *Zero Breach*. I was a fool to use his company to secure my labs, but he played a clever game. I'll grant him that. He had me fooled for years, but it seems he got desperate in the end, even recruiting careless kids for his *IgNiTe* rebel group." He laughs dryly. "After the night you came to my house, I began to suspect something wasn't right. He always refused to join my ranks. I thought he was organizing his own faction, and I was okay with that. Our kind has pulled toward the same goal for a long time. We've trusted each other, like lions hunting together, knowing that in the end we would share the spoils of the chase.

"But the closer we got to The Takeover, the more our factions solidified and James *had* to choose a side. It didn't make sense for him to refuse me, not when I'm the leader of the most powerful faction. He denied being with Hailstone, tried to make me believe there was some other group he was part of, but I knew better.

"That's when I decided it was time to end our business agreement. We even began transitioning our security measures, but it wasn't soon enough. Such a loss. But never mind that. The fact remains . . . there were *other* cameras and they weren't connected to the main system, which means I *saw* you there. I know you are partly responsible for the senseless destruction. I know you're part of IgNiTe," he says with clenched teeth.

Elliot comes away from the desk and leans forward to look me in the eye. I press my back against the chair. The scent of his cologne is woody and expensive. He licks his lips.

"But you see," he says, "there's so much more I don't understand. So much more that boggles my mind and keeps me up at night as I try to make sense of things."

In spite of the cold, a drop of sweat slides down my breastbone. A nervous thrill runs down my legs. He's too close. My head hums like a piano string, unrelenting and louder than with anyone else. Elliot lifts a hand. I flinch, expecting a slap but, instead, he presses an index finger to my temple and pushes it in, making my head bend to the side, digging his manicured fingernail into my skin.

"But things make no sense at all," he says in a whisper, his neutral breath blowing over my nose. "You're one of us. James is one of us. Can't hide that. Can't fake it. It's in here." He drives his finger with more force until my neck feels like it's about to snap and his finger is about to break through and puncture my brain.

I do my best to repress a groan, determined not to give him the satisfaction.

"So why?" he asks raising his voice and finally pulling away from me. "Why would you betray your own kind? What could humans have offered you? And what witless hope do you harbor that makes you think you have a chance against us, a chance to ever enjoy what they have promised you? Tell me. Make me understand."

His face has become a mask of anger and frustration. His British cool and superiority are gone, utterly erased by his dogged desire to understand, to see the pieces of the puzzle clearly. Here is someone who is used to knowing everything, used to being in absolute control. Not seeing how we fit in his scheme must be driving him crazy.

A strange satisfaction washes over me. He doesn't know about Symbiots. He thinks we're full-fledged Eklyptors, traitors to the cause, to *The Takeover*. And for that to be possible, humans must have offered us something, must have bribed us, somehow. And that's the rub—the how—because what could weak humans possibly offer Eklyptors? It would be like cats banding with mice against a mighty pride of savannah lions.

"SO?" In a raised tone, he demands the explanations that will be like sleeping pills to his unrestful nights.

"I don't know," I say, a smile stretching the corners of my mouth, "I sort of like the idea of IgNiTe keeping you up at night, so . . . you can stuff your questions up your ass, you *bloody* bastard."

Calmly, too calmly, Elliot takes a step forward, then slaps me across the face. My head snaps to the side. A string of saliva flies out of my mouth and lands on the carpet. The room dissolves into wavering shapes. The headache I'd managed to ignore flashes like a sun flare. My stomach roils and I wish I could vomit all over Elliot's shoes, but I'm hollow. I don't even remember the last time I ate. I wipe my chin across my shoulder, leave a red stain behind.

He procures a handkerchief from his breast pocket and wipes

his hand. "We can do this the easy way or the hard way, my dear girl. No matter which, you will tell me what I need to know. You have five minutes to make up your mind."

"Why wait? I can tell you right now."

I work up an answer in my dry mouth. It takes a few seconds, but when it's formed, I spit it out onto his legs. Elliot jumps back, horrified. A trail of pinkish saliva dribbles down his tailored pants, right along one perfect crease. The expression on his face is priceless.

"Your crassness is so perfectly American," he sneers.

"Oh, get over yourself!"

"Very well. I shall do just that." He walks around his stately desk and picks up the phone. "Stanton, get things ready down below. Our *guest* needs a break from me."

His golden eyes sparkle and—though his mouth never reflects it—I know that, on the inside, he's smiling with immense satisfaction.

"I think it's time for her to get acquainted with dear *Doctor Sting*." He holds the last syllable with relish, almost making the word vibrate. "Ms. Milan needs someone more to her . . . level, someone rough around the edges. Please come fetch her, and when she's finally ready to talk, do let me know."

Elliot sets the receiver down, satisfaction dripping off him like drool off a hungry dog. He adjusts his right cuff again and says, "Ask and you shall receive."

My skin crawls with a million scuttling insects. I lower my head, averting my gaze, trying to brace myself for what's to come. I'd rather die than tell him anything.

I hope I can.

Chapter 24

Pain.

Pain.

Pain.

It flares and flares, coloring everything red, demanding my attention, which I'm desperately trying to keep elsewhere.

Beep, beep.

The Road Runner is fast.

Fast and evil.

Evil.

Evil.

Evil.

More comes.

Damn you, pain. I knew you. At least I thought I did. I've hurt before. Hurt a lot. But I really didn't know. Really didn't.

Xave. Where are you?

Hazel. Beautiful hazel.

God, I was so wrong. I didn't know. Not at all.

A scream rips through my throat, slashing my vocal chords, betraying the strength I thought I had. But I have none.

None none none.

No one. One.

Someone, please.

"Ahhhhhh . . ."

Meat.

Roasted meat.

I hold my breath. That smell is my leather pants and me combined. It's my thigh, burning, sizzling like a young pig skewered through and through.

"Let's try this again," he or she says in a high-pitched voice. I have no idea if this thing hovering over me is male or female, all I know is that it's a thing, a thing that *stings and stings and stings.*

The creature, appropriately named Doctor Sting, is holding up another knife, large and with a wide blade. Its tip is bright orange like the tip of the first one. "This one is also nice and hot. Right off the pit. Where should it go?" He—I decide it's a he, because of the Adam's apple—asks, as if trying to figure out where to put a freakin' floral arrangement.

I clench my teeth, brace myself, pretending to get ready for the pain, but there is no getting ready. Not for this. Not in a lifetime.

With the long, double-jointed fingers of his free hand, he touches a tender spot above my clavicle and says, "Maybe here."

The creature's hands feel rough, even though they're covered with smooth-looking skin. He licks his scaly lips. They're peeling. Flakes of skin hang loose at the corners of his wide mouth. His eyes are large, too large for a human face. They're round and bulging, with thin, horizontal pupils like a goat's. They are also far apart, almost on the sides of his face. A mess of two-toned hair sits on its head—reddish brown and white. The colors make an unnatural pattern, nothing even the best stylist in the world could accomplish with such precision. This hair *grew*, the way calico-colored fur may grow on a cat.

Twenty minutes ago, Stanton and some other guy snatched

me from Elliot's office, hit the "S" button in the elevator and delivered me here: a cold, disused room with a dank smell and thick pipes running along the ceiling. They hoisted my squirming body onto this restraint chair: a modern-looking contraption that can—with the push of a button—adopt any position between flat and upright. Before leaving, they clamped wide leather straps to my wrists, ankles and head, rendering me immobile, and flicked a bright light that hangs over my head.

Minutes later, this monstrosity showed up, reeking of sweat and something too close to sour milk not to be sour milk. Such a far cry from Elliot's expensive cologne. It's hard to reconcile the two, unless I imagine the Whitehouse faction leader as some sort of ringmaster with his wild and filthy, but necessary, menagerie.

"Or maybe here," my torturer says, purring. He gently touches a fingertip to my eyelid.

I flinch, try to melt into the chair.

No. Please. No.

Eyeball. Burning.

Not there. Not anywhere.

Suddenly, the palm of my left hand sears. On reflex, my fingers splay open as Doctor Sting presses the hot blade to the center of my hand. My skin sizzles like a piece of chicken on the grill. Waves of agony roll through me. I twitch as if with a seizure, wishing for water, snow, ice. Anything to make the infernal pain stop.

Cold peaks.

Mount Rainier.

Hands patting snowballs.

Frosty was a happy, jolly soul.

Hot tears slide into my ears. Shadows leap from one thought to the next, chasing, ready to devour them. I can't let that happen. I have to fight.

Fight the shadows. Fight the pain.

My thoughts jump at a prodigious speed—random images flashing in front of my eyes—a strobe-light at its highest setting, blinking in and out.

"Your choice, *girl*," Doctor Sting says. "Talk or burn. It's easy." He laughs and I think of The Penguin.

Superhero.

Need a superhero.

Clark. Xavier. Xave.

The shadows chase and fail. My thoughts are fluid enough to give me some control. Once more, I focus on the creature's hand and think of it twisting, stabbing one of those hideous eyeballs. Again I fail. There's pain. Enough pain. There's peril. Imminent as needed. My skills should activate, but I'm weak, starved and beaten.

Death today.

Coffin tomorrow.

I can't tell them about IgNiTe. I won't. So if this is to be the end, I accept it, welcome it even. I tried. For Xave. I did my best to hold strong and keep going. Now it's over.

Doctor Sting sets the knife down. "Umm, I need to find a better place for the next one," he says, yanking my jacket's zipper down.

I buck, thrust my hips upward and to the side, but it's useless.

"The abdomen is always *so* sensitive," he says with delight.

"Are you ticklish?" he asks, raking jagged fingernails lightly over my stomach. A shiver ripples through my skin.

"You sick freak," I growl as I twist uselessly from side to side.

He picks up the knife again without really looking, those soul-less eyes providing remarkable peripheral vision. As he holds the blade up for inspection, the creature frowns.

"Well, it's gone cold," he pouts. "Let me get another one."

He walks to one corner of the room where an antique wood burning stove sits; the kind with a grated, small metal door. His steps *click* short and dainty on the polished concrete floor.

Whistling a tune I don't recognize, he pokes the fire with the knife, leaves it there and retrieves a second one. He takes his time, and the wait, the throbbing in my leg and hand, the way the pain morphs from dull to sharp and back again, are driving me to insanity. My fear builds and builds with the knowledge that more is coming.

This delay is intentional, I realize. He wants me to ponder, to second-guess my decision not to talk, to break under the pressure of the tense minutes ticking by.

I want to scream.

Just slice my throat.

NOW.

Red. Lots of it. All over. Life seeping away. But not this.

Except I know it will be a lifetime before that happens. An eternity of ghastly, whistled tunes, questions I don't want to answer and choices I don't want to make. Will he seer my lips? Seer my eyes? Seer my life away?

The creature prances back, steps clicking at the rhythm of his own whistled tune.

"This one is perfect." This time he holds a small, narrow poker. Smoke wafts from its bright red tip. "You know, this particular one would work better in your fingers." He waves at me to demonstrate. "Hands have always interested me. They're so intricate and important. It's a wonder they are constructed in such a delicate way. That's why I had to do something about mine." He wiggles his fingers again.

"Rams have thick skulls capable of withstanding 800 pounds of force, you know?" he continues. "They have to. It means their survival. They fight over the females with their beautiful horns to ensure they can pass their genes to their offspring. I'm considering growing a pair of my own." He absently pats his head. He's quiet for a minute, lost in thought.

He blinks back to the moment. "Where was I? Oh, yeah, fighting for survival. All animals have their means. Fangs, claws, poison. But for men, survival means fighting with their hands. So tell me then why these *tools* evolved to be so fragile? It's paradoxical." He looks at the ceiling, frowning. "At any rate, mine are strong, now. And, nonetheless, still capable of finesse. So it's not impossible to have both."

He takes my hand tenderly to demonstrate.

"See. I can take one finger like this, and angle this very thin rod, like so."

My lungs forget the meaning of slow. I need deep, measured breaths to stay in control but, instead, they race, tripping over each other.

The tip of the metal rod is face to face with the tip of my forefinger. Doctor Sting's inhuman hands are steady as a surgeon's.

"Do you know that your fingertips have more pain receptors than any other part of your body?" He looks at me, but I only have eyes for the sharp, hot object that's about to impale me.

"I guess you didn't know that," he says. "Well, we will correct that. When I'm done with you, you'll possess firsthand experience in the matter. I assure you." And with that, he pushes the rod under my fingernail and the world turns to liquid agony.

I scream, my throat torn open, my neck corded. My lower back arches. My bindings strain. Time stands still. There is no beginning and, certainly, no end. I will swim in this misery forever. A trail of fire shoots up my arm. The universe converges in the tip of my index finger—all space and time shaped from pain and pain and pain. Never-ending. Absolute. An entity that has me by the throat.

Shadows gather, one behind the other.

They aren't attacking. They're just there, bearing witness to my misery, as if my agent were relishing every single second of it.

"Ooops," Doctor Sting mumbles. "Fragile, like I said. That nail just popped right off. Not very fun. Lucky for me, there are nineteen more. I thought I'd leave the little one for last, but it's so cute, I can't resist. Unless . . . you've changed your mind."

He waits, savors my terror. I clench my teeth together, hold back the traitorous words that rest there.

I'll tell it all. ALL!

"I guess not," the creature shrugs. "The merrier for me."

Another scream fills my ears. There are a million—no, an infinity—of nerve endings in one fingertip. I *know* that now, because they are all on fire, shrinking my existence to a centimeter of my body. I'm reduced to almost nothing. There are no legs, no torso, no head, only a single searing nail bed.

My eyes roll to the back of my head. The shadows are still content to just leer, mouths agape with huge, jagged teeth exposed to form sinister grins.

"Ready to talk *now*?" Doctor Sting asks.

"W-we'll blow all, all, all of you to pieces," I stammer, my lips trembling, my mouth stringing together whatever it can, because I have to say something, anything to slow this down and prevent traitorous words from escaping.

He takes my ring finger this time. "Have it your way."

My eyes flicker to the side, to the wood burning stove. The fire pops and crackles. I focus on its sweltering center. Several other sharp weapons sit in the middle of the flames, approaching white-hot levels with every passing second.

Slowly, the poke stabs my finger, embedding itself under the nail, searing the sensitive tissue as Doctor Sting pushes with a steady thrust. My agony reaches new levels. I used to think pain was pain. I had no idea it could compound, testing its limits just to find that there were none.

Tears blur my vision as I scream myself hoarse.

Can't take it. No more.

Spill.

All the beans.

But I can't. I mustn't. Anger twines with my pain. A spark of strength flares in my chest. I hold on to it, kindling it, stoking it with the never-ending source of agony my hand has become.

I stare at the large knife Doctor Sting returned to the fire a moment ago. I harness the pain, holding the desperate command that rests on my tongue for just a little longer. Energy crackles within me. I feel it like a gentle, tingling current, barely more than a head-to-toe shiver. It builds. It feeds. Then it's ready.

"Stab," I murmur.

The knife trembles in place for a moment, deep in the bowels of the stove. It seems to shimmy, trying to get free from the log into which it's been embedded. I give the command again, hope slipping. Then, without preamble, my perspective changes, and I'm suddenly free from the restraining chair. I'm not a constrained body anymore, but a free, undulating force that knows no doubt or fear or pain.

I'm the flame.

Fluid. Ethereal.

I lick the air, consume its oxygen, savoring it, growing stronger. I dance in a dazzle of shifting colors, a million shades of the most beautiful reds, oranges, yellows, even blues. I'm in control and it's exhilarating. Magnificent. Because fire can be anything and, in that moment, I choose to be a hand.

The flames coalesce into me. As one, we take shape. We rage and revel and, finally, grab the knife and throw it across the room. It spins end over end, true to its target.

With a gasp, I snap back into my body. Pain welcomes me and clasps its tentacles all around me. The poke is still pushing deeper and deeper, over my knuckle, tearing skin and flesh, scraping bone. A wicked smile reveals Doctor Sting's large, squared-off teeth that are the size and color of yellow Chiclets. I hold my breath as the knife hisses through the air.

Those bulging eyes widen a bit, then swivel to the side almost imperceptibly. A knowing glint appears in their depths and, in one swift motion, Doctor Sting's hand jerks upward and bats away the knife.

Both useless blade and slender poker clatter to the floor, their echoes reverberating through the sparse basement. Doctor Sting stares from the fire, to the fallen knife, to me. For a long moment, he seems incapable of words.

I whimper, like a lost dog, my throat emitting a high-pitched sound that barely sounds human. Pain still soaks me through and through, but there's a difference. My strength is gone. I'm undone, unraveling into a useless heap of nothing.

"What do we have here?" Doctor Sting says after his deliberation comes to an end.

From a distance, I feel every part of me melting, my flesh, my molecules, even my thoughts. Giving up is okay, I think. No one can blame me. I tried. I really did.

If I close my eyes and I just . . .

—Finally! Mine!

My eyes spring open, searching light.

NO.

Shadows descend over me, a crazed swarm that has finally found its opportunity. They jump onto my every thought and stick like tar, drowning me.

NO.

I was fire.

I was flame.
Now, I'm
Nothing.
I'm
Eclipsed.

Chapter 25

I run through pitch-black.

I scream with no voice.

I cry with no tears.

Shadows chase me. Endlessly.

I've been running, dodging, hiding forever, too confused to fight and afraid of being shadowed like it happened once before. They want to imprison me. I won't allow it. Not again. Not ever. I remember vividly what it felt to be in their clutches—shadows encasing me, trapping my consciousness in a bubble inside my own brain, keeping me from the physical world while the agent, this infectious parasite that has taken residence in my brain, snatched the reins of my body.

All hope would end if they catch me.

I morph to smoke, slide from one synapse to another. The chase takes a lifetime . . . or maybe just one second. Either way, I adapt and learn and find the best places to hide, the untouched crevices inside my consciousness where not even the agent has thought to send its specter army.

For now, I hide, skulk.

If I succeed, maybe later I can prowl.

At the moment, *I* am the shadow.

Why did this happen? Would this have been James, Aydan, Rheema's fate if Doctor Sting had tortured them? Maybe I'm just *that* weak. Maybe I held on longer than they ever could.

"What are you saying?" A question echoes through the cavernous space where I hide. The whole world seems to vibrate with the sound.

I cower. Where is it coming from? Is it an echo from the past? A memory, maybe?

"Just what I said." A second voice. "She threw a knife at me. With her mind. She was strapped to the chair. She looked at the knife. The knife flew in my direction. I stopped it just in time."

God. Oh, God. I can hear them.

I whirl, searching for the source of the voices, but they're all around me, *through* me and, at the same time, nowhere at all. They permeate the utter darkness that surrounds me. And it's worse, much worse than simply being blind while an unseen world revolves around you.

"Strange," the first voice says, clearly disbelieving the knife story.

The British accent registers for the first time. Elliot.

"Well, is she ready to talk?" he asks.

"I don't know. She passed out."

"Let's wake her, then."

Steps. A splash. Gasps. "Argh, fuck!" A curse word spoken in . . . *my* voice.

A curse word I didn't say. God, the agent!

"Your hand looks a mess, Marci," Elliot says. "For your own sake, I hope you *are* ready to tell me what I need to know."

"That fucking bitch, bitch, bitch." My stolen voice again.

The sound is eerie, like a bizarre dream from a bizarre universe. And I know that if I had a body, chills would be rippling down my skin. But I'm nothing. Nothing.

Suddenly, light explodes around me, consuming the darkness. I want to hide, but there's nowhere to go. The brightness subsides by degrees as I struggle to comprehend what is happening.

"I understand the need to insult me," Doctor Sting says. "But I'm clearly male, so I'd say the only bitch here is you."

"Not you," my voice, hoarse and weak. "The human. The little witch bitch. But she's gone now, and I'm free, free. If I could just find her, catch her, trap her, I'd—"

My agent sounds deranged, rambling, repeating everything. God, is this what's been living inside of me all this time?

"What game is this?" Elliot demands.

"No game. Nope. I'm ready to talk. Ready to tell it all. All. All. Isn't that what you want? Huh? Huh? And when you hear what I've got to tell you, Elliot Whitehouse. You'll shit a brick. A big, fat brick."

Chapter 26

Chuckles ring in my space with a familiar timbre. My own.

Elliot will know everything and he'll hear it in my voice, from my lips. Layers and layers of horror wrap around me. What will this monster of a man do with all the secrets I should have protected? I have to stop it, but how? How?!

I'm still reeling when, suddenly, dark shapes slither around me.

No. The shadows have found me.

I shrink, defeated, waiting for them to encapsulate me. I thought I could fool my agent, figure out a way to regain control, but there's no hope.

To my surprise, the shapes don't attack. They just sit there, their dark masses shifting slowly, gaining depth, becoming sharper and distinguishable. I wait, trying to understand. Then, all at once, I realize what they are, and that knowledge is all I need to make them snap into clear focus.

Elliot and Doctor Sting hover over me, staring with twin, perplexed expressions on their faces.

I can see them. I'm not blind anymore!

I don't know how or why. Maybe because the agent hasn't been able to trap me, but it doesn't matter. I can see and it'll help me fight. It will be a reminder of what it is to be alive and why I should battle to take control back again. Not being shadowed allows me access to my hijacked senses.

I resolve to watch and learn. Watch and learn. All isn't lost yet.

"Well, I can hardly wait to hear your tale," Elliot says sarcastically, his golden eyes narrowed to slits.

"Unstrap me then. Go ahead, go ahead. What are you waiting for?"

Elliot leans forward, wearing a chilling expression. "I suggest you stop making demands and start talking. NOW." He shouts the last word, pushing his leering face right in front of mine.

No, not *my* face. This body in which I'm a prisoner isn't mine any longer. I'm trapped in a dusty corner of my mind and what used to belong to me is now under the command of an *infection*: a parasite that knows how to operate my brain, and has turned me into a negated variable inside a hacked program.

In the distance, I perceive a strange humming that is somewhat familiar. I strain to recognize it and then it hits me. It's the buzzing I always felt whenever I was around Eklyptors. The agent is sensing Elliot.

A general state of submission flows all around my space, as if through that mental signal Elliot is stating his superiority. Could it be that the buzzing somehow establishes a rank among these creatures? Is that its purpose?

"All right. All right," the agent says, growing meek. "Maybe give me, give me something for my burns. They hurt. Hurt like the devil."

A blank stare from Elliot.

Another plea. "Okay, okay. Some water then, to clear my throat."

He considers for a moment, then concedes. The agent's voice sounds rough enough to justify a small nicety such as water.

After some rattling off to the side, Doctor Sting comes back and presses a metal cup to my, *her, our*, lips. There's a swallowing noise followed by gurgling, which makes me aware of other sounds, like the rhythmic thudding of a heart and the constant *whooshing* that must be blood coursing through the agent's veins.

"Thanks." She sounds pathetically grateful. Or at least pretending to be because, from what little I've witnessed so far, such qualities aren't part of the crazy creature usurping my body.

"Now," Elliot takes the cup away and throws it to the floor, "You'd better start talking, Marci."

"No, not Marci. I'm not Marci. Call me *Azrael* because I'm her angel of death, and she's gone, gone, gone. GONE!"

Azrael? Really? I guess this stupid parasite doesn't remember Gargamel's cat? It's true I haven't watched *The Smurfs* since I was five, and I've read about the archangel of death more recently in social studies at school. But still.

"Stop this nonsense!"

"Sorry. Sorry. I'll stop. Right now." Azrael does a whine in the back of her throat like a chastised dog. Her voice has lost its initial edge and now sounds groveling and deeply submissive. I seethe in anger at her slimy cowardice. "But when I'm done, could you, could you unstrap me?"

"TALK!" Elliot screams, wrapping a hand around Azrael's neck and squeezing.

"Okay, okay," Azrael croaks.

Elliot lets go.

Azrael coughs and begins, "Uh, you want to understand why she, why I, she would betray her own kind. I can explain. Yes, I can." A pause.

Elliot stares, unimpressed, impatience written all over his face.

"It's 'cause she's different. Different."

No. No. No.

Elliot can't know.

Azrael continues, my protests nothing more than words written in invisible ink. I'm a glitch in a computer with an operating system I can't hack.

"This body's different. I've been in here since she was nothing. Just two cells. In-vitro job. Should've been in control when she got a brain. She never let me. I tried and tried and tried. Nothing worked. Nothing. She was a step ahead. Always," Azrael says bitterly.

"That is impossible," Elliot says between his perfect, clenched teeth.

"No, no. It isn't. They called themselves Symbiots. Fuckin' Symbiots."

STOP.

I fight to make myself heard, imagine growing a mouth, lips I can bite until they stop speaking, until they bleed. But all I manage to do is give my position away. Shadows reappear. They come after me and, this time, I don't run. Instead, I attack, slicing with imagined swords but, when one specter breaks, another appears, then another and another.

"James is a Symbiot," Azrael says, sounding winded. "There are three others. Three more. Yeah, three."

SHUT UP. SHUT UP.

I kick and punch, attacking the thoughts as they form, trying to scatter them just the way the agent always scattered mine.

"No no no, you little hack. She's still here," Azrael says, jerking from side to side on the restraining chair. "I won't let you. Never let you. I have you now. You're mine. Mine."

More shadows swarm, pouring, seeping, obscuring everything. I fight, visualizing arms as fast as windmills of light, slicing with speed, but still failing to make a difference because this fight is immaterial.

"The little bitch is fighting." Azrael catches her breath. "But she won't win. I'll tell it all. All. You hear?"

Elliot's mouth twists in distaste at the sight of what must look and sound like a psychotic Eklyptor. Is this how they all behave when they first come into being? Or have all the years trapped inside my head driven Azrael insane?

Gaining a bit of hope, I fight harder, faster. And it seems I'm making progress until my strength dwindles, slowing me down, then finally bringing me to a halt. I'm spent. I've been through hell and back, and the wisp that I've become only seems to get more ethereal the harder I fight. So much that I'm afraid I'll disappear. So much that the shadows stop and just stare at me. I collapse inwardly. And I think I've become the ghost of a ghost. And I think maybe this is it. This is death.

Azrael exhales in relief. "She's . . . she's done for. Done for."

"Go on, then," Elliot orders.

"Yeah, yeah. Symbiots. I was talking about those Symbiots. Those little fuckers. Flukes. They can resist us. Not sure how. Can't tell. It's all jumbled up in here. Guess there had to be a few worth a damn out the millions. Filthy millions. James says there aren't many. Nice little blessing, that."

Elliot's expression has shifted. His head is cocked to one side, his eyes alert. "So, I could sense *you*, but the human was in control. You couldn't overtake the body?" He still sounds skeptical, but less so than a minute ago.

"That's right, right, right," Azrael says.

"Remarkable," Doctor Sting butts in.

Elliot puts up a hand to silence him, eyes flashing with irritation.

"And that thing, that thing she did with the knife," Azrael says, "the little bitch has been using *me*. They all do it, then call themselves Symbiots, 'cause they use us. They steal. She punished me,

171

made her mind so empty, empty. Tortured me, the little creep. Damn her. Felt so special making things move, but she's not special. She's nothing without me. NOTHING."

The sounds of agitated breaths join the fast thumping of my stolen heart.

"Can we trust this?" Elliot asks.

"It would explain why she was fighting alongside the humans and the rumors we've heard about superpowers during some of the battles against the *Igniters*," Doctor Sting says with a shrug.

Elliot looks almost convinced.

"Trust me. You can trust me," Azrael blurts out. "And you will. I'll tell you where their hidey-hole is. Yes, I'll tell you. It's made of glass, of light. Right under your nose, all, all, all this time. Tried to tell you, but you couldn't hear me. Unstrap me. To go there, go and tear it all down. Make them pay, make *her* pay."

A maniacal laugh erupts out of Azrael once more. Elliot and Doctor Sting watch with mild distaste. The laughter grows more deranged, almost like an involuntary spasm. She's crazy, crazier than the game room at a psychiatric ward.

"It's perfect," Azrael says. "Just perfect. I'll go. I'll kill them all. The best part? She'll see everything and be able to do nothing, nada, zilch."

Slowly, all the shadows around me pull away as if they can't see me, leaving me alone. I imagine myself shrinking, folding into myself, reduced by fear and remorse. I thought that being able to hear and see from this prison could help, but now I know I was wrong. This is worse than being shadowed, cut off from all sights and sounds. Because this wisp that I've been reduced to—this state of *knowing* without really *being*—is the most excruciating torture imaginable. And Azrael knows it and intends to use it against me, intends to make me watch all the destruction and death. Worse yet, she plans to let me drown in guilt, because whatever happens to IgNiTe after today is my fault.

All my fault.

Up until now, I had thought my life was pointless. Now, however, I wish it really was, because the knowledge that I was born to bring destruction to humanity's only hope is far worse than having no purpose at all.

Chapter 27

I am the spectator of a 360 degree nightmare. No eyes to close. No ears to plug. No escape. I'm immersed, soaked through and through in the macabre proceedings that will lead to the end. Even the rank smell of the twenty or so bodies pressed against Azrael permeate to my secluded corner and the tattered remnants of my being.

Azrael is jittery with excitement, packed inside a large army truck. The roof is a thick green tarp. The sitting arrangements: two long benches facing each other. When she looks down, I see her knees, bouncing up and down, the fingernails of her good hand worrying at the bandages through the burned hole in her leather pants. I feel the threaded texture of the bandage in a detached sort of way.

"He said 'kill them all.' Every single one of them," Azrael says.

God, she won't shut up. I command her hands, *my hands*, to strangle her. They remain where they are.

"Can't wait to see it. Can't wait. They deserve to die. Slowly would be better. Oh, yeah. When I—"

"Shut up!" a deep voice rumbles like a diesel engine with a lisp. The command sounds more like "ssshudup".

Azrael startles, looks to the left. She's packed in the back,

174

surrounded by Eklyptors in varying degrees of grotesqueness.

The one with the threatening voice has curved tusks sticking out of his mouth. A strong electric buzz runs through Azrael's head. I feel her shudder and shrink. I guess that means he's the leader of this group? The more I see her reactions compared to the intensity of the buzzing, the surer I become the annoying trait indicates rank.

"Shut your mouth unless you want me to throw your ass out," the tusked creature says, spittle flying in all directions through his *unclosable* mouth. All the words ending in "s" give him trouble. He sounds like Sylvester the Cat.

Sufferin' Succotash.

For the first time since Azrael took over, the crazed yapping stops. Quiet fills my space. I focus on the thumping of her heart—no, not hers . . . *mine!*—a heart I must somehow reclaim. As I listen, a level of calmness suffuses me and not even the horrid faces that materialize in my space as Azrael looks around seem to matter. Not hearing her blabber on and on has to be the closest thing to bliss in my situation.

In the quiet, I have time to pay better attention to what Azrael sees. First, it's the bandages around her torn fingernails. I don't feel the pain the same way I used to, but I sense it. The wounds will heal fast, but she can't be happy about inheriting the pain. Then, I notice how everything looks muddled, as if through a dirty window. It's the same for my other senses. They are there, but somehow subdued.

Okay, Marci, think.

How do I get out of this? I'm trapped, yes, but my senses are all here. I can see, taste, hear, smell, even if it's just what Azrael chooses to. It's like I've switched places with the agent. Something similar or worse has happened before, so I have to be able to do it again. The glitch needs to become the operating system again.

Maybe I just need to rest, to gather. Maybe I'm spread too thinly, hidden too well in the untouched corners of my brain.

Azrael's eyes begin to swivel back and forth, from one ugly face to the next. I have front row of her perspective, even if a bit dull.

As distracting as my situation is, I do my best to pay attention, because I never know when Azrael will decide to stare at her fingers again and I will miss something important. As the scene unfolds before me like a movie, I notice that creatures of similar features sit together. I think of herds, flocks, prides, murders. Divisions like the ones we humans create. We've always found reasons to segregate each other—things as stupid as skin color. It seems they do the same. I wonder, if they're anything like us, can they be united enough against humanity to finish their orchestrated assault? Up until now, they must have had an easy job, because most people didn't have a clue. We were sitting ducks.

After a good look at everyone, Azrael stares at the tusked guy, the only unique specimen. There aren't others trying to go for the wild pig look. Hogzilla has nothing on him. His vibe is strong, though, and that's what seems to make him the leader. It's hard to miss everyone's surreptitious looks his way, including Azrael's.

He sits there, practically grunting through his huge nostrils, drool running down his chin. It's disgusting. I assume he hasn't had enough time to morph his face properly to avoid that little inconvenience, because I doubt he wants to add bibs to his required accessories. But what do I know? It's not like I understand why they want to look like animals. Having night vision, lithe muscles, extra strength, all of those things, I can grasp, but tusks? Beaks? Goat's eyes? I really can't. I know many of them are still in the process of morphing, but why put up with half-formed, disgusting features for so long?

Point in case, the gray-looking trio at the very back. I don't know what they're going for, but they look sick, I-just-smoked-forty-packets-of-cigarettes kind of sick. Their skin is no longer . . . well . . . skin colored. It's dry and thick and a shade of pewter. One of them, the youngest, has only managed to grow a few patches and looks like some sort of Dalmatian mutt.

Azrael seems particularly interested in the couple across from her, a male and female with bare, furred torsos in a striped pattern that resembles a tiger's, *if* tigers were black with orange stripes, instead of the other way around. Their hands are tipped with claws, and their ears are larger than normal and rounded at the tips. The female is slender with small breasts completely covered in black fur the exact color of her skin. Her face is still human, except for her penetrating green, round eyes which, at the moment, are almost all pupil. She bares her teeth at Azrael, flashing a set of sharp canines.

"What are you staring at?" she hisses.

"Uh, like your look," Azrael whispers. "How long did it take?"

Tigress, which is what I decide to call her, lets pride into her mean expression.

"Three years. And don't you dare think of copying me. I'll paw you to shreds," she says with a French accent that almost sounds like a purr.

"No no no. Wouldn't dream of it. Just admiring. Felines are cool. Yeah, very cool. So, how far are you going with it?"

Tigress coolly lifts a furry hand, examines it, and sets it back down on the machine gun on her lap. "Nothing that would prevent me from pulling the trigger on this petit bébé."

For the first time, Azrael focuses her attention on the guns. Her eyes flicker all around, showing me a quick glimpse of more weapons. I fear what is headed IgNiTe's way, wish there was a way I could stop it. Azrael told Elliot where to find their headquarters while all I could do was float in dread and impotence.

"They didn't give *me* one. They didn't," Azrael says, sounding like a kid who's been denied an ice cream cone.

"Shouldn't even be here," Tusks grunts, clearly the ice-cream snatcher in this picture. "But if Whitehouse wills it, so it is."

Just because there's a pecking order doesn't seem to mean every Eklyptor is happy to follow it. Not different at all from the way it works for us humans. Azrael makes a soft noise in the back of her throat—clearly another Eklyptor displeased with the chain of command. If I could, I'd mock her.

"Screw you," Azrael says under her breath.

"What was that?" Tusks demands, spittle flying from his ugly mouth.

"Nothing. Just, I wish I had a bigger gun than yours," Azrael says.

"I bet," he grunts.

She wants a gun to kill all I have left: my Symbiot family— if I can call them that. Anger ripples through me. I'm inside this brain, occupying the same space the agent does, presumably using the same cells and synapses to transmit information, and I can't do anything to fight back. At the thought, a surge of energy thrills through me. What if, somehow, I can intercept some of the commands this brain sends to the rest of the body? Not all, I'm not greedy, but some—important ones maybe. And what if I can find the agent itself and . . . and . . . ? Do what? I don't know what, but trying to do *something* is preferable to folding over, waiting without hope for all hell to break loose.

I set into motion, sliding along what I imagine as gray passages, while the outside world—seen through Azrael—goes on its merry way around me.

"Where are we going?" Tigress asks in a low growl, eyeing Tusks from the corner of her round eyes.

"To kill some human vermin. Nom, nom." Azrael excitedly pats her thighs. Tigress exchanges a look with her partner.

Azrael cups a hand around her mouth. "There'll be regrettable casualties. Sad sad sad. I know what those poor bastards are suffering." She points at her head. "Wish they could be brought out, given a chance. Bastards never had one. But too dangerous. Those *Igniters* have powers. Especially James. He's evil."

"What in the devil is she talking about?" Tigress's partner asks, also in a French accent. His upper lip lifts in sync with one of his eyebrows while his irises—or what little can be seen of them around the dark, dark pupils—glint vivid blue.

Trapped in my reduced world, I go, passage after passage, searching, finding nothing. The corridors are endless and empty. I speed forward, like the wind, hoping something around me changes, catches my attention. But it's all the same.

The hiss of hydraulic breaks echoes throughout. The truck rocks after the squeal of wheels against asphalt. The sounds of something breaking, crashing, twisting, follows. Everyone pushes to the edge of their seats. They sway from side to side as the truck tilts, taking what looks like sharp curve after sharp curve. Following another crash, the truck lurches to a stop.

"We're here." Tusks stands—head hitting the canvas cover—and starts spewing orders. "Go, go, go. You!" He points at Azrael. "C'mon," he says as he opens the tailgate and jumps out.

Tigress stands and looks at her partner. "Allez, Dillon." He gets to his feet and follows. Bodies press against each other as they rush out of the cramped space. Azrael stands, gets caught in the fray and is practically carried outside.

Lost in my gray world, I come to a halt. What little attention I've been able to bestow on my search is promptly snatched away by Azrael's new surroundings.

"Now, open it." Tusks's hand jerks to point at something. A

long string of slobber hangs from the corner of his mouth. Azrael stares straight at it for a moment too long, then turns, following Tusks's arm to a panel on the wall.

The view completes itself in stages. First, I realize the panel is a bio reader, then I notice the elevator. We really are here: the entrance to IgNiTe's safe haven, the place for which Azrael has just the right handprint and retina to gain access.

The place where death will soon rage.

Chapter 28

"We don't have all night!" Tusks takes Azrael's hand and presses it to the flat screen on the bio reader. A blue light runs from the top to the bottom of the screen. After a rapid set of beeps, a line of red text appears announcing: "ACCESS DENIED."

My biodata has been invalidated. A surge of relief mixed with hurt whirls in my space. Both emotions are strong and real, and the last one tears me apart.

"What the hell?!" Tusks exclaims. "You were lying about being able to get us in."

"They removed my access. Bastard. Bastard. Bastard." Azrael goes on a rant, repeating the same word over and over like a scratched CD.

"Never mind you," Tusks pushes Azrael out of the way, propelling her against the wall.

There's a light crunch as her head bangs against it. Then her view of things changes dramatically and all I can see are blurry legs and boots. Azrael blinks and blinks, then gets back up. Tusks is in front of the elevator that leads underground to what used to be one of James's best-kept secrets. Today, though, everything lies out in the open. The existence of Symbiots, James's head-quarters, the fight to find a cure. Everything. Azrael told them

181

all there was to know, and it's my fault for not being strong like Xave said I was, for getting captured and eclipsed.

Tusks slides his fingers between the closed elevator doors. If I could, I would laugh. The elevator might as well be the door to a bank vault. There's another entrance, a way for the crew to bring vehicles in and out when Rheema works on them, but, gratefully, I never used it and don't know how to access it from the outside, so Azrael couldn't tell them about it. My hope is that, by now, they've been alerted to our presence and are well on their way out of here. Not that Tusks has any hope of prying the doors open with his bare hands.

A sudden crunching sound shatters my train of thought as well as its validity. Tusks's massive back is bulging and his cylinder-shaped fingers are wrapped around handfuls of twisted metal. Growling between clenched teeth, he pushes the elevator doors out of the way, biceps the size of cantaloupes, veins popping everywhere like live electric wires.

The whine of twisting metal bounces against the concrete walls of the underground parking area and echoes down the elevator shaft as Tusks pushes the obstacle out of the way with one final exertion.

He whirls, face drenched in sweat. "You!" He points at a small woman, thin and short as a middle schooler. She steps away from the others, her movements jerky and tentative.

"Send the elevator up," he orders her.

The woman gives a curt nod and, without hesitation, runs toward the ravaged opening. Azrael follows her trek, unblinking. Several yards before reaching the elevator, the woman launches into the air. A pair of white, angel-like wings spring from her back. She glides into the shaft, dives—chin tucked against her chest, head pointing straight down—and disappears into the darkness.

For an interminable minute, Azrael's heart pounds. Tusks stands in front of the hole, feet shoulder-length apart, chest ballooning like giant bellows every time he inhales. His small eyes, almost nonexistent under his encyclopedia-sized forehead, throw furtive, furious glances this way.

A ding sends everyone's attention to the top of the elevator door. The "up" arrow blinks red.

"Voilà," Tigress says, shifting her weight from one slender leg to another. "Ready for action?"

Dillon, her feline partner, leans into her. "Oui," he says with a rakish, cat-like smile. "I like the taste of vermin," he adds with a dirty look for Azrael.

As soon as the elevator cabin appears, casting a bright light onto Tusks's immobile shape, he orders half his team through the door, and quickly files in after the last one. Azrael follows, keeping her eyes downcast, hoping to sneak in undetected, but Tusks presses a large hand to her chest and pushes her out.

"Not you. Come in with the next group. Or stay here. That'd be better," he sneers.

When the elevator returns a few minutes later, Azrael gets pushed out of the way as the rest of the Eklyptors rush in. When the cabin begins to descend, leaving her behind a second time, she snatches a knife out of the sheath of a bug-eyed Eklyptor.

"Hey!" he exclaims. "That's my favorite one, you bitch."

"Idiot," Azrael screams, stabbing the air repeatedly as if an invisible person stands in front of her. "You wouldn't be here without me. Oh, no, no. *I* deserve to go. No one else. Hope he does his *speed* thing on your ugly ass."

With everyone gone, Azrael paces in front of the crumpled doors, cursing. "Gotta get in. Gotta get in." A growl of frustration tears through her. She sticks her head into the shaft and yells, "Send it back! Send it send it send it!"

As if on cue, the cables groan and the elevator begins to climb.

"Yes!" she exclaims, gripping the knife with both hands and brandishing it in different angles.

My wisp of a being shudders. Azrael is just *one* crazed Eklyptor, but something about her determination sets me on edge. I have to do something to stop her. I get on the move again, trying to find a way, any way, that can give me some control over her actions.

Even before the cabin levels with the door, Azrael hops inside and frantically pushes the down arrow. "C'mon, c'mon."

As the elevator makes its way downward, an insistent sound becomes apparent, then grows louder and louder the deeper she goes. At first, it's just an unrecognizable screech, but soon I realize it's the ear-splitting bellow of an intermittent alarm.

When the elevator reaches the bottom level, Azrael rushes out and—through the thick glass window—surveys the chaos below. Eklyptors run loose between pods, knocking down heavy equipment, then shooting at it. Sparks fly as servers, monitors, and electron microscopes short circuit. Glass from beakers, test tubes, light fixtures, and cubicle partitions shatters and flies in all directions. Boisterous commands ensue out of Tusks's mouth as he orders everyone to check the entire area and find the *damn vermin*.

Azrael turns and takes the metal steps two at a time. Once at the bottom, she pauses, looks around, then surreptitiously turns toward the sleeping quarters, making sure Tusks doesn't see her.

No! I have to stop her, and maybe I can. I feel sturdier now. I've had some time to understand the boundaries of my own brain, like a fish getting acquainted with its bowl. Determined, I scramble, speeding faster and faster still finding no hint of anything that could help, no idea of how to use this bit of strength I've regained. Curse words infused with all my frustration fill me. They swell and swell with no way to get out and relieve my fury.

I will explode. I can feel it. Blow up until what little I've become scatters into less than semi-dreams.

"Shit! Shit! Shit!" Azrael swears. She stops abruptly, presses a hand to her mouth, looks around.

The pressure deflates.

What just . . . ?

Did I do that? Did I make her curse? I try again, conjuring the foulest curses I can think of. I let them build, then wait.

Nothing.

Azrael shakes her head and turns down a narrow hall. From the looks of it, no one has checked this area yet. She hurries to the first door, throws it open and flicks the light switch. The room is stark, occupied by a small, unmade bed in the corner. No other signs of life but the rumpled sheets suggest that anyone has occupied the room. No discarded clothes or shoes, no wall hangings. Nothing but a sad bed. She moves to the room across the hall, goes for the door knob, but notices a movement out of the corner of her eye: the slight shift of a venetian shade behind the window of another room.

Frozen, Azrael watches the shades for more signs of life. There's a soft metallic click. Her eyes flick to the door. It cracks open. A head pokes out.

Oso.

"Marci," he whispers. One of his hairy arms urges Azrael to join him in the room.

No. No.

He thinks it's me. He doesn't know. How could he possibly know?

Azrael looks back the way she came, then tentatively approaches. When she's close enough, Oso snatches her and wraps her in a bear hug, his wide torso obscuring the view into the room.

"You're okay," he says. "Aydan said they captured you, but I knew you'd escape." He holds her at arm's length with a nervous smile. "What the hell is going on out there? I had my headphones on and just realized the alarm is blaring. Where's everyone?"

His gentle brown eyes examine Azrael's face. I don't know what he sees there, but he frowns. "Are you okay?"

"I'm fine, real fine, real fine," Azrael says.

Oso's frown deepens. His eyes flicker to the knife as it flashes in Azrael's hand. His eyebrows shoot upward. He tries to step back, but the blade is already moving, headed straight to his abdomen—a wide, sure target in his massive torso.

No.

Not Oso.

Not him!

I cast myself outward, willing my ghostly being to grow and swell and expand . . . explode if necessary. Anything to give this gentle man a chance; to stop him from getting hurt, from losing it all.

He has time only for surprise. He looks so shocked, betrayed, rendered the perfect victim for a vengeful coward.

The sharp blade cuts through Oso's stomach once . . .

NO. NO.

I expand and expand, thinking of the weapon in her hand, *my* hand, using the strength I've managed to gather.

. . . twice, three times. A strangled cry escapes from his mouth as the shock in his eyes morphs to denial.

"Marci?" he says in a weak, wet voice.

Azrael says nothing. She hasn't shut up all night and, now, when her crazy rants could prove to Oso that this isn't me, she remains quiet.

Oso's face goes deathly white. He stumbles, wavers on his feet. In one swift motion, Azrael switches the grip on the knife, holds it over her head and drives it down toward his heart.

NOOOO.

I expand more and more and then . . . an explosion.

Suddenly, I'm infinite, covering the expanse of this universe and all others. And still I'm dissolving, becoming nothing but empty space and going dimmer, dimmer, dimmer. Whatever I was is gone in a big bang and I'm so scattered that I'll never be one again.

And that's okay.

I deserve to disappear, because, tonight, a good man has paid for my mistakes.

Chapter 29

Wet. Thick. Slick.

Everywhere.

It shouldn't be. Shouldn't be.

Red wiggles in front of me.

On . . . my fingers. *My* fingers.

I stare at them, hypnotized for an instant.

I'm back. I'm back in control!

My body shakes. I fall to my knees and discover that Oso is on the floor, dark blood staining his shirt, turning it crimson at a staggering speed as its fibers soak his life away.

A voice rings, saying the same thing over and over again.

"No. No. No. No . . ." My lips are moving and I think the voice is mine.

A shadow falls over me. I recoil, too weak and lost to fight the agent anymore. My head turns toward the door, functioning on muscle memory alone. It's not the agent. There's someone standing by the door.

James.

I try to say his name, but my mouth won't obey and just keeps saying *no*.

His storm gray eyes go from my hands to the knife on the

floor to Oso's immobile shape. Next I know, James disappears. A blur hits me. I fly across the room and land in a heap. My head spins. I blink and see James kneeling by Oso.

"Oso, big guy," James says, fingers pressed to his friend's throat.

The agitated pumping of James's chest stops as he tries to get a pulse. His Adam's apple bobs up and down. He inhales deeply and shakes his head. Trembling, he closes his eyes and lowers his chin. After a heavy moment, his gaze swivels to mine in slow motion. Hatred twists his features into a horrifying grimace.

In the next instant, he's on top of me, his large hands wrapped around my neck, squeezing. My throat closes with the pressure. Saliva pools in my mouth. Time stretches, painting everything a vivid shade of red. Blood seems to slide down the edges of my vision: the life of an innocent man. Oso's life, a waste that will forever remind me of my failures. Did he have a family? Have I left a child without her father? I don't even know that. I *don't* want to know that.

Tears gather in my eyes and I think that I deserve to die. That this death James will give me is cleaner than any other I might have encountered so far, cleaner than the one I deserve, anyway.

I'm torn between the instinct to fight and the justice in letting James kill me. Then I realize my body has already decided and my blood-streaked hands are wrapped around his wrists, battling to pry him off. But he's strong. His modified skeleton and muscles are no match for my ordinary human body.

Just die, Marci.

No one

will

miss

you.

My hands fall to the side. I give up. For good.

I'd decided to live for Xave, because he believed in me. But, it

189

turns out, he was wrong. I'm not strong. I'm nothing like he imagined. In a world with no real hardships, it's easy to pretend you're all-mighty and able to withstand whatever crap life throws your way. But this grisly reality is more than I can take. It has true fangs and claws. It has ripped off my façade, exposing the weak girl that I've always been; the silly girl who thought herself special, worth all the things a mother, a brother, a boyfriend, and a few friends had to offer.

God, I never knew what I had and now it's all gone.

Gone.

My lungs ache. My neck feels like a desiccated branch ready to snap in two. I'm limp in utter surrender.

Looking into James's eyes, I beg for forgiveness. His intense gaze falters. Doubt enters his expression, dissolving a measure of his hatred. The grip around my neck eases a fraction as indecision and determination seem to battle within him.

Marci, he would never kill.

The creature that killed Oso, on the other hand, he would gladly asphyxiate a thousand times over. I know he thinks I'm lost, trapped inside this body, but I wonder if he thinks there's still hope for me.

Whatever the case, he shouldn't stop.

I give him what he needs to help him make up his mind. I bare my teeth like an animal and attempt a growl through my constricted throat.

All doubt is erased from his expression, but his previous fury and determination don't return. Instead, pity and regret take their place. Regardless, his hands tighten once more. Agony cinches around my throat as his large fingers dig harder and harder into me. A strangled sound gurgles through my mouth.

James's eyes waver. A tear rolls down his cheek. He knows he's doing me a favor, but it isn't easy. We've all become murderers, directly or indirectly, justified or unjustified. The parasite in my brain has no business being there and doesn't deserve to live. James is right to do this. If I was still under the agent's control with no hope of return, I wouldn't want to live—not after I failed Oso. And even now, as I've risen from the shadows, James is still right. I shouldn't be allowed to go on. So I don't struggle, even as tears streak his cheeks, even as my nails dig into the carpet and I stifle the instinct to fight.

My lungs scream for oxygen. My legs twitch as if electrified. A heavy fog falls over my eyes, obscuring everything. The world fades away and, for the first time in forever, I get a glimpse of peace, an end to the pain and loneliness. I can finally let go.

Images of a happy past flash across my mind. Dad twirling me around. Mom laughing. Xave holding my hand. A smile stretches over my lips. This isn't so bad after all.

Strange, distant sounds interrupt the calm. The happiness is cut off as excruciating pain returns. I'm lying on my side, sputtering. Wheezing and sucking in air like gulps of water. My neck throbs in sync with my heartbeat. The room tips and I start to slide.

I'm suddenly on my feet. Someone shakes me.

"Where the hell did he go?"

Spittle sprays my face. My head lolls. I blink my eyes open and stare into a pair of curved tusks dripping with slime.

"He was just right here." Tusks lets go of me and whirls around the room. "Find him!" He bellows. Hurried steps sound outside the room.

I sway, then drop to the floor with a thud, arms limp, head dangling like a wilted plant.

"At least you were good for something," Tusks says, gesturing toward Oso. "I thought they'd all gotten away." He kicks the fallen body in the ribs.

Possessed by ire, I try to stand, to tackle the beast away from my friend, to stop him from defiling one of the kindest souls I've ever met. I lurch forward, then fall on my face, an insult stuck in my aching throat. Tusks frowns, regarding me as if I'm the most useless creature he's ever known.

"Should have let that traitor kill you." He spits the words out. "Now I have to haul you back. You might still be useful, though I doubt it."

He stomps out of the room. "Bring her! Whitehouse will want a report and will probably want her back."

Tigress and Dillon walk in the room. I look up. Their shapes blur into one.

I'm going back when all I want to do is die.

Chapter 30

"It wasn't my fault." Tusks stands at attention in front of Elliot's desk. I slouch behind him, flanked by Tigress and Dillon. "He really is fast as she said. One second he was there. The next he was gone. There must have been another way out, which she conveniently failed to mention." He points at me.

"Is that so?" Elliot asks, giving me a cold, suspicious look.

"She killed one of them," Tigress interrupts, her left ear twitching. I stare at it, realizing for the first time that it has small hairs sticking out from the tip, like a bobcat's.

Tusks glares at her over his huge shoulder, his nose scrunching upward, revealing coarse hairs inside his nostrils. It's gross. I wish I could dim the lights to hide all these new details that I never saw from Azrael's perspective, and to stifle the awful pain wreaking havoc inside my head. The buzzing seems louder than ever, more so now that I'm aware of the different pitches everyone puts out. Elliot's is shriller than ever. My perception has changed—like I had a *buzz-o-meter* upgrade or something.

"Is that so?" Elliot says again. He doesn't sound impressed, but his suspicion seems to ebb. I give Tigress a sideways glance, wondering why she would choose to help me.

"We did destroy all their equipment," Tusks adds a little louder, trying to affirm his authority. "Computers, servers, microscopes, papers."

"I certainly hope so." Elliot is a tough customer to please, which clearly rubs Tusks the wrong way. I expect nothing short of James's death would impress the bastard.

Tusks isn't ready to give up yet, though. "I left guards in place, in case they come back for any reason."

Elliot waves a hand in the air. "Bah, they won't be back. At least it wasn't a total waste of time." He stands and walks around the desk. The buzzing in my head gets even louder as he approaches. Tusks and my two feline guards lower their heads. Elliot gives Tusks a pointed look. The thug moves his massive frame out of the way to allow his leader a better look at me. Tigress and her partner take two steps to the side. My knees shake and I feel I may collapse again.

"You're very quiet," Elliot points out, looking me straight in the eye.

I should spit on his haughty face, but the idea of going back to "Doctor Sting's Chair of Agony" shakes me to the core. I was more than willing to die a swift death at James's hands, but torture and the distinct possibility of falling under the agent's clutches again is more terrifying than anything I can imagine.

"James," I say, making my voice hoarser than it already is after nearly being strangled. I put a hand to my throat, which surely must be bruised. "He almost strangled me. It hurts. A lot." Remembering Azrael's crazy rants, I add, "A lot, lot, lot."

Elliot makes a skeptical sound. I do my best to keep eye contact, even though his intense golden eyes make me want to crawl under the desk.

"Who was this person you killed?" he asks.

I have to sell this. If I don't, I'll find myself back on that chair, my fingernails yanked out from their beds one at a time. "Some good for nothing," I say, bile burning in my throat at the awful words.

As if Oso hasn't been defiled enough already. I'm a coward, a despicable coward.

Elliot turns on his heels and walks off toward a glass box that I hadn't noticed before. A warm yellow light shines behind its clear walls. I stare at the back of his head, barely containing my rage and desire to scratch his eyes out. But if I die right now, he will go on, the way Oso can't go on.

If I stay, though . . . I look around the room, an idea taking shape.

If I stay . . . I could have revenge, a revenge that will be sweeter for the wait and cunning it would take. Because I've just realized: I can be a Trojan, a perfect computer virus working from the inside to cause a lot of damage.

A lot, lot, lot.

Elliot leans his face into the glass box—some sort of terrarium, I decide—to admire whatever pets he's keeping in there. He gently taps the glass and smiles with fondness. He whispers something over the cover as I strain to see what he keeps inside. Something black scuttles sideways as if performing a little dance for its master, much like everyone else around here does. I squint to make out the shape of his mascot and realize it's a rather large scorpion with pincers the size of quarters and a huge, curved stinger on the end of its tail.

Figures.

"A good for nothing, you say?" Elliot asks without looking at me.

Sell it, Marci. Sell it. For revenge's sake.

"Yeah, he was the driver, the cook. Terrible, terrible cook," I say, my brain trying to find the exact brand of crazy that Azrael treated everyone to, the one worse than a room full of caffeine-deprived hackers. "Syrupy sweet, always sticking his nose where no one invited him, like everyone's good ol' uncle, or something. That one there," I point at Tusks, "didn't want to let me go in. Nope. Didn't even give me a weapon. You know I wanted to kill me some Symbiot scum, but couldn't do it. The cook was a worthless human, a waste of space."

Tusks scoffs. "Takes one waste of space to know another."

I ignore him and brace myself for my next words, which, I suspect, might be the only thing that will sell my act. Heartlessness seems to be Azrael's most predominant trait, so I have to show them that. Symbiots are unprecedented to Elliot. He would have never trusted me if I hadn't served him James on a silver platter. He knows *I* would have never done that. He must believe I'm still Azrael, someone he can marginally trust. "Sliced him like a chunk of steak, like he used to cook." I let out a cruel laugh that colors my soul two shades darker than it already is. I fear acting this way will bring Azrael back, but what choice do I have?

"Good riddance," I add. "Next is James. He's the one. Yeah, he's the one I wanna cut and cut and cut." I brandish my hand in the air as if slicing someone with a knife. In the excess, I lose my balance and fall to my knees, dizzy from both shame and weakness.

"She's a waste of space *and* time," Tusks says.

Elliot comes away from the terrarium, his features not as pinched as before. "I wouldn't be so sure." He wraps a manicured hand around my upper arm to help me stand. "She shows more determination than *most*."

The buzzing in my head moves to the brink of an explosion. My cranium will burst and brains will decorate Elliot's cravat and entire office. Lovely. My knees start to bend. I will fall again. But I can't. I have to stand.

STOP.

The loud command rings throughout my subconscious, willing the maddening droning to go away. With effort, I look Elliot in the eye.

You have no control over me.

I am not one of you.

Not. One. Of. You.

Then—not like lowering the volume, but like pulling the plug—the buzzing stops. I gasp and cover my bewilderment by feigning surprise at Elliot's touch, as if he's some sort of god who has deigned to bestow his gifts on me. I look for a reaction, wondering if he can't sense me anymore, but he gives no signs to indicate that anything has changed. It seems the change goes only in one direction.

A discontented growl sounds in the back of Tusks's throat. He's not happy to see his leader's attention toward me.

"The human girl who once owned this body," Elliot says, "was strong. Something quite rare among them, but she was. I'm sure it took a similar level of strength to finally escape. Am I right, Azrael?" The name makes me shudder, as if its mention will wake the monster inside of me once more.

Elliot's golden eyes twinkle. Without the buzzing in the way, his questions come across loud and clear, but I'm still reeling, still shocked by the fact that I've turned the droning off, so I don't answer.

Elliot raises his eyebrow in exasperation.

Focus, Marci. Focus.

"Damn right," I say.

Satisfied, he turns to Tigress. "Lyra, take Azrael with you, find her a spot in your ranks, then show her where she can . . ." he twists his mouth in my direction, ". . . wash off and rest. She's had a rough day. Keep an eye on her, okay? Make sure she's *comfortable.* She's an interesting *specimen.* Doctor Sting might be able to learn something from her."

So Elliot doesn't quite trust me and I'm to have a babysitter. Great. Tigress, or Lyra, looks as pleased as I do about the arrangement.

"What a stupid name," Dillon says with a smirk as Lyra and I head out. "Did not your host watch *The Smurfs*?"

I give Dillon a mean look. He chuckles and calls me an "idiot" under his breath. I return the favor.

This stupid name is not my fault, but I'm stuck with it, regardless. Having everyone think of me as Gargamel's cat isn't as threatening as I'd like, but appropriate since it fits my intentions of revenge just as well.

I turn to leave, surprised to still be on my feet.

Rest. Elliot mentioned rest. Just the word makes my eyes close.

Since that night at the dojo, I haven't slept. I can't remember eating much. I've been beaten, tortured, imprisoned inside my own mind. I've lost my family and . . . Xave.

I flinch inwardly. Just recalling his name tears my heart open all over again. What I wouldn't give to see him one more time. My world has gone from chaos to *clustermess* in a handful of days and has left me no one to fight with. Of course sleep sounds good. Awesome, really, especially if it is the never-waking kind. So, right now, I'd follow Lyra wherever she wants as long as a bed is involved. And maybe, just maybe, after I wake up, I'll be able to hatch a plan to make any angel of death proud.

Chapter 31

Tigress escorts me out of Elliot's office while Dillon and Tusks stay behind. Above the door, there's a number: 1006. I memorize it. To the right, there's a secretary's desk with file organizers and a phone with a hundred buttons. The area is carpeted, clean smelling and professional-looking. Corporate America in all its glory.

I went through this area before, but I didn't have a chance to notice much given my anxiety at making Doctor Sting's acquaintance. I wonder where the hell I am. I haven't seen the place from the outside. Both times I came in while I was passed out, and the one time I went out, I was in the back of that army truck. It's a tall building. I know that much. The elevator has thirty-two buttons: thirty-one regular floors plus a service one. I shudder. I'll kill myself before I go back down there. It's a promise.

"There are empty beds on my floor," Lyra says, her French accent clipped and thicker than before.

Normally, I would simply nod, but I have to keep the charade. Any amount of suspicion could prove disastrous. "A bed. Yes, a bed! Don't remember the last time I saw one of those. I wanna sleep sleep sleep." Not that I really deserve to sleep, not when others are fighting or dead because of me.

We come to the elevator. It's guarded by the same two squat, barrel-sized men I saw on my previous visit. They look like they're either trying to morph into brown bears or dwarfs, I can't decide—twin dwarfs, that's my best bet, judging by the matching long beards and tomato-shaped noses. They both growl like guard dogs as we walk up. Lyra ignores them. I do the same.

"Well," she says, "sleep while you can, before Elliot decides what to do with you." Her strange green eyes watch the elevator numbers go up. Elliot's office is on the tenth floor. I take a mental note of that as well. The elevator opens and we go in.

"What d'you think they'll do?" I ask, trying not to come up with any scenarios.

The doors slide shut and Lyra presses a button.

"They'll let me go after James. Right? Right?!" I add. "'Cause I wanna catch me some traitors, make them pay."

Her gaze meets mine. We're the same height, so we see eye to eye. Her small, furred breasts move up and down. We're so close I hear her slow exhales. The elevator dings and the doors open on the sixth floor.

"What exactly did they do to you?" she asks before we step out into a small lobby area. "They didn't tell us much. They never do." Her last words sound bitter. Another disgruntled party in the ranks?

As we walk down a windowless, long corridor, I tell her about Symbiots and how they manage to keep the agents prisoner while "taking advantage of us". I tell her about meditation and how it's the most horrible type of torture. I tell her how I'll make IgNiTe and every one of its members pay for all that pain and misery. It's no secret anymore. Tusks knows. I'm sure it will get around. All thanks to me.

"I had no idea that was possible," Lyra says, her eye as rounds as nickels.

"Better believe it."

"Well, you might feel safe here, but don't get too comfortable."

I almost laugh. I'm as safe as a guest at one of those parties at Elliot's house.

"Where's everyone?" I ask.

"Sleeping," Lyra says. "It's 2 A.M."

"Oh."

She guides me through a set of metal doors. "Young Eklyptors are protected at least until they are able to develop a few useful adaptations. That's if you make it that long."

"Humans are useless like that." I roll my eyes like a pro. "But they're in their place now. Yep, they are. Shouldn't have been in control so long. Puny bastards! Brains *aren't* everything to stay on top. I'll show 'em some brains and then some. Might just grow me a set of sharp claws to shred their tender, little throats." I make slashing sounds by pushing air through my teeth.

Lyra grimaces in my direction and I wonder if I've gone overboard with my act. But when she says, "I'd rather not even touch them. They disgust me!" I realize she's just as fastidious as any feline.

"Voilà," she whispers, putting a finger to her lips to indicate silence.

I follow her gaze and blink a few times to adjust to the dim light. After a moment, an expansive area that seems to be as big as a basketball court takes shape. There are beds lining the walls on both sides.

Lyra walks forward as silent as a cat—which she almost is. I follow her, surveying the setup which makes me think of army barracks, except modern and better equipped. The bed linens are gray, just like the walls. The beds themselves are of decent size with thick mattresses that rest on top of wooden frames with built-in drawers underneath. Each bed is sandwiched between a dresser and a small desk. And, of all things, the desks have computers. I try not to salivate.

I count fifteen beds on each side, all occupied by lumps that, for the most part, look human. However, a few drastically different lumps under the sheets unsettle me, making me think of Komodo dragons or larger-than-life horned beetles. Maybe unicorns, but I doubt it.

I wonder how long these people have been here. Did they just move in? Or were they here long before The Takeover? From the looks of it, Elliot makes sure his faction members are comfortable. Maybe that helps with retention factors? He might rank as a leader in the buzz-o-meter, but rank doesn't seem to guarantee loyalty or respect, not judging by Tusks's attitude when the attack on The Tank didn't please.

Still shocked by the fact that my head is not buzzing, I wonder if that hellish side effect is gone for good and if that's an advantage or disadvantage. I'm too tired to ponder that right now, though, so I push the question aside for the moment.

We reach the end of the room. I run a hand through my hair. "Where do I crash?" I whisper, suddenly feeling the fatigue deep in my bones.

"That one is empty." She points to the very last one on the left. "This is mine." She walks to the bed next to mine, sits and begins to unlace her tall boots. "I will take you to get clothes tomorrow. Sleep in those now."

With hope for rest so close in sight, my body finally becomes unhinged. My shoulders slump. My legs go limp—my very insides seem to collapse. I don't care if my clothes smell and look as if I've been inside a Dumpster. I stagger forward and fall on the mattress face first. The pillowcase smells fresh, much better than the one at the fleabag motel where Aydan found me.

Aydan.

He must have gotten away. I keep thinking he did, keep wishing he fried those meatheads to a crisp. I wish I could call him to make sure, but I never knew his phone number. Not like I have my cell with me, anyway. It's in my backpack together with my laptop in the rear seat of his Jetta.

My heavy eyelids open and close in slow motion. I glance at the computer monitor on the narrow desk next to my bed. Ideas swim through my head, but they're foggy and I can't get a hold of them.

"You stay in the barracks," Lyra says from very far away.

"Count on it," I mumble, willing sleep to take me. I'm exhausted enough it shouldn't be hard to simply pass out, but my mind gets busy imagining the creatures that lie on the many beds in the room.

God, I shouldn't be here. This shouldn't be my life. I should be home, worrying about homework, learning something useful from a father who never died, arguing with my mother about the holes in my jeans, or on the phone with my boyfriend planning our next date.

My chest clamps tight. I fight the tears that seem to be at the ready for the moments when I can't help but think of Xave. I curl up into a ball and push aside the memory of his pale face and empty eyes. I will not remember him that way. His hazel eyes could express so many emotions, so I think of him smiling, of his fingers brushing my cheek, of the first time we kissed.

Loneliness engulfs me. My short happy past can't fight this horrible present.

The future doesn't look much better.

Chapter 32

I'm sitting up in bed, rubbing my eyes as I listen to the strangest Eklyptor I have ever met. Again. Like every morning for the past week since I got here.

Ten minutes ago I was lying down, staring at the ceiling after another awful night of restless tossing and turning, when Onyx, whom I met on my second day here, walked up to the foot of my bed and started chattering.

Now, she's lying by my feet, reclined on one elbow, complaining about the fact that all her mutating efforts are spent on growing long hair and boobs. I stare in disbelief, unable to utter a single word. The last six days have been immensely informative, and I've gone from knowing nothing about Onyx, to knowing way too much.

I get out of bed and, nodding vaguely as Onyx talks away, turn off the buzzing in my head. It's a relief to be able to control that infernal noise, especially since I'm stuck here, and I don't think I could survive this place otherwise. After I managed to tune Elliot out that first time, I practiced the skill until it became as easy as flipping off a switch. Now, if I could only figure out how to stop *them* from sensing *me*. That could be really useful.

Sitting on the chair in front of my small desk, I wake the

computer up, pull up "Space Invaders" and begin defending the Earth from alien enemies. On the next bed, Lyra grunts in irritation.

Onyx ignores her and continues her rant. "It just isn't fair," she whines, a phrase that seems to come out of her mouth at least once an hour.

My fingers flicker over the directional arrows of my keyboard as I absently play the old, arcade-style video game. It's been seven days since the attack on IgNiTe's headquarters, since this bizarre stay under Elliot's roof began. No one has come for me, as I'd imagined they would. Not Elliot. Not Tusks. Not even Lyra who seems too busy to bother with a feeble-minded Eklyptor, though she still keeps a tight eye on me.

It seems that, after I gave Elliot all the information I had and helped bring James's operation to a catastrophic stop, I've become not only useless but also invisible. As long as I don't try to leave the building that is, because all exits are well-guarded and only authorized personnel leave the premises. I tried. I didn't get very far, even the elevators and emergency stairways are sealed off to anyone without a security card. Not being sensed would really come in handy to sneak around this place, but nothing I try makes the buzz-o-meter shut off both ways. Luckily, he's also forgotten about turning me into a pincushion, interesting specimen or not.

But being forgotten has suited me just fine. Because during this time, I haven't been idle and I've learned all manner of things about Eklyptors and the Whitehouse faction.

For instance, Onyx confirmed my suspicion that the faction has been operating from this location since way before The Takeover. She's also talked to me about the situation beyond these walls: the ongoing fight between humans and Eklyptors. IgNiTe is fighting, standing their ground, even defeating Whitehouse's man-hunting teams at times and sending the few survivors back with their tails between their legs. It's damn good to hear.

She also enlightened me about the fact that agents possess gender identities. They either perceive themselves as male or female. In her case, she was "unjustly deposited in a horrendous male body," her words, so all her efforts are spent solely in changing her appearance and anatomy to that of a woman. It'll take her years to be *anatomically correct*, but she's determined.

"I'm tired of shaving," she says, running a hand over thick stubble. She normally has a discernible five o'clock shadow, even before noon.

"Why not morph into a female of a species with less differences between genders?" I ask.

"Sorry, but I'm not into that animalistic *stuff*—no offense to anyone, especially Lyra, she's lovely—but I want to be a woman, smooth and curvaceous and glamorous." She flicks her nonexistent long hair over one shoulder.

The rumor is that Onyx is crazy. As crazy as me, according to conversations I've overheard in the mess hall and in the showers. That's why I've befriended her and make her feel welcome whenever she wants to talk. It helps divert everyone's attention away from me. No one wants to mess with the crazies. Being her friend has made me even more invisible and gives me plenty of opportunities to watch and listen, without raising suspicion.

Onyx is nice, for an Eklyptor, anyhow. Nicer than the whole bunch put together. Plus she's civilized, which is probably why the rest of these savages don't like her. They tolerate her, though. She runs the kitchen and mess hall and does such a great job with the meals that no one dares upset her for fear of the food quality going down.

It turns out, the man whose body Onyx occupies was a young chef at a five-star hotel. So with his knowledge, she keeps the kitchen working like a well-oiled machine and serves meals that make everyone happy. According to Onyx, her host was a fiend, one of those tyrant chefs who oppress their underlings and make their jobs a living hell. Judging by the permanent sneer on Onyx's face—one she's working very hard to erase—I can very well imagine the type of person he was. It doesn't justify the fact that he was supplanted by a parasitic infection, but it's somehow easier to swallow since the supplanter seems a harmless individual.

"You're so lucky," Onyx says, continuing her rant. "I'm so jealous of your curves."

"Be patient, Onyx. Patient, patient," I say without taking my eyes off the computer screen.

"Easy for you to say." She lets out a huge sigh. "Don't you get tired of playing that game?"

I shake my head. "Nope, nope, nope."

This game is my cover. When people are around, I play and play and play. It makes it look like it's the only thing I do, like it's just another crazy thing about me. And the more obsessive I appear about the little aliens on the screen, the less anyone pays attention to what I'm doing.

There are thirty females in this barracks, most are tall, muscular, and mean-looking. I guess they weren't handpicked for their delicate manners. For the most part, they look human, recently infected, but there are a few veterans, judging by the level of their *deformities*. There's a tall Amazon creature with small, curling horns on the side of her head; a woman as wide as a barrel, with bony protuberances sticking out of her spine and poking through holes in her shirt; another one with a long, barbed tail; several with mismatched eyes or pointed teeth.

A vet's dream.

So, when any of them are close, I have to be careful while at the computer. The rest of the time, the pretense ends and I have no time for games. I work tirelessly, then, hoping no one figures out what I'm up to. It's been hard and nerve-racking, hiding my progress, sometimes running my programs in the background while I play this stupid game—just like I'm doing at the moment. Still, I've accomplished a lot in these past few days.

The fact that I—Marci Guerrero, better known as Warrior in hacker circles—am allowed to have access to a computer is surprising. Or I should say: perfectly ironic. If Elliot only knew about my abilities, there'd be no way he'd let me near a keyboard, no matter how well I've played my part in deceiving him. I'm just fortunate Azrael never had a chance to mention anything about my expertise. I flinch at the thought, setting my mind in alert once more. I'm now more vigilant than ever. Paranoid, really. I'm determined this hideous, disgusting thing that lives inside of me will never come out into the world again.

I make *pow, pow* sounds as I shoot at little pixelated figures. I tap the space key repeatedly, sending neon-colored death rays all over the screen. I've actually gotten pretty good at this. Beats watching hideous creatures that run around the barracks in all degrees of undress after they wake up and hurry to the showers. I only wish more of them were going for Onyx's glamorous looks, but I've seen some weird stuff. Gratefully, the majority of them are on this side of human.

Onyx stretches out luxuriously. She's wearing a miniskirt that shows three quarters of her long, muscular legs. She says she has a time shaving their coarse black hair and complains about nicks and cuts every morning.

"I can't wait until we get those human rebels under control." She sighs.

I'd like to curse at her so, to disguise my anger, I stare at the fingernails Doctor Sting tore out. New ones are growing already.

After a moment, I say, "You know you start every other sentence with 'I can't wait until . . .'? Do you? Do you? Huh?"

"Do you know you repeat yourself a lot?" She squints her smoky eyes at me.

Every day her make-up skills seem to get better, all thanks to her avid perusal of YouTube videos. In spite of the chaos everywhere, the digital world keeps on ticking. It seems The Takeover motto—which I've heard several times since I arrived—has paid off for them.

"The world as is. No less. And eventually more."

Once it's all said and done, they don't want a world in shambles. No, what they want is the world we humans built with all its modern comforts and technology. They just don't want *us* in it. That's why they meticulously took over everyone who knew anything about anything, even though it took them decades. Engineers, pilots, chemists, doctors, farmers, people who could keep things going. Of course, they also took over politicians, CEOs, generals, journalists, and other pretty useless individuals.

I guess it also helps they're not in any hurry to change our class system with its endless social injustices. If anything, they're all for it and then some. Survival of the fittest is quite literal with them and their buzzing chain of command;, their swarm mentality as straight forward as the social arrangement inside a beehive. So the world goes on almost flawlessly—which for a hacker like me is a plus.

An apocalypse without computers would really have cramped my style.

"Die, die, die!" I exclaim, practically pressing my face to the computer monitor.

"I mean, I'm not complaining," Onyx says, her voice as whiny as any complainer I've ever heard. "I don't mind taking care of

Whitehouse's personal army, but how much longer will this last? A month? A year? What do you think?"

"Not that long," I say. "Kill them all. Kill them all." If she knew who I'm killing, she wouldn't be smiling so big. Not in the least.

A small light blinks at the bottom of my screen. My heart does a flip. My program is finished. I itch to find out if it worked. I throw a nasty glance in Onyx's direction, wishing she'd leave.

"Has Lyra found something for you to do yet?" She holds a hand up and examines her black tipped fingernails.

"Nope. Nope. Been too busy to bother with me."

Not to mention that, when Lyra or anyone of rank is around, I act as crazy as a bat and try to make myself scarce. Out of sight, out of mind. So far it's worked. They all have bigger fish to skewer. In their minds, my usefulness has expired.

Oh, are they in for a surprise.

"You could help in the kitchen," she suggests.

"Want me to lick all the spoons? I will. Like lollipops." I make licking motions at an imaginary spoon.

"Gross!" Onyx exclaims.

It's laughable the stuff she worries about when they have slobbering freaks like Tusks leaving trails of drool everywhere they go. Though all the members of her kitchen staff can keep their saliva throughput to a normal level; I'll give her that.

I hum something tuneless, hoping she'll get bored and leave but, apparently, she's on a roll.

"I can't wait until we get rid of all those Igniters. At least, we got rid of President Helms pretty quickly, that should make things move faster, don't you think?"

"Fast isn't fast enough," I mumble.

"Being in this body is all wrong, but at least I'm glad I didn't get stuck in one of those *Fenders*." She shivers. "You poor thing.

I can't even imagine what you must have gone through stuck for so many years."

Fenders is what Eklyptors are calling Symbiots. Thanks to me and my weakness, they all know about the rare humans who are able to fend off their agents. Thanks to me, Symbiots are being hunted. Yet another shining item I can add to my list of accomplishments. Maybe, in the annals of history, I'll go down like the person who singlehandedly caused humanity's extinction, more despised than Judas Iscariot—if there are any humans left to despise me, that is.

President Helms fought the shadows. It was through his State of the Union address that James finally got my attention when he was trying to recruit me. It feels like another lifetime. I wonder what has become of him. I don't like any of my guesses.

I shake my head, trying to dispel the rising guilt.

"You okay, Azrael?" Onyx asks.

"Just fine. Fine, fine."

She seems content with my answer. "I guess I should go." She sighs. "Got to work on the menus for next week." She gets up from the bed and jiggles, pulling her skirt down.

"I want a flan, make me a flan," I demand.

"I'll see what I can do. Eggs have been scarce. Do you have any idea how limited your recipe choices are without eggs? It's ridiculous. I don't know what they think I am. A magician?" She leaves mumbling to herself and waving her hands in the air.

If eggs are the only food items that are scarce, The Takeover was way too effective. Food comes in every day without fail. Eklyptors have good control of the entire supply chain from the ground up: farming, packaging, distribution. They calculated their population's needs to perfection and ensured they had their people in all the key places. That they miscalculated on eggs, lettuce, and Twinkies is a minor mistake. In the end, it's all the leftover humans who will starve to death.

I watch Onyx out of the corner of my eye. When she exits the barracks only three Eklyptors remain, all on beds closer to the door. Steadying my hand, I press ALT-TAB and switch screens.

I grin.

Chapter 33

It took a week to build a safe haven inside of Elliot's network, but I've done it.

And not just that. I've found Aydan and he's fine.

My code is disguised, hidden and camouflaged, using all the tricks of the trade I know to make my hack undetectable. Maybe Elliot and his clan destroyed James's servers and any means of communicating with IgNiTe that way, but the night Aydan came for me at the motel, he gave me another option: the computer in his car. He was using a hotspot and—even though he's also used all the tricks of the trade to protect himself—I've found him. I truly have.

My heart beats hard and fast. My hands shake, knowing that everything hinges on this moment. Will Aydan talk to me? Or will he want to strangle me like James did? A million explanations pile up inside my mind, all ways to justify to the crew what I did. They're all excuses. Garbage.

I stare at the screen for a moment. I know as soon as Aydan realizes I've tracked him down, he will disconnect. He won't take any chances but neither will I. I've prepared a file. It's small, just a simple text message that will take a split second to transmit.

Even if he disconnects right away, he will get it and, hopefully, what I have written there will be enough to plant doubt in that thick brain of his. It's a slim chance, but it's all I've got.

I pull up the small subroutine I wrote last night. It will connect to Aydan's computer and immediately transmit my text file.

Holding my breath, I lift a finger over the keyboard, then hit enter and say a prayer. My cursor blinks next to the word "CONNECTED" followed by an IP address.

I'm petrified in the space between agonizing hope and fatal resignation. Three seconds pass. The connection is still active. Maybe he's hesitating, torn with doubt. Another second. I straighten, staring at the blinking cursor as if it were a life raft.

DISCONNECTED.

I let out a pent-up breath. I slump on the chair, losing the strength I'd gained during that short instant. Fist clenched, I try to hang on to what little hope is left. I knew this would happen. It's exactly what I would have done in his place. That's why I sent the file.

Just take a deep breath and wait.

He's probably reading what I wrote right now, weighing all the options, trying to decide whether or not to believe me. At this instant, these are the words staring at him:

Aydan:

I know what you must be thinking as you read this message. I've put myself in your shoes and there's only one logical conclusion you can reach. I've given you and the others all the evidence you need to think me lost to the agent, and I was. I lost the battle and, now, Oso is dead because of me. Because I wasn't strong enough to stay in control.

So, no. You shouldn't trust me. Not even for a minute,

because I'm weak and I couldn't stop the agent when it mattered most. It took over me. They tortured me and I couldn't hold it back. I tried to save Oso, but I was too late. His blood was on my hands when I came to. His blood will always be on my hands.

Tell everyone I'm sorry.

Tell everyone I want to make it all right. I want to help, if they'll let me.

I managed to convince Elliot I'm still an Eklyptor. I'm on the inside, on his network. I've found all kinds of valuable information that should help us fight him.

Please, I'm willing to do anything to prove myself. Please, let me fight.

Let me take revenge.

Marci.

An hour passes with me staring numbly at the computer. The letters on the screen have stopped making sense. I only know they spell "the end".

I think of all the ways I could have died in the last two weeks, both at the hands of my enemies and friends. What good did it do for me to survive? At night, I curl up in my bed and cry silent tears. I lost Xave. I lost my brother, my only friends, my only parent.

I miss Dad more than ever—his firm, reassuring love. He made me feel safe even from the shadows and the terror they viciously unleashed into my five-year-old mind. When they attacked me, he always held me tight, stroked my hair and trained me to breathe and think of other things. He stayed with me until the shock passed, then reassured me he would figure out what was wrong with me. He was a doctor. He could have done it. I never doubted him, not even for a moment. He'd just started looking into it, running tests and asking questions to his colleagues, then he died.

I wonder what he would think of all of this. How much he would suffer over Mom's loss? He was the reason she stayed sane after my brother was kidnapped from the NICU. He was the reason I had five wonderful childhood years. I really can't blame Mom for never thinking I was enough to replace Dad. I'm really not.

What good would it do to continue? No one. Absolutely no one would miss me if I disappear. Or maybe Luke would. He wanted something from me, begged me to go with him, promised he would help. But it's a puzzle—one that perhaps is best left unsolved.

So why not go out with a *bang*?

Suicidal ideas flash through my head. Most people die for no reason, so what better fate than to die for a cause?

Something blinks on my screen. I look up and my hope revives as if hit by a 3000 volt defibrillator.

$> CONNECTED ...
$> Meet me at Gas Works Park. Midnight. Come alone. A.

I put a hand over my lips as they curve. My face feels strange with the corners of my mouth stretched in opposite directions. My cheeks are stiff and seem to crack like two patches of arid land. So weird that I still remember how to smile. So utterly right that I don't care if this meeting is only a trap. I also don't care that getting out of here will be extremely hard. My life is only worth the risks I'm willing to take to make things right.

I shut off the computer and go over the different possibilities. There are three ways I can get out of here. I just need to decide which one offers the smallest chance of detection. New ideas bounce through my head, dispelling the fog of my gloomy thoughts.

Already I feel different, decisive and eager.

But most of all, full of a kicking-and-screaming type of hope.

Chapter 34

This place never sleeps. There are Eklyptors on patrol everywhere, always watching. No one leaves the building without marching orders. No one is trusted 100%, and they've got *me* to thank for that, too. Now anyone can be a traitor, a Symbiot, a mole in their midst.

They should pay more attention.

I hold back a chuckle. Nothing seems to be without a sense of irony. I hate myself for what I've caused, for the people who have suffered and died. But, at least, I've also managed to bring unrest to their lot and, who knows, it could prove beneficial one day.

I throw off the covers and sit up in bed. Making a big show as I rub my eyes, I shuffle drunkenly toward the bathroom. The large sleeping quarters is dark but for the lamps on a couple of desks. As I pass each bed, I surreptitiously glance at their occupants to make sure they aren't watching me. Lyra looks dead to the world, so does everyone else.

On the third bed from the door, a long tail sticks out from under the sheets, drapes over the mattress and falls to the floor. The barbed appendage belongs to a particularly nasty Eklyptor named Lamia who is always giving me malicious glances. She does that to everyone, though, so I don't take it personally. She seems to have spent all her morphing efforts on her enormous tail as the rest of her body remains untouched.

When I enter the bathroom, I make sure it's empty. Satisfied, I lock myself in the last stall and take off the oversized pants and shirt I sleep in. Underneath, I wear my leathers, which aren't in the best shape after all I've been through, but they are, at least, clean. I sneaked out one night and gently washed the pants and jacket in one of the bathroom sinks, then hung them in a broom closet at the end of the hall where they remained untouched and unnoticed until today.

In spite of all the holes and scrapes in the leather, they smell fresh and, most importantly, they belong to me. They are the only clothes I have from my previous life and, as stupid as it sounds, I feel closer to my real self in them. I'm tired of wearing the nasty uniforms that are delivered to our barracks. It doesn't matter that they've been laundered, not when my clothes have been tumbling alongside Lamia's or, god forbid, Tusks's. The thought disgusts me.

I stuff my sleeping clothes behind the toilet tank. After making sure they're completely out of sight, I step on the rim of the toilet and haul myself on top of the stall's partition. As it wobbles under my weight, I position my boots on its thin edge and stretch until I reach the overhead vent. Without its securing screws, the grill comes off easily. It pays being prepared and this escape route has been part of my plan since two days ago when I found the building's blueprints in one of the file servers.

I lug myself up the vent, enjoying the pull on my muscles, then set the grid back into place. I take a small flashlight out of my back pocket, click it on and clench it between my teeth. Finding supplies in this place is easy, especially when everyone purposely ignores me for fear of catching my crazy. Being touched in the head is *so* convenient when you need to swipe useful gear.

Inside, the vent is wide enough for me to crawl comfortably. I move slowly, though, trying to make as little noise as possible against the metal flashing. There's no telling how many Eklyptors have enhanced hearing in this place and I'm taking no risks. I can pace my progress. I gave myself enough time.

Adrenaline courses through my veins and, for the first time in days, I feel truly awake. It feels great to finally get on the move, instead of just sitting in front of the computer.

After a few turns, I reach the end of the vent where it connects to an elevator shaft. I pull out the small screwdriver I swiped from a maintenance person in the mess hall, and get to work on detaching the grid. I make good time and soon find myself going down a service ladder. At this time, the elevators are stationed on the first floor, so hopefully no huge metal boxes will come whizzing by within inches of my ass.

Feeling confident, I begin taking the metal rungs two at a time. I'm just getting into a rhythm when my boot slips. I falter, hands grasping desperately. My body slams painfully against the ladder as my hands find purchase. I yelp as the impact knocks out some of the air from my lungs. Hooking my forearm through one of the rungs, I try to catch my breath.

I've barely gotten rid of the cold shiver down my back when the elevator below comes to life with a crank and a whirl.

"Damn!"

The cables in the middle of the shaft groan and tremble with tension. I look down, then up. I'm too far to go back. I judge the distance from the wall to the edge of the approaching elevator. There's barely a one-foot gap between the two, but I'm on the ladder and that about cancels any life-saving space. Oh, hell! I'm going to end up like shaved ice, if I don't do something.

I could hop on top of the elevator and catch a ride, but that only guarantees a trip back to Doctor Sting's chair. I'd rather be smeared like a bug than go back there.

The elevator is only a few feet away! I almost hear the *Muzak* playing inside the cabin. As the top of the giant box comes within inches from the soles of my boots, the solution strikes me. With one push, I swing backward, one foot and one hand still hooked to the ladder like hinges. As my back hits the wall, I reach my free leg out and brace my foot to the corner, where the walls meet. I press my body to the wall, turn my face to the side, and make myself as flat as possible.

The elevator glides right in front of me, taking its sweet time. My legs shake. A white light shines on top of the cabin, casting a ghostly glow that leaves me blinking. When the elevator finally clears me, I swing back onto the ladder, panting. Sweat moistens my forehead. I sigh in relief and start moving before that happens again.

When I reach the bottom, I do everything I did on my floor, but in reverse. I open another grid, get back into the ventilation system and follow it to the receiving area where delivery trucks unload supplies.

At the end of the line, I come out through an air vent in a small, dark office. I land in a crouch on padded carpet. Staying low, I move past a desk and sidle to a window next to the door. Through a set of vinyl venetian blinds, I survey the outside. The area looks like a warehouse. There's a rolling ladder, a forklift, tons of wooden crates stacked on top of each other, and even a military Jeep Wrangler with what looks like a 50 caliber machine gun mounted in the back.

I watch for a few minutes and see no activity. With a deep breath, I turn the knob on the closed door, let it swing open, and step outside. Heading straight, I walk with purposeful steps, as if I belong in this area. From a set of schematics I found while perusing Elliot's network, I know there are a few cameras down here. So I walk with confidence, telling myself that I won't raise suspicion if I don't act suspicious. I stop by a set of crates and pretend to check a few labels. I feel like an idiot. The Eklyptor in charge of monitoring the feeds is probably asleep, too confident in his ivory tower to think anyone would dare do anything illicit.

But this is the last time I skulk around. My next order of business when I come back—because I have to come back, no matter how much the idea scares and repulses me—will be to hack into the security system and make it my own. I wish I could have gained access to it already, but that server and a few others are guarded behind stricter measures. I'll break in, though, and next time, I'll have a security pass with the highest clearance and a way to disable the cameras, so I can be free coming and going as I please. After that, the other extra-secure servers are coming down, too. The additional care they've taken in guarding them has me practically salivating to find out what Elliot and his faction are hiding there.

For now, I have what little I've found in a thumb drive. It won't give IgNiTe much more than Aydan can already get from public records, but it's something. A peace offering at the very least.

Heart beating at double speed, I amble down the crate-lined corridors, making my way toward the loading dock where trucks back in with their deliveries. A cool breeze hits my face, alerting me to the open rolling steel door. Relief washes over me. I'd checked the logs and found that a few deliveries were expected tonight. I'm glad to see the information was accurate. Most deliveries happen at night—something to do with conserving gas during low traffic hours.

I peer around a crate. So far so good. Now I just have to sneak past the two armed guards who are standing at each side of the wide entrance.

The men are facing the outside. The trees that line the service road sway in the breeze, casting moving shapes onto the concrete. My own shadows poke around the edge of my vision. Automatically, my thoughts jump. The specters disappear almost immediately.

A pair of headlights approaches down the road. The guards adjust the grip on their weapons. I wait patiently out of "buzzing" range until the delivery truck backs into the loading dock. The guards stand stiffly and at the ready until the driver and his assistant step out of the vehicle. As soon as they recognize the newcomers, the guards relax and boisterously greet them.

"Hey, Flick," one of the guards says to the driver. "You're a sight for thirsty throats. You got my stuff?"

The driver nods, pulls what looks like a bottle of booze from behind his back and shakes it tauntingly at the guard. "Sure do, what about you?"

"Right here," he says, patting his breast pocket.

So much has changed, yet so little. The same pleasures and vices that have plagued humanity for millennia still endure. It seems that, for some, the urges of the flesh will always overrule the brain. It's nice to see that, in that way, our humanity can still control them.

Once the guards get hold of the bottle, they waste no time opening it. I wait as the first guard takes a swig, then reluctantly passes the bottle to his partner. Guns slung over their shoulders, they walk outside, joking and drinking, their worth as guards completely obliterated in the presence of alcohol.

I tiptoe, staying out of their line of vision and exit on the other side of the delivery truck. There's a fancy dark sedan parked off to the side. Its polished paint job reflects the streetlights. I run and hide on the other side of the car, squatting. After a moment, I peek around the corner, but the guards are too distracted by their booze to notice anything else. They never even knew I was here. There's still the matter of sneaking back in, but I'll worry about that later.

Right now, I have a date with hope. Without it, nothing else really matters.

Chapter 35

The sky is a gray massive cloud, threatening rain. The moon glows behind a fuzzy curtain, diffused, tempered. I sit on a bench, waiting, my buzzing switch flipped on to make sure I sense Aydan's approach. Lake Union expands before me: a darkened mirror of gently rocking waters. To my left, sprawl six metal giants, old and guarding a history that is all their own. Gas Works Park with its domed-shaped towers is, indeed, an interesting sight.

We remember so little, forget what really matters and hold on to the wrong things. Here, in this beautiful piece of land at the edge of a magnificent lake, is a post-industrial monument to a dead technology. But what of the lives? What of the people who worked here? Who suffered or laughed? Who are now gone, never to be immortalized by anyone?

And what now? Now that fewer remain to care and remember?

A cloud pulls aside and lets a few rays of moonlight fall onto the preserved structures that are the remains of an old coal gasification plant. Metal pipes extend toward the sky. Nozzles protrude from metal edifices that used to be generators or something of the sort. There are picnic tables in what used to be the boiler house where the steam was produced for the process of converting coal into gas for heating or lighting. Such a strange place. Kids play inside what used to be an exhauster building.

Kids? What of them? I shiver at the thought. How many are infected? How many never stood a chance? And how about the ones who still do? The ones we must keep safe. And what of new generations, especially those born to Eklyptors, meant to always be vessels to parasites?

Water laps the shore. A salty breeze kisses me. I lick my lips and wait, wait, wait.

There used to be a 4th of July fireworks display here every year. I came to see it once. I wonder if that will ever take place again. Xave and I had planned to see it together, but that's one of many things that will never happen.

My bike clicks behind me as it cools. The sounds are comforting and make me glad I decided to go by the motel to pick it up. After I ran out of Elliot's headquarters, which to my surprise ended up being in the middle of downtown, right across Pacific Place, I left in a hurry, glancing over my shoulder every two seconds to make sure no one was following me, amazed at the fact that Whitehouse was operating from that location well before The Takeover. They hid in plain sight. All along.

Once I felt safe, I found a van in a public parking lot, hot-wired it, and drove it to the fleabag motel where I'd left my ride. The place looked as deserted as the last time I was there, and I had no trouble getting in and out. In fact, most of the city looked deserted, though there was plenty enough proof of the chaos that marked the first few days of The Takeover.

I rode cautiously through streets that actually felt like mine-fields, with their scattered debris: rolled over cars (some still spewing acrid smoke,) felled traffic lights, discarded ballistic police shields, an alarming amount of castoff shoes. It took me twice as long as it should have to get here, but I feel lucky no one jumped me demanding to know my faction allegiance—though a small pack of dogs scared the crap out of me, barking like lunatics when I interrupted their systematic attack of a large garbage bag. Most of them bared their teeth and yapped until I was out of sight; though the smallest looked at me with sad brown eyes that seemed to beg for a bowl full of kibbles.

I check my watch. It's already fifteen minutes past midnight. I stand and look around. The wind whistles as it blows past the rusted-looking monument.

"Where are you, Aydan?" I whisper.

I rub my hands together, trying not to come to any conclusions, but they pop inside my head anyway, like heated popcorn kernels.

Maybe this was a joke and he never intended to meet me. Maybe he was captured, hurt, killed on his way here.

Squeezing my eyes shut, I take a deep breath and let my thoughts jump in other, less gloomy directions—more out of habit than due to a present threat.

Wile E. Coyote runs by the bottom of a cliff and gets smashed by a rock.

He always seems to make an appearance in my mental images. Not good. I can't let my thoughts get predictable and make it easier for the shadows to figure out a pattern. Not that the agent has felt particularly threatening lately.

God, how I hate all the *maybes*. I'd like more certainty.

I wait for another fifteen minutes and still he doesn't show. Feeling defeated and betrayed, I stand to leave. Maybe there is an explanation why he isn't here. Maybe he'll give me another chance. I walk to the lakefront and gaze into the water. I think of the whole world drowning, of only a few untainted humans remaining. Maybe they would survive and repopulate the earth. Or maybe they would kill each other. It's a toss-up.

I whirl at the sound of footsteps behind me. Someone coming from the old gas plant.

Aydan!

I recognize his gait. He's been here all along, hiding by the towers, probably watching me, trying to determine if this is a trap and if it's safe to get close. I wonder how he got there. His car wasn't in the parking lot. He must have left it somewhere else and walked.

Just as my head begins to buzz with his presence, he stops.

"Hey," he says. He's dressed all in black, a hood over his head, a backpack strapped around his shoulders. One hand is inside his hoodie, the other one making a fist at his side. Under the shade of his hood, his expression is unreadable.

"You came," I say.

"I had to." There's no doubt in his voice. This is something he *had* to do.

I nod. "Have you been there the whole time?" I gesture toward the plant.

He ignores my question. "I have a test. I need you to draw some blood and show me the result." He takes something out of his front pocket and tosses it my way. I catch it and give him a questioning look.

"It's a test Kristen developed," he explains. "You've taken it before. She's just made it portable. It will tell me if you're an Eklyptor or not."

"Okay," I say, feeling relieved. This will be a lot easier than I thought. I walk back to the bench and dump the contents of the small bag onto my lap. Two small packets fall out.

"Prick your finger, fill the capillary tube, put everything back in the bag and throw it back," Aydan instructs.

I get right to it, without hesitation. He needs to see I have nothing to hide. Ripping the shorter package open, I take out a small lancet and stab my index finger with it. A gleaming drop of blood beads up. I tear the second package with my teeth, take out the thin capillary tube and touch its tip to the blood. Red rises within the tube's clear walls like fruit punch through a straw.

I glance at Aydan. He's watching me closely, a deep scowl forming a crease between his thick black eyebrows. There are a million questions I'd like to ask him, but I bite them down. His lips are shut tight, holding back the insults and threats a traitor would deserve. I lower my gaze. There's no trust in his expression. I can't blame him.

The tube is full. I place it in the bag and throw it back to Aydan.

He catches it with one hand and pulls it close to his chest. His other hand is still inside his hoodie. "Stay where you are," he commands.

I put my hands up. "I will," I say. "No sudden moves. Don't worry."

Aydan takes a knee, pulls his hand out of the hoodie and slowly sets a gun on the ground. Taking no chances with my abilities, he steps on the weapon.

I scoff. "I don't know if you've had better luck than me, but I can't use my power at will. It comes and goes when it wants to. Your gun's safe from my so-called telekinesis."

He doesn't respond. Instead, he gets to work on testing my blood. I have the feeling he's probably mastered his electrifying powers by now. He has no problem with meditation. More than ever, I don't dare do it on my own, not after Azrael made her unwelcome appearance.

I look away and stare at the skyline across Lake Union; the clouds have cleared a little, revealing Mount Rainier in the distance, a giant silhouette that seems to somehow float over the haze. Closer, the city glows electric under the dark firmament.

The Space Needle seeming taller than any other structure from this angle. The eerie sound of screams appears to travel on the breeze. How many are suffering? How many are praying to be spared the horror? How many think even begging God is hopeless?

We. Humans. Masters and rulers of the Earth.

Have we truly come to an end? Has our cruelty met its match?

We've endured so much, built so much, destroyed so much. Maybe it is our turn to face destruction. Maybe we deserve it.

Out of the corner of my eye, I see Aydan stand. The gun is back in his hand and this time he's pointing it at me. My eyes move from the weapon to the discarded testing implements on the ground, to his face. I get to my feet, hands still up in the air.

"You lying, bitch." His hand shakes. His face contorts with disgust and the same brand of doubt I saw in James's face when he was strangling me.

"Wait!" I exclaim.

I failed the test? Why? How?

"If I failed the test, then it isn't working. Don't shoot, please. I swear, Aydan. It's me. It's me." Whatever levels the test is checking are probably still high in my system. Or maybe it's looking for antibodies released when the agent took over. If that's the case, then I'll forever test positive. Aydan is smart, though, he must know this.

"I figured it was a lie, but I had to be sure."

"I'm *not* lying! Something's wrong with the—"

"You gave us away to Elliot," he cuts me off. "You killed Oso. You took Marci." His voice breaks. "That's why I came . . . I came to kill you."

And with that, Aydan pulls the trigger.

Chapter 36

Time stands still, milliseconds stretching into millennia.

My hand goes up in a weird salute meant to block the inevitable.

"NO!" I yell.

A loud pop echoes in my ears, hollow but fierce. My instincts refuse this, but I think maybe it's better this way, so I shut my eyes and brace myself.

One million years pass. Then two.

My fingers curl. Confused, I lower my arm, fist clenched around something hot. Shaking, I look into my palm. The bullets rest there, burning my skin. I tilt my hand and drop the projectiles to the ground, choking on my own astonishment.

Aydan's face twists in horror. "Aren't you just full of lies? It seems you *can* use your powers just fine."

"No," I say in a whisper, my eyes on the grass and the slugs at my feet. "Not at will. Only sometimes. When a life is at stake. Do you . . . do you think I would still have powers if I was an Eklyptor?" I try to puzzle it out in an impassive, logical way. "The Symbiotic relationship would be broken, right?" I have no idea how it would work. This is unprecedented.

Aydan steps back, still threatening me with the gun.

"No, don't leave," I plead. "You have to listen to me."

But he doesn't. He keeps moving away, dragging what's left of my hope with him.

At the sight of his retreating figure, anger made out of pure impotence overpowers me, making my whole body quake. With the heat of the slugs still in my hand, I imagine the gun flying out of Aydan's grip. Astonished no longer, I watch the weapon sail across the night and into the waters of Lake Union. He curses, turns tail and runs. I sprint after him, thinking he stands no chance in a race against me. He's just a geeky hacker who's desk-bound from dusk until dawn.

He runs up the steep mount in the back of the park, the one they created for people to fly kites. I hike behind him, slipping on the dew-coated grass, touching my hands to the ground to help me stay up right. He gains several yards on me.

"STOP," I yell. He only runs faster.

Crap! He's not slow at all. I push upward as hard as I can. When I reach the top, I see that he's doubled the distance between us.

"Stop," I yell again but, this time, I imagine him tripping. And, to my relief, he falls and lands against the concrete sundial that paves the top of the mount. He scrambles to his feet and starts to run again, except I've slowed him down just enough to catch up.

I haul myself against him and wrap my arms around his waist. We land hard on the other side of the mount and roll, one on top of the other, down the hill. As we slow, I maneuver him so I end up on top and straddle his hips. He bucks like a wild horse, trying to throw me off.

I block his punches and clamp my legs around him. "Just stop, will you?" I scream, doing my best to catch his eye, but he's beside himself with anger and hatred. He's not thinking. Not at all.

In one quick move, I slip a hand between his wind-milling arms and slap him across the cheek. He slows down, but only a bit, so I slap him again, jump off him and take a fighting stance.

"You can get up," I say, "but if you fight me or try to run, you're going down again. You may be a fast runner, but unless you know karate or can zap me with your electric powers, you need to stop and listen."

Aydan watches me from the ground, blinking as if I'm blurry and he's trying to get me into focus. He stands without breaking eye contact. His black hair curls over his brow. He wipes sweat off his forehead and pushes the obstruction aside. His chest heaves up and down.

"I'm not armed," I say. "I came alone. I just released you." I point demonstratively at the ground to remind him. Slowly, I abandon my fighting stance, holding my palms up to show him I mean to be peaceful.

"I know there's no way for me to prove I'm not one of them," I say. "I wish the test had helped erase your doubts, but clearly it only works if you've never been *eclipsed*."

He frowns at the new word but knows exactly what I mean.

I run a cold hand over my heated forehead. "But, trust me, it's inaccurate if you have been. However that test works, it's never been used on someone like me and you well know it. So don't go putting all your faith in it.

"If you want concrete proof that me, *Marci*, is still in control of this body, there is none. You're just gonna have to trust me and the fact that I haven't killed you."

A muscle in Aydan's jaw jumps. One of his dark eyes narrows as he takes a moment to think. Finally he says, "You haven't killed me because it isn't me Elliot wants, it's James. But I won't help you. He doesn't even know I'm here."

What? He came without letting James know? Really? I guess

James would have probably brought a sniper, if our last encounter is any indication of how dead he wants to make me. Or, at least, he would have forbidden an encounter. So I guess Aydan's telling the truth.

Why would he take a risk like this?

"Okay," I say. "Um, that's good, 'cause I don't want *anything* from you. On the contrary, *I* have something for *you*." Making my movements as gentle and obvious as possible, I pull the thumb drive from my pocket and hold it out gingerly.

"I told you the truth in my note. After what happened at The Tank," I say, lowering my gaze with shame, "they took me back to Elliot. By then, I had fought my way back, but I didn't let on that anything had changed, and they still believe I'm one of them." I pause and swallow. "I realize everything that happened is my fault."

Aydan smirks. His expression conveys a clear message, "I don't buy your act."

I press on, telling myself I would behave the same way if I was in his shoes. "If I'd been strong enough, if I'd been able to stop the agent from taking over, Oso would still be alive." I press a hand to my temple, fighting back tears. If I cry, Aydan will think it's part of some twisted performance, so I can't. I can't be weak any longer.

My words keep coming in spite of the knot in my throat. "I was ready to give up, but when I found myself back with Elliot, I resolved not to. Aydan, I'm on the inside and I've gained access to his network. This thumb drive has what I've been able to collect so far. It's not much because it took me a while to get everything set up. And, as soon as I did, my priority was to find you. But now that everything's in place, I'll be able to find out more. There must be something we can use against them."

Aydan eyes pierce me like bullets. "You're telling me that in an entire week all you've managed to do is get a thumb drive with *not much* in it? That's likely."

His know-it-all demeanor rubs me the wrong way like it always has. I take a deep breath and tell myself that at least he's listening and not trying to run.

"Thanks for your vote of confidence," I say.

He scoffs.

"Hey, under normal circumstances, sure, I would have it all mapped out," I add. "But I had to start from zero *and* I can't use the computer whenever I want to. I have to sneak around. There's always someone watching. But I can probably be in the building's security system by tomorrow. There are a few servers with extra safety measures around them. That must be where they keep all the stuff to control the alarms, the cameras and who knows what else.

"For now, I found the blueprints to the building, delivery schedules for next week, daily menus, stuff like that. Here, take it." I offer him the thumb drive. When he doesn't take it, I aim at his face and throw it. He catches it on instinct.

"Yeah, *really* useful stuff." He has the condescension and twist of his mouth down to a science. He should probably patent the sentiment. "*Eau de Aydan, sneer like no other!*"

"Use your imagination. That *can* be very useful, if you're trying to poison them."

"That's twisted." There is a certain tone of approval in his voice. I can feel the scale tipping in my direction. Please, please.

"Just make sure to let me know, so I can skip taco night," I joke.

Aydan is quiet for a long moment. One of his eyelids twitches, and I tell myself it's because his thoughts are whirling, trying to come up with logical reasons *not* to trust me.

Finally, he says, "Let's say *I* believe you," he starts.

My chest tightens with a surge of emotion. Does he? Does he really believe me?

"No one else will. In their minds you . . . *Marci* is gone, just like Oso."

"I understand."

"No, I don't think you do. The secrets you gave away about Symbiots . . . Whitehouse made sure IgNiTe heard about that."

"Oh." But why am I surprised? Anything less wouldn't be worthy of Elliot's evil.

"Thanks to you there's distrust in our ranks, and we have to be more careful than ever. After all of that, they hate you, Marci."

He said *they* not we. It almost hurts to hope I might have one ally. He can help me convince the others once I've proved myself. My legs feel weak. Overcome with emotion, I turn to face Seattle's skyline and let myself collapse on the grass—my back to Aydan.

"I've got nothing else to make life worth living. There's only payback. For Xave, my brother, my mother, Oso. The whole freaking world."

A tear rolls down my cheek. I fight the urge to swat it clean and give away the fact that I'm crying, falling apart like the weak little girl I refuse to be. The droplet tickles as it slides down to my chin. The breeze dries its moisture.

Aydan says nothing, but I feel his depthless gaze on me.

I'm dying to change the subject, to let my emotions cool and Aydan's rekindled trust grow. So I ask the first thing that comes to mind, "Talking about my family, did Kristen have time to analyze Mom and Luke's DNA?"

He takes a deep breath as if ready to offer an answer but, again, he says nothing.

I peer over my shoulder. There's a certain look in his eyes that sets me on edge. It's a mixture of pity and indecision.

"What?" I ask. "She did, didn't she?" I stand and face him.

His gaze wanders away, gliding over the surface of the lake. Tiny lights glint in his black irises as if somehow the bright skyline has shrunk and gotten lost in his eyes.

He nods once without looking at me. "There was no match."

"No match? What do you mean?"

Aydan sighs. "Kristen said that . . . that you're not related."

And, even though I feared something bad, the revelation still breaks me inside. My real twin is still missing. Max is, once more, the infant who was stolen from his family.

My real brother is, once more, an unsolved mystery.

Chapter 37

The knowledge sits with me for only a moment before I start to question it. "No DNA match? None at all?" I ask.

Aydan looks like he has something else to say, but I'm too lost in my own reasoning.

"But, Luke looks *so* much like Mom. How is that possible?" I ask.

"Because," Aydan answers in a very quiet, very careful tone, "because he *is* her son."

I shake my head. "You're making no sense."

He lifts an eyebrow and inclines his head, prompting me to think a little deeper about what he just said.

"Wait, you mean . . . you mean *I* am not her daughter." I wanted it to be a question, but in the end my tone flattened, hammered down by the weight of a deeply seeded understanding, a truth that, somehow, I've always known in some deep part of my mind.

"You are no match to Luke or Karen," Aydan clarifies.

I grab my head, raking stiff fingers into my hair. "What the hell?" My mouth opens and closes, taking in air to form words, but finding nothing to say.

Finally, Aydan's pity wins and he finds it in himself to say the things that I can't even babble.

"None of it makes any sense. The whole situation is crazy. We all discussed it and can't come up with any explanations for Hailstone's interest in your family. James had me look up birth and police records, also news articles. Your mother gave birth to a male and a female on December 3rd at Northwest Hospital and Medical Center. The male was born first, followed by the female, ten minutes later. The male had complications, was taken to the neonatal care unit. The female required no such care. The male, Maximilian Victor Guerrero, was abducted eight hours after birth. The female remained safe with her mother and father. On paper, Marcela Victoria Guerrero went home with Brian Scott Guerrero and Karen Guerrero and has lived at the same address her entire life. On paper, you are Karen's daughter, but biologically . . . There's zero percent chance you're related."

Which, of course, means Luke isn't my brother either. We are not related in spite of the connection I feel with him, a connection I must have imagined. And then there's . . .

"Dad," I say, and it's strange that all the pain I feel is for the parent I lost ten years ago—not for the one I was living with just days ago. If Karen isn't my mother, does that mean Dad wasn't . . . ?

I can't even finish the thought. He's the only parent I ever felt close to. "I look just like Dad, though," I whisper and can hear the loss in my own voice. And I hate, that on top of everything else I've lost, I'm also to lose my identity? My heritage?

"Without his DNA, there's no way to confirm or deny paternity," Aydan says, trying to be helpful, but adding salt to the wound instead.

I grasp at straws. "He was Hispanic. I look Hispanic. He has to be my father. It just . . ."

It just . . . nothing. It means nothing that we share traits such as skin, hair and eye color. Millions of people do. How could I be his daughter and not Karen's?

It makes no sense. My life's inside a tumbler, rolling down a steep hill.

But I can't accept it. "So they didn't just lose a son?" I say. "They also lost their *real* daughter? Was I switched? Is the real Marcela Guerrero somewhere out there?" I point toward the city. "It's like a freakin' soap opera."

Xave was the first person I told when I found out Luke was my brother. Now Xave's not here to tell him it was a lie. The thought makes me explode. I whirl and scream toward the sky, tendons bulging in my neck, soul drifting into nothingness. I pound my thighs and rage, baring my throat to the heavens and cursing God for his sadistic streak.

The universe against Marci, or whoever the hell I am . . . Azrael after all, I suppose.

My chest feels as if it will split in two, overwhelmed by the deformity of the emotion trapped inside of it. How can one person bare so much pain? How can someone lose so much and still be able to find herself in the chaos left behind?

The world dips, then rocks back and forth. My head pounds with each backswing. Pain is a hammer and it falls, falls, falls, shattering my will into dust.

But I can't. I can't. I can't.

I refuse to believe this! Karen never tired of telling me how much like Dad I look. Hell, I can see it myself in the pictures that are left of him. He *is* my father. I know it in my heart.

"Shhh, it's okay," a voice whispers in my ear.

Soothing words exist and they find their way to me, to the one who, since the night Xave died, has known nothing but the purest forms of agony.

I don't know how long it takes me to realize that I'm on my knees, rocking, almost touching my forehead to the ground every time I move forward, that Aydan is kneeling next to me, an arm over my back, telling me that everything will be all right, that not all is lost.

When the storm passes, the shock of having him near me mixes with my other emotions. I look him in the eye and see something I have never seen in his black gaze.

Tenderness.

Disarmed by the warmth radiating from him, I press my cheek to his chest and cry more freely than I've ever done in years. I have always been strong, if only on the outside. It is how everyone saw me, how *I* used to see myself. This vulnerable child in Aydan's arms is like a newborn in a new, terrible world.

He smooths my hair down my back. "We'll find a way," he's saying. "We'll make everything all right."

"I'm sorry," I say, pulling away from him.

We kneel, facing each other without saying anything for a long moment.

"You believe me?" I finally say, even though I shouldn't risk mentioning it. There's no telling how fragile his trust is and how likely I am to break it.

"You are one of us," he answers and gives me a small smile.

"Thank you." The words come out clipped as I fight not to cry again.

"Well, the others . . . don't get your hopes too high," he says, not without some of that tenderness I saw in his eyes just a moment ago.

"I won't. I'm just glad there is *some* hope, no matter how small." I smile sadly.

"You'll understand if I don't tell you anything about our plans."

I nod several times. "Of course. Of course. I don't need to or want to know anything. If I'm eclipsed again, we can't risk Elliot finding out any new information. Although, I'd die before I let that happen. Now, it will be *his* information coming your way, as soon as I go back."

"Marci," he shakes his head. "Going back is crazy. I don't think you—"

"I have to. Having someone inside will give IgNiTe an invaluable advantage."

He sits on the grass, worry shaping his face. "I know, but it's too risky. What if—?"

"I have to do this." The thought of going back scares me to the core, but I can't waste this opportunity. "I have to redeem myself." I sit cross-legged, facing the lake, looking into the distance.

"What happened wasn't your fault. It could have happened to any of us."

"No. I was the weak link. I can't meditate on my own. If I'd been able to, I would've had better control of my agent."

"We can blame James for that."

I look at him. I don't remember Aydan ever taking my side.

He shrugs. "He shouldn't have kept you out. You needed our help. It was our job to protect you. You're only sixteen. Not some sort of soldier in an army. He was so damn bent on secrets and rules." He looks at the ground, wearing an angry frown.

"Clearly, he had a reason."

"Well, he screwed up and he knows it. If he hadn't pushed you away, you would have been with us when it all started." Suddenly, Aydan seizes my hand and sets his intense black eyes on me. "Please, Marci, don't go back. It's too dangerous. Come with me."

"You said it yourself, they hate me."

"Not you, Marci. Not *you!*" His fingers squeeze mine so hard it hurts. "You can prove to them it's still you."

It's very tempting. I'm scared enough to want to go with him, but it isn't an option. Not even close. "I can't. Maybe in a different life, but in this new world, I have a responsibility. Everyone who's still human does, and you know it." I pull my hand away and stand. "I should get back before anyone notices I'm gone."

Aydan stands. The clouds have moved and moonlight reflects on his black hair. There are circles under his eyes and he looks years older than he did a week ago. Each day has been a lifetime since The Takeover, even for him.

"At least tell me, is everyone all right?" I ask.

"It's been rough, but we'll get through it. We will." Certainty shines in his eyes and, for an instant, he makes me believe everything will be all right. He gives me strength—just what I need in this moment.

I take a step back. "Take care."

"Please be careful. And if you don't find anything or if you find something big, just get out. Promise me you'll do that."

Promise him? Why would he demand a promise? We were never friends, and promises aren't something acquaintances, teammates, or whatever we are, demand from each other. Yet, when I give him my word, it feels strong and definite. Truer than anything I've ever said.

It seems that, under the circumstances, we humans owe each other a great deal. More than ever, we owe each other respect. We owe each other honesty.

We owe each other survival.

Chapter 38

I sit in the mess hall, staring at a mound of mashed potatoes. They're cold, topped with chives—not much different in appearance to what they used to have in the school cafeteria, though a lot tastier.

My eyes burn from another sleepless night. As if I didn't have enough worries to occupy my mind, now I'm trying to figure out a way I can sneak home to find a picture of Dad. I'm even wondering if there is anything at home that might contain some of his DNA: an old army uniform, a lock of baby hair saved by his mother. Anything to provide concrete proof to back what my heart already knows. For the *nth* time, I push the thought away.

Eying the Eklyptors sitting at the next table, I wonder when they'll start serving raw steak or live bugs. They certainly look as if that type of menu would agree with them better. The guy with a nose as shiny and black as a bloodhound's sniffs his food and seems disappointed.

I smirk at the thought of a roach leg sticking out of Gecko Man's mouth. He has emerald green bug eyes that stick out of each side of his face and, instead of lashes, he has these weird little spikes that travel over his nonexistent eyebrows and continue over to his forehead, temples and thinning hairline. A long, fleshy tongue flicks out of his wide mouth and practically licks his eyeball. My stomach churns and the smirk dies on my face.

"Where's Redbone?" Gecko Man asks his table companion.

Bloodhound's nose twitches and dips to an inch of his plate. "Dead."

Gecko Man grunts. "That bad?"

"Those fuckin' Igniters are going to pay," Bloodhound says.

I seethe. Bloodhound loves nothing more than to discuss their hunting expeditions and to recount his favorite ways of dispatching humans. When he does that, I have to leave, which isn't easy—not when I want to undo him with a butter knife.

"I'm more worried about Hailstone," Gecko Man says. "It's all so counterproductive."

Good! This is the third conversation I overhear that carries news of the state of things out there. IgNiTe keeps fighting and defeating Eklyptors more often than expected. What is more surprising, though, is the fact that territorial disputes between factions are also taking a toll. Eklyptors thought the city was in their pocket right after the initial Takeover. They were so sure of it that the different factions started fighting each other before they had a true foothold on the population. The idiots.

"Something the matter?" Lyra asks, taking the chair across from mine.

I look down at my dinner. "Hate mash potatoes," I say. "The human liked them, ate them like candy, so I hate them. Really, really hate them."

"I thought you might be *malade*, sick," she says, taking a bite of roast in a manner too dainty for someone with such huge canine teeth. She sounds as if she wishes I was malade. Back at you, bitch.

I bite down my anger. "Sick of potatoes, yes!"

The sound of silverware against plates fills our silence. I'm surprised these creatures actually use utensils rather than lick their plates in circles, except everyone in Elliot's private army has all the right parts to handle a fork. Maybe he grew up too posh and can't handle slurpy eaters. Perhaps the better question is: why don't we have a pastry fork and a caviar spoon?

"Where were you last night?" Lyra asks, pushing the carrots to the edge of her plate.

I stick my fork in the mash potatoes and swirl it around, avoiding eye contact. "Last night?"

"Oui, I woke up and you were not in your bed." Lyra takes a sip of milk, then licks her lips. Her left ear twitches.

"Bathroom, I guess. Had to pee like thirty times. Pee and pee and pee, couldn't hardly sleep." I figure exaggerating is my best bet.

"Mmm," a sound in the back of her throat that seems neither approving nor disapproving.

To make a point, I pick up my can of Mountain Dew and guzzle it all down.

"Maybe you should not drink so much soda before bedtime." Lyra offers this advice in a neutral tone that makes me think she believes my excuse.

Last night, sneaking back in was surprisingly easy. I parked the van—my bike stuffed in the back—where I found it, then hurried back to the delivery entrance. To my immense relief, the door was still open and the guards drunk and passed out on a crate. Nothing else seems to go my way, so I am grateful for small favors. By the time I got back to my bed, it was 3 A.M. I lay down just for pretense. I knew I wouldn't sleep, not with all the questions about Luke and Mom—*Karen*—making endless circles inside my head.

This afternoon, however, more than its fair share has worked to my advantage. It took me over two hours, but I gained access to the building's security system, so there will be no more sneaking out for me. I can waltz out of here whenever I want to. Now, all I need to do is make a few *adaptations* to the smartphone I just swiped, then Elliot's small world will be mine.

"Azrael." Lyra sets down her fork and cleans her furry black hand on a napkin. I examine the orange stripes on her arms and notice they haven't made it past her elbows. I wonder how far she intends to go with them. "Are you good at anything?" she asks.

"Good? Good?" I say, knowing where this conversation is going. Lyra is meant to find me a job around here, but she hasn't had time. I wonder why, all of a sudden, she's decided to find out if I'm good at something.

"Oui, do you have useful skills?" Her green eyes are hard and unreadable.

I think for a moment, unsure of what to say. I don't want to be assigned any tasks that will take time away from my plans, but, if I don't pull my weight, they might get rid of me. Mind racing, I try to think of things that wouldn't bind me to one spot and would, instead, allow me to roam the building unmolested and unsuspected.

"I—I can clean," I say, making circles in the air with one hand. "Deliver things. envelopes, tools, food, drinks, Mountain Dew." I sound eager to do these things and work myself into a sort of frenzy, listing random things that pop into my mind as if I'm thought-jumping. "Organize, I can organize. Sharpen pencils. I can do that, too. Yeah, yeah!"

"Ça suffit!" Lyra snaps.

I think she means that's enough or something equally biting.

"I will see what I can do. If you want to stay, you have to contribute." She holds my gaze to make sure I get the message.

"Stay, yes. I want that." I let my eyes wander toward the exit and try to look afraid of leaving, even as every fiber in my body wants nothing more than to bolt out the door, plans be damned. "Stay with you and go out and kill more Igniters. I'd love to do that." I can't forget to mention that. Not with a name that means *angel of death*.

"I hate to burst your bubble, but I doubt you will get a chance to do that." Lyra resumes her dinner.

"Why?!" I whine so loud that several heads turn my way.

"There is no point in lying, so I will tell you straight. You are not squad material, Azrael. Most around here cannot decide whether to trust you or hate you. As for the ones who *have* decided, it is a toss. I think," she says, *think* sounding more like *zeenk* , "you'd do much better *here*." She puts a special sort of emphasis on the last word that makes my skin prickle. She sounds as if she knows what I'm up to.

I pull back, observing her body language, trying to understand her meaning.

What do you know, Lyra?

Yeah, Azrael isn't squad material. I agree with that. She is insane, but so are the majority of Eklyptors from what I can tell. So why does she think I should stay *here*? Maybe she wants to keep an eye on me, wants to catch me doing something that will undoubtedly involve my fingers deep inside the cyber jar, just where Elliot seems to be hiding some very tasty morsels.

I throw my hands up in the air and make a sound of disgust. "Bunch of selfish bastards. Wanna get all the glory to themselves. All of it. But they don't know those Igniters like I do. They know nothing."

"Do not take it personally," Lyra says, jamming a large piece of meat in her mouth. "It is a hard situation," she mumbles, waving a hand to let me know this conversation is over.

I stand in a huff, snatch my tray and march to the conveyor

belt. Looking over my shoulder, I give Lyra a dirty look. She lifts her cup of milk in a toast, her eyes smiling as if to say "you're welcome," like she's doing me a favor. I turn and frown at the dirty dishes as they glide away on their way to being washed.

What's with the look?

She definitely suspects something and is trying to make me nervous. I take a deep breath and crack my neck. If she thinks she can intimidate me, she's wasting her time. After what I've been through, only a few things scare me. They scare me shitless, sure, but I plan to do something about one of them. And I hope Aydan will agree to help me.

I head toward the exit, stomping my feet. As I push the door open an angry voice echoes through the mess hall. "Where the hell is my phone? Did anyone see my phone?"

I pat my front pocket and smile.

Yep, thank God for small favors.

Chapter 39

This time Aydan's car is in the parking lot, so I'm not surprised when I seem him waiting on one of the benches that faces Lake Union. I walk purposefully to make sure he hears me coming. As soon as he does, he stands and turns. His shoulders are tense, his face shadowed by his hoodie. I know he's nervous, but I'm glad to see him, glad to be out of Elliot's lair, if only for a little while, glad to be with someone who's still human.

The night is clear, unlike the time we met last week. A full moon shines directly above, scattering glimmering stars over the water. I stop several paces away from Aydan. He drops his hood and gives me a single nod.

My throat is dry and stiff. I feel the need to prove myself all over again, to scream at the top of my lungs that I'm still me. But trying too hard would only accomplish the opposite. I wish there was some sort of proof I could give him every time we meet. Maybe a secret that the agent couldn't get to. No such luck. Everything I know, Azrael knows, whether I want her to or not.

I wonder why it doesn't work the other way around. Why I don't know anything about her besides what I witnessed when she took over. I guess there isn't much there, just a cluster of cells that needs *me* to think, store memories or be anything at all.

Words escape me at the moment, so I pull the new thumb drive I've prepared and hand it over to Aydan. He takes it without saying anything and slips it in his front pocket. Sighing heavily, he sits back down.

"I wish the test would work," he says.

For some reason, the sound of his voice reassures me and the stiffness around my throat goes away. I slump next to him. "It's a damn thing," I say, "to pretend I'm not me most of the time. And then, when I can finally be myself, to have no one believe me."

"I want to believe you," he says. "But it isn't easy."

"I know, and I thank you for that. I know we never quite saw eye to eye, so it means a great deal that you're here . . . trying."

"Sorry I was always such a jerk."

"I'm sorry, too," I say with a smirk. He *was* a jerk, and I don't mind agreeing with him.

"Ha, ha."

I chuckle and, placing a hand dramatically over my heart, I add, "I'm glad you've changed."

Aydan ignores my theatrics and responds in a serious tone. "Well, it's a different world. I have to be a different person with those who warrant it. The person I should've always been." He exhales. His shoulders dip and stay down, letting go of all the tension I first saw.

The mood between us grows somber and heavy once more. Will we, humans, ever be able to laugh freely again? Will we ever feel the careless abandon we took for granted?

"I'm into Elliot's security system," I say. "The new thumb drive has the schematics in it. I can leave any time I want now, so it will be easier to meet, if we have to."

"Good," he says in a flat tone that makes me think security schematics for one Eklyptor building means nothing to IgNiTe— even if said building is Elliot's lair.

251

I really want to give them something they can use, something that can make a difference in this fight. "There's a file server I'm still trying to reach. It's giving me fits, but I'll get it. Whatever they keep in there must be important, 'cause the security around it is tight."

"Sounds promising."

"I'm doing my best."

"I know you are."

Angling my body in his direction, I clear my throat. He tears his dark gaze from the rippling lake and watches me take two chocolate bars out of my jacket pocket and place them on the bench between us. He frowns at them.

"I was wondering," I say, "if you could help me."

He cocks his head to one side. A strand of black hair falls over his pale forehead. Moonlight catches his eyes making them look like mirrors for an instant. Goose bumps erupt on my forearms and travel up to my neck as it occurs to me that this may not be Aydan anymore, but a cynical Eklyptor who—taking advantage of his pale skin—has decided to morph him into a vampire or some other creature of the night.

I shake my unease, telling myself that if he's not Aydan anymore, humans are one step closer to extinction, and there's nothing the likes of me can do to save us, so it wouldn't matter.

"Help you with what?" he asks.

"Meditating."

"Here? Now?"

"Here. Now." I say firmly.

Aydan angles his body in my direction until our knees almost touch. "Do you think that's a smart idea with what you've been through? The agent *has* to know more about you, now. What if it isn't safe?"

"I won't lie and tell you it doesn't scare me, but I have to try.

I want to be able to control my telekinetic powers. They're so unpredictable I can't rely on them at all. Meditation is the only thing that will help me do that." One meditation session unleashed my skills, if I can manage a few more, maybe it'll get easier. "Besides, I beat the agent, and since then the shadows seem to be easier to keep at bay. Please, help me get the hang of it. After that, I'll do it on my own."

My gaze wanders to the chocolate bars resting on the bench. Asking for help is such a foreign thing that it makes heat rush to my cheeks. "I brought pick-me-ups." I point at the chocolates, trying to drive his intense eyes away from my face. "They'll help me bounce back, if I fa . . . fail." I was going to say *faint*, but I've already dragged my pride through the mud enough tonight.

"You're right about one thing," he says. "Meditation *does* help and quickly. Though you have to keep doing it. All the time. Once or twice isn't enough. If you stop, the effects go away. But it does the trick." Aydan extends a hand and holds it between us. He squints, a fringe of long, blank lashes hooding his eyes. His breathing slows and becomes audible. After a few beats, a ball of blue light crackles to life on his palm. Miniature lightning bolts flash and strike his fingers, dancing and skittering in a small, contained universe of their own.

"Wow," I say. "That is just . . . wow."

He raises his hand, bringing the light toward his face, catching the storm in his eyes. Mesmerized, he watches as the colors shift from white to yellow to blue. He frowns and seems to ponder for a moment, then flicks his wrist and sends the ball of energy flying above the grass and into the lake's ever-shifting waters. As Aydan's tiny storm touches the surface, it hisses and spreads over the small waves, making a dazzling pattern. My breath catches as I'm reminded of that 4th of July a few years back when I watched the fireworks reflect off the mirror-like lake. It's hypnotizing.

"Did you know it would do that?" I ask.

"I shouldn't have, but I did," he whispers.

"It's beautiful."

We watch in silence as the pattern slowly dissolves. When it's all gone, Aydan looks at me, a small, satisfied smile stretching his too-red lips.

"Let's do it, then," he says. "You need to know how to control your powers. It's—I don't know how to explain it—liberating. It feels so right, like all the pieces falling into place."

"Yeah? I don't think I would know *right* if it bit me on the ass. It's seems all I ever get is the broad side of wrong."

"I had a head-on collision with *wrong*. So don't expect me to feel sorry for you," he says, using some of the spunk and banter from when I first met him. And, even though he used to drive me crazy with those snide comments, I smile, feeling a strange relief wash over me—like he's comfortable with me, like it's okay to be ourselves, like we can finally be friends.

I dare hope and wonder about his life, about all he's been through. And, suddenly, I want to know everything, but I know it's too soon, so I just keep hoping.

Chapter 40

"Hey, hey,"

Someone pats my cheek three times. I moan and shrink away, squeezing my eyes.

"Marci, you did well."

My eyes spring open. Aydan is hovering over me while he holds my head up, a hand at the nape of my neck. I'm on the ground, moist grass tickling my arms. I blink, trying to understand why we're in this awkward position.

"You did well," he says again.

I clear my throat and paw my way back to the bench, away from this *closeness*.

"Here." He tears the wrapper off one of the chocolate bars and hands it over.

I take a huge bite and let it melt on my tongue. "I feel weird." I crack my neck. "I felt in the zone for a little bit there, then I just . . . I don't know."

Aydan walked me through it all, instructing me to wipe my mind clean, to focus on my diaphragm and the way it moves up and down. Little by little, I cleared my mind, dismissing every thought that tried to push its way through, feeling lighter as nothingness reigned. For a few moments, air was the only thing

255

that mattered, as it traveled in and out of my lungs, cleansing me, making me feel infinite and absolutely at peace.

Then, an image of Xave filled my vision and all the peace turned to loss and chaos. And, after that, I guess I passed out. Still, maybe some benefits will come out of trying, even if I ended up twitching like a half-dead bug.

I put a hand over my forehead and squeeze.

Aydan pushes my other hand toward my mouth. "Take another bite."

The bittersweet scent of chocolate fills my senses.

"You managed to hold on for a few minutes," he says. "Much better than the last time. What broke your concentration?"

I shake my head, not wanting to discuss it, afraid of the pain and its sharp, sharp edges. "Was it like this for you?" I ask.

"It's been like this for everyone, even James. You know that."

They told me this before, but I can't help feeling it should be easier.

"How long before I can try this on my own?" I ask.

"A handful of times. That's not so bad."

A brackish breeze blows from the lake, making me shiver. Aydan pulls his hoodie's zipper all the way up.

"You know, I still have your backpack. It's been in my car since they took you. I haven't looked in it," he adds in a hurry.

"Do you mind keeping it? I can't bring it with me. There's only one thing in there that really matters to me. It's a book. It was my dad's." I don't know why I'm telling him this.

"I'll keep it safe." He never questions how a simple book can be so important to anyone.

"Thank you." His offer moves me, and I find myself wondering about him again, wanting to know who he truly is. I know little about Aydan or anyone else in IgNiTe. When I was with them, I was so focused on understanding Eklyptors and what it meant to be infected that I never spared a moment to think of anyone else but myself.

God, how selfish.

Suddenly, I'd like to change that, except I'm not sure how. I've never known how to be open with people. I grew up keeping secrets even from those closest to me, and I think it must be the same for all Symbiots. Secrecy as a way of life. But what else is there to hide at this point? I'm tired of it.

"How, how is your family?" I ask, then regret it. I don't even know if he has a family.

Aydan gives me a sideways glance and, for a moment, I fear my lame attempt won't go anywhere. But in the end, he seems as willing to come into the open as I am.

He stares at his hands. "I wish I knew, but I haven't seen them in a while. I left before they decided to disown me, or lock me up." He chuckles sadly. "After I was infected, I became a big disappointment to them. You know how that goes."

I nod, finding that—for the first time—I understand someone one hundred percent.

"I'm the youngest of three brothers," he continues. "They both excelled in college, and when I couldn't stay on that path, my parents weren't very happy with me. My father came from Italy when he was five years old. His parents struggled—not knowing the language and all. Dad never got a chance to go to college, had to start working at an early age to help out. When I couldn't follow in my brothers' steps, he didn't know how to deal with it. I was seventeen when I was infected by a teacher, someone I was supposed to trust. I tried to cope but, at first, I had no idea how. I did my best, but my parents freaked out."

Aydan pulls up the long sleeves of his hoodie to expose his arms. Even in the dim light I can see the scars criss-crossing his forearms. There are hundreds of them. He puts his head down, embarrassed and with a faraway look in his eyes as if he's remembering his family's reaction to his self-inflicted injuries. I had suspected this, had imagined he'd used pain to keep his focus, but hearing him talk about it leaves me feeling raw inside.

He pulls the sleeves back down. "They sent me to so many doctors I lost count. When nothing worked and my grades kept slipping, they started talking about this place where people with *problems* go for a while. Even as confused as I was, I knew a place like that wouldn't help. I knew that wasn't the answer, so one night I left. All I took was my laptop and the clothes on my back.

"I spent a few months in homeless shelters. When I was having a good day, I'd go anywhere with a free Wi-Fi connection and try to find others going through the same, but . . ." Aydan shakes his head to indicate how futile that was. "There are so few of us," he says in a quiet, dismayed tone. "So very few."

Without thinking, I lift a hand and rest it on his shoulder. I understand him so perfectly. I feel the loss of his family, his despair, the struggle he went through, as if they are my own. Because in a way they are. I know exactly how he felt every step of the way.

He accepts my touch, acknowledging it only by slightly turning his face in my direction.

"I gave up looking and instead started using my moments of clarity and control for other purposes. I did small jobs online to earn some money. Hacks, you know. I saved every penny I got and eventually got enough to rent a little place of my own. Coding helped me. I became more stable, almost . . . functional. I lived like that for a little over a year. Then *Silica Rush* had a hacking contest. Whoever got through their firewall first got a job with them. By then, I'd gotten really good. The agent helped, I guess. So I won. That's where James found me."

"Impressive," I say, then feel like an idiot for not offering something better than that.

"You would have gotten through, too," he says.

"Before you?"

He shrugs. "Probably not."

I laugh and he does, too. We're quiet for a moment, until I finally decide to give something back. "I hope your family is okay. They would be proud of you now. I've lost everyone, too," I say, trying not to choke on the knot in my throat.

"Not everyone." Aydan looks me in the eye and holds my gaze. For once, I don't feel so alone.

"Thank you."

I gaze at the distant electric skyline of a city that looks normal and perfectly ours. We made this place, this world. Not Eklyptors: the damn cuckoos who want to steal our nest.

"What will happen to our city? To the world?" I ask. "It seems so hopeless."

His gaze drifts over the lake with mine. The illuminated buildings reflect off the water, creating the silhouette of a submerged, phantom city. The moon, round and brilliant yellow, shines to the right of the Space Needle: a postcard-perfect view. So beautiful.

Except, it isn't. The city is at war. Eklyptors are hunting the other half of the population, killing them if they resist, infecting them if they are captured. I fear the possibility that they already outnumber us, fear the day when *everyone* becomes nothing but a vessel.

But even if some people are naive enough to seek help with the "authorities" others aren't going down without a fight. Several groups have formed, banding together to protect each other, militias whose members dig old weapons from under their beds, raid supply stores for ammunition, and engage in street fights where the law is kill or die. It's all Elliot's men talk about in the mess hall. Their conversations both excite me and terrify me.

"Everyone is trying very hard," Aydan says. "Don't lose faith."

It's hard to keep your conviction after you've lost everything. I think of Xave, and also Dad whom I might lose twice if I don't hold onto him, to the memory of his strong presence and his love for me. *"His eyes lit up every time he saw you,"* Karen told me many times, jealousy thick in her voice. Even she could see the invisible bond between Dad and me. So if her coldness toward me means she knew I wasn't her daughter, then Dad's unconditional love must mean the opposite.

If there's any faith left in me, this is what I choose to believe.

I face Aydan. His angular profile is stern and hard, but oddly comforting. "Do you? Still have faith, I mean?"

"We have Kristen." A concise, confident answer that makes me feel steadier, capable of more. I imagine her in her lab coat, working tirelessly to find a cure, a vaccine, *something*.

Stuffing another piece of chocolate in my mouth, I stifle the many questions that crowd at the tip of my tongue. I wish I could learn all about IgNiTe's efforts, but I can't, and it would be unfair to ask.

So all I say is, "Keep her safe."

Chapter 41

Slipping in and out is easy now. The building is huge, with many emergency exits, not all of them watched by a guard at every moment. They are relying on the security system—alarms that would blare if the doors are opened without authorization, something my swiped cell phone has no trouble providing.

I crouch behind a hedge, waiting for the guard on this side of the building to move on. He's been leaning against the wall, smoking a cigarette and staring off into space—not doing a very good job at guarding, feeling as safe as houses. His chest is the size of a barrel, protected by a thick layer that makes me think of crabs and their barbed shells. I've seen him in the mess hall. He makes strange creaking sounds as he walks.

Through the leaves, I watch him take a deep drag, then flick the cigarette to the ground. He sighs, looking bored out of his mind, and resumes his patrol. As soon as he rounds the corner, I use my phone to trigger the lock at the nearest fire exit. As it clicks open, I leave my hiding place, run for the door and ease myself inside, then use my phone to activate the alarm once more.

The hall is dark, two of its overhead fluorescent lights have burned out, just the reason I picked this as my point of access. I sneak into a broom closet where I left my pajamas, put them on and ruffle my hair. Before leaving, I check the first floor security cameras through my phone.

I was gone for a little over an hour and it's now 2 A.M. Nothing looks out of the ordinary until I check the cameras on my floor and spot someone walking down the hall away from the barracks—someone that moves with grace and stealth. Lyra.

I rush out of the closet and run down the hall. She must already know I'm not in bed and, if she's looking for me, she'd better find me on our floor. Because, at night, the elevators and emergency exits are off limits, accessible only to those with security clearance.

As I near the staircase, I send an unlock command through my phone and rush in. Taking two and three steps at a time, I climb six flights of steps. My calves and thighs burn. When I reach my floor, I press my back against the wall and check the nearest cameras outside the stairs. My breaths echo against the concrete walls. My heart beats in my throat.

After making sure no one is outside, I ease the door open and step into the hall. Sweat glides down my forehead. I wipe it off with the hem of my shirt and begin walking at a careless pace. My legs itch to sprint back downstairs and out into the night, but this is the only place for me. I will either succeed or die trying.

As I pass an emergency box with a rolled up firehose inside, some strange feeling in my gut prompts me to stop. I open the small, glass door and, quickly, hide the phone inside. I've taken only a few steps away from the box when Lyra turns a corner into the hall.

Pretending not to see her, I shuffle forward, scratching my butt and doing my best to look like a zombie.

"What are you doing?" she booms.

I jump, looking surprised.

"Hey, Lyra, Lyra. Can't sleep either?"

"Where did you come from?" she demands.

"Been walking around. I played some games. Wanna play?" I act all perky at the possibility of playing with someone else.

Lyra narrows her green eyes, shooting me a glare that feels like a laser beam. "I was down this hall already." She takes my arm, twists me around and presses my face against the wall. After kicking my legs apart, she presses a hand to the nape of my neck, letting her sharp claws prick me.

"Whoa. Not a friend. Thought you were a friend," I say in a half angry, half scared tone. "What's going on?"

"You tell me." Her hands move down my body, frisking me.

The emergency box sits only a few inches from my face. I make a point *not* to look in that direction.

Lyra takes me by the shoulders and whirls me around. "You are up to something. Where were you playing games? What games?"

I point down the hall, the way I came. "Room 614," I say. It's a small office with a computer which should at least have solitaire on it.

"Show me." Lyra pushes me in that direction.

"Why are—?"

"Silence. Show me!"

"Sheesh, okay."

When I reach the office's closed door, I turn the knob, not knowing whether it will be locked or not. When it opens, I walk in the room and head confidently toward the desk. Lyra flicks the light on. I cover my eyes and groan.

"Were you in here with the light off?" she asks.

"Yeah, it's 2 A.M." I yawn and fire off the computer. When the screen lights up, I sit and blink at the monitor. I type "solitaire" in the search box. Two games show up, plain Solitaire and Spider

263

Solitaire. "Which one do you like?" I ask, opening the second one without waiting for a response.

I begin clicking and stacking cards on top of each other, acting as if Lyra has gone up in smoke. When she puts both furry hands on the desk and leans into me, I act startled and reluctantly look at her. I wait as she ponders what to say and seems to measure her words very carefully.

"Whatever you are doing, you will get caught sooner or later." Her nose twitches. She's mad which makes her accent more pronounced and causes *later* to come out as *latair*.

There are little dots on her cheeks, close to her mouth. I stare at them intently, pretending her words mean nothing to me, even as the echoes in my head ring loudly of the truth. She almost caught me tonight. I got lucky. I can't risk leaving the building again—not until I find something that can help IgNiTe fight Elliot and his faction.

I lift a finger toward her cheek. "Are those whiskers?" I ask, looking as fascinated as a child poking an ant pile.

She slaps my hand away. "You better watch your back," she says, then leaves the room without a backward glance.

I mechanically play solitaire for twenty minutes, her warning writhing in my mind like an angry snake. I need to get this done, before Lyra's whiskers get too long and she sticks them too far into my milk bowl.

Chapter 42

To my dismay, the next day I find myself under Lyra's supervision.

"Your vacation is over, petit fille," she yells, yanking the cover off me.

I look up, my head pounding from lack of sleep. It's only 5:30 A.M., but she's fully dressed and acting like a drill sergeant— nothing like the gentle kitten she appears to be.

Moaning, I roll over and refuse to get up. But she isn't taking no for an answer and gets me out of bed by putting a boot on my back and pushing me off.

I land on the other side with a thud. "Hey, what's the matter with you?"

"You need to start earning your keep. Get up unless you want to deal with someone higher up than me."

I jump to my feet and give her a nasty glare. Mumbling foul curses, I get ready and follow her out the barracks. Everyone is up already. I guess I was lucky to be left to my own devices for a short while. Getting roped into their schemes was only a matter of time.

After a quick breakfast of eggs for me and ten links of sausage for Lyra, she drags me to the service level and into a large room full of crates. Several people mill about moving boxes.

"Unload those," she orders, pointing at three large, wooden crates. "Crowbars are over there. Contents go against that wall."

She moves on to bark orders at some of the others. I look around trying to figure a way out of this, but several Eklyptors are watching me closely and Lyra throws mean glances in my direction every few seconds.

Resigned, I get a crowbar and set to work on one of the crates. I wedge the metal tip under the wooden lid and put my weight on it. The top pops with a crack and a crunch. I peer inside. The crate is full of army green metal boxes. I pull one out. It's much heavier than I expected. Yellow letters on the side spell the contents: 1000 CRTG 9MM.

Fury clenches my stomach. My jaw grinds. This is the level of control they have over our armed forces. I turn and look at all the unopened crates behind me. There are hundreds of them— more than enough for an army.

A wolfish man reaches inside a crate and pulls out a machine gun. Grinning from ear to ear, he admires the weapon, petting its side. As I seethe, imagining the muzzle inside his mouth, I sense Lyra watching me from the side. It takes all I've got to mold my expression of disgust to one of yearning. I stare at the machine gun longingly, full of envy. Flicking my gaze down to the box of ammunition in my hands, I try to convey a feeling of "and this is all *I* get?"

Acid fills my throat, burning like hot coals. I feel vile, unsure whether all these traitorous performances will pay off. Who knew I had such thespian talents? I guess only time will tell if they're worth a Tony.

I begin lining the ammo boxes against the wall, while vomit keeps crawling up my esophagus. After only ten of them, I can't take it anymore. I won't sit here organizing the bullets they will use to exterminate us. I pull another box from the crate. The last one I intend to handle. I undo the latch on the side and take a bullet out. I stick it in my pocket and imagine I've saved *one* life.

As I ponder what to do, three marching figures enter the room. A wet, hissing voice resounds through the storage area, issuing orders. I recognize it immediately. My mouth curls. If I vomit, I'll be sure to aim for Tusks's boots.

I turn, the open box of ammo in my hands. One thousand cartridges, one thousand lives.

More innocent blood.

Spilled.

With my help.

My hands go limp as self-hate renders me useless. The box crashes to the floor with a loud *clank*, followed by the scattering of bullets as they skitter away like metallic bugs.

Heads snap in my direction. I stare at the mess with a crazed smile on my face. "Pretty," I mumble.

"What the hell are *you* doing here?" Tusks stomps in my direction, boots kicking bullets left and right.

I don't respond, just continue to gaze at the mess, mesmerized.

"Hey! I asked you a question." He takes me by the arm and shakes me. "What the hell are you doing here?" Saliva flies from his mouth and barely misses me.

His tusks look bigger than the last time I saw him. I lean back, afraid he'll poke my eye out. Still, I don't respond, wanting only to spit on his grotesque face.

"Look at the mess you made, you little shit." He squeezes my arm so hard I feel my pulse beating in my bicep.

"I brought her to help," Lyra says from the back.

Tusks doesn't take his eyes off me to acknowledge her. "I don't want you here. Get down and pick those up, then get the hell out of my face." He pushes me down, trying to force me to my knees.

I resist him and manage to stay on my feet.

"Get down, I said!" he rumbles deep in his chest, a beast that somehow has gained the ability to speak. He slaps his massive hands on my shoulders and pushes me down until my legs give way and I fall.

Pain shoots up my knees all the way to my groin. I clamp my lips together to stifle a cry.

Tusks watches me, expectant. I clench my fists, refusing to follow his command.

"Pick. Them. Up!" he repeats.

"No," I say, a resolute word, spoken with all the weight of hours, days, weeks of anger and impotence.

"What?"

"I said no," I repeat. "*You* pick them up, fork face!"

A few onlookers snicker. Tusks's face goes red. Spit flies out of his horrid mouth as he bellows. "I'll teach you to obey me, you worthless rat."

Fast for such a large creature, he pulls one foot back and unleashes a vicious kick to my side. The steel toe of his military boot drives into my ribs, making pain blossom like a giant flower. I fall to my side, limp, and barely manage to cover my face as he unleashes kick after kick and paints my world with bright red pain. As I curl into a ball, he batters my shins and forearms until he decides stomping me like a cockroach is a better option.

The heel of his boots digs into my kidney. I bend backward in pain, the protection of my hands involuntarily falling away from my face. I reel from the pain on my back, then wince as I realize my mistake.

A hammer-like blow lands on my temple. The room spins. Scattered bullets shine in my vision, slowly going black. Muffled jeers from the onlookers ring in my ears.

"Take this piece of garbage out of here," Tusks orders.

Someone grabs my arms and hauls me to my feet. The world feels like a spinning top even as they dump me on my bed.

Chapter 43

Onyx presses a bag of frozen peas to my head. "He's a beast. I can't wait until somebody hangs his ass from those hideous tusks." She flutters around my bed, fussing with my covers. She wears a tight-fitting mini dress. Well-toned arms poke through the spaghetti straps. Her shoulders are wider than her hips, but her upper lip seems to show less of her usual five o'clock shadow. Her morphing efforts seem to be paying off. Nothing but mosquito bites in the boob department, though. She's worse than me.

My head pounds with every one of her flustered words.

Lyra glares at me from her bed. "A little extreme, no? Taking a beating to get out of *work*."

I would say something, but since it'd be a waste of time and it'd make my head pound harder, I keep my mouth shut.

"If it's work she needs, why send her with Rooter?" Onyx asks. "She could help me in the kitchen with something."

Rooter? I guess that's Tusks's name.

"Rooter root Rooter. Rooting for truffles. Oink, oink," I say, even as my head pounds like a giant's heart.

Onyx laughs and even Lyra can't hide the crooked smile that comes to her lips.

"You have a death wish, Azrael. Do not think I'll forget." Lyra points at one of her eyes, then at me. When I give her a blank face, she stands and leaves the barracks, looking disgusted.

"What is *her* problem?" Onyx asks, without really expecting an answer. "Are you comfortable?" She accommodates my pillow for the third time.

"Yes, thank you." It feels strange to be grateful to this Eklyptor, but I am. She must be an aberration. Maybe that's how it works with them. They're naturally evil, and when "something goes wrong" they turn decent.

She sits by the side of the bed with a sigh. "I don't understand why everyone has to act like a savage. At the least, they should reserve the violence for the humans."

My hand turns into a fist under the covers. There goes whatever gratefulness I was feeling toward her.

"I'm glad Elliot isn't like that," she adds, pulling an emery board from her back pocket and getting to work on her fingernails.

"What is *he* like? I mean, I've only seen him a few times." I try to sound like it's all the same to me if she tells me or not, but I'm very curious.

"Oh, he's an English gentleman. I wish I'd gotten a host like that—a woman, mind you. A Hollywood star or a princess would have been wonderful. Think of that. Anyway, Elliot Whitehouse was a young aristocrat. His parents were extremely rich. He was attending Eton when he was infected. Talk about a powerful Eklyptor from the beginning. He kept the name. He was already somebody, so why mess with success."

She holds her hand against the overhead light, checks her progress, then attacks her thumbnail with the file. "He went on to Cambridge from there, recruited a select few and started *making friends* in very high circles."

271

Making friends? Nice euphemism for injecting parasites up people's spines.

"He knew what he wanted from the beginning and accomplished it in a very classy way, don't you think?" Onyx turns away from her nails and looks at me.

I feel like puking all over the sheets but, instead, I say, "Classy? *Pfft*. I'm all for handing *my enemies* their ass."

She scoffs and stands. "Of course. That's why you're in bed with a bag of peas on your head. Well, gotta go. I'll bring you something to eat later, just take it easy." She smiles, winks, and then leaves. I wish I could lie here to nurse my pounding head, but there's no time for that. Not with Lyra breathing down my neck. Not when getting even is all that matters.

I hobble to my small desk, angle the computer monitor toward the wall and get to work. I pick up where I left off, poking and prodding around that too-secure file server. Whoever set up the stupid thing knew a thing or two. They have actually configured security, for one—it's ludicrous how many servers out there use stupid passwords like "password123" for their admin accounts— and the firewall is tight, rejecting everything I've thrown at it so far. My fingers itch as one attempt after another fails to crack the damn thing open.

Something desperate builds inside of me and I feel like a water balloon, filling and filling and filling until my outer walls are thin and ready to tear open. I have to find something. I have to make a difference and prove to IgNiTe that I'm still Marci. Because if I don't . . . if I don't . . .

I shudder just to think of the possibilities, of dying in this place—or worse, of living in it surrounded by monsters, questioning my own humanity day in and day out until it doesn't seem worth it anymore and I decide that holding on is just denial, like a frog stuck in a snake's throat, still dreaming of hopping out.

My hands move from the keyboard to my forehead, trying to squeeze out my headache. As another idea occurs to me, I type a few commands to try yet another technique. I bite my knuckles as my options run out. What if I can't break in? What if I fail and lose what little is left?

I wait.

After several long minutes, my program comes back.

No luck.

My eyes sting. Failing hurts. I fight the urge to fling the monitor across the room, to trash the entire place.

Something flashes on my screen. I look up and my heart skips a beat.

$DR. V> Still you?

Something warm spreads slowly from the center of my chest to the rest of my body, a feeling of familiarity, of home. I smile, even if this longing feels like a knife to my throat.

$Warrior> "Dr. V"? Really? What happened to Specter?

I choose banter over the need to ask for help, for acceptance.

$DR. V> I've been awarded a PhD
$Warrior> By whom?
$DR. V> Myself
$Warrior> In that case, I'm an astronaut and I'm out of here on the next space shuttle. Can't be any worse out there.
$DR. V> I figured why not? M.I.T. isn't a viable career plan anymore. I have double dibs anyhow
$Warrior> How so?
$DR. V> Anyone with superpowers is entitled to use

"Doctor" in their superhero name
$Warrior> You're a TOTAL geek, Dr. Varone
$DR. V> Oh no. That's not it. But you may call me Dr.
Volt, if you dislike the abbreviation
$Warrior> scratch "TOTAL" . . . insert "ABSOLUTE"

I'm smiling, a wide grin that I wouldn't have thought possible anymore. It's weird how many things it used to take to make me feel content and how, now, all it takes is a little attention from someone who understands *exactly* what I'm going through.

$DR. V> Hanging in there? Got to that server yet?
$Warrior> No
$DR. V> Can I help?
$Warrior> I don't think so. It's tight. I've tried everything
$Dr. V> That sucks!

He doesn't ask me what I've tried, showing professional respect for the first time since we met. No taunts. No insults to my intelligence. I feel grateful for this implicit trust, especially since it has arrived when I need it most.

$Dr. V> Wait a sec

Throwing glances over my shoulder, I tap the edge of my keyboard and wait. I take a deep breath and wince as my ribs smart. I run my finger over a tender spot on my side, willing it to heal even faster than normal.

After a moment, Aydan begins to type again.

$Dr. V> The building schematics show the network configuration. You can track the server and hit it directly, if it's safe

You stupid Marci. How did you forget about the schematics?

I thought that finding the physical location of the server would be a waste of time in such a large building, but with access to the damn schematics it's a different story.

$Warrior> I'm an idiot. I forgot about the schematics
$Dr. V> What is the name of the server?
$Warrior> SEA-SF1006
$Dr. V> Okay, if this is accurate, that particular server should be on the 10th floor, room 1006. Could you get to it?

Shit! Not Elliot's office.

Chapter 44

I'm crawling through the ducts again, trying not to sneeze. The tenth floor is always guarded and not by the same over-confident jerks they keep elsewhere. Elliot's personal guards know what they're doing. I've already climbed up the shaft to his floor and, now, I'm trying to move away from the elevator area as quickly as I can. I don't know if the twin dwarfs are still guarding the floor, but I'm not taking any chances at being heard or sensed.

The ducts grow narrow, and I'm forced to slither like a snake. When I reach the vent in Elliot's office, I rest for a moment, eyes closed, breaths slow and deep. I listen and wait. Nothing. Good.

I get to work on the vent's screws with a pair of pliers. Through the slats, the room beyond is dark, empty, just as I expected. I don't know Elliot's schedule, but I figured he wouldn't be here at dinner time. Besides, with Lyra watching my every move at bedtime, I didn't want to risk coming here in the middle of the night. She's at the mess hall right now and should be there for at least thirty minutes. She thinks I'm in bed still recovering from Tusks's beating, so I need to hurry.

The screws are tricky. I have to get them out backwards, so it's lucky I can see their pointy ends. I work methodically, paying attention to every turn of my wrist. I can't rush this. My every move has to be planned, purposeful. Any small mistake could get me killed.

The first screw falls with a small *clink* on the other side. I curse inwardly. I pushed the screw too far out. In a place where there are beasts with enhanced senses, even the tiniest sound can give me away. I sniff myself for the fifth time, worried about someone catching my scent. In spite of the sweat caused by the exertion, I still smell fine, at least to my perfectly human nose. Hopefully, there aren't any bloodhounds around.

As I work on the next screw, my vision tunnels.

I blink, shake my head, and wait for it to pass. The same thing happens as I try again. I frown at the familiarity of the feeling, and it takes me a moment to realize what the eerie sensation is. This is exactly what I felt the night I helped James open the lock to the cryobank.

One meditation session with Aydan and already there are benefits? I press the back of my hand to my mouth, pondering. If only . . .

I remove the pliers and, this time, allow my senses to take me wherever they want. My body tingles. Again, my vision focuses and I can almost *see* the screw, turning, slowly making its way out of its threads. I nearly feel myself twisting, but only at the edges, not entirely.

"C'mon, c'mon," I murmur.

I swallow the sharp curse that springs to my lips. These freaking abilities are frustrating. I can stop bullets, but not release a miserable screw. The meditation session seems to have helped, but it's hardly enough. I close myself and take out all the screws the hard way. By the time I finish, my forehead is slick with sweat and I'm as jumpy as a damn Mexican bean. At least, I didn't drop anymore of the screws inside the room.

I ease the vent off and pull it in, grinding my teeth at the scraping sound of metal. I wait for a moment, imagining stomping boots and angry voices outside the closed door. No one comes.

The vent is so narrow that my only option is to slither out of the hole. Head first, I squirm and wriggle until I'm expelled like a piece of waste. It's a seven-foot drop. I break the fall with my hands at the same time that I tuck my head in. As I hit the floor after tumbling like a weed, my ribs scream in pain. I grab my side, nursing it, grateful that Tusks's steel toe boots didn't split me in two.

I crouch, glad Elliot's office has no windows. The only light in the room is the yellow bulb inside the terrarium. The large black scorpion skitters over the sand and presses its pincers to the glass. On top of the glass tank, there's a mesh basket filled with chirping crickets, ready to be devoured alive. A shiver runs down my spine. I feel like one of the poor bastards, just waiting and waiting to be discovered, plucked and fed to a hungry monster. Because isn't that the way this new Eklyptor world works?

Eat or be eaten.

For so long we've tried to be civilized, to help the weak, nurturing the young and comforting the old. And here we are, back to square zero, reminded of the first lesson in survival: the strong take the spoils.

And it's hard to accept that we aren't strong after all, even if we thought ourselves indestructible and all-knowing. The truth is: our ways only made us weak, easy prey to those who understand how nature works, those who care nothing for helpless creatures that can only chirp and twitch all the way to the dinner table while the mighty scorpion waits for its terribly fresh meal.

I get the urge to snatch Elliot's pet and crush it under my boot. I imagine the *crunch* it would make, the way its guts would stain the carpet, and Elliot's expression at discovering his little pet turned into pulp. I smile a twisted smile.

A slight shuffle by the door catches my attention. I hold my breath, heart beating in my throat. Two shadows shift under the door. I look back toward the vent. Crap! I have no time to climb back and replace the cover. And even if I did, the buzzing will give me away as soon as they come in.

I'm dead. Dead.

A key slides into the lock. From my crouching position, I shuffle to the side like a monkey, hands and feet maneuvering me behind a leather armchair in the corner. I curl into a ball, back against the wall, thighs pressed to my chest.

I fumble through my mind, imagining flips and switches in all sizes. I turn them all off with a giant hand that is clumsy with fear. I don't sense anyone, but I have no idea if they can sense me. God, please. This is a two-way street. If I can block one side, I should be able to shut the other one, too.

My mouth is at the brink of letting out a desperate scream when the door opens. The lights come on. Someone walks in the room. My eyes flick toward the vent again, the wide-open escape route that can give me away as easily as the buzzing.

Don't Don't Don't—the chant of a dead person.

Even though the shadows are barely there, my thoughts jump in all directions as my heart speeds up. I hold my breath, wish I could also hold my heart to stop it from thumping so loud.

Elliot, I assume, sits at the desk, picks up the phone, dials.

I'm frozen, disbelieving that I'm still here and he hasn't sounded the alarm. Did I block my signal? I must have. That's the only explanation. Unless . . . unless he's being cruel, letting me believe I'm getting away with murder.

"Hello."

Yes, it's Elliot, his cool, commanding voice is unmistakable.

He barks several orders, demanding more updates on *the situation*, whatever that is. He makes two more calls, sounding unhappy with everyone, then slams the phone down.

A drop of sweat slides down my temple. If he discovers me, I'm done for. Does he really not know I'm here?

There's silence for a long moment.

He's sensed me, seen my boots. He's laughing inwardly, thinking of the most theatrical way to let me know how screwed I am.

Elliot heaves a heavy sigh, then dials another number. I press my knuckles to my lips and squeeze my eyes till they hurt.

Calm down, Marci. You did it. He can't sense you. He can't.

"Mrs. Zara Hailstone, please," Elliot says.

My eyes spring open.

"Elliot Whitehouse, returning her call."

I lean slowly toward the edge of the couch, peek with one eye. Elliot's high-back executive chair faces the wall opposite mine. All I see is his arm resting on the desk. A cufflink twinkles in the light as he drums his fingers.

"Mrs. Hailstone," he says, diplomacy dripping from his refined British accent. "I understand you have a proposition for me. I'm all ears."

A proposition? Super hearing would be nice right about now. This can't be good.

Elliot stops drumming his finger and begins to trace lazy circles on the desk.

"You have my attention," he says, sounding extremely interested in whatever Zara has just told him. A pause.

"I understand. I suggest a meeting, then. Here. And to prove my good faith, I promise full disclosure and cease of hostilities until the meeting takes place. Does that sound fair?"

Elliot's chair swivels. I pull back and hold myself tighter than before.

"Excellent. I will work out a date and let you know. Until then."
He sets down the phone and stands.

His steps are muffled by the thick carpet, but he sounds like he's headed for the door. Suddenly, he stops, clears his throat. He's close enough I can hear his breaths. I put a hand over my nose and mouth and don't breathe. Of course asphyxia might be useless because he already knows I'm here, because the buzzing gave me away the minute he stepped into the office, because he's just playing a vicious cat and mouse game with me.

"Are you hungry?"

The sudden sound of his voice startles me. He moves away, toward the terrarium to feed his pet. He talks to it in strange hisses that make the primal side of me shiver.

When he leaves, turning off the light and closing the door behind him, I stay frozen, unable to move. Minutes ticks by.

Get up. He didn't sense you. He really didn't. Get up!

I only have fifteen minutes before Lyra gets back from dinner. And I have no doubt she'll check on me then. I have to get moving. There's no time for relief or shock. I have to do what I came here to do before the door opens again and some giant hand pinches me out of the room and throws me into the gaping mouth of some hungry beast.

And, even as my legs tremble under me, I get to work.

Chapter 45

When Lyra marches into the barracks, I'm curled up in my bed, holding my middle and facing the wall. I've pulled the covers over my head, intentionally trying to look like a lump.

"Azrael," she yells.

I don't move, don't even breathe.

"That little . . ." She grabs the cover and yanks it off.

"Hey!" I exclaim, wincing and moaning as I hold my ribs. The pain isn't nearly that bad anymore, but she doesn't need to know that. "I was trying to sleep. I was almost out. Ow. Ow. Ow."

She grunts and marches out, leaving the cover on the floor.

"Could use my cover back. They keep it too damn cold in here. Too damn cold!"

I sit up and pick up my blanket. Several Eklyptors are turning in for the night. Crashing on their beds, looking exhausted. Down toward the door, Lamia is changing, her vicious eyes casting glances my way. Her long tail springs out of a hole in the back of her pants. She wears a long braid that makes it look as if she actually has two tails. They swing in unison as she moves around getting her bed ready. When she sits to take off her shoes, her tail beats the pillow, fluffing it. I stare at her additional extremity, fascination and disgust clashing in my gut. Her upper lip curls.

I avert my eyes toward a woman as tough-looking as Lamia. Except for Onyx and I, everyone here resembles a soldier.

Once more, I find myself wondering how much longer it'll be before they get rid of me. I should probably take Onyx up on her offer to work in the kitchen; maybe I could even slip rat poison in the soup while I'm at it.

I'm not ready to leave yet, and when I am, it'll be on my own terms, and not before I've done all the damage I can, which includes stealing whatever information Elliot keeps in the server under his desk.

Before I left his office, I plugged a thumb drive to a USB port in the back of the computer. When he logs back in, a little program will run and capture every keystroke he makes, including his password. After that, getting in will be a breeze.

So for now, I may as well try to sleep and dream that my hack will help save the world somehow. I close my eyes, imagining life before The Takeover, willing things to fold into a shape I recognize. Beyond my closed lids, I see my room. I pretend I hear the cooling fans of my computer humming. I think my alarm clock is set for 5:30 in the morning and I'll get up and go to the dojo for early practice. After that, there'll be school, and I'll suffer through that with dignity, trying not to slobber on my books as I nod off. When school finally lets out, I'll hop on my bike and drive to Millennium Arcade where Xave . . . where Xave . . .

My eyes spring open as I snap back into my detestable reality, while my past is obscured by a thick fog. Peaceful sleep fails me once more. There are no good dreams—only nightmares all around.

* * *

When I get up in the morning, I stretch, testing my ribs. The pain is practically gone. I talk to Onyx before she leaves to guide her troops in the preparation of breakfast. I tell her I want that job in the kitchen, washing dishes, cutting vegetables, whatever. I tell her my ribs should feel better by tomorrow and I can start then. She's delighted. No one treats her with any respect or friendliness. The fact that I do seems to make her happy. I think that's why she wants me around.

As soon as the barracks are empty, I check my sleeper hack. So far, there's been no activity, but it's early. Someone will surely log in after breakfast. I wait all morning, compulsively checking for signs of life on the server. Nothing.

I pace in front of my bed, biting my nails and going stir crazy. I try Aydan a few times, hoping for a chat, but there are no signs of him. Just when I think I might lose it, Elliot logs in and, just like that, I get his password. A warm feeling spreads inside of me: overdue satisfaction of an exquisite vintage.

"I got you, now," I say under my breath.

He doesn't stay logged in very long, but he gave me all I needed.

After an hour perusing files, emails and schedules, I understand why they took extra measures to secure this information. This is what I've been hoping for. This is enough to show James and the others that I'm worth a second chance, that I can help them make a difference in this fight.

I download every last bit of data, the warm feeling inside of me spreading to every corner of my body. I think if I were to lie down right now, I would finally sleep the way a person with a clear conscious sleeps. I might even start to believe I deserve that kind of peace.

* * *

I'm dying to see Aydan, to deliver into his hands what I've found, but I can't. I can't leave. Not with Lyra breathing down my back the way she's been doing. So I put out a signal for him, ask him to connect at lunch or dinner—as soon as he can. I think of my stolen phone still hidden in the fire hose case, probably out of charge. I wish I could text him, but I can't risk anyone seeing me with it and hiding for more than a few minutes to charge the thing and text isn't possible, not with Ms. Pussy Cat checking on me when I least expect it. Here, out in the open, pretending to play silly video games, is my safest bet.

So I wait and wait again, going even crazier than I was going earlier, itching to tell someone that we can tip the scales in this fight, that one sixteen-year-old girl that wasn't strong enough when it counted most can fight a little harder and still make a difference, that maybe they shouldn't give up on her. Not just yet.

Aydan doesn't contact me until dinner. When he comes online, I feel like tearing into him, demanding what took him so long, as if he didn't have anything better to do than sit there waiting for me to solve the world's problems with my flawless hacking skills. Instead, I find myself wondering where he's been, what he's been eating, what fears keep him up at night.

$Dr. V> Is everything okay?
$Warrior> I got in the server, found something huge. I need to see James
$Dr. V> I don't think that's a good idea
$Warrior> This is big, Aydan
$Dr. V> Whatever it is, I can get it to him
$Warrior> I'm sorry, but I will only give this to him
$Dr. V> You don't trust me?
$Warrior> I do trust you, but that isn't the problem
$Dr. V> What then?
$Warrior> James doesn't trust ME. I plan to change that.

I can help IgNiTe from the inside. He needs to see that.
$Dr. V> I'll try, but I can't promise you anything
$Warrior> I know

Again, I have to wait. At first, I thought I'd just give this to Aydan. I know it's reckless to make demands, to leave when I'm being watched so closely, but James and the others *have* to know I'm with them. They have to know I'm trying to make up for my mistakes. They have to understand I'm still one of them.

A human who thought herself strong and, in doing so, made an irreversible mistake, one she will take to her grave, even as she dies fighting to erase it.

Chapter 46

They wait for me under the cover of shadow. The gasification towers loom behind them, relics from a past that seems more distant every time I come. The tip of a cigar glows bright as James takes it to his lips. They stand shoulder to shoulder. James, muscular and bald-headed. Aydan, lean, with a full head of black hair as thick as the night. A large Harley is parked to the side, ticking as the engine cools off. The night is cloudy. A humid breeze makes the air feel thick, like a wet wall.

I walk in their direction with firm steps, even though my knees feel like rubber. My heart races. I curse my need for this man's approval. I curse the fact that I ever met him, that I ever let him down.

About five paces away, I stop, head buzzing. James drops his cigar on the ground and steps on it. A cloud of smoke whirls around him. An awful burnt vanilla smell wafts through the air. He once told me he smoked to keep his monsters under control, even if it is a hideous habit that might one day kill him.

I wait for them to say something. Aydan nods, but that's all.

"Hello, James," I say.

His only response is a narrow-eyed look.

All the explanations I've ever imagined telling him crowd next to each other inside my mouth, but I know they're all unnecessary excuses. He will make up his own mind about me. He will believe I'm in control or he will not. Either way, he might still blame me for my recklessness or for my weakness, for the death of his friend. I have no idea which way it'll go. What I do know is that nothing I tell him will make a difference.

"I assume Aydan has explained my situation," I say.

James gives Aydan a sideways glance. "He has."

I put my hand in my pocket. James tenses, his eyes sharp, attentive to my every move. I've brought them a new thumb drive loaded with a large database full of names and addresses. My fingers play with the small device, rolling it end over end, but I don't pull it out. Not yet.

"I've gained access to Elliot's private network, and I've found some information that I think can be key in our fight against his faction."

The word "our" feels sour in my mouth. Every human resisting the Eklyptors shares the same struggles, so, in that sense it is "our" fight. But I'm not part of James's team. And that is the "our" I am referring to—a possessive adjective I can't use without his permission.

"Get to the point," James says curtly.

"Yes, of course." I pull my hand out of my pocket, the thumb drive between my fingers. "I have a list of every reproductively capable Eklyptor in Elliot's faction."

I let that sink in. A million thoughts seem to pass behind James's eyes, all revealed by a tightening of his expression and a slight twitching of his upper lip. He exchanges a loaded look with Aydan. They understand better than anyone what this can mean.

"I have their names and addresses," I continue. "Most of them stay together under Elliot's protection. Here, in Seattle, there are about twenty safe houses, and it's the same elsewhere. Proportionally to Eklyptor numbers, the reproductively capable are not as many as I had imagined. If we strike, if we take them out, they wouldn't be able to infect anyone else. We would slow down their progress. Then it would just become a matter of fighting and winning. Of body count. If they can't turn anymore of us, they become a fixed number. Their armies would stop growing.

"And there's something else you should know. Elliot is planning a meeting with Zara Hailstone. The Seattle resistance has weakened them, right? So I think they want to join forces. And if that happens, I doubt the city will stand a chance. I know they will meet at Elliot's headquarters. I just don't know when, but it will be soon. I may even be able to find out the exact day and time now that I have access to his personal calendar and email."

James takes a step closer. "Aydan may trust you, but I find all this very hard to believe. I saw you kill Oso. The girl I knew would've never done that."

My fingers wrap around the thumb drive and hide it inside a clenched fist. I remember the wet stickiness in my fingers as I fought my way back. I remember Oso's shocked expression. I remember James's hands around my neck. Does he remember the same? Will he ever be able to pretend it wasn't me?

He takes another step, forcing me to look up. "I say you're here to trick us, to lay a nice little trap to draw us out and *finish* us."

My vision wavers with unshed tears. In this moment, I hate James McCray with all I've got. I hate that he reminds me of Dad and that I doggedly look up to him even when I'd rather not.

"James—" Aydan begins.

James puts a hand up to silence him. "What do you have to say for yourself?"

"There's nothing to say." I inhale deeply and don't blink. "It's my fault that The Tank was destroyed, that Oso is dead. I tried to be strong, and I was . . . in the end. But it wasn't enough. I live with it every day." Tears find their way out against my will. I rake them away, angrily running my forearm over my face.

"Marci doesn't cry," James says.

"Fuck you," I say between clenched teeth.

He smirks. "And I'm not sure she curses either."

My fists shake with anger. I want to punch his teeth out, but he's too damn fast. I wouldn't even be able to hit his shadow.

"She does have a temper, though." James puts a hand on my shoulder. "For all our sakes, I do hope it's you." He puts his other hand out, asking for the thumb drive.

I part with it, not without a nonsensical possessive feeling gnawing at my stomach.

"I never wanted you to have to go through this, *Marci*." He emphasizes my name. The way he says it makes it feel detached, as if this is something he *would* say to Marci, if she was here.

"I should have . . . kept you safe." He drops his hand from my shoulder, looks at the thumb drive. "Thank you, if thanks are deserved. We will look into it *very* carefully."

He hands Aydan the thumb drive, walks to the Harley and mounts it.

"You understand why I can't invite you to come with us," he says, and it's hardly a question.

I do and I don't. I guess one meeting is hardly enough to regain his trust. This time, however, I'd hoped I could go with them, hadn't I? The realization tears me apart. This is why I asked to see James. This is what I had truly hoped for.

Aydan takes a tentative step in my direction. James kicks the pedal, brings the engine roaring to life.

"Let's go, Aydan," he orders.

Aydan ignores the unequivocal command and walks to me. For a moment, his black eyes are tight pools of pure darkness.

But, when he blinks, a blue sparkling light shines inside of them, very much like the fireworks display he cast on the lake the last time we met.

A half smile tips his lips. "I've been practicing finesse," he says. "What do you think?"

"Nice," I say, almost mirroring his smile, but not quite.

He takes my hand, surprising me. Threading his finger with mine, he gives them a reassuring squeeze.

"You won't go back, right? You promised you'd leave, if you found something big. This is big," he says. "Hide. You've done enough."

I shake my head. "I'm sorry. I don't think I can do that."

"Yes, you can."

"I'd rather die fighting, than hide like a coward."

"No one could ever call you that," he says.

I pry my hand away from his. "Do what you have to do, and I'll do the same."

"I would take you back if it was up to me."

"I know."

He wraps me in a tight hug as if he'd never let me go. My arms stay stiff at my sides, while inside my every muscle and bone disintegrates into pieces.

"Someday, this will end, and I won't rest until everyone understands your sacrifice." He lets go, turns his back, hiding his eyes, and rides away with James.

Chapter 47

Waiting and not knowing is excruciating—at times, more so than the torture I endured at Doctor Sting's hands. For the first couple of days, I held out the hope that James would contact me, that he would realize the information is real and would be grateful and ready to take me back. But that hasn't happened, and all I got is silence, even after I found out the details of Elliot and Zara's meeting and passed them along to Aydan—who didn't seem to have much time for me either.

Now, hope has abandoned me for good, and I find again that life can very quickly lose its meaning when there's no one left to look up to, to argue with, to love. So, every minute, I die a little and feel, not like a Trojan, but like a parasite among parasites.

I eat their food and shuffle their dishes. Onyx got me a job in her kitchen, and it revolts me—the thought that I've become their servant. I tell myself there's a reason I'm here, that something will happen soon, and—when it does—I'll be ready to make a difference.

"One more day. Only one more day," I murmur, knowing that I won't survive another hour, if I look too far into the future.

"She's talking to the dirty dishes again," a lanky girl with eyes like a lynx says. She's in charge of keeping the kitchen clean, picking up spills, taking out the garbage, scrubbing the sinks.

I ignore her, so does everyone else. This place runs from 4 A.M. to 11 P.M. nonstop. No one has time for the crazy girl who repeats everything she says—not if she keeps the conveyor belt flowing and the industrial dishwasher pumping out clean pots and dishes, which I do, flawlessly. So well that even Lyra seems to have lost interest in me, even after I went missing for two hours the night I met James. I guess she's now bored of always finding me where I'm supposed to be, even when she pops in at the oddest times.

It has been a week since that night, and all I've gotten for my efforts is a big fat zero. Elliot's meeting with Zara is tomorrow in conference room 103. I will wait until then. If nothing happens, I guess it will be time to take Aydan's advice and leave.

"One more day," I repeat under my breath.

Wiping my hands on my dirty apron, I head back out into the dining area. It's dinner time, the busiest meal of the day, when the creatures are back from chasing the humans who fight back, when their hunting stories are the loudest and I'm more likely to stab someone's eyeball with the tip of a sauce-smeared table knife.

I keep my head low and walk between tables, picking up trays and delivering them to the blue conveyor belt. Most, if not all, don't pick up after themselves. The pecking order is clear. Everyone has a rank and, with that, no need for manners. If Azrael takes over me again, at least I can be consoled by the fact that her rank will have her doing dishes for the rest of her life.

A large leg appears in my path. I stop, look up and find that it's attached to Tusks.

"I see you've found a job that suits you," he says, stretching his horrible mouth in a twisted, foul grin. There's greasy sauce on his chin and half-chewed food visible past his tusks. He smells like a pork chop. How anyone can stand to eat with him is a mystery, and a good one, judging by every occupied seat at his table.

I ignore him and try to walk around. He scoots his chair and lifts his leg higher to better block my way. I turn to go back the way I came, but he stands and plants his massive body in front of me.

"I have another job for you," he says. "My boots need shining. I want you to clean them . . . with your *tongue*."

Everyone at his table laughs as if they've never heard anything funnier.

"C'mon, what are you waiting for?" he demands, sweeping my feet from under me with one swift kick.

I land on all fours and, again, find myself face to face with his massive scuffed boots. My ribs hurt with phantom reminders of his vicious kicks. I try to stand, but he puts a foot on my shoulder and keeps me down. His dinner pals snicker.

"Lick. My. Boots," he orders me, his foot crushing me down.

My arms tremble as I try to keep myself from collapsing on my stomach. I push upward, but he's too heavy. My elbows buckle. My face is inches from his boot. I work a thick ball of saliva in my mouth and spit it on top of the shoelaces.

"Lick them yourself, if you can, you dirty hog," I say, ready to get trampled again, because I'd rather die than stoop any lower than I already have.

Someone at an adjacent table cackles. "Nope, I don't think he could get the boot past that regrettable grill."

Both tables burst into laughter. Tusks lets out a guttural growl, pushes his foot out and sends me rolling to the side. I hurry to my feet, turn to run, but his enormous hand takes me by the neck and reels me back in. I duck to one side, get free and throw a round kick to his stomach. He grunts, but that's it. It's like hitting a heavy bag, not someone made of actual flesh and blood.

I throw another kick. He blocks it, grabs my leg and hurls me on top of his table. Drinks and plates fly in every direction. Everyone scatters. Tusks lumbers in my direction, his pig eyes glinting with murder. I paw the table and come up with a handful of spaghetti dripping with red sauce. Aiming for his face, I fling the food and hit the mark.

Tusks swats noodles off his eyes. Snarling like a beast, he pulls me down, grabs me by the neck and winds his fist back. I close my eyes.

"I said ORDER!" a commanding voice shouts.

The room goes utterly silent. Tusks's fist freezes midway, and it is then that I notice my head has started buzzing just a little louder.

Chairs scrape against the floor as everyone stands to attention.

Elliot is in the room.

Chapter 48

Elliot's golden eyes go over the crowd, then stop at the spilled drinks and food. His mouth curls in distaste. He smooths his gray suit as if he's been soiled by association. Lyra and Dillon move into my field of vision among the other curious onlookers. Elliot's gaze settles on Tusks for a moment. The mammoth creature seems to shrink several inches. An anxious grunt escapes through his nose as his dime-sized eyes stare at his leader's polished shoes.

At last, Elliot's eyes settle on me. The expression of disgust on his face doubles. "I had quite forgotten about you," he says.

I stare at his shoes, too, even though I want to crawl under the table and make myself invisible; the way I might have if it wasn't for Tusks, The Brutish Boar.

"I guess I shouldn't be surprised to find out you're causing trouble." Disdain drips from Elliot's tone.

What? So *I* get the blame for this?

Tusks stretches back to his normal height.

My anger gathers, boiling down to a single point. It feels powerful, like a laser beam I could use to sever Elliot's head off. My heart hammers. My face grows hot. I could kill him now, tear those creepy eyes out, even if his freaks make a feast out of me afterward. I take a step forward.

Lyra and Dillon move to flank Elliot.

"This way, please," Lyra says, pointing to the back of the room where a handful of empty tables sit above the rest on a sort of dais.

Elliot's attention snaps away from me, and he leaves as if I've blinked out of existence. Tusks looks put out. My anger finds itself trapped, and I feel as if it might blow through the top of my head, spilling brain matter everywhere.

I step back and slip from the crowd as everyone follows Elliot like a magnet they can't resist. He climbs onto the raised dining area and faces his followers.

A shiver crawls up my back, and I notice the temperature has dropped a few degrees. Cold air blows through the overhead vents. Elliot fusses with the cuffs of his shirt, then the sleeve of his jacket. It's a strange habit I've noticed before. It makes him look uncomfortable in his fancy suit—odd considering the fact he's always dressed like he's going to a state dinner.

He addresses the crowd, around eighty Eklyptors of his personal army. "The fight beyond these walls persists. *You*, my generals and captains, continue to direct the troops, purging Seattle as well as other key cities in which we have strongholds. Some are doing better than others. London's Takeover is a great example of efficiency from which you can all learn. I wish to visit, so I expect improvements on this end as soon as possible, so I may do so."

A thick-skinned man near me mumbles under his breath. "It's an island, of course it was easy." A few around him grumble in approval.

"I'm disappointed at the inability to crush the resistance. These IgNiTe rebels need to be dealt with sooner rather than later. We have waited long enough to get here. Are you not ready to cherish the spoils of this centuries-old struggle?"

"Yeah, yeah." Several pump their fists in the air.

Centuries? Have they really been planning to take humans over that long? All while we killed each other through God knows how many wars? How is it possible to have been so blind?

"Several cities have been particularly troublesome," Elliot continues, "though none as troublesome as this. IgNiTe has succeeded in recruiting too many people."

My heart beats harder at this news. It isn't new, but coming from Elliot's lips it feels more real. If he's worried, it means I can at least allow myself a few cocky smiles, even as I rinse his dishes.

"Our progress in converting the rest of the population is *not* satisfactory!" The veins behind his ridiculous, ever-present cravat bulge like ropes.

Converting? What are they? Evangelists? They're a revolting, parasitic infection. Nothing more. Nothing less. They're infecting us, contaminating us, robbing us. They need to call things by their name.

Elliot paces, eyes fixed on nothing in particular. "This is why, we've had a cease in hostilities with the Hailstone faction. It is counterproductive to battle each other over territories that haven't been properly cleansed. This is why we will be combining and focusing our efforts with them until further notice."

Protests go around the room.

"Silence!" Elliot commands. "We have come too far to risk failure. Humans might be weak, but they are resourceful. We cannot underestimate them. There are rumors about a vaccine, even a cure against us."

"What? No way!" the guy next to me says. Murmurs move in a wave across the room.

The world of my past, the one I try to picture every night, seems to lift out of the fog that always obscures it.

A Cure?

Is it truly possible? Could there be a cure already? Did Kristen finally do it? My heart thuds and thuds, each pump trying to resuscitate my dying faith.

"It is my belief that, at the moment, that is all they are, rumors," Elliot says with conviction. "And we need to ensure it stays that way. Consequently, our *interim* alliance with Hailstone. I will hold a meeting with their leader tomorrow. This is our course of action until further notice. Understood?"

Reluctant grumbles are the only response to his question.

"Understood?" he repeats, punctuating each syllable.

Everyone changes their tune, filling the room with forced positivity.

"Yes."

"Of course."

"Understood, Sir."

I ease away from the crowd, back toward the kitchen. A resolute feeling swells in my chest. IgNiTe is fighting, others are fighting, fiercely enough to prompt Whitehouse and Hailstone to worry about their success and form an alliance. Every human out there—whether as part of a group or alone—is making a difference, so why can't I?

It was feeble to think I should leave this place if James didn't call me, didn't ask me to be part of his team again. But it really doesn't matter if I'm with him or not. There's no way I would give less than everyone else is giving. So even if I have to do it by myself, even if my efforts don't go a long way, I will stay and find a way to make a difference.

Every drop counts. If we must bleed to win, my blood is as red as any.

Chapter 49

A gun and a large case of bullet clips wait for me inside the broom closet in the first floor. Lyra should have never showed me their arsenal. It was too easy to sneak in and out and get what I needed.

I wring my hands together as I sit at the edge of my bed. I check my watch again, something I've been doing compulsively since I woke up. Elliot's meeting is in thirty minutes. The barracks are empty. Everyone in charge of anything is in position for the event. Today no one will slack. There are guards in every corner.

One hundred strong.

One hundred.

Against one.

My stomach tumbles. I press a hand to the spot and will my nerves to settle. A presentiment of something bad to come, I suppose. How useless these feelings are. What is the point of a premonition when the actions that will lead you there are inevitable?

I slip the bullet out of my pocket. It's the same one I snatched from the metal box the day Lyra made me stack ammunition. I rub my thumb against its cool, golden metal, imagining it traveling through the air, spiraling toward Elliot and striking him right in the chest.

The thought of ending his life leaves no guilt behind, only satisfaction. True, Oso is dead because I couldn't fend off the agent, but it was Elliot who caused my lapse.

I picture him crumbling to his knees, shocked that I've been the one to deliver the killing blow—much the way Oso was. I think I should feel evil, but I don't. Instead, I feel at ease, like everything will be all right with the world once Elliot's gone.

I've killed before, but it was in the heat of the moment, to save James and myself. There was no premeditation, no plan. So different from now. Funny how uncomplicated it is to become a murderer. I wonder if I'm not sane anymore. How could I be?

Time ticks by as I stare at my boots lined up perfectly next to each other. I wear a black uniform like everyone else. The boots are a match. I wait—breaths even, mind made up. A certain calm has come with resignation. I will probably die within the hour, and that's all right. I will make my stand and, if it's the last one, I'm okay with that. At least, my life won't be given up in vain, like Oso's life, like Xave's.

The ache of remembering is raw; an open wound that won't close, no matter how much I pretend it's not there.

I pull my boots closer, set my bullet between them. I slip one foot in, then the other. My fingers move calmly around the shoe-laces, tugging and tying.

One bunny ear.

Two bunny ears.

I remember Dad teaching me. What would he think of me, now? Would he be proud? Would he ache seeing what's become of his little girl?

The bullet goes in my pocket. I stand, throw my head back and take a deep, deep breath. I march out of the barracks, my steps echoing through the empty room. At the entrance, I run into Lizard Woman, a.k.a. Lamia. Her tail swings up and out of the way to let me pass. I don't acknowledge her, but I can feel her eyes on me as I firmly walk away. I turn the corner, leave her behind and retrieve my gun and bullets.

I'm ready for this.

One hundred and ten freaking percent.

* * *

I'm a mole in more ways than one. I've crawled through these dark tunnels, the bowels of the building, once more. Now, I sit here in the dark, waiting. I'm a ghost, a nonentity, forgotten by everyone, even by Lyra.

The conference room is beyond me. Through the metal grate of an air vent at floor level, I see everyone in the room. Shadows envelop me inside and outside. I breathe in deep, deep, deep, then hold it. I think of freedom.

Blacktop sliding by . . . Xave's laugh behind me.

Wind blowing on my face . . . Small kisses on the back of my neck.

His arms wrapped around me as we ride.

It's an ever-present memory that I've pushed away many, many times. Today, I embrace it. I savor it. Maybe there is a heaven and today I'll see him. And dad.

That isn't bad at all. I smile.

My buzz-o-meter is off. Both ways. I'll do this as a human.

The gun is in my hand.

Ready.

In the room, Tusks, Lyra, Dillon, and the tall, horned Amazon from my barracks stand at attention in different corners of the room, waiting for the meeting to begin. All four look like warriors. Either muscular or lean, there's a deadly quality in their gazes.

Vertical blinds hang shut, blocking the view outside the room.

After a moment, the door opens and Elliot walks in, alone.

"They've arrived," he says, taking the seat at the head of the long table. "Keep your eyes open, but no one make a move unless they do. Understood?"

"Yes, Sir."

After a moment, Elliot stands, walks to the thermostat and turns it all the way down. He returns to his seat. Cold air blows through the vents with a sudden *whoosh*. For once, I welcome the chill.

Steps sound outside the room. A few silhouettes are visible behind the blinds. The conference room door opens again and a petite woman with copper-colored hair and a narrow face enters. She looks familiar. I've seen her before, somewhere. It was at the nightclub, wasn't it? She was with—

My thoughts stop short as the answer to my question walks in step behind her.

Luke—blond, tall and calm—is also here.

* * *

"Welcome, Mrs. Hailstone." Elliot stands and shakes the woman's hand.

She inclines her head in a very refined way.

Animals with manners. Who would have thought?

"Thank you, Mr. Whitehouse," she says in an accent that sounds just like Lyra's.

Zara Hailstone is French? My mind reels with possibilities.

"Let me introduce you to Luke," Zara Hailstone says. "He is my second in command and my son."

My body goes limp. The gun falls to my folded legs and slides down toward the metal flashing that makes up the tunnel. I catch it and clutch it to my chest, breathing hard.

Her son? Luke isn't Zara Hailstone's son. Aydan said Luke's DNA matched Karen's. Was Zara the one who raised him? Ernest Dunn's wife? But Luke said his mother abandoned him after he was born. None of it makes any sense, especially the way he came into our lives and wrecked everything. Why? To what end?

I force my lungs to slow down. They will hear me if I don't get it together. I'm here for a reason and one reason only. This doesn't change anything.

I struggle to get myself under control. My hands are shaking. *Breathe, breathe, breathe.*

Slowly, my heart rate calms. In a minute, it will be back to normal and then . . .

"Please, take a seat," Elliot says.

Zara sits closest to Elliot, and Luke next to her. I see his profile. He eyes the guards at each corner.

"Our guards remained outside," Luke says. "Is this really necessary?"

"My dear boy, *you* requested a meeting with *me*," Elliot says as if he's talking to an elementary school brat. "Therefore, this will happen on my terms."

Luke's jaw twitches. Tusks smirks in the far corner.

"This is fine," Zara says, pronouncing *this* as *dzees*, "as long as a conversation in front of them is prudent."

"It's quite all right. These men and women have my complete trust," Elliot responds in a tone that suggests that whatever they're about to discuss doesn't warrant risking his life by dismissing his guards.

"Very well." Zara inclines her head. There's something lithe about her movements. Her eyes seem to smile in a cunning, amused way, like she knows something no one else does.

"So you said you wanted to discuss an alliance," Elliot says.

"Yes," Zara assents. "Several of our bordering territories are

304

experiencing a level of conflict that is quite worrisome at this stage in the game. Things aren't proceeding the way they should as far as humans go. The Takeover has been more difficult here than in other areas. So, naturally, some adjustments are necessary."

Elliot nods over his steepled fingers. "I quite agree."

I lift the gun and stare at my hand. It's finally steady, as steady as it'll ever get. My bullet is ready. It's the first one. I lower my ski mask, a souvenir I found tucked in one of Lyra's drawers. If I survive this, maybe staying anonymous will be helpful. With one last look through the grate, I flick the gun's safety off. When I look up, Luke's face is slightly turned in my direction. He's frowning, his blue eyes darting from side to side.

"Something the matter?" Elliot asks.

Luke rolls his chair back slightly. "I . . ."

He suspects something. I don't know how, but he does.

I take one last deep breath. This is it.

Kicking from a sitting position, I jam my boots against the vent cover with all I've got. The grate flies into the conference room, tumbling end over end on the floor with several loud, metallic *clanks*. I shoot out, head first, and roll to one side. I come up on one knee, gun searching my target. Elliot's startled eyes meet mine. He's frozen on his tall leather chair.

I don't hesitate.

I pull the trigger.

Chapter 50

The bullet leaves the gun in a rush of power. I feel the shock in my hand and up my arm. Elliot is an open-mouthed statue and I'm the bullet, sure and true. I will not miss.

Shattering my certainty, Tusks flies from the corner and lands on Elliot's lap, pushing him out of the way. The massive guard jerks as the bullet strikes him in the back. The chair rolls away with the impact. They hit the blinds, send them swaying from side to side. Elliot cowers behind Tusks.

I adjust my aim, ready to pull the trigger again. Zara and Luke jump to their feet. Luke's eyes lock with mine. A tremor runs down my spine, as the sense of recognition thrills through me.

Lyra and the other guards train their weapons on me. Elliot peeks from behind Tusks who's trying to struggle to his feet, but isn't allowed. For an instant, we all stand still, digesting the moment. Lyra's eyes shine. She makes the first move, angling her gun toward Luke. Dillon does the same. The tall Amazon never takes her eyes off me.

"Shoot them," Elliot screams.

I jump out of the way. A shot zips by my ear.

"No!" Luke whirls and knocks the gun out of the Amazon's hand. A shot rings from Lyra's gun, but misses Luke.

The Amazon swings and lands a jaw-breaking punch. Barely stunned, Luke rams into her, wraps his arms around her waist and knocks her down. Her gun flies out of her hand. Zara goes for it, but Lyra kicks it out of the way and without hesitation shoots her. Zara jerks but doesn't drop to the floor. Instead, she launches at Lyra, growling like a small dog.

A million steps sound outside. Others are coming; if they get in here before I kill Elliot . . .

The bastard is still clinging to Tusks, using him as a shield. I step to the side to get a better angle. Several shapes rush behind the vertical blinds. Unable to get a clear shot, I rush forward, ready to shoot over Tusks and at close range. Elliot screams and pushes Tusks off, finally letting him go. He crashes against my legs. I lose my balance and fall backward.

The twin dwarf guards burst through the door. I aim at Elliot's head. I'm about to pull the trigger when suddenly the whole floor rocks with an explosion. In spite of the blinds, glass flies inward from the floor-to-ceiling windows. Pieces of false ceiling rain down. Everyone ducks, covering their heads. The electricity goes out and emergency lights come on.

Shots erupt outside.

Suddenly, it's full-on war.

* * *

I bat a piece of ceiling tile off my face. Tusks moans and pushes rubble out of the way. I pull my legs from under him and scramble to find my weapon.

"Give me that," Elliot says, snatching a gun away from one of the dwarfs.

I crawl under the long table still searching. A bullet explodes through the tabletop, nearly slicing my neck off. I scuttle away from Elliot toward the opposite end. A volley of shots follows in my wake, sending splinters flying in all directions.

The rapid fire of machine guns comes from outside the room.

"What is happening out there?" Elliot demands.

No one answers.

I stop and make myself as small as possible. From here, I see Zara lying on the floor, a hand pressed to her bloody chest. Luke and the horned woman are also on the floor, fighting each other, rolling, punching, grunting.

"You did this," Elliot screams to Zara. "Kill them both. The other one, I want alive," he orders.

Guards surround the table, their black, military boots shuffling and stomping all around me. Someone heaves Zara to her feet. The butt of a rifle smashes against the back of Luke's neck and he falls limp to the side.

"We didn't do anything," Zara says. "Don't hurt him." Her voice is pleading and desperate, the voice of a scared mother.

"Get the other one," Elliot orders.

The rolling chairs are wrenched away.

Dillon crouches from a distance, pointing a gun right in my face. "Get out of there." He flicks his gun slightly in a beckoning motion.

Sweat soaks my ski mask, itching, making me want to pull the damn thing off. I focus on that stupid detail and ignore the gun that's staring me in the face. The room is now filled with Elliot's armed beasts. There's no use in fighting.

Or is there?

More shots ring outside, sounding closer and closer.

Maybe there is.

"Get the bloody bastard from under there," Elliot screams.

Suddenly, the table above me shifts. I scramble away as one side of the massive piece of furniture tips upward. The sound of a feral growl fills the room, then the table lurches and crashes on its side. People scramble out of the way. Tusks stands, back hunched, chest heaving after the impossible effort. Something smolders in the depths of his small eyes. His tusks seem sharper than ever, dripping with sweat and saliva, poised to charge.

Adrenaline tingles through my limbs. I'm crouching, guns and beasts alike aimed in my direction. This is it. I've failed.

I stand very slowly, arms loose at my sides. My heart drums and drums while the events of the past five minutes replay in my mind, showing me all the things I could have done differently to succeed. I should have planned better. I should have—

Bullets fly in from the outside, peppering the walls and the overturned table. Everyone ducks for cover. Two of the guards fall to their knees, then on their faces. Tusks drops, goes for the gun at his hip. I jump over the table and scramble along its length. Shots ring behind me.

Fire shoots through my calf as a bullet grazes me. I lose my stride and fall flat. More shots whiz by right above me.

"I got you," someone says from this side of the table.

I look up. The horned Amazon has her gun aimed directly at my head. I close my eyes. It's time, and I'm *not* ready. If only I hadn't missed . . .

Suddenly, a deluge of bullets criss-cross the room. They strike one after another like fireworks. I open my eyes. Amazon woman lies on the floor, groaning. She tears her shirt open, cursing, baring her teeth in pain. I back out and round the table as she fights with her Kevlar vest like it's on fire.

"Shoot him!" The cry comes from outside the conference room, full of a desperate quality that spells defeat, like whoever they're trying to kill isn't an easy target. Not at all.

My heart surges. Could it be? Is *he* here?

An image of James blurring into nothing pops into my head.

It's a stupid hope. This has to be a trap from Zara. Maybe she is *that* stupid. Maybe she really thought this would work: attacking Whitehouse on his own turf.

Elliot's guards hide behind overturned chairs, shooting through the broken windows, shredding the blinds.

I press my back to the table, suddenly forgotten as everyone takes cover. My calf throbs. I press a hand to it, clench my jaw at the surge of pain. My fingers come away bloody.

It's just a scrape. Just a scrape.

I look toward the vent. I can escape that way.

"Get me out of here," Elliot says. "You and you and you, cover us. The rest come with me."

I peer around the edge of the desk. Elliot is rushing out the door with Amazon Woman and the rest of the guards shielding him. Tusks, Lyra, and Dillon stay behind, shooting in the opposite direction at the unseen enemy.

Bullets hit fast. Not missing a mark. I pull back, pressing closer to the floor. Tusks gives a loud grunt of pain. I hope someone hit the bullseye, right in the middle of his hideous mouth. I peer once more. Luke helps Zara to her feet and, in the confusion, ushers her out of the conference room in the same direction Elliot left.

I smile; a twisted thing that's made of pleasure. They won't get away. I *won't* let them. Patiently, I wait for a few beats. When the next volley of bullets comes into the room, I crawl toward the door, shots zooming overhead, and pick up a discarded gun. With a quick look back, I notice Tusks on the floor, his massive body still. I guess someone did hit the bullseye. Good riddance.

I keep crawling past the door. Once outside, I turn on my buzz-o-meter in case I run into any Eklyptors. I stand and run down the corridor, ignoring the pain that shoots up the back of my leg. The fight rages behind me, its sounds becoming muffled the further I go. Elliot may think he's getting away, but a second wave of rage is coming at him and, this time, it won't fail.

Chapter 51

I catch up with Zara and Luke first. Her arm is around his waist as he helps her, carrying her forward. I slow my pace and try to control my agitated breaths. They continue, hobbling, unaware of my presence.

My fingers tighten around the gun. I take a knee. My injured calf trembles as I go down. Blood has soaked my pants down to my boot. I relish the pain, let it fuel me, let it spur my hatred. There, only yards away, are the leaders of the Hailstone faction. I can kill them both.

I lift the gun, aim for Zara, for the space between her shoulder blades, right under Luke's arm. She deserves to die as much as Elliot does. She's as responsible for the chaos in the city, for the deaths, for the humans trapped inside their own heads while parasites puppeteer their bodies.

Slowly, I apply pressure on the trigger. It should be a small opposition, but the curved piece of metal feels like an immovable thing against my finger, a mountain, the faith of a true believer. My hand shakes. I can't line up my sights.

I am a killer.

I *am* a killer.

My hand falls to the side. I may be a killer, but I can't shoot anyone in the back. Not even an Eklyptor. Luke opens the door to the mess hall. As he helps Zara in, he looks back, sees me kneeling on the floor. His blue gaze locks with mine and, once more, a thrill of recognition passes between us. He looks down at the gun, understanding my inability to do what I should.

He lowers his gaze and turns his head toward the door. Frozen in place for a moment, he seems to ponder a million possibilities. Finally, he shakes his head and rushes into the room.

Why couldn't I pull the trigger? She's not any different from Elliot.

Elliot . . . Elliot . . .

I have to go after him. I can still do some good tonight. This can't all be in vain. I struggle to my feet, calf shaking.

There's a sound behind me. I spin, gun outstretched and ready to shoot. A lone figure stands in the darkness, an orange emergency light at his back. A knot forms in my throat. He's also holding a gun, but his hand rests at his side. I should pull the trigger but, again, I can't. Some worthless morality stops me. Instead, I take a step back.

Sweat drips into my left eye from the soaked ski mask. I blink and, in that instant, the figure blurs and disappears. Something hits my hand, and the gun flies off and slams against the wall. I whirl, but see no one. From behind, an arm wraps around my neck and squeezes, lifting me off the ground. I try to speak but only a choked sound comes out.

"Which way did they go?"

He releases his hold just enough to let me speak.

I cough. "James, it's me, Marci." Hand shaking, I pull the mask off.

James lets me go. I slump against the wall, a hand to my throat.

"What are you doing?" he demands.

I touch a hand to my neck and swallow.

He inhales. His chest swells up, then comes down. He's wearing his IgNiTe jacket, just like the one he got for everyone. It fits him as if they used a mold of his torso to make it.

When I get my voice, I say, "Same thing you are." I push matted hair off my forehead, straighten. I look him in the eye. "Trying to kill Elliot. I almost had him."

There's still suspicion in his eyes, but we don't have time for that.

"He went this way." I pick up my gun and head for the mess hall's double doors, doing my best not to limp. "Zara did, too." I don't look back, don't wait for him. This mission is my own. He can stuff his distrust.

Opening one door slowly, I peek inside. The area is empty and dark, illuminated only by two sets of bright emergency lights. I push inside, gun at the ready. James follows behind me.

"They must have gone through the kitchen." I point toward another set of double doors in the back. "There's an exit that leads to the back of the building."

I run forward, press my back to one of the doors and crane my neck to look through its small window. At the end of the long kitchen, Luke moves slowly forward. He's now carrying Zara, who seems to have passed out.

"I see them," I stage whisper. James is standing in the middle of the mess hall. A deep frown splits his forehead in half. He's probably wondering if this is a trap, if I'm leading him straight into Elliot's arms.

"For God's sake," I say, "stop standing there. He's going to get away."

He just stares at me, unmoving.

"Fine!" I exclaim and head into the kitchen. Luke is at the far exit door, already making his way out of the building. I've taken only a few steps in pursuit when a gust of wind rushes past me, sending my hair into my face. I push loose strands away from eyes. James has crossed the long distance to the exit door and is now holding it open. He takes a quick look outside.

He presses a finger to his ear. "Retreat. Target has exited the building. North side." His words echo gently through the kitchen, almost too soft to be heard.

I blink.

He's gone.

Chapter 52

"Damn!" I curse.

James is gone. Just gone.

My legs pump, pain forgotten as adrenaline spikes and floods my system. Blood trickles down my ankle, spurred by my sudden outburst.

I reach the door, don't even stop to peek outside, just erupt into the night, brandishing my gun and looking for a place to take cover. Bullets whiz by in every direction. I keep running, not knowing which way leads to enemy lines. I roll on the blacktop and take cover behind a Dumpster.

A light rain falls from the black-gray sky, sending a bone-deep chill through me. The street gleams with moisture.

Back pressed to the Dumpster's cold metal, I try to get my bearings. I wince at the poignant stench of wet garbage. Shots blast all around, near and far. Elliot's guards, Zara's people, and IgNiTe, all in one place. Of course, all hell has broken loose.

The main fight seems to be happening on the east side of the building. Twisting my neck, I look around the edge of my hiding place, but I can't see much besides guns popping in and out of all the nooks and crannies capable of sheltering a person.

The sound of rapid footsteps slapping the ground reaches my

ears. I pull back, heart hammering. A man wraps around the west corner of the building and takes cover, pressing his body against the concrete wall. He's so intent on whoever is after him that he doesn't even register the chaos going on at this end. I've seen him in the mess hall before. He's an average-size Eklyptor of human appearance, a fairly new specimen.

Without any brusque movements that might attract attention, I scoot to the other side of the Dumpster. Newbie doesn't notice me. He's too busy looking scared, head pressed against the wall, lungs pumping as if oxygen will run out in the next hour. Then, without notice, he jumps out and begins shooting back the way he came, screaming like Tarzan. His rifle *cracks, cracks, cracks*, one bullet after another, the muzzle swinging from side to side as if he's wielding a water hose.

Suddenly, a ball of lightning hits him in the chest and he flies five feet in the air. His arms shoot back and he glides backward as if crucified. He lands on the asphalt with a heavy *thwack*, back arched, legs twitching. He goes on jerking for a moment, then goes still.

Aydan.

IgNiTe must be fighting in that direction. The urge to run toward him takes over me. He's the only one who trusts me, the only one who seems to understand. I shut my eyes, resisting the desire to leave my position. But no one ever manages to run away from their problems, right? Not me, that's for sure.

More Whitehouse soldiers round the corner, chased by blue-white bolts of light.

I've got to move.

Fighting a wave of dizziness, I scoot in the opposite direction, turning my back on the temptation of running toward Aydan. I smile bitterly at the idea that *he* has become my only friend. Who would have thought? Life is truly a sardonic bitch.

A delivery truck is parked against the building. I run from the Dumpster and sneak between the vehicle and the wall. I walk sideways in the narrow space until I hear voices. I freeze. The tones are low and almost lost in the din of battle, but I can still make them out.

"You'll be in charge now." A female voice, barely audible.

"Just stop. You'll be fine. Tauro and the others are coming to help us," the other voice, one I recognize, says firmly, though without true confidence.

Luke and Zara are by the front of the truck.

I can see the top of her head from where I am. She's lying on the ground, while Luke kneels next to her, his back turned. Zara coughs. Luke presses a hand to her forehead.

"Just hold on," he says. "I called them. They're coming," he insists.

"You know what . . . you have to do," Zara says.

"Yes, but there's no need for that." Luke smooths her hair back.

Something twists in my stomach as I feel his emotions wash over me. He's in pain. I can sense it as if it were my own. We share no twin connection and I can still feel him. I turn, shut him away as best as I can together with all the questions that spring into my mind.

I will not witness this. It's impossible to think these beasts have loved ones. I figure them as snakes, laying down their eggs and abandoning them to their fate.

I retreat as silently as I came. Maybe I'm incapable of shooting her in the back, but not beyond wishing her dead. If that also makes me a beast, so be it. Xave was killed by one of the creatures at her club. She leads an army of predators. She deserves to die this death.

There's no pity when you're fighting for survival.

I rush out the other way and run past Luke without looking

back. I don't know if he notices me or not, and I don't care. I pass one of Elliot's men hiding behind a wooden crate. He startles and points his gun at me, but doesn't shoot. I recognize him from the mess hall. He must recognize me, too.

A bullet tears my shirt sleeve and strikes the ground behind me. I run a diagonal line and squeeze between two tall hedges that make a delineating barrier between this service road and the one for the adjacent building. A branch cuts across my cheek as I sidle by. When I come out on the other side, two guns are pointed straight at my face. They stay there for a moment, then slowly go down as their bearers notice my matching uniform. A man and a woman stare at me with wide eyes.

"What's the situation?" I ask, trying to sound in command.

They give me a strange look, probably wondering why the girl who buses their dishes is carrying a gun and acting in charge. Still, one of them answers.

"We need to get Whitehouse out of here," the woman says. She has a broad back, almost as large as her companion's. Her dark hair is tightly braided to her head.

"Tell me something I don't know," I say, irritated.

"Well, he's trapped inside his getaway car," she adds.

"Yeah, most of Hailstone's people are on the other side," the man says, pointing east. "But I hear shots from the west end, too. They've got us surrounded, but they are still on the other side. So why are our people falling like flies? It makes no sense!"

Of course it makes sense. James is here and, from the sounds of it, he's taking people out faster than bullets can. Still he's only *one* man.

"All right," I say, gesturing back toward the fight. "Let's see what we can do."

They nod and turn. I take the man out first, slamming the butt of my gun to the base of his neck. As the woman turns, surprised, I jam an elbow right against her temple. She crumples like a *stringless* marionette and falls in a heap on top of her partner.

James may not think so, but he's not alone. At least one member of his crew is here to help—whether he likes it or not.

Chapter 53

The hedges are six feet tall. I can't see over them. Shots continue to fly by, too close for comfort. The plants provide a good hiding place, but the foul-smelling Dumpster was better cover. I have to move.

A bullet slices a branch in two and sends leaves raining down all over me. I drop to my knees and crawl to the nearest gap. My calf screams as I creep forward. I ignore it. From this vantage point, I can see Elliot's men—maybe eight or ten of them, I can't be sure—hiding behind crates, air conditioning units, and a fire escape stairwell. Their guns are trained east, past the dark sedan that I noticed the night I first sneaked out to meet Aydan.

The car's tires are all flat and the paint job is peppered with dings. More projectiles hit it, but barely manage to make any dents. It's the *getaway* car, bulletproof and with Elliot inside. I expect the sedan to tear down the road at any moment, but it just sits there, as still as a hunk of metal at a junk yard. Something tells me IgNiTe is responsible for this lack of escape-worthy qualities.

I imagine Elliot cowering inside, while his people risk their skins to keep him safe. What an outstanding leader he is. He deserves a medal—right through the eye.

Kneeling by the hood of the car, Amazon Woman discharges one magazine after another. Her curling horns stick out, giving away her position. Bullets whiz over them, doing nothing to slow down her furious, trigger-happy finger.

Beyond the car, guns flash, engaged in the crossfire. If the guards I just knocked out are right, those are Hailstone's people, here to save Zara and Luke. I look back the way I came. Luke still kneels by the woman, probably imploring death to spare her, while my prayers stack in opposition.

I focus my attention back on the battle, holding all the variables, except one.

James.

Where is he?

I see no evidence of his presence, not that this means anything. He moves faster than the eye can see. Except there are bullets criss-crossing the plane, also faster than the eye can see. So if he's moving within the field of battle, how long until he gets hit?

I guess I could shoot all of Elliot's men in the back, but it's safe to say I won't be able to do that. And even if I had the guts to try, the first shot would give me away, and then what? Eat leaves? They would shred the hedges so quickly they would find chlorophyll behind my eyeballs.

Here is yet another occasion when my stupid *skills* could be extremely useful.

"C'mon," I say under my breath—a lame pep talk that never works.

I focus on the man closest to me. He's crouched behind an air conditioning unit, slipping a fresh magazine inside his pistol. As he clicks it in place, he sticks an arm around the large metal box and starts shooting in an erratic, desperate manner.

Imagining the way his gun would feel, I concentrate on it. There's a mechanism inside of it, gears and pins and springs that I can almost see as I reach a hand toward it. Now, if I could just . . .

I can nearly sense what to do. It's right there, like an almost-remembered word at the tip of my tongue. Maybe if I just jam the bullet, give it a little push. I focus with all I've got. A familiar energy tingles through my body for a moment, then dissipates, leaving me bereft.

Crap. Why couldn't something other than meditation be the key to these stupid abilities?

In the next instant, the gun falls out of the man's grip and hits the ground. He looks at his hand as if it just grew out of his wrist. He curses and reaches for the weapon.

One moment, he's poised to retrieve the gun, the next his face is flat on the blacktop, utterly immobile. My eyes dart around in all directions, looking for a disturbance in my plane of vision, for the least little blur that may reveal James's presence. Nothing. He excels with his skills at the same level that I fail with mine.

It's infuriating. I may as well play the lottery. I'd have better chances with those odds.

Another guard falls flat on his face, this time by the fire escape. James is taking them down, but not fast enough. Without encountering real resistance, the Hailstone people are getting closer. And, once they get here and realize what is really happening, they'll likely join Elliot's men against IgNiTe.

Superpowers would be nice at the moment. But I've been fighting this battle for years, way before I even knew what I am. I may not be able to shoot them in the back, but I can fight them. It is time to make another stand, and I'm still willing to make it my last one.

I rise to my feet, calf shaking so bad I almost don't make it. I take a step forward. Another step. My head spins. My vision blurs. I look down. The bottom half of my pant leg shines crimson.

Ignoring the pain, I slip the ski mask over my head and rush through the hedges, a crazed cry tearing out my throat. Elliot's men shift their attack and aim my way. They hesitate for a moment as they notice my uniform, but only until someone yells, "Shoot!"

At the word, I shoot too, not at all reluctant to return the favor.

Chapter 54

Shots blast past me. I shoot back, incensed, blood tracing discernible paths through my every limb, renewing my energy. I pull the trigger, changing my aim after every hit. My martial arts training kicks in and I move, fluid, confidently—my hand a mere extension of my very thoughts: a precise tool.

Two men go down. I roll behind a crate, next to one of the fallen bodies. I round the wooden box and come out on the other side, aiming for a third enemy, but he's down already, eyes open, staring blankly at the dark sky. I run and take cover next to him. Crouching low, I let my lungs pump for precious air while my veins run afire with adrenaline. I take a few deep breaths and ready myself for another attack. Every time I stick my neck out there, I hang my life from a fraying thread.

It feels right. It feels worth it.

Before running out, I check how many bullets I have left. Only three. Cursing at the delay, I take out a new magazine from the side pocket of my cargo pants. I'm about to reload when a series of *clanks*—like ice skates moving on metal—breaks my concentration. My eyes snap upward and spot movement on the fire escape, about four stories above.

A dark shape stands out against the cloudy sky. It's large, but moves at a prodigious speed that seems to defy the laws of physics. In a flash, it leaps over the metal railing and into open space. A pair of wings splays open, and the creature dives head first in my direction, plummeting like a meteor.

I scramble back, out of the way, dropping the magazine. The creature lands just inches away, its leathery appendages behind its back still flapping. The wings are small relative to the creature's size, as if they're not done growing yet. Large joints protrude through the thin, stretched out membrane that covers them. I think of a bat, then of the creatures that attacked Xave when he was our lookout during the assault.

A shock of black coarse hair hangs over the beast's forehead between two horrendous ears the size and shape of soup bowls. It's perfectly round eyes shine black, like gems. It's bloated mouth makes chittering sounds through two rows of long, pointed teeth. The thing wears no clothes and, although it still seems human in places, it isn't. Not one bit.

This is an animal, a terrifying predator of the night.

As it crouches over me, the beast stamps huge talons on the ground, making terrible, pecking sounds with them. The hum in the back of my head intensifies in response to its closeness. It assesses me, its huge ears cocking to one side while it chitters and chitters. I cower, trembling like a scared mouse.

Without warning, the thing flaps its wings and flies backward, away from me. I stare, petrified, the gun useless in my stiff fingers. The thing thinks I'm an Eklyptor and, now it moves on, probably looking for human victims.

Panic froths in my chest, a heavy foam that seems to expand and expand. The only humans I can think of are Clark and Blare. But what if there are others? Fresh recruits? New allies I never got a chance to meet. James is the leader of our IgNiTe cell, but there are others. I rise with the jolt of my panic. We've already lost Xave and Oso. We can't lose anyone else. Every single human here is more precious than anyone who's been tainted, Eklyptor *or* Symbiot.

I barely have time to reassess my position when more metallic *clanks* come from above. They are fast, one after the other, like bullets raining on sheet metal. My gaze snaps upward. A half-dozen bat-like creatures have appeared on the fire exit, their clawed talons scraping against the staircase. They jump down, spreading wings that vary in size and span anywhere from four to ten feet in width. Some land on the pavement, others swoop low, then fly in different directions, talons held at the ready, like those of falcons diving for prey. Some even hold rifles.

Oh, hell!

There is no nightmare worse than this reality.

Ignoring the cold numbness, the horrible premonition in the pit of my stomach, I turn to look for James. Of course, I don't see him anywhere, but there's evidence of his work. Only one of Elliot's men remains upright, still shooting toward the advancing Hailstone soldiers. He's across the street, screaming for backup into a handheld radio to soldiers who are otherwise engaged. I run in his direction in a diagonal line. He jumps when he sees me and changes his aim. I pull the trigger at the same time that a ball of electricity flies past me and strikes him in the chest, sending him into convulsing spasms that bring foam to his mouth.

I throw a quick glance over my shoulder, expecting to see Aydan, but I don't. All I see is a couple of bat creatures swooping down, shooting their rifles, raining bullets on what I assume are IgNiTe fighters. But I can't worry about Aydan or anyone right now, not when I'm so close to Elliot's car.

Amazon Woman is the only one still shooting at Hailstone. She is so intent on her targets and so good at what she does that she hasn't noticed every single member of her backup team is out of commission.

For no apparent reason, she stops shooting and goes eerily still. Then, in one sudden motion, she whirls, her eyes swiveling in all directions, searching for danger. She seems to be focused on the air in front of her, but when she doesn't see anything, her eyes move further down the line and spot me running toward her.

We aim at each other.

I shoot.

She shoots, but, inexplicably, her arm jerks upward, and the bullet goes wild.

My shot strikes the car, right next to her hip. She rolls to the side, and I shoot again. I cut to the right, expecting her attack, but instead, she shoots to her left, toward empty space.

I stop, my heart collapsing to the bottom of my chest, cognizant of what's just happened before my mind has a time to grasp the situation.

As if by magic, James materializes next to Amazon Woman. Eyes wide, he staggers backward and hits the ground. A starburst of blood blooms on his chest.

Chapter 55

"James!"

He's crumpled on the floor, unmoving.

My eyes snap back to the Amazon. She's staring at James's body as if hypnotized.

A growl reverberates in my throat, but I can't scream. Large blotches burst in front of my eyes, the color of rage. Fueled by pure hatred, I spring forward, aim, and pull the trigger.

The gun clicks.

Empty.

I hurl the weapon at the Amazon. It smashes against her cheekbone with a crunch. Slowly, she shifts her attention toward me and, for the first time, I notice she's shot. Blood seeps from her side. Her body begins to turn, her gun changing targets. But she's too slow.

I jump and round kick her extended arm. The gun pops out of her grip, hits the ground and skids under the car. As soon as my feet hit the blacktop, I release another kick, taking advantage of my momentum. The Amazon blocks it with both arms. She flinches, but barely stumbles back. I land in a crouch, and find myself in a defensive position as she throws a kick of her own.

She's taller, with muscles as big as a bodybuilder's, but she's hurt, and I've got James to worry about. So I don't think it a cheap shot when I jab her side, dig my fingers into the bullet hole and try to rip her in two. Blood spurs from her wound coating my hands. She yells and recoils in pain. Lowering her head, she rams forward and slams her curved horns into my ribcage. Air *whooshes* from my lungs. My side throbs with pain as if I've been slammed with a club hammer.

We roll on the ground. I maneuver myself on top and—from somewhere, even though my lungs ache and struggle for air—I manage to get the strength to pound my fist into her wounded side. Her eyes roll to the back of her head. The color drains from her face. Seeing my chance, I leap to her chest, take her by the horns with my bloodied hands and slam her head against the pavement. Her eyes go blank for good, rolling like two white balls on a pool table.

Wiping the blood on my pants, I stand and look at Elliot's car. Its windows are tinted and cracked in a mess of spider webs caused by so many bullets. I can't see inside. I waver between helping James and finishing what I set out to do today—what James, himself, set out to do. The last thought makes my decision easy. I walk to the car and reach for the door handle.

Before I can grab hold of it, however, the retractable delivery door begins to roll upward, filling the night with the sounds of whirling gears. Hand frozen in midair, my attention snaps to the widening gap between the loading dock and the door. The whole building seems to be yawning its mouth open, promising to vomit all its wrongness on top of whoever happens to be outside.

Before I realize I've changed my mind, I'm limping toward James, kneeling next to him and shaking him. "James!" I press two fingers to his throat and find a heartbeat. "JAMES!" I scream, right into his ear.

He blinks his eyes open and slams a hand to his wounded

chest, wincing in pain. His fingers turn red as if they've been dipped in paint.

I spare a quick glance to the delivery door. It's halfway open. Two bright lights shine from inside, blinding me. What the hell? I look away, my retinas flashing with the imprint of two white circles. Hailstone's people, who are now upon us, split their attention between Elliot's car and the opening gate.

"James, we have to get out of here." I shift positions, plant my feet on both sides of his head and slide my hands under his arms. Leaning back, I pull him the way I came. James is so heavy I barely manage to move him a couple of feet. My calf smarts, making itself known again.

"Help me, damn it!" I order in the most commanding voice I have.

James shakes his head, seems to come to his senses, and begins pushing with his legs, trying to stand. All he manages to do, however, is shove himself backward, which isn't much help.

The whirring from the delivery door stops. I look up, blink at the bright lights shining from the inside of the loading dock. My heart drops, limp with horror. The bright spots are headlights, the halogen lamps of the military Jeep Wrangler I saw in the weapon storage area, the one with the 50 caliber gun mounted at its back.

Behind the huge gun, a massive figure lets out an incensed war cry and proceeds to rip the night apart by unleashing a hellish bullet storm meant to annihilate anyone who stands in his way.

As it turns out, Tusks isn't dead, after all.

Chapter 56

The sound is deafening—hammer blows inside my head, one after another, drilling, pounding, shattering my every thought. A million projectiles rip through the open gate, piercing the night indiscriminately.

Bullets strike in a semicircle as Tusks sways the huge gun in an arch. They hit the pavement, the hedges in the back, Elliot's car and, in the end, swing all the way to the other side where Hailstone's soldiers fall slack to the ground: flies trapped in a cloud of insecticide. Frantically, electrified by an unexpected source of strength, I drag James close to the wall, completely out of Tusks's line of sight and the reach of his monstrous gun.

I kneel next to James, chest aching from exertion, vision blurring. My calf throbs like the heart of a giant. I half collapse against the wall, teeth bare as I hiss in pain. If I could rest for just a moment, only a short moment . . . but I can't.

With a deep breath, I push away from the building, pull off my ski mask and throw it down. "You have to get out of here," I say, bending over James to catch his gaze.

His eyes fight to focus. He blinks and examines my face carefully. "Marci," he says.

It's just my name, but it says it all. It says that he understands, that he *sees*, that he trusts. I nod. Something passes between us, wordless, but heavy and more meaningful than a thousand explanations, excuses or justifications.

A few Hailstone soldiers still stand. Tusks continues to unload bullets in a frenzy.

I press my mouth to James's ear to make sure he can hear me over the maddening din of the battle. "Take a deep breath and get out of here as fast as you can. That way." I point west where IgNiTe is still raging its own battle against the flying nightmares. Maybe James won't be better off that way, but his people are there. They should be able to help him better than I can. Besides I have a job to finish here.

Two actually.

"Do you understand?" I ask.

"No." He tries to sit up and moans in pain. His torso is bathed in blood; his face as white and lifeless as a porcelain plate. "I can help."

"*Pshaw*. You're no help here," I forcefully say. "We need you alive, so you get out of here. RIGHT. NOW."

I don't want to think of what would happen to James if he doesn't get out of here. The torture I went through at Doctor Sting's hands will be nothing compared to what they'll do to him.

"But—" James's protest is cut short by the sound of the Jeep's engine roaring to life, followed by the unmistakable hum of the vehicle backing up. The brightness from the headlights retreats. Tires squeal. Tusks is retreating into the building, and I can only think of one reason for that.

"James," I grab a handful of his IgNiTe jacket and shake him, "you get out of here. Don't let my efforts be in vain. You hear me?" I don't wait for his answer. Instead, I take the gun from the holster at his hip. I check it for bullets. It's empty, but I have an arsenal in my pockets and luckily it's the right match.

I stagger to my feet and limp a couple of steps to the door. When I reach it, I aim, my arms inside the building over the waist-high loading dock. The Jeep has retreated to the very back of the room. The mechanical sound of shifting gears echoes through the crate-filled area, then the vehicle speeds forward, tires whining, the acrid scent of rubber filling the air.

The Jeep rushes straight toward me, its headlights two beacons of doom. Pressing my entire body weight to the wall, I lean forward, aim high, and shoot. The Jeep's windshield shatters, but the vehicle doesn't slow. As it nears, I shoot at the tires and radiator. When the Jeep is only a few feet away, I drop backward and, lying on the ground, discharge the contents of the gun on the undercarriage as it hurls through the air above me.

For a moment, there's absolute silence. The car's tires spin uselessly against empty space. I blink in slow motion, watching the Jeep's underbelly glide overhead, soaring like some strange bird from a parallel universe.

When tiny rain droplets pepper my face and the gray sky reveals its gloom, I roll to my stomach and watch as the Jeep slams into the ground, its temporary wings revoked by the laws of physics.

Barely rattled by the bone-jarring landing, Tusks jumps out of the driver seat and hops behind the machine gun. I struggle to my feet, hurry toward the Jeep and slam my back against its grill, just as the beast starts shooting, not even aware that I'm here. The whole car vibrates against me with every shot: a lethal massage device.

As I ponder what to do next, I throw a quick, worried glance toward James, but to my relief, the only thing left is a dark bloodstain. I hope he has enough strength to get out of here. We can't lose him. I don't see any hope for humanity if we don't have enough people like him fighting for our survival.

Tusks's machine gun bellows, imparting death on Hailstone at the speed of light. Spent cartridges *ding, ding, ding,* as they hit the ground. After a few beats, the weapon swings west, massacring the building in the process. I look to my left. It seems the remainder of Hailstone soldiers have retreated. I didn't mind Tusks's killing spree against his own kind, but now his efforts are focused in the wrong direction, the way I told James to run, and I can't allow that.

Besides, I do have it in for the bastard.

Making up my mind, I scoot alongside the Jeep, my back pressed tightly against it. As Tusks imparts his indiscriminate carnage, the few that still fight on that side of the battle retreat, rounding the building as fast as they can. Bat creatures flap their wings and fly to the top of the roof for safety. A handful of men drop to their knees, then fall over dead, huge bullets piercing their backs.

I think of James, hoping to God he made it out.

Unable to help myself, I then think of Luke and wonder if he'll make it, too. I hope he doesn't, but it's not important.

Tusks's cackles are audible between bursts of bullets. Spent casings continue *dinging* on the ground: tiny bells presaging death.

As I make it to the driver's door, I take a deep breath, push away from the Jeep and aim to shoot. Except the element of surprise I thought I had was an illusion and, as soon as my sight is set, Tusks's leg kicks out and knocks the gun out of my hand. I freeze, regretting my overconfidence for only an instant. With no time to dwell, I go on the offense.

Determined to get him from behind that gun, I step onto the Jeep's running board, grab hold of the roll cage and swing my legs. Carried by my momentum, I sail sideways and smash my boots against Tusks's face. He stumbles backward, away from the gun, but doesn't fall.

Unbalanced by the impact, I begin to drop into the back of the Jeep, but manage to spring back and land outside in a crouch, ready for the beast's fury, which is sure to come.

I stare at him, waiting. His hands are pressed to his face, eyes oddly vacant. He takes a few more steps back, swaying. I stare confused, until his hands fall away and reveal the problem. Only one of his tusks remains. The other one is gone. It takes me a moment to compute what just happened: the tusk, I've kicked it straight in. I couldn't have done that if I'd tried. For once a big favor, not a little one. His head rolls back limp, then his body topples, lifeless, over the back of the Jeep and onto the street.

For a moment, there is quiet. I look left and right. The place is empty, and I think it's almost over. I straighten and turn to face Elliot's car.

The moment has come, I think.

Limping, I move toward the sedan, searching the ground for a gun.

"Just a little further," I mumble to myself.

At least that's what I think until an incensed growl breaks the silence. I turn and face the building. Lyra and the long-tailed Eklyptor, Lamia, stand on the delivery platform, looking down on me with evil in their eyes.

Whipping her fifth extremity up in the air, Lizard Woman jumps from the loading dock and runs in my direction, a huge serrated knife in her hand. Lyra follows, taking huge leaps that put her ahead of Lamia in an instant. I look frantically at the ground, but the nearest weapon is too far.

Knowing my luck has finally run out, I look up to find that Lyra has already covered the separating distance between us. She stands in front of me, arm pulled back. How did she move that fast? Like a stone from a slingshot, her furry fist flies through the air and slams on the side of my face.

For a moment, I stand there, my whole world oddly numb and weightless. Then my legs give out and I collapse. In my last thought, before I pass out, I wish for death, because I know that what will be waiting for me when I wake up will be much worse.

Chapter 57

When I wake, the first thing that registers is a pair of eyes, staring into mine from ten inches away. I think of how odd they appear, of how terrifyingly familiar. At the idea, my brain awakens all at once and my heart lurches, slamming against my chest.

Not this!

Doctor Sting straightens, pulling his sour milk breath away from my nose. I'm lying on a bed with white covers.

"Good," he says with a smile that reveals his squared-off teeth.

Whatever is capable of giving this creature pleasure can't be good.

"She's awake." He addresses someone whom he regards sideways with those goat-like eyes of his. I refuse to look in that direction and stare at the false ceiling instead.

My mouth is bitter with fear. Images of endless, empty corridors flash before me—the passages that will, once more and forever, become my prison. I won't be able to claw my way out again. I know it. My arms jerk protectively toward my chest. The covers rustle and I'm surprised to find I'm not restrained.

"Hello, Azrael," an unmistakable, accented voice says from my left.

Elliot walks to the foot of the bed and regards me with raised eyebrows. His gold-flecked gaze sparkles with satisfaction.

He's still alive. He's still alive.

My throat closes. The rhythm of my heart becomes anything but steady. A whimper tries to force its way out of my mouth, but I cage it behind clenched teeth. Death was too much to wish for. Death, I don't seem to deserve.

"Shall I be on my way?" Doctor Sting says, his words an almost incoherent noise to my ears.

"Sure, sure." Elliot waves dismissively.

Doctor Sting walks away from the bed. My eyes dart around the room looking for his *implements*. He reaches a door. I imagine a closet full of pokes, knives, and cattle prods. But when he opens it, it's just a regular door—one he uses to leave.

My whole body sighs with release. Whatever they plan to do to me won't happen just yet. As my gaze reluctantly moves back to Elliot, I notice another person in the room: Lyra, sitting on an armchair. She acknowledges me with a curt nod, then stands and takes her place behind her boss. I remember Lamia rushing in my direction, but Lyra getting there first and knocking me senseless.

Fear returns, rolling in waves, crashing against the pit of my stomach with nauseating force. They watch me with small smiles on their faces. And I know I'll melt into a puddle of tears and blood, if they don't stop staring. My cowardice embarrasses me. After all I've been through, I should be tougher than this, but all I can think of is the one thing I won't have.

A quick, painless death.

"Your performance last night was *noteworthy*," Elliot says.

Oh, I'm sure it was. He has taken note, and I've been found exceptionally disappointing. I don't even want to imagine the punishment he has in store for me.

"You will serve as an example to everyone," he adds.

So that's what I'm to be. An example. A reminder of what happens to those who dare get in his way. My gaze flicks to Lyra's green, round eyes. There's a strange vibe in them that doesn't feel quite right.

"Sounds grand," I tell Elliot, my eyes cutting back to him, my voice steadier than I imagined possible.

Elliot tilts his head to one side, looks at me with amused curiosity. Behind him, Lyra puts a furred finger to her lips, indicating I should stay quiet. The gesture is odd. Not like a warning to keep my mouth shut, but a request to guard a mutual secret.

Slowly, I push up on the bed, look around. The room is clean and private—not like the barracks or the basement. The walls are painted a cheery shade of green. The bed is a regular bed, not a cot or a torture chair. There are paintings and lamps and armchairs.

My attention drifts back to Lyra. Her mouth tightens ever so slightly, as if repressing a smile. What is going on?

"You saved my life, Azrael," Elliot says. "Of course it is *grand*. Our faction owes you a big debt."

I saved his life?

"Lyra told me how valiantly you fought against those IgNiTe rebels and how you stopped Rooter. He went quite mad with rage in the end. Some of those large bullets actually pierced my car. If you hadn't intervened in time, I loathe to think what would have happened, where our faction would be at this moment."

My mouth forms a big "O". I press my lips together and try my best to look smug, rather than shocked and incredulous and stupefied.

"That crazy son of a bitch," I say, voice shaking. "Made him eat his own tusk. That, I did!"

"That, you did," Elliot says, looking a bit put out by my response.

If he was expecting Crazy Azrael to have died alongside Tusks, he's asking way too much out of his "example".

"Well," he claps his hands together, "I simply wanted to offer you my *thanks*."

"My pleasure," I say with a smile.

I can oblige any time, Elliot. Much more easily now that I find myself under your good graces.

But I guess I shouldn't get ahead of myself, not without knowing what game Lyra is playing. And what about Lamia? What role does *she* play in all this?

"I'll be on my way," Elliot says. "Make yourself comfortable. You deserve a rest."

He turns, gives Lyra a nod and walks out. She follows him, but before exiting the room, she mouths the word "later" then closes the door behind her.

I collapse back on the bed, wincing at all the parts that hurt.

Well, that was unexpected.

I close my eyes and try to tell myself that, today, it's okay to sleep.

It doesn't work, though.

Not when the sting of failure and questions about Lyra drive me to restlessness.

Chapter 58

The creature known as Elliot Whitehouse still walks the Earth.

Sitting on my bed, back in the barracks, I close my eyes, take a deep breath.

Failure is a funny thing. It beats you down. It gnaws at your bones, deep and relentless. It coats you with shame and anger. It leaves you raw.

But it also gives you focus, and a better clarity and understanding of your goals. Before, I knew Elliot had to die. The knowledge was logical, justifiable in every sense. Now, however, my understanding is much more than that. It's an undeniable certainty, a breathing, living thing that has gotten its claws into me, and will make sure this aching need to destroy Elliot becomes a reality.

I don't know where. I don't know when. But I do know why and, perhaps, I even know how.

"Azrael," someone says.

I open my eyes. Lyra stands in front of me. She tilts her head to one side, gesturing for me to follow. Without a word, she turns and walks away. I follow.

Yesterday, I spent the entire day in that private room, trying to push Elliot and my failure out of mind. I slept for the first time in weeks. It wasn't the undisturbed rest I used to enjoy before The Takeover when, in spite of thinking myself crazy, life felt full of possibilities and a future, but it was good enough sleep.

I also ate two delicious meals. They didn't come in a tray with the average food served at the mess hall. No. I had fine china, a crystal glass, shiny silverware, even a cloth napkin. My favorite meal was dinner: prime rib, braised potatoes, aromatic rice, soft rolls, and creamy cheesecake—all cooked and delivered by Onyx herself. I allowed myself to enjoy the treat because it came from her. While I ate, she sat with me and talked about everything except what had happened the night before. She has no interest in those things. She's a free spirit. I guess they come in all sizes and shapes and species.

That was yesterday, and it was decent—for lack of a better word. Today, however, is different. Rest is over, and I'm hungry for more than food. I want, I *need* Lyra's answers.

We ride the elevator without saying a word. When we reach the ground floor, she walks with firm steps toward the front exit. Our boots tap against the marble floor in unison. My calf is bandaged tightly, aching deeply, to the bone. I limp, but it won't be for long.

Everywhere I look there is evidence of the battle: bullet casings, chipped tiles, bloody prints. The glass windows and doors by the entrance are shattered. The wind whistles as it rushes into the building. My hair blows backward and I catch it in a ponytail and tuck it in the collar of my jacket.

None of the guards stop me when I walk outside, but they look and whisper.

Outside, the sun is aglow on a baby blue sky. I look up in awe, squinting at the passing clouds. I don't even remember the last time I was out during the day. It feels like several lifetimes ago.

At least two, at any rate. I was someone else for what felt like forever, after all.

We cross the deserted street. More evidence of the battle is out here. The hole-ridden vehicles are the most apparent. To see that many cars—private property once respected—savaged, torn to bits, leaves me oddly frazzled. I understand it's all just collateral damage, nothing compared to the loss of life, of humanity. Still, this chaos is too perfect an example, too keen a demonstration of how much has gone wrong, of how the order and way of life I once knew is now gone.

Lyra presses forward, kicking bullet casings in her wake. They skid out of the way, twinkling golden in the sun. After a few blocks filled with nothing but eerie ghosts of a past life, she seems to relax.

"I cannot stand that place," she says. "Not that it is better out here."

A million questions fight for first place inside my head. They're all strong and important. Big bullies. The one that finally presses its way out seems just as good as all the others.

"Why did you help me?"

She stops and faces me. I do the same. Her eyes are all green with only black slits for pupils. Her black fur shines under the sun. Her right ear flickers. She puts her hands out, demonstratively and says, "Because I am human."

If she'd told me her mother was a parakeet, I might have laughed, but this joke is too much.

"You know I'm not really stupid, right? It's all just an act," I say.

"Oui, I know." She gives me a crooked smile that makes me notice her now-longer whiskers. She's really going for them. How *human* of her.

"Then you're joking, but it isn't funny."

"Non, not joking." She stuffs furry hands in her front pockets and resumes walking. "Unless you think I look like Puss and Boots." She chuckles to herself as if that's exactly how she sees herself.

"Maybe you should try a hat with a feather," I say.

"Ahhh, that would be a nice touch. Either way," she sighs, "it's true. I *am* human and I did this to myself. On purpose. A Symbiot can alter her body just the same as an Eklyptor's. But you know this already. You belong to James McCray's IgNiTe cell. He must have explained."

James modified his bones, tendons and muscles to become as fast as he is. Rheema grew fangs and can use them to deliver a deadly neurotoxin. Yes, I know Symbiots can alter their bodies. But this? I never even considered anyone taking it so far. And just like that, I believe her. It's the only sensible explanation to the fact that I'm still alive.

"I did it to earn their trust," Lyra says as if reading my thoughts. "No one thinks I am anything but an Eklyptor. You never did. It is brilliant, really." She gives me a satisfied look.

"Apparently so," I say.

"It is all reversible, after all. A small sacrifice to ensure the survival of our species."

Reversible? I hadn't thought of that either, but it makes sense. If she can command her body to grow fur, she can also tell it to stop.

Lyra continues, "You kept me on my toes, Cher. You gave away the location of James. I thought for sure you had gone Eklyptor all the way. Though, I started to suspect you were up to something shortly after. For some time, I even thought you were a Hailstone spy."

"I did go all the way." My voice is bitter, revealing how guilty I still feel.

Her whiskers twitch as her eyebrows go up. "And you came back?" she asks in disbelief.

"It wasn't easy."

"It could not have been. I am impressed. Vraiment." There's no sarcasm in her tone. She genuinely seems impressed.

Lyra slaps a metal lamppost as we walk by it. A metallic *ding* resonates for a few seconds. "I thought I recognized you in the conference room. The ski mask looked familiar." She smirks. It was her ski mask, after all. "But mostly, I acted on instinct when I knocked you out. Then had my people check with James's people, and they vouched for you. By the time Elliot got around to asking for explanations, I knew I could trust you. It was not hard coming up with a story. Rooter went mad. I guess being used as a shield can do that to some people. And Elliot was cowering so low inside that car he didn't see a thing. He truly thinks you saved his life." Lyra laughs a strange, hearty laugh that almost sounds like a hiss.

I take a large step over a trailing heap of black potting soil from an overturned planter. "Do you know if James is okay? He was hurt during the battle."

"I could not tell you. Did not know to ask."

Not knowing is eating me up. He has to be okay. He just has to be.

"What about Lamia? Is she buying it?"

"I think she suspects something, but she will do whatever her leader tells her to do." She waves a hand in a very French way to indicate that Lamia is inconsequential. "I am also part of IgNiTe, by the way," Lyra adds as an afterthought.

"What?" I know there are other cells, but I find this hard to believe. Since we met, I've seen Lyra as the enemy. To think that we're both IgNiTe members is hard to process.

We come to a café. It's closed and its front window is obscured in a spider web of hairline fractures; still, the outside tables are inviting. I sit. I have a feeling this will be a long story, and I'd rather look Lyra in the eye as she tells it. Yearning for my lost life, I imagine the smell of roasted coffee beans wafting through the air.

"I am part of the strongest French IgNiTe cell. Dillon is also with me. The Hailstone faction has been our focus for many years. In other words, Zara Caron and Tom Hailstone. They married twenty years ago, lived in France and began to build their little Eklyptor Empire. Over seventeen years ago, they based their operations out of Seattle—Tom was originally from here. At the time, we thought that was why they had moved. That and the fact that we were getting very close to them back in Paris. A year later, a son came into the picture, however."

A son came into the picture? That's an odd way to put it.

She must be talking about Luke. I prop an elbow on the table and press a fist to my mouth. How much does Lyra know about the "twin" brother situation? If I had a million questions before, they have taken the liberty of multiplying themselves by two.

Still, I dare not ask a single one. I don't want to give anything away. At the moment, my best option is to shut my mouth and listen. I press my fist harder into my mouth, until my teeth hurt. I stare at a large planted pot with its sad shock of wilted pansies.

"This son was unexpected. Adoption is not an institution Eklyptors subscribe to. They are used to taking who they want, when they want."

"Are you talking about Luke Hailstone?" I ask, unable to help myself.

"Yes. Precisely. Your twin brother."

My chest goes tight as if I've been punched. I feel oddly transparent and fragile, like I've been sanded down to one millimeter

347

of my regular thickness. I'm a piece of glass and, soon, the tension around us will shatter me into dust.

I wonder if Lyra knows we aren't a DNA match. It seems she doesn't.

"Zara was never pregnant," Lyra says. "And one day, she and Tom just had a kid. We had no idea where the boy came from. They kept the details of the *adoption* very quiet. It all remained a mystery to us for years, until just recently, when Ernest Dunn died and we learned that there had been no adoption at all, that they had, instead, kidnapped a baby—which made even less sense."

So the man my mother always blamed had little to do with what happened to her son. The memory of Luke's sorrow-stricken face at Dunn's funeral appears before my eyes. I scoff. And to think I felt sorry for him. To think I hugged him, tried to comfort him.

Doctor Dunn . . . a shocking idea runs through me as the cogs in my mind begin to turn at full speed. Here, between the lines of this convoluted twin story, lies the truth about my biological parents.

"I knew who you were the minute I laid eyes on you," Lyra continues, throwing a wrench in my thoughts. "I followed you many times after the news came out about a long-lost bébé reunited with his family."

"You did?" I feel like a complete idiot. I never suspected being followed. Although, at the time, I had no reason to be paranoid. That was when life still seemed en-route to a better future. Well, at least *a* future.

She nods. "It was a waste of time. I still have no idea what Luke, you, the kidnapping, Dunn have to do with Hailstone's plans. The little blond bâtard got away, but we will get him. For your sake, we will get him."

"For my sake?"

Her eyes do a little roll, flat-out calling me stupid. "You are somehow part of their scheme, Marci Guerrero. I would hate to be against you, but if it comes to that, je suis désolé."

A threat then. It comes down to a threat and my part in Hailstone's plans, whatever they may be. What scheme could have possibly began sixteen years ago? I shudder to think of it.

The sound of a car approaching steals my entire concentration. Lyra tenses ever so slightly, then turns to look at the dark SUV riding in our direction. When the vehicle passes by, the driver dips his chin to acknowledge us. My brain buzzes identifying him as an Eklyptor. He continues on, unconcerned, headed down Olive Way.

"Quel con," Lyra growls. "They will not get away with this. We made this world into what it is. We'll take it back or take them down with us."

I don't know if her threat is even possible, but I do know I'll die trying to make it so.

"What are Hailstone's plans?" I pick up the thread of our conversation.

"The same plans we have been trying to figure out for almost twenty years." Her low tone is a purr of frustration. Her ears and whiskers twitch in unison, outward signs she doesn't seem able to control.

I gesture with one hand to indicate her answer isn't helpful.

"Before they moved to America, a rumor began deep in the bowels of Hailstone. We had spies within their walls, even then. They said Zara and Tom had discovered a way to rid them of the need for hosts. In other words, the need for humans."

An involuntary breath escapes through my half-open mouth.

"To this day," Lyra adds, "the rumor has continued and we aren't any closer to finding out how in the world they intend to do that, and what it means to us. They are parasites, so what could they mean by needing no host? It makes no sense. Their plan, if it is more than just a rumor, is too secret, too well-kept. That is why we stopped trying to figure it out and, instead, decided to kill everyone suspected of knowing. We got to Tom five years ago. Dunn just recently and now Zara. It took too long to get to them, but we did. So . . . I'd like a little Bordeaux with that, please." She gestures toward the closed café door and laughs bitterly.

"I don't think getting to the kid will be as hard, though," she adds. "I wish I had not missed. He is next and, when we have no more use for Elliot, he will join the front of the line."

Chapter 59

The moon is huge and watchful, teasing the surface of Lake Union with its magical shimmering brush. It is as it must have been since the beginning, since before there were humans to spoil the horizon with concrete towers.

It is unchanged.

The view invites thoughts about my life and this struggle, of how, before I knew what I am, emotions seemed absolute and insurmountable.

I had no concept of change. Not really. I thought everything was "the most" I had ever and would ever experience. The most dangerous. The most terrifying. The most intense.

Everything was superlative.

Everything was new.

Before I knew about Eklyptors, I never thought that anything could surpass my intense desire to figure out what was wrong with me. For years, that need drove me, lit a fire in my heart that kept me searching and asking questions. A desire that led me to IgNiTe even when James gave me nothing but secrets, even when joining him seemed like a monumental mistake.

Now, however, I know better. "The most" doesn't exist.

I've been through too much, and now there's only the knowledge that anything can *always* be worse: pain, guilt, desire for revenge.

For the latter, there is, at the moment, a blinding force, a powerful flame that ignites me. A heat that burns hotter than molten lava, an intensity that is restless, determined and dogged in its single-mindedness. A desire that has grown from a concept to an overwhelming drive for payback, for justice, for one eye in exchange of another, and for *hours* of pain in payment for mere seconds.

Because, in my revenge, in this new driving force that grows and grows, there's no decency, no morality. I'm stripped raw and, in the flesh, in what is left, I am primal. I know no codes.

My need for revenge has become a cancer that seems to encompass more and more every day. Its fuel is hatred, and there's a never-ending supply of it. I can feel its tendrils reaching, finding new targets, but keeping two in particular at the very top, at all times.

One: Elliot who has taken so much from me.

Two: Luke who stole any chance I ever had to make right with Karen—even if she wasn't my real mother—and, above all, to love Xave for a full, happy lifetime.

Revenge suddenly is a beautiful word that rolls off the tongue, that matters more than anything else, that gives me lucid moments like this one—where the moon seems within reach, where it's not *the most* beautiful I have ever seen, but it's, at this moment, beauty itself.

I pick up a rock, test it in my hand, place it just so between my fingers. With a quick flick of my arm and wrist, I cast it against the surface of the lake. It skips four times, kissing the water and sending ripples that will go on for longer than I can imagine.

"Good shot," Aydan says from behind me.

I whirl, heart thudding. "You're here." My voice breaks. I didn't know if he would get my message, if he would come. Since I became Elliot's *savior*, I can come and go as I please. Meeting with Aydan was the top priority on my list.

He's pale under the moonlight; a figure carved out of wax, the planes and angles of his face symmetrical and strong.

I open my mouth to say something, but before any words come out, Aydan covers the distance between us and wraps me in his arms.

He doesn't say a word. He just holds me, tighter and tighter until my body arches backward, and I can hardly breathe.

I don't hug him back. I can't.

Whatever relief I feel to see him doesn't compare to his. The intensity of Aydan's emotion is spelled in the curve of his arms, the strength in his muscles, the warmth of his cheek against my temple. There's much in his embrace, and it freezes me, my thoughts, and a world of possibilities. And it could be one of those "most" type of moments, but I don't know anymore, so I just take what I can from it and allow the burning flame of my revenge to grow dimmer and less important than the here and now.

I close my eyes.

"You're okay," he says, voice vibrating in his chest and against mine. "When I saw your message . . . I just . . ."

My skin begins to tingle. Something crackles. I open my eyes. A light glow traces Aydan's shoulder. I lift a hand and stare at it in awe. My fingers are silhouetted in light, like tiny electric bulbs that could illuminate the world.

"Wow," I say in a whisper.

Aydan pulls back, stares at my hand. His lower lip trembles. His eyebrows can't decide whether to go up or stay down.

"That was . . ." he begins, sounding embarrassed.

"Beautiful," I finish for him.

He smiles halfway. I do the same.

"I . . . we . . . thought you didn't make it," he says.

"Did James make it?" It's all I want to know.

"He sends his regards and his thanks."

A long exhale rushes past my lips. "Good. Good. I wished I'd known you were going to attack." I don't want it to sound like a reproach, but it does.

"I wanted to tell you, but—"

"No, you don't have to explain. I understand. I'm just glad James trusted me enough to take a risk with the information I gave him. I wish we could have gotten to Elliot, though." My voice betrays my anger. Something burns a little hotter inside me.

"Oh, we did," Aydan says. "We got to him all right."

I frown, confused.

He walks to the closest park bench and sits. With an extended hand, he invites me to take a seat next to him. I shake my head and shrug with impatience, demanding an explanation.

"He can't be happy right now." Aydan's expression is satisfied; something I haven't seen in a while. "All thanks to you. That list you gave us, we used it. Almost every single one of those reproductively capable Eklyptors is dead."

My mouth falls open. "How? When?"

"The same night of our attack on his building. It was a concerted effort. James gathered as many people as he could and we all attacked at once. It had to be done that way. If we didn't get to everyone at the same time, Elliot would have moved them, would have put them under tighter surveillance. With their deaths, he has lost decades. It's a huge blow to his faction, if he can even boast of having much of one anymore." Aydan's smile is huge and satisfied—nothing *halfway* about it, now.

I'm smiling, too, and walking back and forth in front of him, eyes darting in every direction as I realize the magnitude of what he's saying.

"He can't grow in number anymore," I say.

"No. And everyone he loses from now on is one more he won't be able to replace, not for a while, not if we keep striking and do our best to stop others from reaching reproductive maturity."

I think about it, frowning. It's far from perfect. Too small of a victory.

Aydan seems to read my thoughts. "There are still many battles ahead of us. We just have to win most of them, and we just won a huge one."

"I know that. But it seems so hopeless sometimes." I finally sit, pressing my restless body against the bench's cool metal. "Maybe we'll get our city back, but what about the rest of the world? What about other factions? Hailstone may have a plan."

I tell him about Lyra, how she rescued me, how they suspect Hailstone has some sort of grand plan, how it might involve me, all of it.

Aydan just nods, but he looks like he knows something.

"What?" I ask.

"Nothing. Just that James mentioned it. He's aware of it and he seems to be worried. Worried enough to," his voice breaks with too much hope, "ask you to come back. You've done your part. You've paid your dues. It's time to think of yourself first."

The irony of it is too much. This is what I've wanted all this time, and I now can't.

"No. I have to do this. I have to keep fighting."

"It's not all up to you. I know you think you're alone in this, but it's not true. You have us. We'll be your friends, your . . . family."

I hide my face from him. I feel so broken inside, so consumed by this desire for revenge that I don't even think friends and family could soothe the raw edges this fight has left on me.

"Everyone's fighting, Marci," Aydan continues. "The entire world. James also passed the list you gave us to his contacts in London. They weren't as successful as we were. They didn't get to everyone, but it was also an effective attack."

"That's good, but we need more from *everyone*. More than anything, we need a cure," I say, hoping to veer the conversation in a different direction. I peer at him, knowing he can't share this type of information with me.

"Yes, we do." Aydan returns my gaze. His dark, dark eyes tell me nothing.

I look away and stare at my boots. Silence weaves itself between us. To my surprise, it's a comfortable thing, like a blanket wrapping us in one single space.

After a moment, he asks, "Please, Marci. Come with me?"

Come with me. Not us. *Me*.

I want to believe that he doesn't mean anything by it, but the hopeful tone in his voice makes me doubt. "I can't," I say. "I can't." Especially knowing that my work as a mole has had such an impact in this war.

"When, then?" he asks, and his tone suggests there may not be another chance.

But I'm okay with that. I have felt truly ready to die. That changes something inside of you.

I'm not the same person I was.

I am more, and I am less.

I am what I need to be.

Acknowledgements

A huge thanks to Eleanor Ashfield for all the amazing input and attention to detail. It has been fun and a pleasure working with her and the amazing team at Harper *Voyager*. As always, I owe my family all the time they let me borrow from them to hammer away at the keyboard and type every word in this series. You guys are *happiness* itself.

I must always thank my friends Billie, Subu and Bret for being such supportive beta readers. Bret, thanks for always straightening my prepositions.

Lastly, I'd like to thank all the readers and bloggers who have supported me and have so enthusiastically cheered this project. Tony, Olivia, Sanovia, and many others. You guys are the best.